The Cornish Widow

The Cornish Ladies
Book Four

Fil Reid

ARE YOU SIGNED UP FOR DRAGONBLADE'S BLOG?

You'll get the latest news and information on exclusive giveaways, exclusive excerpts, coming releases, sales, free books, cover reveals and more.

Check out our complete list of authors, too!

No spam, no junk. That's a promise!

Sign Up Here

www.dragonbladepublishing.com

Dearest Reader;

Thank you for your support of a small press. At Dragonblade Publishing, we strive to bring you the highest quality Historical Romance from some of the best authors in the business. Without your support, there is no 'us', so we sincerely hope you adore these stories and find some new favorite authors along the way.

Happy Reading!

CEO, Dragonblade Publishing

Chapter One

W ITH CONSUMMATE EASE born of years at the helm, Captain Jack Trevelyan brought his new lugger, *The Fly*, a boat he'd only taken possession of a month ago, past the dangerous Enys Rock and into the shelter of Bessie's Cove. She handled like a dream, and not just thanks to the experience of his crew. Their combined skills helped, of course, but the fact that they were working with a sleek greyhound built for speed and easy handling played the biggest part. Jack had found, to his delight, that *The Fly* responded almost to his very thought, like some living sea creature given into his hands. He patted her gunwales with a proprietorial hand, as though she were a woman, grinning as she skimmed through the shallower water towards the beach.

As they lost the wind between the cliffs, *The Fly* slowed, and her crew took down her now sagging sails. They worked together like the well-greased cogs of a clock, and he had no need to issue any orders. Within minutes, they were as far in as their draft would allow, with an anchor down stem and stern to steady them, as the bo'sun, Jack's boyhood friend, Daniel Bussow, organized the launching of the gig.

Jack raised a hand to shade his eyes as he peered inland. The cliffs here weren't particularly high, but the way they overhung the narrow inlet provided as good a hiding place as any for a none-too-large boat. To see down into the cove from the cliff path, any nosy person had to get right to the edge. And the same went for out to sea. Once in the sheltered waters of Bessie's Cove with their sails furled, no passing revenue cutter would be able to spot them.

No wonder John Carter, Daniel's uncle and the self-styled King of Prussia, had set up business here back in the last century. He was long dead now, but Jack partnered with the man who'd carried on his tradition, his son-in-law, Captain Will Richards. Thanks to the two of them, the well-earned reputation of the Carters lived on.

Was that Will on the eastern cliffs now, watching them un-loading the goods? Most likely. Jack raised an arm and gave the distant figure a leisurely wave. He received a wave in return.

The crew, scarcely needing any organizing from Daniel, unloaded the ankers of gin, brandy and rum they'd picked up in Roscoff into the waiting gig, as she bobbed beside the larger boat, along with a couple of chests of tea and several bails of silk, one of which Jack had earmarked for his own mother's use. Down on the little sandy beach, Will's men were already shoving their own gig into the waves to come out to help.

"Thassa good run," a gravelly voice to Jack's right said.

He glanced at the old man by his side. Old Tummels, grip-ping the ratlines in one hand, rubbed his whiskery chin, as averse to doing any lifting work as always, but forgiven it thanks to his appearance of advanced old age. He paid Jack's father a pepper-corn rent for a tumbledown cottage on the westerly headland that Jack had more than once offered to improve. He'd been turned down every time. For some reason, Tummels seemed to enjoy both his isolation and the conditions he lived in, and, as he only worked when he needed a few shillings for his ale, he wasn't often a member of Jack's crew.

Jack had known the old man all his life. "So it should be," he said, glancing left towards the westering sun. "Be dark soon."

"Cap'n Will—be he a-goin' to store the kegs in the caves ternight? Or mebbe down one o' they shafts?" The old man might well be thinking of tapping off a bottle or two for himself, unobserved. He'd been known to do that before.

Jack shrugged. He'd done his bit by bringing this consignment over from Brittany. It was up to Will to sort out where it went, and how safely stored it was. Jack didn't much care about who got what profit out of it, so long as he made his bit. After all, with what his father had put in trust for him, he didn't really need the money. But he did need the excitement. He wasn't about to stop making these trips back and forth across the channel in a hurry.

With the gig well filled, Phoby Geen, another of Jack's boyhood friends, who'd been steadying her by holding one of the ropes hanging from the side of *The Fly*, settled himself at the oars. Young Harry Richards, Will's son and heir who'd accompanied them on this trip to Roscoff, took the other. The two young men put their backs into it and pulled for the shore.

They passed the other gig on its way over and soon that was being filled with the remainder of the cargo.

Jack swung down from where he'd been standing in the bows, grabbed the last anker of brandy and passed it down. With a grin, he hopped over the gunwales and slid down a rope to land lightly in the gig. "I'll take an oar." This gig was larger than the one they carried on *The Fly* and would take four men to row it.

Hosking, their carpenter, shifted over on his thwart and Jack settled beside him, taking hold of the butt end of one of the oars. As he did so, he happened to glance to his right again, westwards. Movement caught his eye. A skirt billowed. Was that someone else up on the edge of the cliffs, out near the tip of the headland, staring down at them? A girl by the look of it, her gown catching in the stiff sea breeze and her long dark hair blowing out behind her. Where the hell had she come from? The only houses hereabouts were Will's own, out above neighboring Prussia Cove at Porth en Alls, Bessie's Kiddleywink, near where he'd spied Will waiting, Tummel's single story fisherman's hut on the western headland, and that empty thatched cottage some far-off widow-woman owned, standing just back from the cliffs. No one had lived in it since Brewinney Pascoe'd gone over the cliffs onto the rocks below.

So where had a strange girl appeared from?

"Heave ho," Hosking growled, and Jack set to with the other three, pulling for the little sandy beach. With the tide right in, the way it was now, not much of the beach was on show. He had no need to worry about *The Fly* when the tide started to drop, though, Daniel was to take her round to Penzance to do some honest work picking up a cargo of fish to carry round to Plymouth. Not the sort of work that appealed to Jack, so he'd be staying on land until the time for the next run across the Channel to Roscoff came around.

Between strokes of the oars, Jack glanced back at the clifftop again, but the girl had vanished, if she'd ever been there at all. He shook his head. Perhaps she'd been a pisky. After all, the next cove along *was* called Pisky's Cove. Or a figment of his imagination.

The gig bumped on the sand and the men jumped out, splashing through the shallow waves and pulling the gig clear of the water. Jack jumped out as well and lent a hand. Laden with all their contraband, she was a heavy load.

A strong hand clapped him on the back. "Well done, lad, ye've fetched a tidy load in this time, and in broad daylight. Right under the noses of the gaugers, too."

Jack looked up at his friend Will. A big man by any standards, and a good fifteen years older than Jack, lately fine living had given him a sizeable paunch, but not detracted from his fierce good looks. His graying hair still sprouted in luxuriance, giving him the appearance of a trustworthy elder statesman. Which he was, really. The most honest man Jack knew. If you didn't count the smuggling. "Not sight nor sound of a revenue cutter."

Will grinned. "Probably busy round at St Ives and up to Padstow. They'll not catch us down here unless they think to give the Penzance Collector a cutter of his own to play with. And we know they won't do that. Pendennis'll put a stop to any ideas that way."

As Pendennis, the local magistrate, was the one who'd decide whether or not to allot a cutter to Penzance, Will was more than likely correct. The magistrate was not averse to taking a few kegs of brandy that had paid no duty for himself, and was always ready to turn a blind eye on what went on in his jurisdiction. It suited him well to ignore the goings-on to the east of Penzance.

Will slung an arm around Jack's broad shoulders. "Young Harry'll sort everything out here. You come on up to the Kiddley with me for a tot of something that's paid no duty, and tastes all the better for it." Leaving the men to unload, the two captains started back up the narrow path to Bessie's Kiddley, a hostelry named, as many were, after its most famous proprietor. Although nowadays, at pushing eighty, the old lady did none of the work.

FROM THE DOORWAY, Mrs. Harriet Penhallow, widow, surveyed the state of the tiny, thatched cottage her late husband's great-aunt, Mrs. Bolitho of Marazion, had seen fit to offer her and her children. Habitable was not a word she would have chosen to describe it. Neither was clean. A slender woman, with her rich chestnut hair at this moment covered with a demure bonnet trimmed with mourning black, her delicate brows furrowed in a worried frown.

Beside her, the stout and sensible Bertha, who'd been Harriet's nurse as a child, then lady's maid, followed by nurse to her two children, and had now matured into unpaid general factotum cum lifelong friend, heaved a heartfelt disapproving sigh, but stayed silent.

"It's awful," fifteen-year-old Lydia, with no such inhibitions, said, wrinkling her pert nose. "Surely you can't expect us to live *here*?" She pulled a face. "No one should be expected to live in a place like this."

Bertha's lined face settled into a heavy frown that sent Harriet's heart sinking to her boots. She'd been against coming here from the start and had made it plain to her mistress. Now, she must be thinking she'd been proven correct in her doubts. Which in all probability she had.

"You can see the sea," twelve-year-old Theo, ever the optimist, piped up, hopping from one leg to the other as though he might need to find the privy very shortly. If there even was one. "It looks like we're on top of some cliffs, but there might be a beach. With sand and waves. Maybe caves. Can we go and look, Mama? Can we?" His voice rose in desperate pleading.

Harriet sighed, although not so deeply as Bertha had. She might as well let both the children go. It would give her time to form a plan of action with Bertha. Something that needed to be done swiftly as the late September evening was approaching. "Off you go then, but if there *are* cliffs, keep well back from the edge in case they're crumbly. I don't want you having an accident on your first day here."

"First day?" Lydia scowled. "You say that as if there's going to be a second day."

Harriet bit her lip. Of course there was going to be a second day, and a third, and so on into a distant infinity. They had nowhere else to go and were lucky old Mrs. Bolitho had seen fit to offer this… this hovel. No, she mustn't think of it like that. She had to be positive. It had four walls and a roof, at least, which was more than they'd had yesterday. It was going to be their home, come what may. The old adage that beggars can't be choosers sprang to mind. Since Ben's untimely death at Waterloo, they'd definitely become beggars.

But she didn't want to think about Ben.

"Come on, Lydia." Theo, buoyed by the resilience of youthful optimism, grabbed his sister's hand. "Let's go and explore."

Lydia spent exactly three seconds wrestling with whether to join her brother in his enthusiastic explorations before her curiosity got the better of her. However, holding hands with her younger brother was clearly not the way she wanted this to go. She snatched her hand back, and the two children ran off, Lydia holding up her skirts the better to run.

Silence would have descended had the cottage not been on the coast, where the distant rumble of the waves in the cove below was a constant, and so were the raucous cries of the wheeling gulls overhead. A stiff westerly blew, reminding Harriet that it was autumn, and winter would soon be upon them. Before that, they needed to make sure this cottage, whatever it was called, was windproof and watertight. Because they were going to have to make do and mend here, and stick it out, come what may.

Thanks to Ben. But she'd sworn not to think about him.

Bertha set her pudgy hands on her hips and scowled. "Doesn't look like anyone's been living here for a long time."

Harriet nodded. "At least the roof appears to be in reasonable condition, though."

Bertha's expression said that this was small comfort, and Harriet had to admit she was right. About everything.

The cottage did indeed look as though no one had lived there for a long time, with dirty, ragged curtains at filthy windows, tall weeds jostling the foot of the walls, and an unloved, uncared for air about its exterior. But they'd have to make the best of it. Harriet suppressed another sigh. "Well, let's go inside and take a look. We haven't anywhere else to go, so we're going to have to."

She pushed the front door, which might once have been painted blue, wider open and stepped through it, Bertha right behind her. Was this the kitchen? Hard to tell. At least there was a table, dustcovered and littered with the remnants of what had to have been someone's long-ago last meal in the house. And a stone sink. And was that filthy, rust-encrusted object a kitchen range? Could it be made to function?

Bertha harrumphed loudly as she ran a finger through the dust on the table. "Fancy leaving your dirty dishes out like this.

What sort of a person lived here, I'd like to know? Did a moonlight flit, I'd wager, owing rent."

Harriet nodded. "At least Mrs. Bolitho has said *we* don't have to pay her any rent. That was very kind of her."

Another harrumph from Bertha who had formed a low opinion of their benefactor, Harriet's late husband's great-aunt, even though neither of them had met her as yet.

Harriet pretended she hadn't heard. She'd better take a quick look at the rest of the house before the children came back, just in case it was even worse. Although, how it could be worse than this first glimpse lay beyond her imagination.

There appeared to be two good-sized rooms downstairs, if you didn't count the lean-to pantry—was it even a pantry?—tacked onto the back of the kitchen. A huge, inglenook fireplace took up most of the adjoining wall in the second room, sharing its chimney with what remained of the range. Some cobweb-shrouded, high-backed wooden chairs stood in front of it, one with a dirty blanket heaped on it. In a corner, a rickety door gave onto a twisting spiral staircase whose treads creaked with every step Harriet took. She took care to place her feet at the edges, for fear of the wood being rotten.

On the first floor, a narrow landing provided three more doors. To two bedrooms, if you could call them that, and a box room. No beds though, unless that pile of filthy rags heaped in one of them could be called a bed. The small, leaded windows badly needed de-spidering and a good clean, but the plasterwork seemed to be intact, and at least the windows still had glass in them. Really, if she looked beneath the liberal layer of dirt and dust, this was quite a nice house…

Well, it *could* be a nice house. Nothing like the one they'd rented in Bath though. Within walking distance of Lydia's school.

Briefly, the image of the home she and Ben had shared when he was home on leave from the army flashed into her head. Small, but perfectly appointed, with a kitchen in the basement and quarters for Bertha, Mrs. Birch the cook, and Daisy the parlor maid in the attic. How she'd once loved that house… where her children had been born and she'd been so happy in the first year or two of her marriage. Until… No. She wouldn't think about that. There'd still been happy moments in amongst the… No. She had to stop remembering. She just had to be thankful that French dictator had escaped his island prison and set out to reclaim France for himself. Thankful for Waterloo…

This was a new beginning and she had to make the most of it.

She snatched herself out of her reverie. She also had to be practical. This was her reality now, for both herself and her children, and nothing she could do would change anything, and even if she could have changed it, would she have wanted to? She had to be thankful for what she still had. Thankful to Napoleon, and to Mrs. Bolitho, who had come to her aid when she found herself homeless, despite her worry that the lady nurtured some ulterior motive for her sudden kindness. She'd think about all of that later.

She retraced her footsteps down the corridor and creaking stairs and into the cottage's sitting room. If that was what she was going to have to call it.

Running footsteps sounded outside and Theo charged into the cottage, his dark curly hair blowing in the breeze. "I saw a ship, Mama! Down in a beautiful little bay with real waves and sand. And it's a proper ship with sails and sailors!"

Chapter Two

LYDIA, HAMPERED BY her long skirts and a little breathless, caught up with her brother. "We saw lots of men, down in a little cove, unloading barrels and bundles onto rowing boats and taking them ashore."

Theo interrupted, clearly more impressed by the vessel itself. "The ship was *sooo* beautiful. She had all her sails down and was just bobbing on the sea."

Lydia clasped her hands. "The sea was beautiful as well. Such a lovely bluey green. Like the painting we used to have in the parlor. The one above the fireplace." For a moment her face took on a wistful expression as though she were far away, back in Bath.

Harriet frowned. Who could be unloading goods into a quiet cove in the middle of nowhere? Not a question she wanted to know the answer to, because whoever it was must be keen to do it out of sight of the authorities. Even though she knew little about the sea, she had enough sense to know that cargos were generally unloaded in big ports.

"Were they *smugglers*, Mama?" Theo asked, giving voice to her own fears, but managing to sound as though he thought it the most attractive of options.

Bertha harrumphed as though she thought Theo might be right.

"I'm sure they're not," Harriet said, which she knew for an

outright lie. "But nevertheless, do you think any of them saw you watching them?" She had to fight to keep the worry out of her voice. They'd only just arrived in their new home, and already danger threatened.

"I was lying on my stomach," Theo said. "Pretending I was watching out for the Spanish Armada so I could go and warn Drake where he's playing bowls on the Hard. They couldn't have seen *me*." He squinted at his much taller sister. "But *Lydia* was standing right on the edge of the cliff."

Lydia had the grace to blush. "I couldn't help it, Mama. I didn't know there'd be anyone there, and I didn't know they might be smugglers." Her voice rose in panic. "How was I supposed to know? Do you think they saw me? Do smugglers come after people they think have been spying on them?"

Hands on hips, Bertha peered out of the kitchen door towards where the none-too-distant cliff edge lay beyond the trees, perhaps expecting a cutlass-wielding smuggler to come charging over it at any moment.

Harriet patted her daughter's arm. "There, there, Lyddie. They're probably just local fishermen unloading their catch. Your brother's been reading too many boys' adventure stories. But all the same, it would be best for you to stay close to the cottage if there are fishermen about. They might be quite rough people."

Bertha nodded. "Best to keep ourselves to ourselves here, I'd say."

Harriet bit her lip. In the past year Lydia had changed, almost overnight, it seemed, from an awkward, gawky child into a beautiful young woman, with Harriet's luxuriant chestnut hair and her father's heather-green eyes. In Bath, it had been relatively easy to keep young men away from her, mainly because they hadn't known any, and didn't mix with people who had sons her age. But Harriet had a feeling that here in Cornwall, things might well turn out to be different. And fifteen was far too young to be considering matters of love, which no doubt an innocent young girl would do if introduced to a handsome young fisherman. Or even a not-so-handsome one who took the trouble to pay her court. Or, heaven forbid, a smuggler.

Lydia pouted but didn't demur. Perhaps she'd felt more than curiosity on spying the unknown ship down in the cove and instinct had warned her to be more wary. She gave herself a little shake and changed the subject. "Mama, we aren't going to have to sleep here tonight, are we?"

Theo smacked his hand against his forehead. "Unless you want to walk all the way back to Penzance. The wagon's gone, remember. What a silly you are."

Lydia clenched her fists. "Don't you call me silly."

Oh no. Harriet recognized the light of battle in her daughter's eyes. She wasn't yet grown up enough to resist a fight with her brother if she perceived herself wronged.

Bertha got in there first, though. "Theo, go and fetch our bags in from where the carrier left them. Lydia, let's see if we can find a broom. Or better still, three brooms."

Harriet heaved yet another silent sigh. Thank heavens for Bertha. What would she do without her?

Shooting her brother an angry glare, Lydia followed her mother from the kitchen into the parlor, her nose wrinkling still further at the state of it. "I think we're going to need more than brooms, Mama. Where are the servants? Surely Aunt Bolitho will have sent a maid to prepare the house for us?" She paused, no doubt because the unlikelihood of this was settling over her. "Won't she?"

"Clearly not," Harriet said, spotting a mangy birch broom leaning up against a wall. "Here. You take this one and sweep out the kitchen. Start with the ceiling to get all the spiders' webs down. Then the walls and furniture and finally the floor."

"Spiders' webs?" Lydia took the broom between finger and thumb as though it were made of something disgusting. "Can't we get a maid in to do that? Why do I have to do it?"

"Because we don't have a maid any longer," Bertha said. "Only me and you. So if you want to spend the night in a house full of spiders, you go and sit on the grass outside."

Theo lugged in one of their well-stuffed valises. "Where shall I put it?"

Exactly. Where in this filthy house should they store their bags? "The bottom of the stairs," Harriet said. They could sweep out the ground floor and then go upstairs, but for now the stairs, dirty or not, were the best place for their bags. "Can you go and get the rest?" She turned back to Lydia who still held the broom as though it might bite her. "And you can get started. Off you go. I'll do the parlor."

"Theo gets to do the easy job, as usual," Lydia moaned.

Theo scowled at her. "These bags are heavy. What did you pack in yours, Lyddie? It feels like bricks. Did you pack bricks? Did you?"

Lydia raised the broom like a weapon.

Harriet stepped between them. "If you persist in arguing, we'll never get this house done by nightfall, and we'll all have to sleep amongst the spiders. Get on with it, both of you."

Lydia let out a little squeal and hopped to one side as though in the process of being attacked. "Spiders?"

Theo snorted with laughter. "What did you think made the webs, then? Fairies?"

"Outside, Theo," Harriet snapped. "Hurry up."

With her two children gainfully employed... well, perhaps... and while Bertha bustled off upstairs, Harriet turned her attentions to the parlor. If you could call it that. In fact, the whole house had an air of not being what she wanted it to be and being proud of it. As luck would have it, a second broom, even less generously equipped with birch twigs than the first, leaned against the wall at the foot of the stairs, where Theo had dumped the first of their bags.

Harriet peered up at the beamed ceiling. Liberally festooned with both spiders and their webs. She wasn't about to admit it, but she hated spiders as much as Lydia did. If only she had something to put around her head. What was in her bag? She undid the clasp and rummaged inside. An old scarf. That would do. She took off her best bonnet and instead wrapped the scarf around her hair, knotting it securely at the back of her neck. Spider protection.

Now to tackle the eight-legged beasties.

She'd denuded the ceiling and begun on the walls, and Theo had been dispatched to explore the shed at the back of the house in search of firewood, when the knock on the door came. Wiping trailing webs off her face, and no doubt a few spiders as well, Harriet set down the broom and hurried into the kitchen. Lydia, too, had stopped sweeping. Her hair was full of dust and bits of web. Best not to tell her.

"Who is it?" Lydia whispered, as though whoever it was might be dangerous. One of the smugglers, maybe, come to silence them. Her eyes had gone round with fear. Surely her fears were unfounded. Harriet shoved all thoughts of vengeful smugglers aside. Things like that just didn't happen to people like them.

However… "Go upstairs and don't come down until I tell you to. It might be best to be as quiet as you can." Why was she encouraging Lydia's suspicions? Of course it couldn't be anyone dangerous, could it? How ridiculous was that. This was 1815, not the Middle Ages. She was quite safe and so were the children. All the same…

Lydia scurried away and Harriet lifted the latch and opened the kitchen door.

A woman was standing on the doorstep. Definitely not a smuggler, she wore a fine muslin gown with a delicate lace shawl about her shoulders and had a pretty straw bonnet set on dark curls gently scattered with gray. Her heart-shaped face hinted at her age, although the lines about her sea-blue eyes and curving mouth spoke of laughter rather than worry. She smiled at Harriet in an open, friendly fashion, as though being greeted by a woman with spiders adorning her head was quite normal. "Good evening. I hope I'm not putting you out by calling to see you like this? On your first day here at Keynvor Cottage."

Harriet closed her mouth, aware that Lydia had not retreated upstairs but was peering through the parlor door, now their visitor had proved not to be dangerous. Bertha's heavy footsteps came clumping down the stairs.

"Not at all," Harriet managed, acutely aware of what a state she must be in, wearing most of the house's dirt, and wishing the woman anywhere but here, nice as she appeared to be.

The woman, a lady by appearance and speech, smiled again. "I heard Mrs. Bolitho had let the cottage and thought I should come down to welcome you to Bessie's Cove." She paused, her eyes flicking to the gloomy inside of the cottage that Harriet and Lydia's labors had done nothing yet to improve. "And I have to admit that I feared you would find the cottage in this state. Mrs. Bolitho must have known nothing of this, I assume, or she would have prepared for your arrival. In truth, I'm here as your neighbor to offer my assistance."

Heat climbed from Harriet's throat to her cheeks, flaming them with mortification that this stranger was here to offer her charity. More charity. Because, of course, this cottage was charity in the first place, and Mrs. Bolitho, aunt or no aunt, had plainly thought her duty done in offering it. Which was true, really, as what did she owe Harriet, who wasn't even related by blood? The humiliation of her situation washed over Harriet and tears pricked in the corners of her eyes.

The woman stepped forward and laid a gentle hand on her arm. "My dear. I'm so sorry. I didn't mean to upset you. I'm here to offer you my friendship."

Bertha clumped into the kitchen.

Harriet fought to control herself at this onslaught of kindness, but the tears wouldn't be denied and, forcing their way out, trickled down her dusty cheeks. For a moment, nothing happened, then suddenly she found herself enfolded in the woman's surprisingly strong arms and pressed against her chest, soothing hands patting her on the back and stroking her hair.

"There, there," crooned the woman. "Let it all out. I can see you need to. And don't worry yourself. I'm here to help."

This show of kindness was enough to have Harriet sobbing, something she'd not done since before Ben died, and then only in the privacy of her bedroom.

"Mama?" Lydia's nervous voice intruded, at last.

She'd never let the children see her cry before.

Harriet extricated herself from her comforter's embrace, swiping at her eyes with her dirty hands, for want of anything else. "I'm so sorry." The words came out in a mumble. "I shouldn't have done that."

"Nonsense," the woman said with the air of someone used to dealing with crises. "There's nothing wrong with showing your emotions. A good cry can do us the world of good. Now, I'd best introduce myself as I've just embraced you. Talwyn Trevelyan of Rosudgeon House. I saw the carrier's wagon pass from my window—there's only the one road into the cove—and decided to come down here to make sure you were all right. And it's just as well I did. Mrs. Bolitho doesn't appear to have made any preparations for your arrival." She snorted in what might well have been disgust. "Not that I thought she would."

Harriet remembered herself enough to bob a curtsey. "Harriet Penhallow. Mrs. Bolitho is my late husband's great-aunt. She owes us nothing. It has been exceedingly kind of her to even allow us to live here. We are most grateful for her kindness."

Bertha, who owed no such allegiance, snorted. "Common decency would've had her make sure as the cottage were in good order though. You'd think."

Mrs. Trevelyan frowned. "Perhaps. But I am here now, and I insist you allow me to help you." She held up an admonishing hand as Harriet opened her mouth to protest. "No. I will brook no refusal from you. You have children." She waved a dainty hand at Lydia and Theo. "You need help. I am here to provide it, as a good neighbor should. Let us go inside and see what is required."

Without waiting to be invited, Mrs. Trevelyan stepped inside, and Harriet followed her back in. For a moment or two, their guest stood staring about herself, an expression of acute intelligence on her face, as though assessing the amount of work required. "You intend to sleep here tonight?"

"No," Lydia put in before Harriet had time to answer.

"Yes," Harriet snapped, shooting an angry frown at her daughter. At least the kitchen was now devoid of cobwebs but dust hung in the air, tickling the nostrils and making her want to cough and sneeze.

Mrs. Trevelyan's gaze lit on the range. "No one has lived here, I doubt, since old Brewinney Pascoe fell over the cliff on his way home from Bessie's Kiddley three years ago. And it looks to me as though no one's been in here to clear up after him."

Theo burst through the door, his arms piled high with dry driftwood, and skidded to a halt on the stone-slabbed floor, eyes wide with surprise.

Mrs. Trevelyan bestowed one of her lovely smiles on him— enough to make his cheeks blossom with color.

"My children," Harriet said, a trifle belatedly, still wiping at her eyes. "Lydia and Theo. And this is Bertha, our maid."

Mrs. Trevelyan nodded. "Work is required in here immediately to render the cottage habitable for you tonight. You are not common mine workers, as Brewinney was, and cannot be expected to live like this." She waved her hand at her surroundings. "When I next see Mrs. Bolitho, I shall have something to say to her about the state of her property."

Oh no. She couldn't be allowed to do that. Harriet shook her head. "Please don't. We are very much reliant on her kindness in allowing us to live here, as I've said. She might well take the cottage away from us if you were to tax her with its state. I'm sure once we have it cleaned it will look much better."

Mrs. Trevelyan's eyes narrowed and her lips pursed. "Well," she said, with a shake of her head. "If you allow me to offer my assistance right now, perhaps I might not bother your aunt about it." She eyed Harriet up and down. "One thing is certain. You cannot do this by yourselves in the few hours of daylight remaining. What do you say?"

Harriet glanced at Bertha and Lydia, who both nodded with determination.

Theo didn't count. He was the sort of boy happy to sleep in a barn.

Harriet swallowed. "Then in that case, dear Mrs. Trevelyan, we will happily accept what neighborly assistance you can offer us. Thank you very much for your kindness."

Mrs. Trevelyan beamed. "It's decided, then. I will hasten home and send down a wagon of supplies for you with some of my hardest-working servants. Many hands will make light work, as they say. You must tell me what you need, because I have plenty of furniture in storage that I can send down." She glanced at the range. "And someone to make sure this contraption works." She gave the rust a poke. "I'm sure it's just on the surface and nothing worse, although kitchens are no longer familiar to me." She benefitted them with her charming smile once more, her eyes fixing on Theo's armful of driftwood. "And I doubt there is much in the way of firewood here. I'll add that to my list."

Chapter Three

ALONGSIDE WILL, JACK strode up the steep track towards Bessie's Kiddley, where it squatted on the clifftop overlooking the tiny cove. Even though it still bore its old name, after the woman who'd established it, and who now presided over the taproom from a big armchair by the fire, by rights the kiddley should have been known as Lovey's.

Lovey Bussow was the wife of Jack's bo'sun, Daniel, himself a nephew of old John Carter and therefore cousin to Will's wife, Eliza. They believed in keeping it in the family here in the Cove. She'd been a barmaid in the kiddley for several years before she'd snared Daniel, helped by the fact she'd been expecting his child.

Old Bessie, ten years younger back then and still a force to be reckoned with behind the bar, had insisted Daniel make an honest woman of the girl and give a name to the babe, despite his protestations that anyone could have been the father. Cado, who luckily happened to be the image of Daniel, had been born six months after the wedding, and little Rosanna two years later. Jack had to admit that the childless Bessie had chosen Lovey as her successor well, and perhaps the forced wedding had been for an altogether different reason than making Lovey and her baby respectable. For Lovey was cut from the same piece of cloth as Bessie herself, and there'd never been any drama in the kiddley.

At the cliff edge, Jack peered over until he spotted *The Fly* bobbing a little further out, where she was in no danger of running aground when the tide went out. A reassuring sight he couldn't resist checking on.

"No doubt your crew'll be coming ashore to whet their whiskers in the kiddley before they're off to Penzance and the law-abiding job of carrying fish," Will said, with a grin.

Jack nodded. They would leave the ship's boy, young Clemo, who was only thirteen, on board to check the anchor didn't drag. Came of being the youngest on a ship—you always got the worst jobs. He'd been in that situation himself as a boy, as had Will in his time, and Daniel and Harry. He'd best make sure his men weren't too long in the kiddley, though, or they'd be sailing into Penzance drunk and in near darkness in his precious new lugger.

The kiddley was a long, low building, perfectly constructed to withstand any gales that blew in off the sea, which they often did in winter. She clung to her position a little set back from the cliffs like a limpet on a rock, a cluster of barns, stables, salthouses and fish presses sheltering behind her where the rising land made a nook for them around a cobbled yard.

He pushed open the solid oak front door and went into the room that served as taproom. Behind a couple of barrels topped by silvered wooden planks, Lovey Bussell herself, a generously proportioned young woman whose cheery expression hid an inner core of solid Cornish granite, was already holding out two glasses of brandy. "Cap'n Trevelyan. Cap'n Will. Good to see you."

Tables made economically from driftwood found in the cove sat higgledy-piggledy everywhere, a few grizzled locals already occupying one or two, nursing their own drinks. By the fire, also of driftwood, Bessie's bulk, increased rather than diminished by age, took up a solid ladder backed rocking chair, a clay pipe clamped between her toothless gums and her gimlet eyes on Will and Jack. "Ye're back, I see." Her loose lips smacked together as she spoke, and the pipe didn't so much as budge.

"Good evening to you, Bessie." Jack touched his forehead in

salute, something he'd done ever since he'd first met her as a boy, on his first sortie into her kiddley with his friends Kit Carlyon and Nat Treloar. Brave boys they'd been, back then, determined to act like the men they weren't, buoyed up by the false entitlement their positions in society had given them. She'd soon put them straight on that.

The peat fire smoldering in the grate, mingled with the aroma of the tobacco smoke, served to fill the room with a thick fug and render it even gloomier, but the old matriarch seemed unaffected by it.

Jack took one of the glasses, raised it in Bessie's direction, and Lovey handed the other to Will. From somewhere at the back of the kiddley came the bump and bang of unloading. Probably a barrel or two going into the kiddley cellars to supply Lovey's customers.

Will knocked back his brandy. "No revenue man'll be showing his nose here to look for our goods. They don't dare. 'Tis more'n their lives're worth."

Lovey refilled his glass. "You never did speak a truer word, my luvver." She chuckled. "D'ye remember when that revenue sloop chased the King o' Prussia's lugger into our cove and he saw it off with those guns he had set up on the headland?"

Will laughed. "Do I remember? I was there, girl, fighting them off."

Jack held out his own glass for a refill. He'd heard this story many times before, but it was one retold, with a few embellishments, almost every time they brought in a cargo of contraband.

One of the grizzled old locals looked up from by the fire. "I were there too. Best day o' my life, sendin' them revenue men off wi' their tails between their legs."

His companion nodded, his head shaking a little as though he had the palsy. "Pity the old King had to tek down those guns. Should've kept 'em. I can still see the face o' that soldier-man when the King told him they was in case the Frenchies tried to invade and all perfickly legal." He went off into a wheezing laugh that ended in a coughing fit, then spat copiously into the fireplace.

Will joined in the laughter. "They came back the next morning but there weren't nothing they could do. Nothing for them to find, neither."

Jack smiled. "I wish I'd seen that."

He'd knocked back a second and third glass of brandy before his men began to drift in, and Lovey set to serving them. He could have stayed a while longer with them, which they'd have liked, but he needed to be elsewhere. Setting his glass down on the makeshift counter, he turned to Lovey. "Can you get Amram to bring my horse round from the barn?"

With a swift nod, she ducked her head through the low door behind her and shouted to the hitherto invisible Amram to "get the captain's horse saddled quick now."

Jack slapped a few of his crew on the back in greeting, and headed for the door. Outside, the sun had sunk low in the sky by now, over in the general direction of Penzance, with a few pink clouds scudding across the sea's distant, hazy horizon, betokening a good day to follow. A breeze blew up from the cove, ruffling his overly-long dark hair, as his eyes of their own volition swiveled towards the cove's westerly headland, where he'd seen the girl as they came into the cove. Nothing there now but a few stunted hawthorn bushes. Maybe she had been a pisky, after all. Stranger things happened.

Shod hooves clattered on cobbles, and young Amram emerged from behind the kiddley. A rather scrawny specimen of youthful masculinity, he had a narrow, pinched face and too close together eyes that immediately gave the unfortunate impression of untrustworthiness, but so far, his service with the Cove Boys had been uneventful. Jack would just have to overcome his natural inclination not to like the boy.

He was leading Jack's fine black gelding, a horse he'd bred himself and had cut late, a decision that had given the animal all the attributes of being a stallion, with none of the problems where in season mares were concerned. Shadow was a lively ride, but sweet as a nut and nothing Jack couldn't cope with.

He took Shadow's reins from Amram and vaulted into the saddle without risking using the stirrup, settling himself comfortably as the big horse fidgeted under him, eager to be off. He'd been cooped in the kiddley stables all the while Jack had been over in Roscoff and must no doubt be keen to stretch his legs.

Amram stepped away from where Shadow's agitated hooves were sparking on the cobbles, a hint of fear in his eyes. Although his main job was the stables, a job which mostly involved hiding pack ponies, Jack knew the boy preferred to feel a ship's deck under him to dealing with the unpredictability of a horse. Not that a ship wasn't unpredictable of course—just that the boy probably had little imagination about what could go wrong at sea, whereas he could see for himself how dangerous a horse could be.

Jack nodded his thanks to Amram and threw him a coin, then turned Shadow up the track that edged the cliffs, keeping a tight rein on the horse. He had no desire for them to end up smashed on the rocks below. Over, just to the left of straight ahead, Tummel's decrepit cottage showed where it sat on the track west around the headland, and to the right of that, huddled amongst a few low trees and bushes, sat Keynvor Cottage… which should have been empty. Was that smoke coming out of its chimney? He did a double take, shading his eyes against the westering sun. Yes. It was. Someone must have taken the cottage. Didn't it belong to an old widow woman from Penzance? Its being occupied could prove to be a nuisance but also might answer the question about who the girl on the cliffs had been.

As the path wound away from the cliff edge, Jack let Shadow trot, although what the horse really wanted was a good old gallop. Not yet. He glanced back at Keynvor. Whoever had taken that on was in for a bit of a shock. They must be desperate, as the place had fallen into disrepair since Brewinney had gone over the cliffs. Probably someone's newly employed farmworker who'd just be glad of a roof over his head and would turn an obliging blind eye on the goings on in the cove.

Passing the end of the track that led down to Keynvor, Jack gave Shadow a looser rein, and the horse sprang forward into a canter as they headed inland. He was almost home when he had to haul hard and bring his horse to a halt. Up ahead of him, trundling along the track in the direction of the cliffs, was a precariously loaded wagon. And walking by the head of the horse pulling it was none other than the gigantic figure of Locky Massen, one of his own servants. Riding on the seat and driving the wagon was Mrs. Keneder, his housekeeper, beside Bronnen, his housemaid. What on earth were all his servants doing out here?

The wagon ground to a halt in front of him, mainly because the track was too narrow to let it pass unless he moved Shadow right up against the hedge. None of his employees looked a whit embarrassed that they'd been caught out apparently absconding with a load of his furniture and what looked like a heap of firewood and a large basket piled with food from his pantry.

Jack frowned at them. "Well? Is anyone going to tell me what's going on?"

Locky tugged his sparse forelock, a knitted hat hiding his balding pate. "'Tis on the orders of the Mistress… Sir." The sir sounded like a bit of an afterthought. These servants of his were inclined to regard his mother as their employer even though she wasn't the one who paid their wages. He wasn't helped by the fact most of them had known him since he'd been in petticoats, when his mother *had* been the one in charge.

Jack sighed and raised an eloquent eyebrow. "What orders would those be?"

Mrs. Keneder leaned forward in her seat. "We're to take all this to Keynvor Cottage on account of a fine lady in straitened circumstances having come to live there, Sir. Your mother, she walked down to see them a while back and met the lady. We's to deliver this and help with the clean up." She wrinkled her nose. "Being as you don't mind, that is." Also an afterthought. When had any of them bothered about what he minded?

Jack sighed again. His mother would only grumble at him if he turned them around, and in his experience, it was best to mollify her sometimes strange whims. "Very well." He guided Shadow into the hedge with a touch of his leg. "You'd best do as she's told you then." He fixed Mrs. Keneder with a stern frown. "I suppose it's cold cuts for me tonight then?"

Mrs. Keneder, whom he knew full well to be fond of him, allowed her face to crinkle into a wide smile. "All set ready for Abigail to serve when you're home, Sir." She clicked to the horse, and Jack watched his furniture and food rumble past, before turning Shadow back for home. He'd have to think about this. An actual lady living at Keynvor Cottage was an entirely different prospect to some local farmhand and his family, who knew to keep their mouths shut about his and Will's smuggling runs.

Chapter Four

HARRIET STOPPED SWEEPING and leaned on her birch broom. A swirl of dust and dirt eddied in the breeze provided by the open windows of what might, if one's imagination were particularly vivid, eventually be considered a parlor. Upstairs, Bertha was still crashing about and, in the kitchen, Lydia and Theo were bickering. Again. This was ridiculous. She didn't have the tools to clean this place nor the skills, and neither did the children. It was never going to be habitable. And she doubted very much if Mrs. Trevelyan had meant what she'd said. She'd probably gone off to her undoubtedly lovely clean home and forgotten all about her impoverished new neighbor.

She swiped a strand of hair out of her eyes and tried to tuck it under her headscarf. If it wasn't for the fact that they'd have been turned out on the streets in Bath, she'd never have accepted this offer, made through her late husband's solicitor. The one he happened to have shared, unbeknownst to Harriet, with his great-aunt. The one who, solemn-faced, had informed them that Ben had left nothing but debts that had taken most of their belongings, leaving them only the tiniest annual stipend on which to live. Buying those stagecoach tickets with almost the last of their money and heading west back to her home county had seemed the most sensible thing to do. Cornwall, both her and Ben's birthplace, had been calling to her, offering her the security of a home, despite the fact her parents were both long dead.

Theo crashed into the parlor. "Mama, Mama, there's a wagon coming. I saw it from the front door."

He ran to the parlor's front window, from which she'd just pulled down the most moth-eaten set of cobwebby curtains she'd ever seen, and she followed. The view to the left showed the track, the ground rising away beyond it towards distant, hazy hills. Sure enough, on that track and heading towards the cottage was a wagon, piled high with what had to be pieces of furniture. Two women sat on the seat and a man walked by the head of the single horse, his hand on its bridle.

Lydia hurried to her side, her hair now also safely under a scarf and her dress as dirty as her mother's. "They're coming here, aren't they? That lady said she'd send someone and she *has.*" Relief tinged her voice as she was no doubt counting on help with all this unaccustomed cleaning. And hopefully a real bed to sleep on that night. Harriet had to admit she shared her daughter's hopes.

The wagon lurched closer. Good heavens. It appeared Mrs. Trevelyan had indeed lived up to her promise. Perhaps Harriet shouldn't have been so doubting, but she was unused to people doing kind things for her. "Theo, run upstairs and tell Bertha. And mind you tread on the edges of the stairs. I don't think we should trust our weight to the centers. Not until we're sure." They didn't need him putting his foot through them tonight, and possibly breaking his leg.

"Even me?" Theo argued. "Bertha, yes, because she's so fat, but not me."

Harriet opened her mouth to reprimand him for his rudeness, but he'd gone, thundering up the stairs and quite definitely not treading carefully on the edges. Instead, she put his bad behavior away to deal with later, smoothed down her dress and retied her headscarf to control her unruly hair before hastening into the kitchen. By the time she reached the open front door, followed by Lydia, the wagon was just drawing up outside.

The man at the horse's head, a giant of a fellow with a kind, weathered face and startlingly blue eyes, whipped his cap off to reveal thinning gray hair. "Mrs. Penhallow?" His voice held the rich vowels of Cornwall Harriet remembered from her childhood, bringing another lump to her throat. What was all this emotion? She'd learned not to show it to anyone in the last sixteen years, but somehow, Cornwall was drawing it to the surface.

Struck dumb for a moment, she nodded, and he made her an awkward little bow.

"Mrs. Trevelyan, she did send us over to help you out. I'm Locky Massen, and this be Mrs. Keneder, the mistress's housekeeper, an' this here is Bronnen, the housemaid."

Harriet surveyed Mrs. Trevelyan's servants. Mrs. Keneder, whom Locky was helping down from the driver's seat, was a stout woman of late middle age, wearing a starched white apron and a matching mob cap. She had a look about her of industry and capability. Bronnen, on the other hand, now getting down from the wagon on her own, had a cheeky air that might well bode trouble—probably for any men she met. She had a mass of auburn curls inadequately contained by a white cap, its strings hanging loose under her chin, and couldn't have been much older than Lydia.

Mrs. Keneder took charge the moment her small, booted feet touched the ground. "We've a wagonload of furniture here that needs unloading." Her gimlet gaze fastened on Theo. "You're small but no doubt strong. You can help Locky get it all down. Set it outside for now, though, while we women make a start on the house." She nodded at Harriet, and Bertha, who had just emerged from the house and was having a sneezing fit thanks to all the dust. "Five of us workin' hard should get it done in no time. We've brought our cleaning things with us. I doubt old Brewinney even knew what a broom was, so the Mistress told me to bring everything I thought we'd need."

"Actually," Lydia said, with the tone of one who'd be happy

to relinquish hers, "there're two brooms."

"Well, that's as maybe. I've brought better ones, along with mops and buckets. We've fuller's earth and fine sand to scrub the floors with and oil for any woodwork as needs it. We want that furniture and the mattresses inside before it gets dark and the night chills start." She glared at the low-set sun as though her gaze might slow its progress.

Oh, what a relief it was to have someone in charge who knew what they were doing and had brought the wherewithal to do it. Harriet relinquished control of the cleaning with a grateful sigh, although Bertha's face betrayed her resentment at the intrusion of another servant of similar standing to herself. Mrs. Keneder began by striding inside and throwing commands out to left and right. Even Lydia didn't object, but set to with Bronnen to wash the bedroom walls and scrub the floorboards on her knees. Who'd have thought it?

And Mrs. Keneder was quite right. Five people working like canal navvies brought about a kind of miracle on the cottage that Harriet would have never thought possible. In a matter of a few hours as darkness closed in, all the windows had been cleaned, inside and out, no spiders or cobwebs remained anywhere, and, best of all, the dust had gone. The floors had all been scoured with the sand and fuller's earth, the walls and ceilings washed down, and Locky had set about putting the rusty range to rights.

Very shortly, they were all able to work together to bring in the furniture. The four beds went upstairs in pieces, to be reassembled in the bedrooms by Locky and his eager apprentice, Theo. "Why does Theo get a room to himself?" Lydia protested while this was being done. "I'm older than him."

"Because you're a girl, you silly child," Mrs. Keneder retorted, unfolding a sheet for the first completed bed with a snap. "And he's a boy. You'll have to share with your ma. He can't. No more than you can share with him."

"Even Bertha's getting a room to herself though. Just not me."

"Bertha only has the box room," Harriet said. "There's barely room for more than her bed in there."

Bronnen snickered, and Lydia glared at her but kept on working, perhaps afraid that if she stopped, Mrs. Keneder would vent her temper on her. Harriet smothered a smile that would have annoyed Lydia still further. This house was going to be very different to the house in Bath where the children had grown up, but at last she was feeling more confident about living here.

Once Locky and Theo were downstairs again, Harriet presided over the distribution of the downstairs furniture: four ladder-backed oak chairs for the lone table in the kitchen—all scrubbed, of course; a faded but still serviceable chaise longue for the parlor and several other well-worn upholstered chairs; a dark-oak sideboard for the kitchen and a box of crockery to display on it; a once brightly colored but now sadly faded rug for in front of the parlor fire, and a rather fine escritoire. Whoever had dispatched the wagon had seen fit to include some ornaments and a few pictures for the walls, which, once distributed, gave the little house a much more homely feel. Could it have been Mrs. Trevelyan herself? Surely not. She was a lady, so more likely they had Mrs. Keneder to thank for these touches of comfort.

Bronnen and Harriet unpacked the hamper: bread, butter, pots of jam and honey, milk in an enamel jug. "You can get more o' that from the farm up the lane, if you takes your jug over with you, an' a basket," Bronnen said. "That's where my ma lives. She do chat on a bit but she's happy to sell to anyone as calls."

Harriet found places for all the goods in the now spruced up and mouse-free larder: cheese, pickles, a large cooked ham, tea, some apples, two sacks of flour and small ones of sugar and salt, and a bottle of brandy that brought a heavy scowl of disapproval to Bertha's face. Had it come in on that ship Lydia had spied, or one like it? Even though she'd been brought up in Truro, Harriet had been well aware that a lot of the brandy the men drank had never paid any duty. The men her father had known had all seemed secretly proud of this fact. Were the children right, and had they found themselves in a den of smugglers? Best not to ask.

At last, everything was done and, under Locky's close supervision, Theo had lit the range, something he'd never done before but took to with enthusiasm. One of the sheds out the back had proved to be harboring a substantial pile of driftwood, which, added to the supply that had arrived in the wagon, would certainly do to start with.

Mrs. Keneder settled her bulk into one of the kitchen chairs with a sigh. "A proper job we've made of this." She smiled at Harriet, the first smile she'd deigned to bestow on her. "A nice cup of tea's needed now, I should think. Fill the kettle, Bronnen, there's a good girl."

The maid disappeared outside to the well that had provided them with the water for their cleaning, and returned in a few moments with a bucket of clean water. This she filled the iron kettle with then sat said kettle on the freshly blacked range, whose fire was beginning to roar. Mrs. Keneder nodded to Bronnen, whose face was covered in smuts from doing the blacking. "Why don't you take the boy down to the cliff edge and show him where to get gulls' eggs from, when they're laying? They make a tidy breakfast for a growing boy."

Theo, also filthy of face, hopped from one leg to the other. "Can I go, Mama? Can I?"

Harriet bit her lip. "Well, so long as you don't go too near the edge. Keep a good eye on him, Bronnen. He doesn't know cliff paths. It's getting quite dark."

Lydia stood up as well. "Can I go, too?" Her enthusiasm might well not have been for the expedition though, rather, effecting an escape from whatever chores remained to be done.

Harriet nodded, and the children, who appeared to have suddenly regained their energy, bolted through the open door behind Bronnen.

Mrs. Keneder spooned tea leaves into the china pot she'd brought, then added the boiling water. "No point in mollycoddling them when there's cliffs to be climbed and caves to explore."

"They're town children," Harriet said. "Not used to being out of doors the way Cornish children are." Not that growing up in Truro had been in any way an outdoor childhood for her, as it hadn't, apart from the riding to hounds she and her father had done.

Locky poured himself a tot of the brandy. "If'n you don't mind, ma'am, I prefer a tot to a cup o' tea at this time o' day."

Harriet waved a hand. "Please. Help yourself. It's the least I can do after all the work you've done."

Bertha fixed Locky with a reproving stare but, undaunted, he downed the brandy and poured another, then stretched out his long legs towards the range and yawned. "That were hard work, 'tis true. Shame on Mrs. Bolitho for lettin' you come to such a place. Mind you, I'm not surprised she done it. Just surprised she let you have it in the first place."

"Me too," Mrs. Keneder joined in.

Harriet's ears pricked. "Do you know Mrs. Bolitho?"

They nodded in unison.

"Not to speak to, like, seein' as we're servants. But to recognize if I was to see her out in Penzance," Mrs. Keneder said. "And to know of her reputation."

"I've never met her," Harriet said. "This was arranged entirely through my late husband's solicitor in London, who happens to be her man of business as well." Bitterness returned to her voice, but she couldn't help it. If she was being honest with herself, then bitterness was what she felt. "He told me she was prepared to let the children and me stay here. She was my late husband's great-aunt." She paused. "I had no idea she had a 'reputation.'" She raised her eyebrows, hoping they'd say more.

Locky nodded. "That explains it a bit, I don't doubt."

Mrs. Keneder poured tea for herself, Bertha and Harriet, dodging Harriet's implied invitation to expand on why her great-aunt by marriage possessed a "reputation." "All the same. She didn't do right by you to let you come down here to this. 'Tain't right. 'Tain't *proper* for a lady like you to be livin' like this."

They sipped their hot tea, and Harriet allowed herself to relax at last. Perhaps a tot of that brandy would be a good idea, but she'd wait until they'd left, and when Bertha wasn't looking. She didn't want them going back to Rosudgeon House and telling everyone she was a tippler. For the first time in ages, she felt as though things might be going to go right and she didn't want to spoil it by gaining a "reputation" of her own.

"If'n you don't mind me askin', ma'am," Locky said, pouring himself a third generous measure of the brandy with a wink at Bertha, whose brows had sunk so low as to almost obscure her eyes. "What happened to Mr. Penhallow?"

Harriet managed a wry smile. The truth would have shocked them so she wasn't about to give them that. "My husband was a captain in the hussars. We thought he'd done well to survive the Peninsular War unscathed, but then Bonaparte took a hand in his fate. The hussars returned to Britain last year, but as soon as Boney escaped, they were off again to Belgium. My husband fought at Waterloo. Fought and fell. He didn't come home."

Locky drained his glass. "Major Treloar, over to Roskilly, a few miles east o' here, he were in the hussars, too, I think. Only he didn't go back to fight at Waterloo on account of his wife being in the family way, I heard. And him being guardian to his young cousin."

"Your husband were a proper hero, my luvver," Mrs. Keneder said, patting Harriet's hand with her plump one. "A proper hero. No doubt about that."

Harriet bit her lip. That was what everyone said, thinking to console her. If they had any hint of how she really felt they'd have spurned her as an unnatural wife. She schooled her face into the correct expression for a recently bereaved widow, avoiding Bertha's gimlet gaze.

Besides, would a proper hero have left his wife and children destitute?

Chapter Five

HARRIET WOKE TO the unaccustomed raucous calling of gulls. For a moment, confusion overwhelmed her, then she opened her eyes and saw the beamed bedroom ceiling above her head. Sunlight streamed in through the curtainless window and she was struck by how homely the barren bedroom appeared. Cozy patchwork quilts decorated the two beds, the hump in the other indicating Lydia's still-slumbering presence, and a bright rag rug lay on the floor between them.

Harriet rolled onto her side and studied the small, now spotless window. Blue sky outside indicated the start of a fine day, which was not always true of Cornish weather, as she well knew. Not a day to be wasted lying in bed. She pushed the covers back and slid out, the old, and now well-scrubbed, boards smooth under her bare feet. No use getting up herself and leaving Lydia and Theo lying in bed. She gave Lydia a shake. "Wake up, Lyddie. Time to get up." Although what the actual time was, she had no idea, as Mrs. Trevelyan hadn't thought to lend them a clock.

Lydia pulled the covers over her head. "It's too early." Her voice emerged as a grumpy mumble.

"If you want breakfast, then I suggest you get up now. We have chores to do and you can help with them."

Lydia groaned. "Can't we employ a maid to do the chores?

Can't Bertha do them?"

Harriet shook her head and dragged the covers down. "You know we can't afford a maid. That we can't even afford to pay Bertha and she's staying with us out of the goodness of her heart. So, you'll have to get up and help me with my stays, then I'll help you with yours. Or neither of us will be properly dressed. Come on. Up you get."

Lydia groaned again, but at least she seemed to have given up on her protest. She sat up and rubbed her eyes. "Very well, but I shall be good for nothing, I promise you. I'm certain this is far too early. Much earlier than I used to get up at home."

Twenty minutes later, both of them fully dressed in worka-day gowns and boots, they woke Theo up, Lydia with untoward relish, and descended the stairs to find Bertha already attending to the fire. The embers from last night still glowed in the range, and a few well-placed driftwood logs soon had it roaring.

Theo came padding down in his night shirt, barefooted. "What's for breakfast?" He rubbed the sleep out of his eyes with one hand and failed to stifle a wide yawn. Had he gone to bed with those smears of dirt on his face? It had been dark last night, and she must have been too tired, to notice.

"Nothing if you don't get dressed," Harriet retorted. "But before that, can you go and fetch us a bucket of fresh water from the well, and I'll put the kettle on."

After a breakfast of milky tea and the remains of the previous day's bread, generously spread with butter and jam, Harriet set Theo to bringing in wood for the stove and sweeping the floors, and Lydia to washing and drying the breakfast things to be followed by helping Bertha with the chores, which, of course, she protested about. Then, her apron removed and her best bonnet secured, Harriet set off, having issued orders to her children to stay close to the house that morning and do as Bertha said. Saying a polite thank you for yesterday's help and furniture was top of Harriet's list of priorities for the day.

Mrs. Keneder had described how to find Rosudgeon House,

so Harriet had no qualms about getting lost. She closed the front door behind her and started up the path inland.

The raucous cries of the gulls permeated the air, joining the steady roar that must be the waves breaking in the cove. That might mean the tide was in. Although she'd been born in Cornwall, as had Ben, she'd never lived near the coast, and the sixteen years of her marriage had been spent mainly in Bath, so she knew little of the sea and her tides. The breeze that had been dancing the branches of the trees around the cottage began to pick up, and a wary glance over her shoulder revealed a dark gray line on the sea's far horizon that might mean bad weather coming. This, she did know, was typical of Cornwall.

To her right, on the far side of the cove, the tiled roof of a good-sized building rose above the surrounding trees, and a narrow path headed off in its direction, probably a sight too close to the cliff edge for her to feel safe on. But the high hawthorn hedges topping the stony banks on either side of the track soon hid the lower part of the building from view. With surprising speed, clouds were blowing in from the sea to largely cover the earlier blueness, but the day continued fine, and quite warm for September. For Cornwall in September, at any rate.

Every so often, she passed a field gateway, and, peering into it, was rewarded by a view of grazing sheep, or golden stubble or cows. In the far distance, a man was driving a pair of sturdy workhorses in front of a plough, but nothing else. A few birds sang in the hedgerows, but not many as it was autumn.

How good it was to be able to walk along a quiet lane like this and see nobody. What a contrast with Bath's busy streets, even those in the less genteel area where she'd lived. Too many people, too many carriages, not enough fresh air and sunshine. This place, despite its many all too apparent drawbacks, would be much better for Lydia and Theo. Why she'd ever let Ben take her away from Cornwall escaped her. She must have been mad—or so convinced she was in love with him she hadn't cared. But that had been sixteen years ago and the passage of time had shifted their relationship beyond recognition. If she'd been able to go back and give her love sick seventeen-year-old self any advice it would have been not to follow her heart in the rash way she had. Too late now. No use berating herself for her own youthful impetuosity.

She passed a few lanes opening off to left and right with hand-painted signs proclaiming "Beare's Den Farm" and, astonishingly, "Trengrouse Castle." This last she had a distant view of, as it was no doubt a lot taller than a farmhouse would be, its fancy turrets rising above the trees that surrounded it. Not the sort of castle a medieval knight would have called home, alas, but more of a medium-sized more recent stately home. Impressive. Who might live there? And might they possibly be in need of a governess for their children? Being a governess was the only thing she considered herself qualified to do, as she was most likely going to have to supplement her meager stipend by working. Or taking in sewing, which would not be a remunerative occupation.

She must have walked nearly a mile before she spotted another turning to the left, between banks of brightly flowering golden gorse, this one signposted Rosudgeon House. Aha. She'd found it.

She set off down this lane with a determined step.

Before long, she passed between tall gateposts and the track widened into a graveled driveway. The house was not as big as she'd expected, being less than half the size of the distantly viewed Trengrouse Castle. Two stone-built wings, with arched windows, must at some point have been attached, one at either end, to a simple manor house, possibly even a farmhouse, giving it a wide aspect and an appearance of opulence. Tall chimneys pointed towards the now threatening sky, and a pillared portico had been built over the front door. Good, not *too* imposing, but then, Mrs. Trevelyan hadn't seemed like the sort of woman who would have an imposing residence.

She approached the front door attempting to exude a confidence she didn't feel. Why did it seem so strange to be going somewhere without Ben telling her what to do and how to do it? She'd done it enough times while he'd been posted abroad with his regiment. What made it so different now? The fact that she was truly alone and always would be from now on. But surely, that was a good thing? She gave herself a mental shake, and tugged on the bell rope.

Somewhere far off inside, she caught the sound of the bell ringing. Would Mrs. Trevelyan have a butler? Was this house big enough to merit one?

It was and she did. A middle-aged man in a smart dark coat and breeches and black stockings opened the door, regarding Harriet from a rather lugubrious face with no hint of any emotion. "You rang, ma'am?"

Harriet pulled herself together in a hurry. "I've come to call on Mrs. Trevelyan. Is she at home?"

The butler stepped back. "If you would care to step into the drawing room, I will go and enquire."

As snooty as any butler in Bath, not that Harriet had much experience of them. She followed him to a door which he opened to allow her through into a drawing room, its walls a powder blue and a Persian rug spread over the polished boards. Behind her, the door clicked shut and she was alone.

She walked across the room to the two large windows and peeked out into what must be the gardens. Immaculately mown lawns stretched away to where tall trees formed a natural boundary and no doubt a windbreak. Most pleasing.

Turning away from the window, she ran her gaze over the contents of the room. What sort of a woman kept a house like this? One with a liking for china ornaments, that was certain. Above the empty fireplace a painting hung, of a young woman in an old-fashioned gown of some thirty years past with a little boy sitting on her knee. The woman, clearly Mrs. Trevelyan in her younger days, was beautiful in a rather wild and exciting way, with her dark curls loose and uninhibited and her gown cut low enough to show her plump, alabaster shoulders and the curve of her breasts. The child was young enough to still be in petticoats, and had an engaging mop of dark curls, very like his mother's, and a willful expression on his face quite out of keeping with his age. The artist had captured both their characters with skill.

Someone cleared their throat behind her.

Harriet spun round. Mrs. Trevelyan was standing only six feet away. "Mrs. Penhallow. What a surprise. I didn't think to see you here this morning." She sounded as friendly as ever.

Harriet recovered herself, aware her cheeks had taken on an uncomfortable heat. "Why, Mrs. Trevelyan, I had to come to express my most sincere thanks for everything you have done for me and my children. Without your help, we would have been sleeping on those dusty boards last night with no food inside us."

Her hostess's blue eyes twinkled, but her face remained straight. "It was the least a neighbor would do for a newcomer to Bessie's Cove. Had I known you were arriving, I would have made sure all those things had been done beforehand. *If* Mrs. Bolitho had thought it wise to inform me, which she did not."

"I fear that my aunt—I call her that as her true relationship is too complicated—would not have thought it fitting to inform anyone that she was allowing us to occupy her cottage. From what your kind servants told me yesterday, she is not a woman who often thinks of others."

Her benefactress nodded. "Sadly, you are quite right, but they should not have relayed gossip to you. Now, what am I thinking of? Leaving you standing here when I should be offering you a seat." She gestured at the elegant chairs. "Do sit down. I'll ring for tea. Unless you would prefer coffee?"

Harriet shook her head, and sat down. "Thank you, tea will be lovely."

Mrs. Trevelyan pulled the bell rope by the door and the butler reappeared as if by magic. "Ah, Crawford. A tray of tea, if you please. Here in the parlor."

She sat down on one of the chairs close to Harriet. "I trust you slept well?"

Harriet nodded. "Far better than we would have done had we been lying on the floor, thank you. The beds were very comfortable." She paused, at a loss what to say next. "Your servants were very kind to us, and we much appreciate you sending them to our aid, so please don't reprimand them for gossiping. It was me, pressing questions on them that loosened their tongues."

Mrs. Trevelyan's brow furrowed. "No need to keep thanking me. If you do, it will become tiresome, and I shall grow bored. Best to leave it at that."

"Of course."

The door opened and Crawford came in with the tea tray. He set it down on a small table near his mistress and retreated.

"That will be all, thank you, Crawford," Mrs. Trevelyan said. "I shall pour." She dimpled at Harriet, suddenly appearing a lot younger than what must have been her fifty years, and much more like the lively young woman in the portrait.

Harriet's gaze slid involuntarily to study the painting again. Was there a Mr. Trevelyan somewhere in this house? She resisted the urge to scour the walls of the drawing room in search of his portrait.

"Ah." Mrs. Trevelyan laughed, a soft, throaty chuckle. "You've spotted my portrait, I see."

"I couldn't help but admire it. Is it by any chance an Opie?"

Mrs. Trevelyan nodded. "You are right. It is. My... son's father had it commissioned when Jack was two." She shook her head. "A long time ago now."

Jack? Her son? Did he live here with his mother or might he be off in the army like Ben, or perhaps the navy, having been brought up so close to the coast? That would be more likely. Harriet didn't like to ask, in case, like Ben, he was dead. Her hostess did have a slightly melancholic air about her this morning as she gazed at the portrait.

Even if Harriet had wanted to, she wasn't about to be given the time to ask any questions. Mrs. Trevelyan leaned forward as she handed Harriet a dish of tea. "Now, tell me all about yourself, for yesterday we had no time to speak of anything but the necessities of life. With them under control, we can progress to becoming great friends, I think. I find it most pleasing to have a new neighbor to converse with."

Mrs. Trevelyan was clearly well versed in interrogation. Before long she had extracted most of Harriet's life story, or at least the parts of it Harriet was willing to divulge: the early marriage to the man she'd seen as her handsome, dashing soldier. A man whom she'd never suspected of being such a gambler, nor of being a… She shut that one off inside her head. No one ever needed to know that. The birth of their children, his departure overseas to fight for Wellington and his country, his death at Waterloo and Harriet's subsequent penury. Mrs. Trevelyan was a sympathetic listener, plying Harriet with tea and patting her hand as Harriet recounted her story. There was something about her hostess that loosened Harriet's tongue more than she would have imagined possible and had her confiding her fears to this woman when she'd no more have told her own dear-departed mother the details of her plight. At least, not quite all her fears.

"You poor dear," Mrs. Trevelyan finally said when Harriet trailed to a close, determined not to let the tears forming in her eyes fall. How easy it would be to succumb and cry again. But if she did, what would her hostess think of her? Once was bad enough, but twice? And besides which, hadn't she suppressed her tears countless times before?

However, when put together like this, her life seemed to be one long succession of things going wrong, so perhaps tears were justified. "At least I have my children. And dear Bertha."

Mrs. Trevelyan nodded, her gaze rising to the portrait above the fireplace. "One's children can be such a comfort in one's hour of need."

Harriet groped for something to say. "Do you have but the one son?" jumped into her mouth. No sooner had she said it, she regretted her impulsiveness.

Mrs. Trevelyan nodded. "Yes, but one son such as my Jack is

more than enough."

So not dead, like Ben. Probably. Really, she'd disclosed an awful lot about herself to her new friend, but had learnt nothing about her in return. Such as where was Mr. Trevelyan? The feeling that he didn't exist swept over Harriet. Perhaps Mrs. Trevelyan was a widow, like Harriet, but she could hardly ask such a prying question. Far too impolite. And where was the son? And the son's wife? And the son's children? Instead of asking all these questions, Harriet waited, hopeful her hostess might divulge some of this information unprompted.

Mrs. Trevelyan's eyes lingered on the portrait a little longer. "Such a sweet child." She gave herself a shake. "So like his father."

For some reason her words had Harriet wondering if he was no longer so sweet as he used to be, and if so, why not.

She was about to discover why.

The door of the drawing room swung open and a man strode into the room. He ground to a halt as his eyes came to a rest on Harriet.

He must have been over six feet tall, with slightly too long, almost black hair and curiously light brown eyes, so light they might almost have been said to be golden. He wore mud-speckled topboots, brown twill breeches and a navy coat.

Harriet blinked. Never before had she seen such a handsome man. His whole persona oozed masculinity and, right at this moment, an annoyance he was clearly struggling to hide. His dark brows unknit from the heavy frown that had marred them, and he visibly pulled himself together. "Mother."

Chapter Six

JACK STARED AT the stranger in his drawing room. She had to be the woman his mother had told him about last night. The one who was to be living, along with her two children, who were bound to be nosy because children always were, in Keynvor Cottage. They would all be perilously close to the seat of his and Will's smuggling operation.

His mother had described her as pretty, but that was a mild understatement. Despite being a mother herself, presumably to the well-grown girl he'd seen on the headland, she had the flawless skin of a younger woman, a cupid's bow of a mouth that looked dangerously kissable, and wide hazel eyes which were right now staring back at him in shocked surprise. The plain black mourning gown she wore accentuated the delicate pallor of her cheeks, where two spots of red had just bloomed.

"Jack, darling," his mother said, a smile lighting up her face. "I thought you were riding over to Carlyon Court to see the Beauchamps this morning?"

Despite a longing to retreat out of the room as though he'd never been there so as not to have to meet his far-too attractive new neighbor, Jack closed the door behind himself and approached the occupied chaise longue. "Good morning, Mother."

Still smiling, his mother patted her new acquaintance's hand. "My dear, may I introduce you to my son, Captain Jack Trevelyan. Jack, this is Mrs. Harriet Penhallow, who will be living at Keynvor Cottage with her children for the foreseeable future."

Oh no, not just a short visit to Cornwall then.

Jack made a polite bow to both his mother and Mrs. Penhallow, muttering a greeting, then straightened up, ready to make a hurried escape.

"Do sit down," his mother said, cutting off his hopes of a polite exit as she waved an elegant hand at the nearest seat. "And I'll pour you some tea. It's quite fresh still."

Unable to refuse without seeming rude, which he might well have done had not Mrs. Penhallow been there, Jack swept the tails of his coat out of the way and sat down on the edge of the seat, facing the two ladies, and wishing himself elsewhere. The lovely Mrs. Penhallow's wide-eyed gaze rested on him a moment too long before she snatched it away, those spots of color burgeoning afresh. For someone who must already be in her thirties, she seemed unusually shy.

"I see from the state of your boots that you *have* been out riding," his mother said. "But clearly not so far as Carlyon Court, or you would not be back here so soon."

Jack took the dish of tea she offered him. "Storm clouds are massing on the horizon, Mother. There's going to be bad weather, so I thought it best to remain here."

His mother, who was fond of Sam and Ysella Beauchamp, smiled. "As Mrs. Penhallow is going to be living nearby, it would be nice for her to meet our friends and neighbors, I think. Perhaps we should invite the Beauchamps over for dinner one evening? And the Treloars at the same time." She turned to Harriet. "The Beauchamps live a good ride away beyond Penzance, but there's a lovely walk along the cliff path to Roskilly, where the Treloars live. They have a little boy who must be about your own son's age, I would think. Mrs. Treloar, Caroline, is a dear friend of mine and will be overjoyed to make your acquaintance, I'm certain." She laughed. "Living down here in Cornwall we can all find the life a little lonely at times, so we relish the arrival of someone new with interesting things to tell us."

"Thank you. I should like that very much," Mrs. Penhallow managed, looking a little shell-shocked by this gushing speech by his mother and not at all as though what she was saying was true. She peeked sideways at Jack from beneath her eyelashes in a way reminiscent of a beaten dog expecting a second blow.

What was she staring at? Could it be that it had been her, not her daughter, he'd spotted on the headland, and she'd recognized him? No, the figure had been that of a slight young girl, not possessed of the full-bodied allure of a mature woman, like Mrs. Penhallow. He had to tear his eyes away from where a lace fichu hid her swelling breasts and chastise himself for looking at a widow in that way. A widow, according to his mother last night, whose husband had been dead a scarce three months. No wonder she was still in mourning.

His mother glanced towards the row of windows that looked out over the lawns and tutted her tongue. "You are right, as usual. A storm is indeed brewing. And I had *so* hoped to keep the garden looking tidy this autumn. If we have a high wind, the last of the roses will shed their petals, and we'll get bits of twig and branches all over the lawns. Again. What a shame. We've had such a good show of blooms this year and the gardens were just as I wanted them to be."

The lovely Mrs. Penhallow set her empty tea dish on the tray, those beautiful eyes of hers wide with a hint of relief as though she were glad of an excuse to leave. "If there's to be a storm, I think I should be getting back to my children, who are no doubt running rings around their nursemaid by now with their excitement at being so close to the sea. I don't want them venturing near the cliffs in a high wind." She kept her gaze on Jack's mother as though deliberately avoiding his presence. "Thank you again, Mrs. Trevelyan, from the bottom of my heart, for all the help you've given us. It is most appreciated and is very kind of you."

His mother squeezed Mrs. Penhallow's hand. "Not at all, my

dear, and do, pray, call me Talwyn. I would much prefer it. Whenever anyone calls me Mrs. Trevelyan, I feel quite ancient. And it was the least I could do to help you settle in. Now you have the cottage all straight, and we are friends, I hope you will come again to visit me. We *are* a trifle isolated here…" Her voice trailed off and she glanced sideways at Jack, an accusatory look in her eyes, as if he were responsible for her loneliness. "It would be a kindness to me if you would perhaps bring your children next time. It's been so long since Rosudgeon House echoed to the sound of a child's laughter."

Were those tears sparkling unshed in their visitor's eyes? Jack looked away so she could deal with them. What sort of a life had this woman led that his mother's small kindness could produce such a reaction in her? Because it was only a small kindness to a new neighbor. Just furniture he'd had in storage and supplies from their own pantry. Nothing, really. His mother would have done the same for anyone she thought might need it, of any class. And frequently did. At his expense.

Young Mrs. Penhallow, her tears controlled, rose to her feet and so did Jack's mother. She gave a tentative smile. "You have been the kindest of neighbors. Of course I will return and bring the children. They would love to come here, I'm sure."

His mother patted their visitor's hand again. "I'm so glad." She glanced at Jack, a glint in her blue eyes that had him worried. "Jack, dear, perhaps you could escort Mrs. Penhallow back to her cottage, as the weather is so rapidly deteriorating. I know Mrs. Pike has been hard at work this morning baking pasties, and I'm sure our new neighbors would like to try them, as they are quite the best pasties in the whole of Cornwall. You can ask Mrs. Pike for a basket and carry them down for her."

Mrs. Penhallow's eyes widened for a moment in what looked like real fear, before she had them under control again. How odd. Did she not want the pasties, the generosity or to be escorted home by him? Or was it just by a man in general?

Fortunately, Jack was well accustomed to schooling his own

face into blank indifference, something he frequently had to practice when out for the occasional unavoidable dinner at some local dignitary's home when the conversation turned to smuggling. He managed a gracious smile for his mother. "Of course. If Mrs. Penhallow doesn't mind waiting, I'll just go down to the kitchens and retrieve the pasties, shall I?"

Relieved to escape at last, but with the reprieve only of short duration, Jack bowed again to the ladies and beat a hasty retreat down to the kitchens, scene of many escapes from duty throughout his boyhood.

Mrs. Pike, who closely resembled one of her own doughy buns, with two deep-set currants for eyes, was just taking a second batch of pasties from the oven of the huge black range. Already, a row of six sat cooling on the large oak table. The scent of savory pasty filled the air, making Jack's mouth water. Molly, the dowdy little kitchen maid, was engaged in chopping turnips for the next batch at the other end of the table and from the expression on her face was as hungry as Jack.

"Master Jack," Mrs. Pike exclaimed, setting the hot tray on the low trivet on the table. "Following your nose, I don't doubt. Be you hungry?" She chuckled, a deep, throaty sound, and her ample body quaked with the effort. "When was you ever not? These ones here are about cool enough to eat."

Jack grinned. "Alas, I'm not here for my own gratification, tempting as your pasties smell. My mother wants to send some of them to our new neighbor as a gift and has sent me down to collect them. If I take the hot ones, they'll still be warm by the time she reaches her home."

Molly, ever nosy, squinted up at him in open curiosity.

Mrs. Pike banged the table at her. "You keep chopping and stop earwigging. 'Tain't good for a girl to go earwigging." She turned her gaze to Jack. "That'll be the leddy your ma sent all the supplies down to yesterday?"

Jack nodded.

"She's stayin' a bit near to the kiddley, I'd say," Mrs. Pike added, fetching a wicker carrying basket from the pantry. "I'll put 'em in here, shall I?"

Jack nodded again. "Thank you."

She wrapped each pasty separately in a clean white cloth. "And chilluns, I hear. Bound to be out and about and seein' what they shouldn't be seein', same as all chilluns. What'll you be doin' about that, I'm askin' myself."

Jack shrugged. "We'll have to see what happens with them there. We can always make the next run after dark, if the tide's right." Mrs. Pike's late husband had been one of the crew on Jack and Will's other boat, *The Black Joke*, and had been one of old John Carter's Cove Boys all his life, so she knew all about what went on at the kiddley and down in the cove and was understandably protective of it.

She tucked the wrapped pasties into the basket then covered it with an oilcloth as she'd probably already taken a look out of the window at the weather. "There. All done. You can take that upstairs to her now, and no nibbling at them on the way. There's some down here waiting for you when you've done your errand."

Jack didn't tell her his mother had commandeered his services as a porter and escort, but picked up the basket, thanked her, and returned upstairs. He found his mother and Mrs. Penhallow in the front hallway, peering out of the open front door at the massing clouds. A wind had risen and the trees encircling the garden bent before the force of it, leaves and branches whipping back and forth. The nearest rose bed already looked depleted of petals.

"Good heavens," Mrs. Penhallow exclaimed, just as Jack came to look outside as well. "I'd forgotten how quickly the weather can change down here."

Her black gown might have had long sleeves and, with the fichu attached, a high neck, but even Jack could see it would offer no protection should the rain begin while they were on the way back to her cottage.

"You must take my thick cloak, my dear," his mother said, her tone one that brooked no argument. "I fear we are in for a downpour." She paused. "Unless you would prefer to wait the storm out here? That might be better."

Jack pressed his lips together. Having a stranger stay in his house, despite her evident prettiness, was not something he wanted to happen. The fewer people who visited Rosudgeon, the better, as far as he was concerned, and here was his mother virtually offering open house to a stranger. Who, odd as this might sound, might even be a government spy. Who would suspect a woman with two children of anything underhand? Well, he would. The sooner she was gone, the better, from both his house *and* Keynvor Cottage. He cleared his throat. "The bad weather could well be set to last several days, Mother. Mrs. Penhallow has already said she needs to get back to her children. Just hurry up and give her your cloak and allow us to leave before the rain starts."

Mrs. Penhallow shot him a sideways glance out of those fearful eyes, but happily received the loan of his mother's cloak, and with a fond farewell for the cloak owner, stepped out into the portico, Jack right behind her. Crawford, who had been standing by unobtrusively, as usual, closed the door behind them with more force than was needed.

The wind immediately snatched at both of them, billowing the heavy cloak out like a sail and forcing her to hold it together as best she could with her hands. Jack had already hooked the basket of pasties over one arm, and now he felt constrained to offer his other arm to her.

She hesitated.

"If you don't take my arm, I can't guarantee you won't be blown away," Jack said, a little gruffly, as this inexplicable reluctance of hers was making him impatient. Surely she had no need to be so reticent and timid with him.

She blinked up at him for a moment, as though weighing him up, then, with a visible stiffening of her backbone, slipped a diffident hand into the crook of his elbow. He clamped it firmly lest she decided to remove it, and they set off down the drive.

The wind whipped around them, pushing her towards him, and she had to duck her head and bend slightly forwards to gain against the power of it. Typical Cornish weather—a storm springing up like this in such a short time. Jack pressed her arm against his body more firmly, to keep her close and support her, his own hair blowing into his eyes. It was far too windy to carry on any kind of conversation.

They'd reached only the halfway point in their journey when the rain began. At first just a few drops fell from the leaden sky, but within minutes, rain was pelting down, plastering Jack's hair to his head and running down his neck. The woman by his side at least had the cloak's hood to cover her, but the heavy raindrops falling with such force must have been soaking into the fabric.

She stumbled on the uneven footing, her hand clutching at his elbow, and Jack dropped the basket and turned to steady her, taking her by her slender shoulders and feeling her inevitable stiffening beneath his touch.

"Th-thank you." She had to almost shout above the wind and rain.

There was nothing for it now. He'd have to put a steadying arm about her to keep her upright. With the rain soaking into the wool of his coat, he retrieved the basket of pasties and pulled her bodily towards him. Under his grip he felt her stiffen again, before common sense must have taken over and she leaned into him, perhaps grateful for his strength. They hurried on as best they could.

After what felt like much longer than it should have taken, they reached the short track that led down to the cottage, the building barely visible now through the sluicing rain. Jack hurried his steps and Mrs. Penhallow matched his stride, no doubt as keen to be out of this deluge as he was. Jack and the wind pushed the door open with a bang, and they both tumbled inside. With his foot, Jack kicked the door shut behind them.

Three people were seated at the kitchen table: a stout woman of late middle-age whose apron suggested she might be a servant; a slender girl, her loose chestnut hair falling almost to her waist; and a small, curly-haired boy with a dab of soot on the end of his nose and wide hazel eyes very like his mother's. If he hadn't known Mrs. Penhallow to have children before this moment, he would have known these two to be hers with no difficulty, so alike were the three of them.

Chapter Seven

HARRIET UNFASTENED THE cloak and shrugged out of the soggy garment. The good thing about wool was that when it got wet, it stayed warm, and despite the wind and the rain now rattling against the door and windows, she wasn't too chilled. However, the hem of her gown was not just wet, but soaked and spattered with mud as well. What a good thing she'd worn her boots and not the dainty slippers she usually wore about the house.

"Miss Harriet." Bertha, after an initial shock that had held her unmoving for a few seconds, lumbered up from the table and hurried to take the cloak. "Whatever were you doin' out in weather like this? We was all worried about you."

Lydia and Theo nodded in chorus. "Where've you been?" Lydia asked, her gaze flicking to Jack's even wetter figure right beside her. Theo's eyes had widened in something akin to outright fear at the sight of a man in their kitchen.

Captain Trevelyan shook himself like a dog, water flying from his hair. He must be soaked through with no cloak on, although his woolen topcoat would have kept him warm as her cloak had. He rather filled the kitchen, large though it was, the top of his head in danger of brushing the now cobweb-free rafters. As tall as Locky Massen, but with only half the width.

Bertha took charge. "Come and stand by the range, the pair

o' you." She caught Harriet's hand and, with the other, ushered Captain Trevelyan to go before them as though she were herding hens. A small smile played on the captain's lips as he allowed himself to be hustled over to stand by the heat, one hand going up to swipe the hair out of his eyes. If Harriet hadn't been so nervous, she might have better appreciated how extraordinarily handsome he was…

She remembered herself, just in time. She really mustn't dwell on her escort's good looks and remember her status as a recent widow, and why she had vowed never to have anything to do with a man again. However, she couldn't deny that with looks like that he was most distracting. She could allow herself, perhaps, to look, despite her vow never to be tricked into love again. "Captain Trevelyan, may I introduce my children, Lydia and Theodore. And this redoubtable lady is their nurse, who is our only servant, Bertha."

Bertha pulled two of the chairs away from the table and set them close to the range, clearly prepared to treat their imposing male visitor just as she would Theo if he'd been out in the rain and come home soaked. "Just you sit down there, and I'll make you some nice, hot tea."

The captain's brows rose, but he took the offered seat, sweeping his wet coat tails out of the way as he sat down.

Perhaps he was expecting some other kind of refreshment now he'd got himself soaked through on her account? That was what men always wanted, wasn't it? "Bertha, the brandy for the captain, if you please."

Bertha's brow lowered in disapproval.

His lips twitched. "Pray don't put yourself out, Bertha. Hot tea will do nicely and warm me better. I find it an excellent pick-me-up in situations like this. Far better than brandy in all ways." He flashed Bertha a charming smile, and Bertha's cheeks, already rosy from the heat, became even rosier, as no doubt she chalked up his refusal of alcohol as being in his favor.

Heavens. Harriet had never seen Bertha react to a man like

this. What was the world coming to? Even an elderly servant could be swayed by good looks, it seemed, and, of course, the refusal of the brandy. Not that Bertha had ever appreciated Ben's good looks.

Bertha added fresh boiling water to the teapot on the range and gave the contents a stir, a definite benign expression on her homely face as she peeped sideways at their guest. Was she, for goodness sake, susceptible to the flattery of a man? Bertha, who'd barely tolerated Ben on his infrequent visits home from the army, and always with an air of resentment at his intrusion into their comfortable domestic setup. Even though she'd not known the half of it. This was something quite new.

About the captain hung a slight hint of resignation, as though he'd decided he had to put up with staying here to warm up a bit, out of politeness, perhaps. But he kept his tawny eyes fixed on the object of his attention—Bertha's stout form.

Why on earth was he fixating on her servant? Harriet frowned. What was going on here? Not that she wanted his attentions herself, but really, this was very odd.

Theo leaned across the table, eyes sparkling with curiosity. "Are you an army captain or a ship's captain?"

"Manners, Theo." Lydia, who also happened to be staring at the captain in fascination, could never resist the opportunity to correct her brother.

Theo shot her a scowl and tried again. "Are you an army captain or a ship's captain, *sir?*"

"Ship's captain," Trevelyan said, taking the cup of tea Bertha handed him with yet another charming, and this time suitably grateful, smile and bringing a fresh blush to Bertha's ruddy cheeks. There was no denying that he'd made an immediate conquest of her servant.

Harriet scolded herself for her thoughts and amended them, because, after all, she didn't want the captain smiling at her like that. Did she?

Theo's face had lit up at the mention of a ship. "And do you have a ship of your own? Sir? I love ships. I want to be a sailor when I grow up, if Mama will allow it. A captain like you. With my own ship. In His Majesty's Navy. Like Admiral Nelson."

Harriet's brow furrowed. Did the captain have a ship, or was he on leave, perhaps, from the navy? There were a few different types of captain he could be, although, looking at him, he didn't have the air of a naval man. Too roguish. She knew enough about men serving in both the army and the navy to suspect the man before her had never been in either. He seemed so very different to Ben and the few friends he'd ever brought to their house.

"I do indeed have a ship of my own," the captain replied, that strong mouth of his twitching again as though he might be finding this conversation with so small a boy amusing.

Theo sucked his lips in and threw a sideways glance at Harriet. "Could I see your ship, do you think? Sir? Please?"

High time to intervene before Theo forged a link between them that would be hard to break. "Captain Trevelyan must be a very busy man, Theo. Too busy to take curious small boys to see his ship, I'm certain. You must stop pestering him." Just because Mrs. Trevelyan had seen fit to bestow her kindness on them didn't mean her son would feel inclined the same way towards Theo. Most men, and this had included her own husband, saw small boys as a nuisance to be avoided. Both children had been very much "seen but not heard" while their father had been in residence, but especially Theo.

To her surprise, Captain Trevelyan shook his head. "Not at all, Mrs. Penhallow. I should be delighted to show Theodore my ship when it's convenient. She's round at Penzance now—in harbor I would hope in this weather—but when I rejoin her, I'd be happy to show your son around." He bestowed a smile on Theo. "I can even take you out to sea if you like. I'm assuming with your surname, you're Cornish born?"

Theo bounced up and down on his chair with glee. "You will? Thank you, sir. Thank you." He beamed back, full of boyish excitement. "I *am* Cornish, only I wasn't born here. Mama and

Papa both were, though. In Truro. And please call me Theo—Mama only uses Theodore when she thinks I've been doing things I shouldn't."

"Which is all the time," Lydia put in, a trifle waspishly.

Captain Trevelyan laughed, the sound somehow too loud and masculine in a kitchen that had shrunk in on itself with him sitting in it.

Too much masculinity by far, and Harriet's skin crawled just a little at the thought of how very male he was. His laugh was more of a guffaw, really, nothing like the way Ben had laughed when… She shook herself. Probably he was used to having to do everything loudly on a ship.

He held out his tea dish to Bertha for a refill. "If you're to become my shipmate even for a day, young Theo, then don't call me sir. Call me Cap'n. That's what my crew call me."

Theo's eyes shone. "Yes, sir, Cap'n." He clasped his hands on the tabletop. "I wish I *had* been born in Cornwall, but Mama left Truro when she married Papa, and Lyddie and I were born in *Bath*." He loaded his voice with scorn for the city's name. "It's a city. Lots of houses and no ships at all. Only a canal and a river, and the sort of barges that go up and down those are pulled by a horse. Not real ships at all."

Harriet frowned, her thoughts elsewhere. Had she not hinted heavily enough that she didn't want Theo having anything to do with the captain's ship? Ships were dangerous, as the present weather was enough to prove, not to mention the plethora of wrecks that surrounded the Cornish coast, that her own long-gone father had told her about as a child. She did *not* want her only son on board a ship, and especially not going to sea in what could be a leaky old hulk. Still, she could head this one off when the moment arrived, by finding an excuse for Theo not to go. She'd think about it then.

She sipped her tea, not quite sure what to say to this imposing specimen of manhood filling the chair on the other side of the range, charming her children and her servant and drinking tea out of one of the cups his mother had donated yesterday and that were probably his in the first place.

Luckily, he spoke first. "Do you intend to stay at Keynvor long, Mrs. Penhallow?"

"I hope not," Lydia said, from the table where she was now leaning on her closed book.

Harriet frowned a warning. "I don't really know." How much had his mother told him? Did he think her an indigent widow woman? Well, if he did, he was right. The mortification of this realization sent heat to her cheeks yet again. Thank goodness they were sitting so close to the range that he would think her pink cheeked only from warming up after her drenching. "We are here thanks to the kindness of my late husband's aunt." She paused, deciding to be honest. No point in hiding their situation. "After my husband died, I discovered he had amassed some… gambling debts. Once these were paid off, I was left with very little, so was most thankful when my husband's solicitor informed me that Mrs. Bolitho had so generously offered us this cottage. I see no possibility of change on the horizon, so we shall be here for some time to come, despite what Lydia would prefer."

Out of the corner of her eye she spied Lydia's resigned scowl.

The captain regarded her from out of those golden eyes, the reflected flames from the range dancing in them, and nodded. No charming smile for her, though. "I see. My mother wasn't terribly clear about your circumstances. She is a rather… disorganized person and often forgets to pass on things she's been told. You have my commiserations for your plight. Might I be so bold as to enquire as to the circumstances of your husband's demise?"

Had his mother not mentioned Waterloo to him? Best to be honest about that too. Not too honest, though. "My husband, Ben, was a captain in the 18th Hussars. He fought in Spain and southern France before Bonaparte surrendered. He returned home…" She faltered. "Then he was recalled this year, when the Little Corporal escaped from Elba, and returned to France. Ben was killed at Waterloo."

Somehow, the retelling of his loss felt cathartic. It was something that needed putting behind her, shut away in a box with no key, so she could get on with her new life without him. But she hadn't been able to, thanks to her anger at the situation he'd left his family in. The situation he'd left his children in. For herself, she could have managed, but with children… how hard it would be for them from now on. She'd had to withdraw Lydia from her school and dismiss Theo's tutor, Monsieur Bulot, in order to teach them herself, something that didn't guarantee family harmony. And on top of that, there'd been the loss of the house she'd loved and where her children had been born…

She sighed. "My husband loved the army, Captain Trevelyan. I know he would have been proud to give up his life for his country." At least that wasn't a lie. He would have seen it as the only way a soldier should end—death rather than retirement. He'd hated those months kicking his heels in Bath, something he'd made abundantly clear, and been overjoyed when Boney had escaped his imprisonment. So had Harriet, but for different reasons.

The captain's eyes narrowed. Could he perhaps read between the lines of the story she was telling? "I believe one of my neighbors, a boyhood friend of mine, was himself an officer in the 18th. Major Nathaniel Treloar, of Roskilly House, whose wife my mother recommended you visit. He might well know of your husband." He paused. "He was not himself at Waterloo having resigned his commission last year and taken on the responsibility of being guardian to his young cousin. And he was just married." He glanced at Theo. "The young cousin he's in charge of is of an age with your son, I think. Perhaps Theo would like to meet him? I could show them *The Fly* together." A small smile escaped him this time. "I know at their age I craved the company of other boys."

Harriet relaxed. That sounded a more acceptable rendezvous for Theo. Better than having him run away to sea with ideas of adventure, as boys his age had been known to do. Twelve was not too young to become a midshipman in the navy, even though to her he was still her little boy.

"That would be lovely," Harriet said. "As your mother was so kind as to suggest it, I think I will walk round to visit them. Not now. When we have settled in and the weather has improved."

Theo interrupted. "I could go there on my own, Mama. Where is Roskilly? Is it far? Cap'n?"

"Maybe a little over two miles along the cliff path," the captain said. "An easy walk for a boy your age."

Harriet shook her head. "Not on your own, Theo. That would be quite rude. All three of us will walk that way in a day or two, after this storm abates, and hope for you to make the acquaintance of the boy who lives there."

The captain rose to his feet. "And now I must leave you, Ma'am. I don't anticipate any let up in the weather, so I might as well set out now, rather than wait." He turned to Bertha, his smile returning. "My thanks to you for the restorative nature of your tea."

Bertha, who had resumed her sewing, colored from her throat right up her face but managed a smile back.

He winked, yes, winked, at Theo, as though they were partners in some clandestine enterprise. "And perhaps we shall see one another some day soon."

Theo beamed back at him as he headed for the door. "I hope so... Cap'n."

Harriet rose to her feet as well. She had to protest at his leaving in such dire weather, even though an overpowering desire for him to depart had swept over her. His size, his imposing personality, and above all his good looks, had produced a distinct disquiet in her. She chided herself that she was a widow and had vowed after Ben's death to have nothing further to do with the opposite sex. "Are you sure you don't want to wait to see if it lessens a little?" Her lack of enthusiasm must have been evident as Theo shot her a puzzled look.

The captain raised an eyebrow at her. He must have heard

her lack of conviction. Heat flared again in her cheeks at her own rudeness and lack of gratefulness for his having escorted her through the rain.

"I can assure you, ma'am, that this weather will not release its hold on Cornwall until at least tomorrow morning. There's no sense in my delaying. I shall make my way home again." He glanced at the still wet skirt of her gown. "And I suggest you change your gown before you catch a chill. Good day to you. And many thanks for the tea, Bertha." He glanced at Theo and Lydia. "Perhaps we will meet again soon."

The door jerked on its hinges as he opened it, pushed inwards by the force of the wind, but before Harriet could go to help, he'd closed it behind him. Instinct had her hurrying to the front window to peer out of the raindrop filled glass as he walked back up the path towards the road. But he didn't turn left to head for his house. Instead, he turned right and disappeared from sight. How very odd.

Lydia banged her folded arms down on the tabletop and everyone turned to look at her. "That's the man who was on the ship Theo and I saw down in the cove."

"Was it?" Theo asked.

"Of course it was, you silly. Didn't you recognize him?"

Theo shrugged. "I was looking at the ship. Silly yourself."

Harriet turned back from the window. "The ship that was in the cove unloading… barrels and things like that?"

Lydia nodded. "The one we thought was a smuggler."

"That was his ship?" Theo's voice rose in excited admiration. "That's the ship he's going to take me out on?"

"A smuggler's ship," Lydia said with ominous glee. "You think Mama's going to let you go out in one of those, with a smuggler?"

Theo's fists balled in indignation. There was nothing for it. Harriet had to intercede. "Nonsense," she said with as much conviction as she could muster. "He's a gentleman so he can't possibly be a smuggler. Either you are mistaken, Lydia, or that was fish he was unloading yesterday. Captain Trevelyan is not a smuggler."

"That's what you think," Lydia muttered, bending her head over her book again.

Harriet pretended she hadn't heard her.

Chapter Eight

JACK STRODE DOWN the track towards Bessie's kiddley, the rain, sluicing in sheets in front of him, rendering visibility at a minimum. At least the wind had diminished a bit. The cliffs to his right hid the cove's tiny anchorage and the rain effectively shrouded anything more than a few hundred yards out to sea in a dull gray curtain.

He turned his collar up and hunched his broad shoulders. What on earth had possessed him to offer to take the boy out in *The Fly*? And young Yves Treloar as well? As if one boy to take care of wasn't enough. On the spur of the moment, it had seemed a good idea to involve their new neighbor's son and thus render it impossible for her to peach on them. But now? Had it been entirely wise to allow himself to make such an irrational offer? Had her extraordinary looks, and that wistful, hunted air blunted his customary wisdom and turned him into an idiot?

He rounded the bend and the kiddley came into view, the smoke from the chimney pooling in the wet air and hanging over the surrounding trees like a tatty shawl. That woman had him foxed. How could someone with two children that age still be the most beautiful creature he'd ever laid eyes on? And he'd be the first to concede that he'd laid eyes on a lot of parts of a lot of women in his thirty years. Not as a boy, of course, but since he'd turned fifteen and had first gone to sea with Will, finding willing women had never posed any difficulty. In fact, women had been part of his initiation into the smuggling life, and still remained an enjoyable part of it now. Although, oddly, not a single face came to mind right now from the many he'd associated with. All he could see was Mrs. Harriet Penhallow's wary visage in front of his eyes.

She was different. She didn't want him and wasn't susceptible to his charms. In fact, he'd had the impression she didn't like men at all and was perhaps a little afraid of him. He'd felt it oozing from every pore of her rigid body even as she'd allowed him to steady her in the wind on the way down from Rosudgeon. It had been clear that only common sense had allowed her to accept his help. At least, however, that must mean she could be classed as sensible. He couldn't abide a woman who wasn't. Heaven help their enterprise if she were to turn out not to be.

So, why on earth was he affected by her at such a deep and intrusive level? Was it because she looked so in need of protection? His mother had certainly picked up on that. He huffed a deep breath. His physical reaction to her in the kitchen had been hard to hide and he'd been glad to be sitting down. Damn it. He needed to stop thinking about her. She was off limits and had made it clear.

He reached the door of the kiddley, its blue paintwork excoriated by wind, sun and rain to a mere hint of the color it had once been, and the wood beneath bleached pale and smooth. Why had he set out to charm her elderly servant? Because he wanted to charm the mistress, and he wanted to do that because he saw her as a challenge to his manhood. That was why. Capture the servant, the daughter and the son, and he might find a way to the woman herself. With a grunt, he pushed open the door and went inside.

On the opposite side of the smoking fire to where Bessie sat, puffing on her pipe, Will occupied one of the tables working on his books, his half-moon glasses on the end of his nose. No sense being a smuggler without keeping your books neat and up to date. Will wasn't just a smuggling sea captain but also an astute businessman like his late father-in-law, and, between them, they'd taught Jack well. Better than the rather hit and miss nature of smuggling west of Penzance, on Cornwall's rocky tip.

A few years back, there'd been raids over that way, with several men killed or transported for their so-called crimes. Kit Carlyon, one of Jack's smuggling friends, who'd narrowly escaped with his life, had retreated back to his seat in Wiltshire to resume his role as the proper, law-abiding Viscount Ormonde, having gained himself a wife who'd by now presented him with several children.

Lovey Bussow rose from a seat behind the plank bar, smoothing her apron down and smiling a close-lipped welcome. So long as she didn't open her mouth to reveal the state of her teeth, she could be considered a pretty young woman and a draw for the kiddley. "Mornin' Cap'n Jack. Tot o' brandy for you?"

Jack shook his head. "Ale if you have it, thank you, Lovey."

She poured him a tankard of ale and brought it over to Will's table, where Jack had taken a seat.

Will looked up at him over the top of his glasses, in appearance every inch someone's diligent clerk instead of the most successful smuggler in Cornwall. "What're you doin' out in this weather? You not got the sense you were born with?"

Jack took off his coat and hung it over the back of his chair to dry. "Doing my mother and our new neighbor a favor."

"Our new neighbor? You mean the lass what's taken Keynvor Cottage? I hear she's a widow-woman, so no man around to bother us but with a pair o' likely children. You seen her already? And your ma's poked her nose in, has she?"

Jack nodded. "You have it spot on the nose, Will. My mother saw her arrive on the carrier's cart and couldn't resist interfering. As is her habit." He took a swig of his ale. "In the event, it turns out her help was much needed as no one's been near the cottage since old Brewinney fell over the cliff." He leaned back in his seat and stretched his wet legs towards the fire. "I fear it might have been better to have left her to get on with things by herself. Then she might have decided not to stay. As it is, my mother, having made free of my furniture and my food supplies, not to mention my brandy and my servants, has managed to make the cottage like home for her. She's staying indefinitely."

Will set down his pen on the table with careful precision. "Ah. That might be a problem."

Jack nodded again. "You can say that again."

From her chair, Bessie snorted and spat a wad of phlegm into the flame, making them hiss. "Wimmin like her allus be a problem. You mark my words. She do need a man to tek her in hand."

Will tipped her a salute. "It'll take a bit o' thinking round. The next run we do should be at night, just in case. Yesterday was risky even with no customs cutter likely to be about."

This made Jack laugh, and the old brindled dog sleeping on the rag rug by the fire lifted its head in curiosity for a moment before deciding Jack had meant him no harm and resuming its peaceful sleep as only an old dog can. "We're not likely to get one down here, not with the influential backers we have."

"You never know," Bessie opined, nodding her grizzled, mob-capped head with all the sagacity of her eighty-odd years and smacking her lips together over her toothless jaws. "Stranger things've happened, I can tell'ee."

Will pulled a disbelieving face. "Not a one of our backers'd want to lose their duty-free brandy. But still, daylight runs aren't the safest to make, even if the tide's in our favor. Could get an unexpected navy sloop down here, outta Plymouth, waitin' to creep up on an unwary free trader. I prefer to make my runs at night, as you know, and I think you're going to have to do the same, my lad. Don't want the widow-woman noticing what goes on right here on her doorstep, do we now?" He paused. "What did you find out about her? All I've gleaned is that she's got no man with her, which has to be good. We can always try frightening her into silence."

Did Jack want her frightened enough to prevent her peaching on them? There'd been such an air of vulnerability about her, leavened with a streak of iron determination, so maybe not. Any woman left alone in the world as she'd been, who'd decided to bring her children to a location like this would have to be strong, despite her nervous demeanor. Or she'd buckle. It might take a lot to truly frighten someone who looked as though she lived with daily fear.

He shook his head. "We don't operate like that. You know we don't. People don't peach on us because they like us, not because we scare them. They keep their mouths shut because we help them. Because we're part of their community. I'd say our best bet is to make her part of all that, so she feels loyalty to us. Make it worth her while to keep her mouth shut, same as everyone else." He drummed on the table with his fingers. "She's got a boy, about the age of young Yves Treloar. He's a likeable lad with a love for the sea in his blood. They're Cornish, all of them, so why wouldn't the sea be calling him? He asked to come and see *The Fly*. I said yes. If his mother thinks he's become a part of our undertaking, she'll not say a word for worrying what might happen to him if we're caught. Then when she feels the benefit, she'll keep silent out of loyalty. Like everyone else."

"Good idea. Work on the boy and the woman will follow."

Jack sighed. That might not be quite as easy as it sounded. "There's a girl as well, though, older than the lad. Pretty as her mother and with a look in her eye of rebellion, if I'm not mistaken. She doesn't like it here. She might be a problem. In fact, she's just at the age where problems start with girls."

This made Will laugh. "Said with all the sagacity of a single man with no daughters and no sisters. What makes you the expert on daughters, all of a sudden?"

"You don't have to have daughters or sisters to know girls. I've been with enough of other men's sisters and daughters since I was fifteen to know what a troublesome one looks like. And that one reeks of trouble. She's missing a father who was always off soldiering, as well as her old home in a big city. And now her mother's dragged her down to the wilds of Cornwall and she resents it, and her mother. She won't be blaming the father, who died in heavy debt, mark my words. It'll all be her mother's fault and she's ready to stand up on her hind legs and argue."

Will sighed. "Girls. I'm mighty glad I only have the one boy. Never could get my head around girls. Not even the wife."

"And you'd best watch your boy around that girl." Jack meant young Harry, twenty years old, good-looking in a rather wild way, and already popular with the womenfolk on both sides of the channel.

Will grimaced. "That boy'd chase anything in a skirt with a pretty face. Maybe wouldn't even need to have a pretty face."

Bessie let out a guffaw of laughter. "You could dress that table in a skirt and he'd run after it."

Jack's turn to laugh. "I rest my case. I can't see our widow-woman being best pleased to have a sailor boy coming sniffing round her daughter. Not one with no respectable intentions, that's for sure."

Will huffed in mock umbrage. "A girl with nothing to bring to a union could do no better than to look to my Harry. One day he'll have all of Porth en Alls and Prussia Cove and be a rich man."

"I doubt her mother'd see it that way. And since when was he the marrying kind?"

"Well, it's not happened yet, so I'm not about to start worrying about it. Harry's round to Penzance right now with *The Fly*, in harbor, I hope, if Daniel Bussow's got the sense he were born with. When they've taken a cargo down to Plymouth, you can take Harry on your next run with you across to Roscoff and keep him out o' harm's way. He do lack a lot in the caution department where girls is concerned, that I'll allow."

Jack nodded. "Wise move."

"And the little lad?"

"He can come aboard when we've done the run, and everything's stowed away neat and tidy where no one'll ever think to look. I'll leave *The Fly* at anchor until morning then take him and young Yves aboard together. Time young Sir Yves got his sea legs now he's growing. Nat'll be happy for me to do it. He told me the boy's itching for adventure." He rolled his shoulders to ease the muscles. "You know that last year the boy set off exploring the mines under Wheal Jenny through that old adit on the beach? Fell in a water-filled mineshaft and had to be rescued by Nat and his wife, before she was his wife, that is. None the worse for the adventure, so Nat told me. By the look of this other boy, they'll hit it off well."

Will shrugged. "Let's hope they do then." He rubbed his temples as though the effort of bookkeeping had tired him. "It'll be good to have a couple of lads aboard for a jaunt. Take us back to our own young days, eh? Not that yours are too long gone." He reached out and ruffled Jack's hair, much as he'd done when Jack was a boy eager to curry favor. "You need a haircut, lad, if you're goin' a-courting."

Jack opened his mouth to speak but no words came out for a moment. He cleared his throat. "I most certainly am *not* going courting."

Will's blue eyes twinkled. "You think not? 'Tis written all over your face, lad. She's got you smitten."

Chapter Nine

THREE DAYS PASSED before the weather improved enough for Harriet to declare they would walk over to call on their neighbors at Roskilly house, as Talwyn Trevelyan had suggested. When she got up that morning, the low clouds had cleared at last, the wind and rain had ceased, and a blue sky was in evidence, promising a good day.

She helped Bertha clear the table of their breakfast things. "There's a path along the cliffs we'll need to follow to Morgelyn beach, I believe. Mrs. Trevelyan told me that would be the way to take."

Bertha snorted. "Along o' those cliffs? You mind you keep well back from the edge then. We don't want you a-fallin' over to your death." She wiped her hands on her apron. "Are you certain sure you know the way?"

If only Bertha possessed a slightly more positive attitude. "Of course I won't be going anywhere near the edge of any cliffs. And neither will the children. I'll make sure of that." She shot a determined glance at where her two offspring were still seated at the table. Theo, who'd been out exploring over the last few days in between bouts of pouring rain, sported a milky mustache on his upper lip. Should she send him over to the farm first to fill their milk can, or let Bertha, who'd made firm friends with the farmer's wife, Mrs. Voas, go instead?

Bertha would see it as a privilege, unlike Theo who saw it as an unwelcome chore, designed to take him away from his favorite undertaking—exploration. Best to let Bertha go if she wanted to be away soon. Theo, when tasked with a chore he didn't like, would not be quick about it.

Harriet smiled at Bertha's concern. "I do indeed know the way. Mrs. Trevelyan told me we're to pass one beach that you can't get down to easily, then a high headland with mine buildings on it, called Penmar Head, and down to a much bigger beach, Morgelyn, which is the one we want. Roskilly House is halfway along and up a track through the sandhills. She said it shouldn't be hard to spot."

"Are you *sure* the cliffs are safe?" Lydia asked, wrinkling her nose and frowning in distrust as she reiterated Bertha's sentiments. "Suppose we fall off them like the old man who used to live here did? It *can't* be safe, or he wouldn't have done that, would he?"

Theo emulated Bertha and snorted in mockery. "*I* shall walk right by the edge so I can look for gulls' nests like Bronnen showed me the other day."

"I don't like gulls," Lydia snapped. "They make such an awful noise with all their shouting."

Theo rose to the attack. "Gulls are really useful seabirds. You can eat their eggs in spring, and they show you where to fish. Bronnen told me. Only someone silly would say they didn't like them."

Lydia, never one to ignore a challenge, opened her mouth for a tart reply.

Harriet cut her off. "I expect the old man fell off because he was old, or ill, or something like that." Best not to suggest he might have been in his cups. She knew all too well what men could do when in that condition. "I doubt very much he just fell off without a reason. And of course gulls are very useful birds, Lydia. But Theo, you are *not* climbing down any cliffs to look at their nests. That would be far too dangerous."

Lydia pulled a face at Theo. "Haha."

Theo sprang to his feet, but this time Bertha interrupted, planting a heavy hand on his shoulder and pushing him back down onto his chair. "Probably the old man was the worse for the demon drink." She had no qualms about suggesting that. With her free hand, she wiped the crumbs off the tabletop. "Like as not, everyone round these parts is, there being an alehouse within spitting distance." Bertha, a Methodist from birth and lifelong abstainer from all things alcoholic, frowned on anyone she considered had debased themselves enough to take to the drink and had soon discovered the proximity of the alehouse. Ben's liking for strong liquor on his infrequent visits home had done nothing to persuade her otherwise.

Lydia sniffed. "All the same, I think I'd rather stay here with Bertha, if you don't mind, Mama? I don't like the idea of walking along the edge of a cliff. It's still quite blowy out."

Harriet eyed her daughter. Lydia had reached the age of straining for some independence long before she'd expected. Best to make certain she stayed around the house and didn't go wandering off on her own. Who knew what might happen if she did. This whole area, bar Rosudgeon House and possibly the old farmer and his wife, who seemed very pleasant, was an unknown quantity, and Harriet intended to explore it herself before allowing her daughter any kind of liberty. Theo, being a boy, was different. Plus, he was of a more boisterous nature, and she'd been happy to let him out of the house to expend some energy over the last few rainy days. "Of course you may stay with Bertha," she said. "There are lots of chores to be done, and you can help her."

Lydia's face fell, but a satisfied smile spread over Bertha's. "That'll be grand, young Lydia. I'm not so young as I was, and an extra pair of hands'll be a godsend this morning. We'll start upstairs."

Theo shot his sister a smug smile, and Bertha removed her hand from his shoulder. "Best get your coat on if you're goin' with your mama."

Harriet nodded. "You can be my escort, Theo, as you are now man of the house."

Bristling with pride, Theo forgot all about his sister and ran to find his coat.

A BARE QUARTER of an hour later Harriet, suitably bonneted and gloved, and Theo, left Keynvor Cottage behind and set off along the same route Harriet had seen Captain Trevelyan take on the first day of the bad weather. At the end of their own track, Harriet turned right, curious to see what might have drawn him that way.

She soon found out. The coast path led right past what had to be the alehouse, where it nestled under the low roof she'd seen when she'd walked up to Rosudgeon House. However, at this time of the morning, nothing appeared to be happening within its stone walls. Not even any smoke issued from the two chimneys. And if she peered over the cliffs in front of it, what little she could see of the small cove was empty, with not a person in sight. The whole place seemed deserted.

"That's Bessie's Kiddley," Theo said, with an air of pride that he knew something she didn't. "Bronnen told me about it, and so did her ma, Mrs. Voas the farmer's wife. Mr. Voas goes there every evening." He pointed to a side entrance. "I met the boy that lives here. His name's Cado and he's as tall as me but only ten. He showed me the way down to the beach, and we went crabbing with a bit of string and a meaty bone he fetched from the kiddley kitchens. He had a bucket and we put them in there until it was full."

So that was where he'd been going off to and who he'd been with. A boy from an alehouse, no less. Was he quite the sort of companion Theo should have? Maybe if she asked Theo to bring him home, she could meet him and form a judgement. That would be best.

Oblivious to her thoughts, Theo grinned. "Bronnen says everyone round here comes to drink brandy in the kiddley. Only Bronnen doesn't, because she's too young and her ma would wallop her if she did. She told me her ma says only loose women go there." He paused. "What *are* loose women, Mama?"

Harriet tightened her grip on his hand and hurried his reluctant steps past. "Not very nice women," she said. "It's not nice for any woman to go into a common alehouse—"

"A kiddley," Theo interrupted.

"—a common kiddley, if that's what you have to call it. No lady with any sense of decorum would go into such a place unescorted, and I doubt even if she had a gentleman with her."

Theo frowned. "As I'm escorting you, couldn't we go in there on the way back and see what it's like? I've only been in the kiddley kitchen, with Cado. His ma wouldn't let him and me go into the taproom, and I'd like to. Bronnen told me her brothers go in there."

He must have seen the frown on her face because his voice became a wheedle. "So… at least, wouldn't it be all right for me to go in because I'm a *boy*. Could I go in there by myself, as you don't want to?"

"Absolutely not," Harriet snapped. "Cado's mother is quite right. Little boys should not go in taprooms. The subject is closed. You are not to go near that alehouse. You're far too young."

"Kiddley," Theo grumbled. "But I can still go over there to see Cado?"

"Alehouse. I suppose you can see your new friend but you must follow his mother's rules. You are not to go into the taproom. Now, let's see where this path goes next." She gave his hand a tug, pulling him closer, and hurried her steps, intent on putting as much ground as possible between herself and the dreaded alehouse. No doubt that was where Captain Trevelyan had repaired to the other day, thus tarring himself with the same brush as Ben. Men. They were all the same. No wonder she wanted to avoid them at all costs.

As they rounded the headland, they came face to face with an imposing granite-built house occupying a spot hard against the top of the cliffs. It overlooked a cove similar in size to the one where their own house lay, sitting square and bleak, as though whoever had built it had focused entirely on making sure it was weatherproof rather than attractive, with few windows in its blank gray walls. As silent and dead as the kiddley. There, even she was calling it a kiddley now. That word had stuck in her head.

"That's John Carter's house," Theo said, with an air of proprietorial pride. "Porth en Alls. Bronnen told me. He was the King of Prussia and Cado's something-or-other uncle. His great-grandma's brother... I think..."

"He was the king of *where?*" This unexpected statement brought Harriet to a halt in front of the house. "Of *Prussia?*" Although, of course, hadn't Aunt Bolitho's man of business in Bath referred to this area as Prussia Cove? There must be some connection. He couldn't really have been the king of Prussia. Could he? Not with a name like John Carter. Besides, wasn't Frederick William III, who'd joined the fight against Napoleon, the King of Prussia?

Theo nodded. "Only he's dead now. She didn't tell me who lives here nowadays."

No one, by the look of it. The house's few small windows appeared dark and forbidding, and its barns and storehouses lay scattered in confusion as though someone had made no plan as to where they should go but rather added another one on wherever there was a space.

"Come along, Theo. No time to stop and gawk, or it's going to take us all day to get to Roskilly." Sensing Theo's reluctance to leave, she pulled him after her along the next bit of the path.

Here, it hugged the clifftop, giving them a view of the rocky foreshore below as the tide was either partly out or partly in. Harriet had no idea how to tell which way it was going. Ahead of them, the cliffs rose higher, skirting around the top of a long sandy beach, but with no apparent way down to it. This must be the beach they had to walk past. The name came back to her. Kennegy Beach.

Out to sea, small fishing boats dotted the deep blue-green water, their sails billowing in the wind, and white foam topped the waves here and there. That same fresh wind tugged strands of Harriet's hair loose from inside her bonnet and ruffled Theo's dark curls. The smell of the sea was strong. What a beautiful day to be out walking, especially now they were away from habitation. The glorious loneliness of the coast settled in a balm on Harriet's damaged soul, washing Bath away as though she were sloughing off a skin, like a snake.

The beauty of the day had infected Theo as well, and he appeared to have forgotten about venturing into the kiddley. She kept a tight hold of his hand though, not trusting him so near to such high cliffs. He was no more used to them than she was, and the fear nagged at her that if she were to release his hand, he'd end up emulating the previous tenant of their cottage. What with kiddleys and cliffs and looking for gulls' nests, danger loomed on every side if you were a small, adventurous boy.

Their way led over the next headland where the distinctive, tall silhouettes of two tin mines could be seen from afar. The sound of their busy pumps rose above the crash of waves at the cliffs' feet and the wind snatched the smoke from their chimneys to drive it inland in stringy shreds.

Theo, ever curious, wanted to know what they were, which entailed a long explanation on Harriet's part of what she knew of the Cornish tin industry. The telling of this, despite the paucity of her knowledge, took them down off the headland and onto what had to be the wide sands of Morgelyn Beach. She could finally release Theo's hand in safety and watch him run about in delight, cavorting like a gangly colt and leaving pleasingly firm footprints behind him in the damp sand. The tide seemed to have fallen further back, exposing the full glory of the beach, so it must be on its way out.

Halfway along, as she'd been told, a narrow, gritty path wove between the low sandhills leading them to a wider track and the sight of a splendid granite-built house in the distance, larger and more imposing than Rosudgeon. For a moment, Harriet quailed in her shoes, unsure whether Mrs. Trevelyan had been right in advising her to make herself known to her neighbors. Whoever lived here must be of great importance to own such a large house.

A side gate led to a winding path between lawns, still leaf-strewn after the storm, before forking at the house, one path leading towards the front and the other heading off towards the servants' quarters and the stables at the back. Taking Theo by the hand again, in case he had the temerity to go running off to explore the garden, Harriet started around the house to the front with some trepidation.

In front of a modern façade and fashionable pillared portico, a young, liveried groom stood holding the reins of a large black horse. As Harriet rounded the corner, both turned their heads in curiosity, the horse's ears pricked and alert. A finely bred, high-crested creature with all the presence of a stallion. The young man tugged his forelock in respect. "Ma'am."

"Good morning." Harriet bestowed a slight smile on him as she headed for the porticoed front door. Theo's head swiveled to inspect the horse as he passed, but she had him firmly in tow.

Her knock was answered by a butler clad all in black, the thin white hair on his head, as well as his unusually pale face, in stark contrast to his outfit. For a brief moment, his appraising gaze flicked over her appearance—smart in her best black dress—before he executed a small bow. "Good day, ma'am."

Harriet had already fished in her reticule for her calling card, a remnant of her more affluent days in Bath. "Good morning to you. My name is Mrs. Penhallow. Might Mrs. Treloar be at home?"

The butler didn't even glance at the card. "If you will allow me to escort you into the drawing room, I will enquire for you, ma'am."

Inside, the house was as up to date as the front façade, decorated mainly in plain white with some expensive ornaments in alcoves and tasteful portraits on the walls. Underfoot, stark black and white tiles gleamed with fresh polish. Whoever ran this household must keep a tight ship.

Harriet and Theo followed the butler into a similarly tasteful drawing room, and he departed with her calling card. As soon as the door closed behind him, Harriet's hard-won confidence deflated. What if Mrs. Treloar wouldn't see her? How embarrassing would that be? She might be the sort who didn't like new people, even though Mrs. Trevelyan had said she was nice. Especially not ones who lived in tiny cottages on the charity of others. One person's definition of nice was not everyone else's.

She didn't have long to wait. The door opened, and a young woman of about her own age entered the room, with a boy by her side. Tall, dark haired, and not what anyone would call classically pretty, she nonetheless possessed an unusual striking beauty. Intelligence shone from her eyes, and, thank goodness, a smile hovered on her lips.

"Mrs. Penhallow, I'm delighted to make your acquaintance." She held out her hands to Harriet. "Please sit down." Her warm hands on Harriet's cold ones conveyed a sense of welcome just by their touch, aided by the kindness in her dark eyes. Was everyone down in Cornwall this kind? Having left the county as a girl of seventeen to follow the colors with her new soldier husband, Harriet had few clear memories of what it had been like to live here. Once her parents had died, there'd been nothing to lure her back to Truro and besides, Ben would never have allowed it.

Harriet perched on the floral camelback sofa and indicated to Theo to sit down as well. However, he seemed to be too taken up with staring at the boy who'd come in with Mrs. Treloar. Clearly a year or two younger than he was, the boy possessed a mass of unruly blonde curls, a mass of freckles and a cheeky upturned nose. And he seemed as fascinated by Theo as Theo was by him.

Mrs. Treloar took a seat on a pink chaise longue. "Sit down, Yves." With a show of obedience, the boy sat beside her, and Theo dropped onto the sofa next to Harriet, his eyes still on the boy—Yves. A rather French-sounding name. Or might it be Breton?

Mrs. Treloar smiled. "I can see both of our boys are eager to make each other's acquaintance. Why don't we allow them to run off together so Yves can show your son around. I'm certain they'd prefer that to sitting here and listening to us talk."

Theo's head swiveled to stare at Harriet, hope in his eyes. She nodded. "Thank you. That's very kind. I'm sure Theo would enjoy that."

When the boys had gone, both a little wary of the other, Mrs. Treloar turned back to Harriet. "My dear, I'm more than glad you've decided to call on me. Roskilly is so isolated we don't get many callers willing to trek out here. I gather you've taken Keynvor Cottage, and that Mrs. Bolitho is your late husband's great-aunt?"

Good heavens. There must be some kind of message system around here that worked even when the weather was bad. "That is so," Harriet said, a little carefully. The idea that she might be the object of gossip disturbed her more than a little. Speculation usually went hand in hand with gossip. Heaven forbid she should be the subject of gossip *and* speculation.

"How delightful," Mrs. Treloar said. "We are quite close together if you use the cliff path—is that the way you came today?"

Harriet nodded. "It is. A beautiful walk on a fine day, but I imagine in the storm, it wouldn't have been the place to be."

Mrs. Treloar nodded back. "We do seem to get more than our fair share of Atlantic storms. It never ceases to surprise me how many brave fishermen put out to sea all year round. If I were them, I would be afraid to do so."

Which made Harriet think of Captain Trevelyan's worrying

offer to take Theo and Mrs. Trevelyan's little boy, Yves, to sea in his ship. Unsure how to broach this, in case his mother didn't yet know, she changed the subject. "Have you lived here long?"

Mrs. Treloar's kind eyes twinkled. "Only a little over a year, so I am quite the newcomer, like you, which is why dear Talwyn suggested you should call. And yes, I spoke to her yesterday when I called on her." She smiled. "Having no wish to keep secrets from you, and as it is common knowledge amongst my friends, amongst whom I hope to claim you, I will freely admit that I first came to Roskilly as governess to Yves, whose parents are both long dead. Then I met the man who was to become my husband, Yves' cousin Nathaniel." She smoothed her skirts, a secretive smile gracing her lips. "And now Nat and I have been blessed with our own child, dear little Nicholas."

Well, that *was* interesting. So, Yves wasn't her son. Harriet opened her mouth to speak, but at that moment the door from the hallway swung open and two men strode into the room. One of them she didn't know, a tall gentleman with a soldierly stance who might have been considered handsome but for the disfiguring scar that marred the right side of his face. The other was Captain Jack Trevelyan.

Chapter Ten

J ACK GROUND TO a halt, staring at the woman seated opposite Nat's wife, Caroline. Unmistakable and every bit as alluring in her vulnerability as he remembered, her slightly wind-blown appearance told him she must have walked along the cliff path to get here. But of course, she had no other mode of transport other than her own two legs. Why was it she seemed to be everywhere he went at the moment?

"Caroline. Mrs. Penhallow." He made a polite, and rather stiff, bow.

"Nat, my dear." Caroline Treloar greeted her husband. "And Jack as well. How lovely." She smiled. "I didn't know you were here, Jack. You seem to have the advantage of Nat and already know our guest." She glanced back at Nat. "May I present Mrs. Penhallow, who has taken Keynvor Cottage. You know which one. That little thatched cottage round in Bessie's Cove. Mrs. Penhallow, may I introduce my husband, Major Nat Treloar."

Nat swept a slightly more flamboyant bow than Jack had done. "Delighted to make the acquaintance of a new neighbor, Mrs. Penhallow. Please forgive this interruption. I had no idea my wife was entertaining."

Mrs. Penhallow managed a wide-eyed stare, reminding Jack for a moment of a frightened deer, but had her face under control in an instant. "And I you, Major Treloar. But it is I who intrude, as I called without invitation."

Jack tore his gaze away from Mrs. Penhallow's face and regarded his friend's wife. "Nonsense. We are the intruders. Or rather, I am. I do beg your pardon, Caroline. I'll go." Anything to get away from the disturbing presence of his rather too lovely new neighbor who, it had to be admitted, appeared to regard him with abhorrence.

"Nonsense," Caroline said, her smile genuine but, nevertheless, firm. "Sit down, and I'll send for some refreshment. It's far too early for brandy, even though I know it's what you men prefer, so will tea do? I haven't seen you for such a long time, Jack. We can catch up."

Nat gave the bell a tug and took one of the upholstered chairs. "Tea will be perfect, my love. We're happy with a lady's drink, are we not, Trevelyan?"

Jack frowned. Damn it. No escape. He'd have to sit down and socialize with them all. He took a second chair, pulled further back so they'd have to turn half round to include him in their conversations, too late realizing it gave him a perfect view of Mrs. Penhallow's rather exquisite profile. What a delicate nose she possessed, and such a high, intelligent forehead. No. He'd best look at Nat's scarred visage instead. Much better.

"What brings you here today, Jack?" Caroline asked, her air one of someone determined to extract every ounce of information from her visitors.

Flummoxed for a moment by his proximity to Mrs. Penhallow, Jack groped for an answer. "The bad weather," he finally came up with. "And how it's affected the crops here at Treloar." Damn it again. That didn't sound at all natural, even though it was true.

Caroline raised a delicate eyebrow as though she might not believe his explanation.

Jack managed a smile. "I hear from Nat it's not caused too much damage to the standing barley your farm manager's yet to get in." How was it he felt perfectly at home on the deck of a ship with his men, or in the kiddley, or in a Roscoff drinking den, when here in a society drawing room, even though it belonged to his friends, he felt more like a tongue-tied schoolboy. Ridiculous. Upper-class ladies were surely like other women the world over. Why should it be so much harder to talk with them than it was with those women he was more used to? Even Caroline, whom he knew well, had suddenly taken on the specter of a daunting obstacle.

"That is fortuitous news after all this rain," Caroline said, ignoring his discomfort and glancing at her husband. "Mrs. Penhallow has a young son, Nat. Yves has taken him outside to show him around. I think it would be nice for our boy to have someone of his own age to play with."

Nat snorted with laughter. "I hope you told them to stay within the gardens. You know what Yves is like, and if he's got another boy to egg him on, they could end up anywhere."

Caroline had the grace to look guilty. "I didn't think of that. I'm sorry."

Jack would have smiled if he hadn't been so on edge. They were boys, for goodness' sake. Hadn't Nat got up to all sorts of mischief as a boy? He was damned sure he had himself. He kept silent on that, though.

Mrs. Penhallow's brows had knit in a frown. "Should we call them back?" She glanced towards the door and her nervous fingers entwined themselves in her lap. She looked as though she'd have liked to jump up and run after them. That boy of hers was far too firmly attached to his mother's apron strings.

Caroline reached out and patted her guest's hands. "Pray don't worry yourself. Yves has enough sense not to go wandering off. I'm sure they'll stay in the gardens."

"Since when has Yves had any sense at all?" Nat asked.

His wife shot him a frown. "Since he has become more grown up and responsible, now he's ten."

Jack again forbore from commenting, which was just as well, because they were suddenly treated to some shouts of boyish laughter from outside. All eyes turned towards the wide, leaded windows, through which the two boys in question could be seen playing with a dog and a ball. The dog, Yves' little russet spaniel, Dash, was barking excitedly around them as they threw the ball to one another.

Mrs. Penhallow heaved a sigh of relief. "Perhaps, Major Treloar, you might tell them not to leave the gardens?" She hesitated. "I am a little more conscious of the precarity of life since I lost my husband. My son, Theo, has a propensity to act impulsively, taking after his father the way he does."

Nat rose to his feet. "If it will set your mind at ease, of course I will." He went to the window and opened it. Leaning out, he called to the boys. "I would prefer it if you boys stay within the gardens for now. Mrs. Penhallow needs to know where Theo is. We don't want to be launching any search parties for you when the time comes, now do we?"

Mumbled agreement could be heard from the boys. It sounded disappointed, so who knew what they might have been planning had Nat not intervened. Boys could be daringly adventurous when they wanted to be, as Jack well knew.

Nat returned to his seat. "I gather, Mrs. Penhallow, that your late husband was in the same hussar regiment as I was. I believe I knew a Penhallow. What was his rank?"

For a moment a haunted look flashed over Mrs. Penhallow's face and in her lap her fists clenched. Whatever for?

When she looked up at Nat, though, her face had gone oddly blank. No emotion at all. The thought that she had to be hiding something washed over Jack. "Captain," she said, her voice as flat as her expression. "Captain Benedict Penhallow."

Nat frowned. "A man of medium height with dark hair? I believe we fought side-by-side in Spain." He touched the right side of his face, where the jagged scar had disfigured his looks. "But, as you can probably imagine, I try not to remember too much about the war. I didn't return for Waterloo." He glanced at Caroline. "My wife insisted that I remain here, and I took little persuading. I've had my fill of war."

Mrs. Penhallow nodded. Was that relief in her eyes? "A wise decision. Returning to his regiment turned out to be my husband's death."

Not a tear glistened in her eyes as she said this. Jack frowned. In truth, she didn't appear unduly upset at discussing a husband so recently lost. Not the usual grieving widow, no matter how black her gown and bonnet. Almost, they might be construed as her armor to keep the world at bay.

"There's another ex-hussar lives in St Ives," Caroline said. "Captain Fitzwilliam Carlyon. He's a cousin of my friend Ysella Beauchamp of Carlyon Court. He also would in all probability have known your husband."

That haunted, wary look flashed back into Mrs. Penhallow's eyes again, only to be swiftly hidden as she lowered her gaze to her hands.

Jack pressed his lips together in a hard line. He had other reasons than whatever hers were to not want that particular ex-hussar officer hanging around this corner of Cornwall. Captain Carlyon now headed up the county militia charged with both the prevention of smuggling and the apprehension of those doing it. Which meant him and Will for a start, not to mention all their men. If Mrs. Penhallow made friends with him, thanks to a connection with her late husband, the fellow, who was unmarried and had a reputation for liking the ladies, might end up coming calling on her. And that would never do.

"I believe Ysella told me that Captain Carlyon is a bit of a rake," Jack said. "Not to be entirely trusted around ladies." He ignored the fact that this might be the pot calling the kettle black. "I would not trust him with a sister of mine."

"You have a sister?" Mrs. Penhallow asked, her face brightening and her attention diverted from what appeared to be the worrying thought of another hussar officer in the neighborhood. With any luck she wouldn't want anything to do with Fitzwilliam Carlyon.

Jack shook his head. "Alas, no. Just an expression of speech." Although this wasn't entirely true. What about Horatia, Honoria and Lavinia? Nat and Caroline knew about them, of course, but he didn't feel ready to share their existence with Mrs. Penhallow. Any mention of their names would inevitably lead to explanations he didn't want to go into. Not with a stranger, beautiful and mysterious or not.

Mrs. Penhallow bestowed a gentle, and slightly bolder, smile upon him. "I myself grew up an only child. So it seems we have something small in common, Captain Trevelyan."

"Are your parents not still living, Mrs. Penhallow?" Caroline put in.

Mrs. Penhallow shook her head. "My mother died when I was twelve, and my father shortly after my marriage, so until now, there's been nothing to bring me back to Cornwall. I should mention that I was born in Truro, and my late husband was also Cornish, so for me if perhaps not for my children, this is a return home."

Caroline nodded. "Your name gives your origins away, of course. But I'm so sorry you've lost both parents. My father died some time ago, but my mother was to come and live here with Nat and myself this spring. She was so excited that I was presenting her with a grandchild at last, but she caught a chill last winter and passed away before she could join us. I understand all too well your sadness at losing both parents."

Mrs. Penhallow bowed her head, evidently a lot more moved by the loss of her parents than the loss of her husband. "I still miss my mother despite the length of time she's been gone." She glanced up at Jack from under her long lashes. "You are lucky to have your mother still living and in such robust health." Her voice, a little bolder again, held real envy.

Nat set down his empty tea dish. "I think you must be the only one here with parents, Jack. I have none, Caroline has none, Mrs. Penhallow has none, Yves has none." He nodded to Mrs. Penhallow. "I suppose we can count your boy, Theo, as having one parent. But Jack, rather unfairly and greedily, has both of his."

Jack suppressed a frown. What was Nat doing, bringing his parentage into this conversation? Mrs. Penhallow's lovely face had taken on a puzzled frown, as well it might with no sign of a Mr. Trevelyan at Rosudgeon.

"Do you ride, Mrs. Penhallow?" Jack asked, in an effort to change the subject before she asked him about his father. "My mother doesn't ride as much as she used to, and her mare is much in need of exercise. I could ride down leading her and take you out to view the local countryside, if you would care to accompany me? Perhaps tomorrow morning?"

What on earth was he doing? If he didn't want to involve himself with this woman, despite his body telling him otherwise, why had he just offered to take her riding? Because, on the spur of the moment, he'd not been able to think of anything else to distract everyone from discussing his parentage. Not that it was a particular secret. Just that he didn't want it bandied about to someone he didn't know. Yet…

Her face lit up as though he'd just gifted her the crown jewels. "Oh yes, Captain Trevelyan. I love horses and rode to hounds as a girl but had no opportunity to do so when I lived in Bath. I should adore to take to the saddle again. Thank you so much." Her hazel eyes sparkled at him, her whole face suddenly brought to life with anticipation, the wary fear banished as though forgotten.

Jack couldn't help the warm feeling that pervaded his chest at having been the one to cause such apparent happiness. This was ridiculous. What was he thinking?

"Bath must have been interesting to live in," Caroline said. "With the remains of the Roman baths to visit and being able to take the water whenever you wished. You were lucky to be there."

The joy vanished, and Mrs. Penhallow's face clouded. "Yes. I suppose I was." But she didn't sound all that enthusiastic about her old home. Another odd thing. Not that Jack would have liked to live anywhere but Cornwall, though.

"Nothing so beautiful as Cornwall on a fresh spring day," Nat said. "Especially after the arid landscapes I saw in Spain and Southern France. Once Cornish, always Cornish. Not something you can extract from your soul and cast away."

Very true. Jack had been away from Cornwall only a few times, and every time he'd returned it had been with relief. His frequent jaunts across the channel to Roscoff and St Malo didn't count, as the deck of *The Fly* felt as much his home as Rosudgeon and just as Cornish.

It was at this point in the conversation that Theo and Yves returned, their faces flushed from being outside and their eyes shining. A reproving hand, held up by Caroline, kept them silent, although their desire to chatter radiated from their eager eyes.

Caroline nodded to Yves, who performed a respectful bow and, after a second, Theo did the same. Jack suppressed a smile, memories flooding back of his own boyhood and how irritated he'd been when he'd wanted to tell his mother something and been prevented from doing so by etiquette.

"You may speak," Caroline said.

Yves began. "Theo says Cap'n Jack's going to take him out in *The Fly* and I can go too."

Drat it. Jack had let their exchange slip from his mind. He'd dug himself a hole there. He should have known an impressionable, adventurous boy would never have forgotten.

Mrs. Penhallow's face fell into an even more worried frown than the one she'd worn earlier.

Caroline looked at Jack, her brow furrowing as well. "You did?"

Oh well. Too late now. He nodded. "I did."

Caroline looked at Mrs. Penhallow. "And you agreed to this?" A slight hint of accusation tinged her voice.

Mrs. Penhallow shook her head with vehemence. "I did nothing of the sort. It was merely a suggestion by the captain that

Theo took to mean was a definite arrangement. I don't mind Theo seeing what it's like on board a ship, but I do object to him going out to sea. He's never been on a ship in his life and can't even swim."

"Best not to be able to swim," Yves interrupted. "Then you drown quicker. That's what Tom Pascoe, our groom, told me."

Nat wagged a finger at him. "A remark not guaranteed to set Theo's mother's mind at ease."

"But true," Yves protested. "And you always want me to tell the truth."

Jack snorted. "I suppose if Mrs. Penhallow allows it, you boys can come aboard the next time *The Fly* is round in harbor at Bessie's or Prussia Cove. But you're not going to sea in her unless Mrs. Penhallow and Caroline allow it."

"Which'll be never," Theo muttered, loud enough for them all to hear.

"And not if you're rude," Jack amended. "Best to apologize to your mother, young Theo." Now he was behaving like a parent himself, when he'd rather have congratulated Theo on standing up for himself. What was he doing? What was the close proximity to Mrs. Penhallow doing to him?

Theo hung his head. "I'm sorry, Mama. I didn't mean to be rude."

Mrs. Penhallow met Jack's eyes for a brief moment. "Thank you, Theo. You will allow Mrs. Treloar and me to decide what is right for you boys and abide by our ruling."

Head still down, Theo nodded. But was that a spark of boyish rebellion Jack spied in his eyes?

Chapter Eleven

HARRIET STOOD IN front of her wardrobe in her petticoat, while Bertha rummaged through its meager contents, her stomach roiling with the effort of preventing her hands from shaking. The morning chill in the air had brought goosepimples up along her bare arms and she shivered. But the cold wasn't the only cause of the shiver, nor the hand shaking. Why on earth had she said she'd go riding with him? With any man? Still less one so obviously masculine and threatening. The lure of being on a horse again had tempted her into a momentary indiscretion, into allowing her heart to rule her head. Into what she could only perceive as a potentially dangerous situation. One she'd vowed never to put herself in again.

"There it is," Bertha declared, emerging with a long, brown-paper-wrapped package over her arm. "Let's get it out and see how time's treated it. The paper should've kept the moths at bay."

She laid the package on the bed and carefully cut away the paper to reveal the blue, woolen riding habit Harriet had last worn on the hunting field as a girl of seventeen. The faint aroma clung to it of the lavender it had been stored with. Bertha inhaled it like a fine perfume. "I don't doubt as it's a bit out of fashion now, seeing as you haven't had call to wear it for nigh on sixteen years." She eyed Harriet's trim figure. "Might have to tighten up your stays a bit to get you into it. Two babies do have a habit of expanding the waist, in my experience."

As Bertha had never been married, nor produced any babies of her own, yet had a waist several times that of her mistress, Harriet considered this an unkind criticism, but ignored it. After all her years of service, Bertha had earned the right to speak forthrightly to her mistress. Harriet managed a shaky smile. "Shall I try it on first before you tighten them?"

But of course, Bertha was right. Harriet was no longer a slender seventeen-year-old, but a mother of three-and-thirty. Much tightening of her stays was required. "Good heavens," she puffed. "Was I really this thin? I shan't be able to breathe properly if you tighten them much more." But at least all this heaving served to distract her from the disquieting prospect of riding out in the company of a man. And such a man.

Bertha stopped pulling and set her large hands around Harriet's waist to measure it. "That should do now. Let's get this on you."

And she was right again. This time the habit fastened everywhere that was required. A little snug in places, but not dangerously so, and, as it was fashioned of good quality wool, untouched by the depredations of the moth community for the past sixteen years, it was unlikely to provide any unexpected embarrassing disclosures.

Harriet set her matching hat, carefully brushed by Bertha, on her neatly coiffed hair and secured it with a few pins. "Will I pass muster?"

Bertha stepped back to admire her mistress. "Indeed you will. Very nice you look too. Could be a girl fresh out of the schoolroom. Sister to young Lydia rather than mother."

Harriet sighed. "I wish I had a mirror, but I daresay that's only being vain. It's just so long since I wore this habit that I'd like to see how I look." She compressed her lips. "And I must admit I feel a trifle guilty that I'm not wearing the black that's expected of a widow."

Bertha, who, despite to Harriet's knowledge never having known the truth about Ben, had also never approved of him, shook her head. "It's been more than three months and this blue's as near to black as you can get and still be dressed to ride a horse. And I refuse to spoil it by trying to dye it black for you. Seeing as it's the only one you've got." She set her hands on her hips. "And you won't be getting another, seeing as he left you practically destitute."

Very true. But the wearing of widow's weeds felt as though she donned armor against the world, particularly men, and today instinct told her she might need that armor. If only she could have thought of a way to avoid this outing. But deep down inside, she was looking forward to being on a horse again, even if it meant having to keep company with a man. There was always the possibility that if she felt threatened she could just gallop away from him and head for home. In extremis.

Harriet picked up her gloves from the bed. "We won't talk about that, thank you, Bertha. And we're not *quite* destitute. I still have what's left of Ben's army pension to rely on, after his creditors have taken their share. And we have Mrs. Bolitho to thank for this lovely cottage to live in. We should practice being grateful, I think, rather than complaining."

Bertha's huff told Harriet she wasn't in agreement.

Harriet ignored it, and, picking up the long trailing element of her habit, marched onto the tiny landing and promptly bumped into Lydia at the top of the stairs.

"Mama, you look beautiful." Lydia clapped a hand to her mouth. "So, you *are* going to go riding with Theo's Cap'n, after all?"

Who had suggested to Lydia that she might not? "I said I was, didn't I?" Harriet almost snapped, still annoyed with Bertha. "He invited me, so I could hardly refuse." Perhaps she was behaving a tad grumpily. It wasn't Lydia's fault Bertha had annoyed her. She let her voice soften. "And I used to love riding."

However, Lydia's face had already fallen. "I didn't mean to be rude, Mama." Her gaze skimmed over the cut of the gown and the smallness of her mother's waist. "Indeed, your habit looks as though it might well fit me."

Theo must have been lurking in his bedroom. "*If* you could ride," he said, poking his head around the half-open door. "Which you can't."

Lydia glared at him. "But I would *like* to. It looks so very easy."

This produced a guffaw of mockery from her brother. "That's what you think. My friend Yves is going to teach me how to ride on his old pony, so I'll be learning before you. He let me sit on the pony yesterday, in the stable but with no saddle. Her name's Blossom. He has a new, bigger, pony, so he and I'll be riding together."

This was the first Harriet had heard of this, and the dangers immediately leapt into her head, not least the fact that he would be being taught by a boy younger than himself. "We'll have to see about that. You should ask me first before you make any such arrangements."

Lydia pulled a far-too smug smile at her brother and flounced down the stairs in front of Harriet. Bertha, tutting to herself, followed behind, her footsteps heavy on the creaking treads.

In the kitchen, Lydia stepped back to admire her mother the better, her head tilted to one side. "A riding habit is so... so becoming. Much nicer than an ordinary dress. Quite military. Did Papa ever see you in it?" She tapped her fingers on the tabletop and her eyes narrowed. "Might you let me try it on to see what I look like in it? Even though we don't have a horse and I can't ride?"

Bertha's snort of disapproval echoed around the kitchen. "Young ladies in your situation can't give themselves hoity-toity airs."

Lydia's brow lowered and her lower lip stuck out in mutiny.

Harriet would have interfered had not right at that moment a sharp rapping on the kitchen door drawn all their attention.

Bertha waddled past them and opened the door.

Captain Trevelyan was standing on the doorstep, dressed in a smart blue coat that perfectly matched Harriet's habit, tall topboots polished to a high luster, and with a beaver hat of moderate proportions on his dark curls. This he removed as he spotted Harriet behind Bertha, in order to sweep them both a low bow.

He straightened up with what could only be described as a roguish smile on his lips. "Bertha, delighted to see you again. I'm here to deprive you of your mistress's company for an hour or two, if you don't mind too much?"

Bertha, almost simpering, which was most unusual, stepped out of the way and Captain Trevelyan's tall form filled the doorway. "Mrs. Penhallow, you look charming. Blue suits you well. I'm glad to see you haven't changed your mind about our ride, as I've brought my mother's mare, Peggy, down here especially for you."

Despite her inner trepidation, Harriet allowed herself a little smile at the thought of being on a horse after so long. He would have no idea how much it meant to her to be about to ride again after all these years. She'd ridden since the age of three, beginning on the garden pony, until the fateful day when Ben had swept her off her feet in his dashing hussar uniform and carried her off to Bath as his wife. And in all the intervening years, every time she'd seen anyone on a horse, her heart had broken a little for want of a horse of her own again. But best not to let her escort know that. Best not to let him know anything at all. Just for a moment, she allowed herself to feel glad she'd accepted his offer and pushed her fears to the back of her mind.

"Good morning, Captain." She peered past him in curiosity. The large black gelding from the other day was standing patiently in the autumn sunshine where his rider had hooked his reins around the low branch of a tree, and beside him stood a smaller, also black, mare, equipped with a side-saddle. A daintier, more finely boned mount than the gelding, a pretty, long white blaze reached to the tip of her nose and one white sock decorated her offside front pastern. Her well-muscled neck and quarters and the slope of her shoulder suggested a long-striding, comfortable ride. She possessed an air of sweet gentleness about her that the gelding didn't, despite his apparent patience.

"She's beautiful," Harriet gasped. "Are you sure your mother won't mind me riding her? I haven't sat on a horse now for sixteen years, and I'm bound to be rusty."

Lydia came to stand beside her. "Goodness, Mama. What a lovely horse. But it looks quite large…" Of course, Lydia and Theo had never seen her ride and were only used to the carriage horses they'd seen about the streets of Bath. Not many people rode within the city limits.

"If you'll come this way, I'll introduce you," Captain Trevelyan said, gesturing with one gloved hand.

Suppressing the impulse to glance back at Bertha and Lydia for reassurance, Harriet followed him to where the mare was nibbling leaves off the branch she was tied to. "Mrs. Penhallow, meet Peggy. She's a lady herself; quiet and willing without being too taxing a ride. A real lady's mount. I selected her myself for my mother, and she was trained by my friend Kit's mother, the Dowager Viscountess of Ormonde, a woman with the skills of a horse whisperer."

Was he a little overeager? Did he suspect her of reluctance to accompany him? Did he think the cause of it might be nerves at riding again after so long? Well, he had that quite wrong.

Harriet ran her gloved hand down Peggy's white blaze, the horse's warm breath in her face. "I imagine I will have ridden horses less quiet and willing in my time." Let him know she was no timid novice. She pulled off her glove so she could touch the horse's silken coat, where just a fuzz of coming winter growth had taken away the shine of summer. "Hello, Peggy. You'll have to be very gentle with me today as it's such a long time since I've ridden."

Captain Trevelyan unhooked Peggy's reins from the branch

and threw them back over her head. "She'll be gentle. That was why I chose her. We have no groom, so I shall need to give you a leg up."

Harriet froze. He was going to have to touch her. Why hadn't she thought of that before agreeing to ride with him? Of course, in the past, *before* Ben, she'd been given leg ups from all sorts of people, so why should she hesitate now? Because she didn't want him to touch her. Not even her booted foot. Because she never wanted any man to touch her again. And especially not this one with his rather wild good looks and air of latent masculinity.

With a huge effort, she wrestled herself under control. She mustn't show him how disturbed the suggestion of a leg up was making her feel. She swallowed. "Thank you, Captain."

He linked his hands to make a step, and with only a momentary hesitation, she set her foot on them, and he launched her into the saddle. Trying not to think of the strength he'd displayed in shooting her into the saddle, she hooked her right leg around the lower pommel and arranged the voluminous skirts of her habit, then slipped her left foot into the stirrup he was holding. Its length felt comfortable, so there was no need to adjust the leather. Thank goodness. She gathered up the reins and patted Peggy's shoulder, but the little mare stood immovable and calm, just as he'd assured her she would. How wonderful it was to have a horse beneath her again. After so long, Peggy's docility might be a good thing.

It became borne in upon her that Captain Trevelyan had not moved over to retrieve his own horse but was looking up at her. The urge to avert her gaze waxed strong. His smile reached eyes that also held open curiosity. "I can see already from the way you sit that you have not forgotten any of your riding skills."

Heat swarmed up Harriet's cheeks, but she managed to return his smile. "I suspect it is a skill one never forgets, although I fear that this evening, and perhaps tomorrow, I might notice aches in muscles I'm not accustomed to using."

He unhooked the gelding's reins and swung himself into the saddle, settling down as though he belonged there, his back straight but his body relaxed. "Shall we go?"

They set off, riding side-by-side, up the track that would take them back towards Rosudgeon, the long stride of the little mare matching the bigger horse easily. Although ostensibly looking ahead at the lane, curiosity got the better of Harriet and she was able to surreptitiously survey Captain Trevelyan as she rode. As this was the closest she'd got to him, and he seemed unaware of her sideways glances, she had the opportunity for a detailed reconnaissance.

He was as handsome as she remembered, his overly long dark hair curling on the nape of his neck and peeking out along his forehead from under his hat. A faint haze of dark stubble covered a strong jaw, and his lips had set in a firm line. He held his reins lightly in one hand, his other resting on his knee, and his body swayed in perfect synchronicity with the movement of his horse beneath him.

Perhaps she ought to speak to him, although from what she'd seen of him so far, he appeared not to be loquacious himself. "Your horse is very handsome. What is he called?"

He turned his head and she had to struggle not to shy away from him. "Shadow. I bred him myself."

"Is that a hobby of yours, then? Did you breed Peggy as well?"

His golden eyes glittered in the sunlight. "It is, and no, I didn't. I purchased Peggy for my mother from Lady Ormonde, as I said earlier, who'd bred her little Arab mare to the Thoroughbred stallion Waxy, a grandson of the great Eclipse. I like a lady's horse with a bit of Arab in it. They're an intelligent breed."

"She's a sweet ride."

"My mother is well pleased with her, but I'm too big to ride her."

Harriet returned her gaze to straight ahead, where the track bent to the right and a narrow path could be seen winding away to the west between the little, stone-walled fields.

"If we go this way," he said, pointing, "we can ride towards Penzance and the beach at Marazion, then return across the moors inland. Do you feel up to riding that far?"

Oh, if only she could just keep on going forever on the comfortable Peggy and leave all her troubles behind. But this was reality, and she had two children who depended on her. Not to mention Bertha, who seemed quite enamored of her escort. "Yes," she said. "That would be lovely. Might it be possible to ride into Penzance so I can call upon Aunt Bolitho to thank her for her kindness?" Best to seize the opportunity when it came along. She could hardly walk to Penzance.

He seemed unfazed by this request. "Of course. The beach there is magnificent for a gallop, if you should so wish. Do you have her address?"

"Her man of business told me she lives in a street called Causeway Head. I have the name of the house."

He nodded. "Easy to find. We'll make that our aim this morning."

Harriet tapped Peggy with her heel as she followed the captain down the path. "How far is it?"

"A couple of hours altogether, depending on how fast we go. It's a pleasant ride with plenty of places to canter. You're certain you're up to it?"

Two hours. But Peggy had a comfortable stride and saddle, both of which were important for an enjoyable ride. The day promised to be a fine one, with little wind blowing and, for once, Harriet felt as though she were a young girl again. "Why not?" she said, unable to suppress the unaccustomed delight in her tone, despite her misgivings at undertaking this in the company of a man. "I'd love to canter again."

Chapter Twelve

THE PATH JACK was following opened out onto rough moorland, leaving the small, stone-walled fields of grazing sheep behind them. Overhead, clouds dotted the blue arc of the sky, and the sun, warm for late September, beat down on his back. He took a quick, sideways glance at his companion. A soft sea breeze blew, gently ruffling the wispy curls on the nape of her slender, all-too seductive neck. That she'd been of two minds about riding out in his company had not escaped him, and even now he could sense the tension zinging through her body whenever he rode too close. What did she think he was going to do to her out on a perfectly simple ride? He felt a little insulted that she so blatantly didn't trust him. He might have a bit of a reputation with women, but never for illtreating them, nor taking what they weren't perfectly happy to give. And the mystery about her only made him the more interested.

"Your mother's horse is truly a pleasure to ride, Captain Trevelyan," she said, turning to look at him, seemingly unaware of his scrutiny. Her cheeks had flushed a becoming pink, and her hazel eyes shone, although Jack doubted for the same reason he was feeling that way himself. As he met her eyes, an inexplicable warm glow that he couldn't fathom started in his stomach and spread through his body in a tidal wave of unaccustomed emotion.

She dropped her gaze in a hurry, as though she might have divined his reaction and been disturbed by it. Even, that she was afraid of it, and him.

He needed to pull himself together; she was just another pretty woman, and he'd known plenty of them. In the Biblical sense. He should make some innocuous conversation to put her at ease. "As we are to be neighbors, and perhaps come to know one another a little better." He kept Shadow at a respectful distance from Peggy, aware that he might sound as though he was gabbling but unable to stop himself. "Would you perhaps feel comfortable in calling me Jack? Everyone else does, and Captain Trevelyan sounds so formal. I should be honored if you would."

Damn it. He'd gone too far. This was a gently brought up and obviously shy young widow he was talking to, not some Breton girl in a bar in Roscoff. Although he'd always been quite happy for girls like that to just call him *Capitan* in their lilting, sing-song accents.

She blinked at him, possibly considering the connotations of agreeing to this. Such as having to allow him, in return, the freedom of her own first name. After a long pause, she bowed her head in what he took to be acquiescence. "I own I am a little reticent at such informality. However..." She pressed her pretty lips together. "As I am already friends with your mother, and she has invited me to call her Talwyn, I see no insurmountable barrier to my addressing you as Jack." She regarded him out of solemn eyes. "And I suppose you are hoping that you might call me Harriet?"

Of course he was. That was the whole point. He almost laughed. She was, he had to admit, beguiling, especially in her snug blue riding habit that showed off her still slender waist and the delightful curve of her breasts. He had an urge to put his hands around that waist and pull her towards him; an urge prevented by the fact they were both on horseback and by the thought that it was a move she wasn't likely to be in the least happy about. Best to still those thoughts. She might be impoverished, but she was not one of the light-moraled women he was used to. "Only if you are comfortable with it… Mrs. Penhallow."

A chough flew across their path towards the coast, too far away to startle the horses, as she appeared to be giving this some thought. At last, she gave a little, almost careless, toss of her head, indicating that despite her apparent wariness of him, she still possessed some daring spirit. "I have decided that you may call me Harriet, if you so wish."

This caused Jack such pleasure that he felt his own cheeks color. Again. What was he? A green boy? He hadn't considered himself one of those since he was fifteen. To distract her attention, he nodded ahead towards a distant outcropping of granite. "We can canter to that pile of rocks, if you like. Harriet…"

She needed no further telling, and, with a momentary delightfully wicked look in her eyes, she sent Peggy galloping up the track between the banks of heather and yellow gorse, crouching forward over her horse's neck to encourage her speed.

Shadow pranced under Jack's tight hold, eager to join in.

Hadn't he said *canter*? The pleasurable thought that he might have taken on some sort of human Valkyrie flashed into Jack's head as he sent the over-eager Shadow in pursuit.

He reached the granite outcropping neck-and-neck with Harriet and Peggy and pulled up to a walk as she did. Both horses' sides were heaving, but Harriet's eyes shone with the excitement of the gallop as she put a gloved hand to her flushed face and windblown hair. At least she hadn't lost her hat, which must have some powerful witchcraft to keep it still fixed to her head like this. Unlike Jack's, which had blown off right at the start, hatpins not being a normal convention in men's wardrobes. He'd send one of his servants out later to find it. Peterkin, the gardener's boy.

"Now that," she exclaimed, "is why I said I would come riding with you. For moments like this."

Was this her true self suddenly on show? A confident, laughing girl taking pleasure in the speed of the gallop, instead of the wary, skittery young woman who looked as though she thought disaster about to strike at any moment.

Jack had to laugh. "I had no idea you were such a neck-or-nothing rider." Shadow pranced under him again, eager to keep going now he'd been given his head once. "Someone after my own heart. You must have been feeling quite deprived when you lived within the confines of Bath."

Her expression sobered as though a cloud had obscured the sun, as though she'd suddenly remembered the persona she was meant to be projecting. She didn't answer as they started downhill towards Mount's Bay, where the little, rocky island of St Michael's Mount could be seen with its grand house clinging to the summit. The tide was right out, and the raised causeway to the island lay visible with a laden string of packhorses trudging across it.

"Is that a real castle?" Harriet asked, her change of subject marked.

Jack shrugged, glad to be able to discuss the view and not have to think how attractive his companion looked with her windblown cheeks and hair. "In a way, I suppose it is. More of a country seat now than a defensive structure, although I believe it's withstood the odd siege in its time. It belongs to the St Aubyn family to whom I'm distantly related." He grinned. "Very distantly, which is how they prefer it."

She shot him a curious look, a little less wary than before, but had to turn her attention back to where Peggy was picking her way between the scattered lumps of weathered granite lying half-hidden in the heather. A bloom of deep purple covered the hillside and the inland hills, only here and there interrupted by the vivid greens of clusters of small, enclosed fields.

The horses reached the foot of the slope, where a grassy track led up to the Penzance Road at Marazion. Jack gathered his slack reins. "Are you ready for another canter? And by that, I mean just a canter, this time, not a flat-out gallop."

The confident girl was back again, as though her other self had been momentarily forgotten and being on a horse had been the catalyst that had brought out what must be her true self. "Was our last gallop a shade too fast for you, perhaps?"

"On the contrary. I feared it might be too fast for you, as you've not ridden for so long."

"Peggy is such a sweet goer I already feel quite at home in the saddle, as though no time at all has passed since last I rode."

She looked it too. If he hadn't known she had a daughter of fifteen, he'd have thought her a girl herself, with her flawless skin and still shining eyes. He'd never known a woman so enamored of riding, apart from Kit's mother, of course, as most saw it as a necessary evil to get from place to place. This was a woman who saw it as the ultimate of pleasures. Well, perhaps not quite the ultimate, but he refused to think about that. He cleared a throat gone suddenly dry. "All the same, just a canter this time."

Her smile widened. "Why, of course, Jack, if that is what you'd prefer?"

The sound of his name on her tongue sent a shiver of glorious excitement ricocheting through Jack's body. What on earth?

But he had no time to ponder on this as she set Peggy into the most collected of canters that seemed scarcely faster than the walk they'd been doing down the hill. Damn her, she really was an accomplished horsewoman. She could easily give Lady Ormonde a run for her money. He hadn't quite expected that of her.

He kept Shadow in a more workaday trot beside her until they reached the road, where a ramshackle gate had to be negotiated, something he did from the saddle with casual aplomb, glad, in a way, to show off his own skills as a horseman. She gave him a round of applause as he finally pulled it shut and looped the ragged rope over the gatepost again. "Bravo. You have a certain skill on a horse, I'll own."

"Such praise, from a veritable centaur."

"I like to think I can spot a real rider, and I can see you're just that." Her gaze slid past him, out to sea, where a ship could be seen breasting the small waves and heading east along the coast.

Jack would have known the ship anywhere. But then, after a lifetime at sea, he could recognize most ships from further away than they were at this moment, especially the St Ives revenue cutter. But this wasn't the revenue cutter. No mistaking *The Fly*, her search for a cargo done, with all five of her sails up as she left Penzance behind. From the way she was breasting the waves, he could tell she had a good load on board, most likely of herring and mackerel stored in barrels, to be delivered as quickly as possible to Plymouth's markets. She'd be returning to her mooring in Bessie's Cove via Jersey in the Channel Islands where she'd pick up a cargo of duty-free tobacco. Then she'd return to the cove to pick Jack up and they'd be off to France to trade the baccie for the brandy that was so expensive here in Britain. The itch to be on board *The Fly*, with the wind in the sails and his hair, and the smell of tarred ropes and the sea in his nostrils, gripped Jack hard.

Harriet spoke without looking at him, her eyes squinting at the glare of the sun on the sea. "Are you as adept with a ship as you are with a horse?"

He gave himself a mental shake, remembering how he didn't like to be aboard at the same time as a cargo of fish. "I like to think I am. But you'd best ask my Bo'sun, Dan Bussow, that one."

She cogitated for a moment, her eyes on the neat outline of his ship. "What kind of a ship is that one? It's such a pretty little thing with all its sails billowing full like that."

Jack smiled to himself, strangely pleased that she liked his ship. "*The Fly*. My own ship, commanded right now by my Bo'sun. She's called a lugger."

This time she did turn to look at him. "A lugger? A pretty ship with a not-so-pretty name."

The Fly was raking across the sea, as sleek as the dolphins they often had chasing along beside them. "It's from the name of her sails. See their shape? Four-cornered with none of the sides parallel."

She nodded.

"Those're called lug sails."

Another nod. "She looks quite small."

Ignoring the apparent insult to his precious ship, Jack shook his head. "No. For a lugger she's large. Bow to stern she's forty-five feet. Add in the spars, and she's nearer eighty, with a beam of thirteen feet and a draft of seven."

"I know nothing about ships. What is she for? I mean, what is her purpose? What do you do with her?" She frowned at him as though trying to connect him to the doings on a small ship in Cornwall, and probably coming up with the wrong answer. Hopefully.

"She transports goods—such as the fish others have caught as she's so swift. And sometimes other goods." Ha. That was an underestimation of what she carried most frequently. "Like you on a horse. She's a flyer."

"Oh." She gazed again, one hand up to shade her eyes, as though the harder she stared the clearer her vision might become. "What is it about the sea that made you want to own a ship of your own?"

Now she was prying, but for the life of him he couldn't dislike her questions. He should, because he didn't want her to know any of this. And yet… the fact that she was showing such an interest pleased him. "I've sailed since I was a boy younger than your Theo. The sea's in my blood. I hear it calling and I can't resist."

Her eyes widened. "Like the call of Cornwall?"

Yes. She understood. He nodded. "Just like it. I could no more live elsewhere than I could give up my ship."

She nodded. "I see." A little frown furrowed her brow.

Perhaps in her head she couldn't see him as captain of a carrier, no matter that *The Fly* was larger than most of the others. He cleared his throat. "I think we've had long enough gazing at my ship. Shall we continue?"

They started down the road in a trot, avoiding the many potholes and stony patches, and the small fishing village of Penzance, beyond the Mount, drew closer. He found where the path twisted down onto the beach, and soon Peggy's and Shadow's hoof beats were muffled by the soft sand the tide hardly ever touched. The beach stretched out before them towards the village, where all the fleet would at present be out at sea, working.

Shadow pranced under his steady hand, and even the well-mannered Peggy skittered and danced, kicking up sand, eager to stretch her legs. "Best to gallop on the damp sand where it's easier going for the horses," Jack said. "But keep her steady to begin with until we've crossed the Red River where the sand can be quite soft and deep."

With the causeway to the Mount and its surrounding rocks behind them, they maintained a steady canter, one behind the other, to where the Red River spilled out over the sand, trotted through its brackish waters, then gave the horses their heads along Long Rock beach, only pulling up when the horses began to flag. Ahead of them, Penzance lay a lot closer now, her stone harbor wall curling out into the sea. To their left the distant waves rolled up the beach, and to the right, beyond the low dunes, the flat river valley spread out green and lush toward the higher, heather-clad inland hills.

Jack swung Shadow around to face back up the beach. "Come. It's best if we return to the road into Penzance to see your Mrs. Bolitho. It's only a short distance from here, and I know Causewayhead where you're aiming for."

Her face, that had been flushed with the enjoyment of the gallop, blanched, and she visibly stiffened her spine. "Very well." But she didn't sound enthusiastic.

What was she so frightened of? Jack knew very little of Mrs. Bolitho, bar the fact that she was a known skinflint just like her late husband had been. Well… perhaps if he'd been going to meet her for the first time, he'd have been as timorous as Harriet appeared to be.

Chapter Thirteen

L ETTING PEGGY TUCK in behind Shadow, Harriet followed Jack up through the low sandhills onto a stretch of scrubby grassland. Rabbits scattered in all directions, but the small, tough-looking sheep with their wooly, half-grown lambs ignored the horses. Across this open grazing land, the Penzance Road cut an unimpressive swathe. If you could call it a road. She'd noted on their stagecoach journey down into Cornwall that the further they strayed from Bath, the worse the roads became, and here it was little more than a stony, pot-holed track and had been an uncomfortable ride in the stagecoach.

"Not far now," Jack said, as they turned to the left and headed towards the village, where it sat, hugging the curve of the bay and astride the coach road.

Of course, Harriet had seen plenty of small villages or towns but never a fishing village like this before. On the outskirts, the main road led between the semi-tumbledown cottages of the poorest inhabitants, but as they progressed, the quality of the buildings improved, and soon they were riding down a wide High Street and into a bustling marketplace.

"Market day," Jack remarked, as though he thought she needed telling. There'd been markets in Bath too. She wasn't stupid.

Shadow and Peggy had slowed to a walk, passing between

stalls selling everything from live chickens to hot pies, possibly themselves made of chicken, a kind of insult to their clucking neighbors. Hurdled pens held pigs and sheep, amidst displays of farm tools, pots of honey and conserves, as well as stalls displaying all-manner of vegetables that were tucked in every possible corner.

The people moving between the stalls were a motley bunch—some of them clearly the poorer members of the community in their drab homespun clothing, the few children barefooted and grubby. Others resembled the better-off working class Harriet had seen in and about the parks and streets of Bath—clean and tidy but in clothes that had seen a good degree of wear. And here and there, the more genteel paraded, women with jaunty bonnets and men in tailcoats and shiny topboots like Jack's. Not many of them though, and Jack seemed keen to avoid meeting them, hurrying the horses away as he spotted them.

"We'd best leave our horses at the *Star*." Jack indicated a reasonable sized inn on the corner of a side road. "I doubt your Mrs. Bolitho will have stables we can leave them in."

Was he planning on accompanying her right up to the house? Somehow, she'd envisioned herself facing this challenge alone. However, the thought of turning up with a gentleman in tow only had the effect of making her quail. What would Ben's aunt think of her? That she was a fast woman who had moved on from Ben in the blink of an eye, that was what.

"Captain… I mean Jack. This is something I have to do alone. I appreciate that you are willing to escort me, but really, I think it's best if I do this by myself."

He'd kicked his feet out of his stirrups about to dismount. "As you wish. But I insist on taking you to the door, and I shall wait outside while you see her." He must have seen the expression on her face. "But have no fear. I shall do so unobtrusively."

She managed a smile. "That is very kind."

He swung down from Shadow and came around to help her down. "Nonsense. It's nothing."

Their eyes met. Was that understanding in his eyes? Surely he wasn't that perceptive. He was a man, after all. She slid down into his waiting arms and felt the strength of his steadying grip about her waist for a brief moment. Before she could recoil, though, he'd released his hold and stepped back, as if instinct had told him how much she didn't want to be held by any man. "Thank you." She smoothed her habit and caught up the loop that would enable her to walk without trailing her skirt in the dust and dirt of the street.

A young ostler in a collarless shirt with its sleeves rolled up above his elbows, over brown breeches, stockings and heavy working boots, emerged from the side gates of the *Star*. "Stablin', Cap'n Trevelyan?"

So Jack was well-known here.

Jack nodded. "Thank you, Jonno. An hour, two at most." He handed a coin over to the man, who took Shadow's and Peggy's reins as though he knew them. "Just a slice of hay. No oats."

The coin disappeared into a leather bag on his belt, and the man saluted, as best he could while holding two horses, then led them through the archway into the inn's backyard.

Harriet looked back at the street, which seemed suddenly more crowded now she was on the same level as the people on foot. Which way? Luckily, Jack knew. Tucking her hand into the crook of his left elbow, he guided her along the edge of the street, keeping as close to the buildings as possible and skirting the main thoroughfare between the market stalls, where the majority of shoppers were walking.

A bare minute or two later he steered her out of the busy market and to the right, up a street only a little wider than a stagecoach. A selection of shops lay to either side—a dressmakers, a milliners, and a tailors, in between more day to day necessaries such as an apothecary's, a chandlers, and an ironmongers. So, this was the oddly named Causewayhead. Less crowded down here, as no doubt most of the townspeople were looking for market day bargains.

Mrs. Bolitho's house lay towards the top of this road, a little back from most of the other buildings which gave it room for a small, iron-gated and stone-slabbed front yard. It stood taller as well, with three main, sash-windowed stories and smaller windows in the roof indicating an attic for servants' accommodation.

Jack halted at the gate. "I've spied myself a coffee house just along the street. I'll leave you here and wish you luck with your aunt." He made a bow. "If your interview is swift, then look for me in the coffee house, and we'll return to our horses together." He released her hand from his arm, holding it for a moment as though unwilling to relinquish it entirely, and perhaps inclined to give it a reassuring pat. Very avuncular.

His company suddenly felt like something Harriet would have appreciated, going into the lion's den as she was. Or worse, to face a dragon, as St George had done, but without a trusty sword. Before she succumbed and asked him to stay, she turned sharply away and hastened up to the imposing front door. No. She would not glance back over her shoulder to see if he still stood there.

A bell rope hung by the door, so she gave it a firm tug. From inside came the discordant clang of it ringing.

Steeling herself, she waited.

After what felt like a long time, the door swung open on a young woman in a starched white apron over a dull gray dress. The white mob cap on her mousey-brown hair indicated her status as housemaid. "Can I help you, ma'am?" She sounded nervous.

Harriet took a deep breath. "I'm here to see Mrs. Bolitho. She's not expecting me, but she knows me and was aunt to my late husband. You can tell her it's Mrs. Penhallow who has come to call."

The girl, who couldn't have been a lot older than Lydia, opened the door wider, her doubtful eyes betraying a certain obvious lack of confidence about letting some stranger claiming a relationship with her mistress into the house. "If you'll wait here, ma'am, I'll go and see if the mistress is seeing people today." And leaving Harriet standing in the gloomy hallway, she was gone up the narrow staircase.

Harriet stared about herself with nervous interest. A few dark pictures hung on the walls, and beneath the stairs stood a door that might lead to the kitchens. If only her heart would cease its infernal hammering she might feel better about this encounter. No matter what she'd thought outside, this was an old lady she was about to see, and not either a lion or a dragon.

The girl returned promptly, her booted feet clattering on the stairs. "The mistress is in the library. She says she'll see you." She gestured. "This way."

The library lay on the first floor, one of several doors opening off an ill-lit corridor with a faded rug running its length. As the maid hung back wide-eyed, Harriet pushed the door open and went in.

A library in every sense of the word. Shelves of books covered every wall, and heavy curtains hung from the sash windows, letting in very little light and making the room near as gloomy as the corridor. A small fire, giving off next to no heat, burned in the grate at one end of the room, and in front of it stood two high-backed, upholstered chairs. In one of them sat an old lady clad entirely in black, her snowy white hair partly covered with a lace cap.

Harriet hesitated, unsure of her reception. Ben had never spoken of his aunt in all the time she'd known him, and the old lady's man of business in Bath had more than hinted that she was a difficult customer.

"Well, girl, get over here and let me look at you." For an old lady she possessed a firm and autocratic voice.

Harriet approached her seat and bobbed a perfect curtsey.

Mrs. Bolitho's face was as lined as an old apple forgotten at the bottom of the barrel, her cheeks sagged and folds of crepey skin hung over her small, hard eyes. Both gnarled hands rested on an ebony cane, a diamond ring glittering on the forefinger of one of them.

Harriet hesitated again, unsure how to address the old lady, and withering inside under her gimlet glare.

"Well, girl, speak up. What are you here for?" she almost shouted.

This was not going the way Harriet had hoped it would. Had the maid not told Mrs. Bolitho who she was? Her hands began to tremble and hot color surged up her cheeks. "If you please, Mrs. Bolitho, I've come to thank you for your generosity."

"Eh? What?" The old lady leaned forward. "Speak up, I said. I'm not deaf, but you're mumbling. Who are you and what do you want?"

Harriet tried again, much louder this time. "My name is Harriet Penhallow. My husband was Benedict Penhallow, your great nephew. A captain in the Hussars. You have been so kind as to allow my children and me to live in one of your properties now Benedict is dead."

The old lady's eyes sharpened. "Oh. You're *that* girl, are you? Come a bit closer and let me have a better look at you." She waved at the other chair. "Sit down."

Harriet perched on the edge of the chair, her hands folded in her lap while Mrs. Bolitho scrutinized her.

This took a while. Finally, the old lady gave a loud harrumph. "You're a skinny little thing. I remember you now. Married to young Benedict. He used to visit me and my Horace down here when he was a boy. Smart little fellow. Smart indeed. And a hero, too." She cleared her throat and spat into the fire. "Shame he's gone. And it leaves you a widow woman with two children, I hear? Benedict's two. And one's a boy."

"Theodore." Harriet's heart had begun to steady. "And Lydia."

Mrs. Bolitho shook her head. "Ain't interested in the girl." She smacked her wet, wrinkled lips together. "But the boy's a Penhallow and the last of his line. My brother Joseph had but one son who lived to adulthood, and that was your Benedict's father, my nephew, Andrew, who also had but one son himself—Benedict."

Where was this leading? Harriet held her tongue and waited, far too conscious of her unsteady heartbeat.

Mrs. Bolitho bared what teeth she still possessed in what might have been a smile but was more like a snarl. "I'd like to see the boy. Is he like his father?"

Now there was a question. In what way did she mean? Yes, Theo resembled his father physically but not in temperament, thank goodness. Probably the old lady would have fond memories of Ben as a boy and be more interested in Theo's appearance. She nodded. "He is very like his father. As is Lydia." The fact that Mrs. Bolitho wasn't interested in Lydia irked.

The old lady nodded her head. "If I like him, then I'll pay for his education. Can't have him growing up in the back end of beyond like a yokel. I'll send him up to Eton like his father and grandfather before him. Do him the world of good."

So this was what the old woman wanted. Control of the last Penhallow. Theo. Harriet bit her lip to stop herself from shouting out a no to this. A strong awareness that it wouldn't do to offend her benefactress kept her mouth shut. "He is very young, as yet, and needs his mother as he misses his father so much." Not true at all about the missing of his father. Theo had always been *her* child, as wary of Ben as she was. Perhaps he'd sensed her own fears. Fears she'd tried so hard to hide.

"Nonsense," the old lady snapped, spit spraying. "Bring him in to see me as soon as you can, and we'll see about him starting school. My man in Bath tells me he's twelve, isn't he? About time he was removed from the apron strings and made a man of."

But not a man like his father. Harriet's insides quaked. "It's difficult for me to get into Penzance," she tried. "I have no transport of my own, and it's quite a distance. Too far to walk." Not necessarily true, but she was clutching at straws.

Mrs. Bolitho's eyes sharpened like razors. "Indeed? And how

did you get here today, then?"

Oh no. Should she lie or tell the truth? Better a half truth. "I was given a ride into the town. Which means I can't be long with you, as my friends will need to return soon." Anything to get away from this grasping old lady who wanted to turn Theo into a reincarnation of Ben.

"Which friends?"

Oh no again. Instinct told her not to mention Jack. Luckily, he possessed a mother. "The Trevelyans of Rosudgeon House. It is quite close to the cottage you've allowed me to take."

"The Trevelyans? *Talwyn Trevelyan?* She's not a woman I would like my niece-by-marriage associating with." She glowered. "And you should not like your daughter to be near her. The woman's no better than she should be and has a 'reputation'."

Harriet stiffened her spine, glad her interlocuter had jumped to the conclusion that Talwyn had brought her into Penzance without the necessity to lie. "I'm afraid I had little choice. I felt I must come in to thank you for your kindness and could delay no longer. We are all most grateful for the cottage and the security of a roof over our heads."

"Then bring the boy to see me. As soon as you can. I shall be awaiting him with impatience."

Harriet nodded. "Of course. As soon as I can procure another ride into Penzance, I will bring him and Lydia to visit you."

Mrs. Bolitho shook her head. "Don't bother with the girl. What do I want with a girl? She'll be off marrying someone and taking his name in five minutes. It's just the boy I want. The Penhallow boy."

"Of course."

Of course not. She had to find a way around this, and at the moment, her one hope was her lack of transport. And insisting that Theo needed his mother. But neither of these excuses would last for long. At some point, Mrs. Bolitho would get impatient and send transport out to fetch them.

Mrs. Bolitho leaned back in her seat. "You may go."

Taken aback at so curt a dismissal, Harriet stared at her.

"Don't look all astonished at me, my girl. You've said your piece and I've said mine. We know where we stand so there's nothing more to say. Off you go before Talwyn Trevelyan comes knocking on my door to look for you. I won't stand for that from her. Be off with you and tell her I said that if you want. What do I care? I'm seventy-four years old and I've earned the right to say what I think."

Harriet rose to her feet, her heart renewing its pounding and her knees wobbly. "Of course, Mrs. Bolitho. Good morning to you."

No reply came, so Harriet walked across to the door and let herself out. The maid was waiting outside in the corridor. No doubt she'd had her ear to the keyhole. Harriet couldn't resist. "Is she always like that?"

Wide-eyed, the maid nodded. "Can be worse, ma'am. I've seen worse, for sure." She peered up at Harriet as they started down the stairs. "Didn't know as she had any relatives though. It'll be news to all of us below stairs."

Harriet pressed her lips together. "I rather wish we weren't her relatives."

Chapter Fourteen

Harriet found Jack, as he'd said, drinking his second cup of coffee in a small, rather smoky coffee house devoid of other customers. He glanced up as she entered, and his face broke into a welcoming smile. Just what she needed after such a disturbing interview.

"Would you like a cup of coffee?"

She shook her head. What she wanted to do was return home to Theo and reassure herself of his safety. She felt, unreasonably, of course, as though Mrs. Bolitho might stretch out her talons, decorated with that ostentatious diamond, and snatch him away from her before she could get back to him. "I'd rather be on our way if we can. If you don't mind."

He tossed a coin onto the table and called a thank you to someone banging about out of sight, then escorted her out onto the street. The fresh air felt good on her skin. She heaved in a deep breath in an effort to steady her nerves.

"What happened?" Jack asked, pulling her hand once more into the crook of his arm. She'd have resisted this time, but he had her gripped tight and it would look bad to struggle. And besides, she had other things to think of.

"She wants my son." The words popped out before she had a chance to stop them.

"Theo?"

She nodded. "She wants to meet him and, if she likes him, pay for his education. At first. But I know what happens in situations like this when a rich relative offers to pay for a fatherless child's education. Very soon Theo would be spending all his time with her and not with me. She wants him for herself as the last Penhallow." Tears were close but she mustn't let them fall. There must be something she could do.

They turned out into the market, and he steered her along the edge. "And you don't want to agree to this?"

She shook her head. "Of course not. He's my son, not hers. She has no sons. I don't want Theo at school miles away from me."

He frowned. "She's a widow, don't forget and he's her closest relation, or so she seems to think. Do you not think it wise to let her do this, as in all probability she'll leave her fortune to him."

Harriet glared up at him. "Do you think me a common fortune hunter?"

He shook his head. "Not at all. But I did take you for a woman of sense. You said yourself you are in straitened circumstances and your late husband's aunt could provide a way out of them for you, and especially for Theo. Do you think that he'll get such a chance again while living at Keynvor Cottage with you?"

What was he saying? Did he think she should take this offer?

He held up his free hand as they stopped outside the Star. "If I were you, I would give it some thought before you turn her down."

She wrenched her hand free of his arm. "You don't understand. Only another mother could. Did your mother send you, her only child, away to school?"

A strange look she couldn't fathom flitted across Jack's face. "I went to the grammar school in Truro. I boarded during the week and was home on Saturday afternoons. She had no opportunity for giving me a better education."

Harriet shot him a triumphant glare and strode through the arch and into the stableyard.

His footsteps sounded behind her on the cobbles. "Jonno, our horses, please."

The horses having been brought, Harriet allowed Jonno to boost her into the saddle and she and Jack rode out into the street. All this while she maintained a stony silence and it was only as they left the hovels at the edge of the village that she turned to him again.

She took up where they'd left off. "And would you want to have been sent to Eton, away from Cornwall and your mother?"

He had the grace to shrug and smile at her. "Probably not. Let's call it a truce. I was only thinking of your future… of Theo's future. I'll keep my opinions to myself from now on."

She allowed herself a slight smile. "Thank you."

"And for now, shall we trot?"

For answer she set Peggy into a lively trot along the uneven road.

They'd gone only perhaps half a mile in a more companionable silence than before, when a shout assaulted Harriet's ears. She twisted in the saddle to look, as Jack did the same.

Trotting along a track to their left came three riders, one of whom, the female of the bunch, was waving her right hand with enthusiasm, as though she thought she knew them. Well, as though she thought she knew Jack, surely? Which she in all probability did. Jack drew Shadow to a halt, and he and Harriet waited while the riders caught up. Who could they be? From their appearance, they must be well-to-do locals, possibly people of quality… but for that hoydenish wave. If Lydia had behaved like that back in Bath, she'd have been swiftly reprimanded. Not that reprimanding her seemed to do much good. And this was Cornwall, with Cornish customs which might well allow someone to shout and wave if they caught sight of a person they knew.

Jack edged Shadow between her and the new arrivals, almost as though he wanted to keep them apart, his dark brows lowering over his eyes in what could have been construed as a disapproving frown. He had a look of someone who would have liked to cut his losses and gallop off up the road. Puzzling, given the enthusiastic hailing from the young woman and the impression he'd given Harriet of not being one to follow social mores.

"Jack!" cried the young woman as she drew closer. A slight, dark-haired creature with a heart-shaped face and wide, brown eyes, she was beautiful by any standards. "How lucky to meet you on the road. Sam and I were on our way to visit Nat and Caroline when we bumped into dear Fitz, and he offered to accompany us." She laughed, a gay, rippling sound that carried through the rapidly warming morning air, and turned her gaze to Harriet, her delicate brows rising.

"Ysella," Jack said, more than a little stiffly. "Sam, Captain Carlyon. May I introduce you to my new neighbor, Mrs. Penhallow." He turned back towards Harriet, and she couldn't miss the displeasure in his eyes. What was it he didn't like about this chance meeting? Surely not the effervescent young woman. "Harriet, may I introduce you to my friends, Samuel and Ysella Beauchamp of Carlyon Court. And this is Ysella's cousin, Captain Carlyon, of the local militia. He's in charge of apprehending smugglers locally, not to mention anyone else who catches the attention of the law."

Harriet kept her face straight, afraid her confusion would show if she wasn't careful. That Jack was not at all pleased at this encounter puzzled her no end. Did he not like any of them? No, it had to be this Captain Carlyon, whom he'd deliberately not included as his friend, he was directing his disfavor against. Ysella, Mrs. Beauchamp, appeared very happy to see Jack, and immune to his look of annoyance, and yet...?

Mrs. Beauchamp brought her little chestnut mare up closer to Peggy. "How lovely to make your acquaintance, Mrs. Penhallow. Oh, fustian. I can't call you that can I? Might I use your first name? I call all my friends by their first names, and I know you'll be one of them. This is Cornwall, after all, so I believe we're allowed." She tilted her head to one side and smiled becomingly, her eyes twinkling. She couldn't be more than twenty or so. Scarcely any older than Lydia. Harriet suddenly felt ancient and world weary.

However, she smiled back, trying hard to ignore the interested, speculative gaze of Captain Carlyon. "It seems formalities are to be dispensed with here in Cornwall, which I own is not a bad thing." She paused. "Ysella. What a beautiful name. Is it a traditional Cornish one?"

Ysella Beauchamp beamed. "It is. Both my sisters have Cornish names, too, despite our dear Papa having hailed from Wiltshire, for the most part at least. Mama insisted, as she was born and bred in Cornwall and says she is Cornish to the core and always will be. Only our brother, Kit, escaped. He's Christopher, you see, but we often call him Kitto which is so much more Cornish. And you are?"

A compunction not to share her name with the wolfish Captain swept over Harriet, but it was too late by far now. She kept her eyes fixed on Ysella, as the hairs on the back of her neck stood on end. "Harriet. My own parents were from Truro but sadly didn't grace me with a name typical of our county."

"Don't hog our new friend, Ysella," her husband said, getting between Harriet and Jack. For some reason, an urge to hide herself behind Jack and Shadow's solid presence rose, and Harriet had to swallow down her fear and stiffen her backbone. She couldn't behave like this in public, no matter how uncomfortable being the focus of a strange man's attention made her feel. Jack's sudden protectiveness endeared him to her, bestowing on him the mantle of knight in shining armor. For the moment.

Surely his behavior had been prompted by the dashingly handsome but cruel-eyed captain rather than the solid and dependable Sam Beauchamp. But as she well knew, you never could tell what a man was really like under the façade they chose to erect for public view. Ben had been handsome and charming when she'd met him...

"Sam Beauchamp, Mrs. Penhallow. Delighted to meet you.

I'd kiss your hand and bow, but, alas, all I can really do is doff my hat whilst mounted. Please imagine I've done my duty."

Harriet managed a small laugh. "Being on horseback does present an obstacle to polite exchanges. I used to hunt when I was a girl, and frequently the niceties of polite conversation had to be abandoned in the heat of the chase." Oh, if only she were that girl again, what wouldn't she do to change her life?

The wolfish captain, Ysella's cousin, who'd been half hidden all this time by Jack and Shadow's imposing bulk, brought his horse around to stand beside Ysella's, giving Harriet her first proper view of him. He held out a hand to her, his dark eyes smoldering in a way that sent heat flaring to her cheeks and made her suspect he knew what she looked like naked. His dark eyes and high cheekbones betrayed his relationship to Ysella, but other than that he was his own man. Tall, taller than Jack probably, with hair that might have started out carefully curled and coiffed but now was windblown, as they all were. Probably, with his looks, he was very successful with the ladies. The windblown hair only served to accentuate his rather devilish handsomeness, although she wasn't blind to the cruel set to his mouth and the coldness in his eyes. He would not be a man to cross. No wonder Jack was wary of him.

With slight hesitation, she took the offered hand.

"Mrs. Penhallow. Might I, too, take the liberty of calling you Harriet?" He smiled, but it wasn't a nice smile as it never reached his intense dark eyes. "It's so seldom we get to meet anyone new down here. So, you're Jack's neighbor. Lucky devil, Jack." His voice had a languor to it, a world-weariness that sat well with his looks. The sort of man her mother would have told her to avoid like the plague.

A shiver ran down Harriet's spine. A not at all pleasant one. The captain's lazy eyes slid sideways to consider Jack as he spoke, cold intelligence foremost in them, as though he was assessing her companion and finding something fascinating about him. "So lucky to bump into you, Captain Trevelyan. I've been wanting to meet you again for some time."

What was there about the way he said this? It had sounded almost like a threat. As though, he, like Jack, didn't like the man before him.

Jack's eyes narrowed. "Pray don't let us hold you up. Harriet and I were going to ride inland a little before turning back to Rosudgeon."

News to Harriet.

She caught the tension in Jack's voice even though she sensed he was trying to hide it. He didn't want to ride with these three. Now why was that? Even if you didn't care for someone, why would it make you so keen not to be in their company? It was Captain Carlyon, she felt certain, who was provoking this reaction. Her mind shot back to the day they'd all arrived at Keynvor Cottage when Theo and Lyddie had come running up from the cliffs with tales of a ship in the cove unloading goods they'd thought might be smuggled. Was Jack keen that his tenants, who might well be the smugglers in question, should remain unthreatened by the revenue men? Was that it? Did he know about the smugglers? Probably, as she'd been sure he'd gone to the kiddley himself, which was bound to be their base, on the day he'd escorted her home in the storm. Confusing.

"Oh, do ride with us at least part of the way," Ysella said, pouting a little. "I would so like to get to know Harriet a little better. You can't keep her to yourself. And you can ride inland any day you choose, Jack, but the chances of us riding over here from Carlyon Court again and meeting up with you like this are tiny." She smiled a sweet smile. "Indulge a poor lonely lady, Jack." This last came out as a wheedle.

Would Jack be rude enough to turn her down?

No.

"Very well, Ysella, we'll accompany you some of the way. You have appealed to my better nature."

She giggled. "And there was I thinking you didn't have one." She flashed him a smile and moved closer to Harriet. "There, it's done. I do hope you won't mind me depriving you of your tour of our countryside and confining your ride to the road?"

Harriet smiled. "Not at all."

"Then we'll be off," Sam said. "I've a notion to be at Roskilly with the Treloars in time for a bite to eat at noon." He rubbed his belly and grinned.

The five riders, reassembled, resumed the road towards Marazion.

Jack, Sam and Captain Carlyon rode ahead, and Ysella and Harriet kept their two mares behind, lagging by some twenty yards, just far enough not to be easily overheard. Captain Carlyon had shown an urge to ride beside Harriet, but, thankfully, Ysella had shooed him away. "Nonsense, Fitz. I am busy making friends with Harriet and don't need you butting in. Off you go and ride with Sam and Jack and leave us in peace. Talk about the things men like." She glanced at Harriet. "Men. They see a pretty face and think that every woman wishes to be flirted with. What nincompoops they are. Now, let me give you the sort of guided tour Jack would no doubt have omitted."

True to her word, for the first part of their ride, Ysella contented herself with pointing out and naming all the points of interest they were passing, but this information rapidly ran out. An inquisitorial gleam in her eye, she turned to Harriet. "Now, you must tell me all about yourself, or I shall die of disappointment. You have about you an air of mystery that intrigues me."

Harriet, acutely aware of Jack's ramrod straight back up ahead, bit her lip. Ysella had about her a hint of not being the best person to confide any secrets to. Of being a flap-jaw. But that could just have been her chatty friendliness and the fact she claimed to have been starved of female company. She did seem very keen to add Harriet to her list of acquaintances. But whatever she was like, Harriet was no more prepared to bare her chest to her than she had been to Talwyn Trevelyan.

"There's very little to tell," she said. "I'm a widow with two children, whom my late husband's aunt has provided with somewhere to live. It's a small cottage but very manageable in my reduced circumstances. We haven't been there long, but it's homely and," she nodded at Jack, "the neighbors are kind and friendly."

"Which is most surprising," Ysella said, keeping her voice low as though she didn't wish to be overheard. "Never was I more shocked to see Jack in the company of a proper lady."

For a moment, Harriet didn't know what to say. "Oh," was all she managed.

Ysella nodded vigorously. "Oh, indeed. Jack is quite the recluse. Sam calls him a bit of a hermit. Not so his charming mother, who has attended all our soirées at Carlyon Court and is quite the loveliest of hostesses... only while he's away from Rosudgeon, of course. But while he's at home, she organizes nothing."

"Where does Jack go when he's away?"

Ysella shrugged her slender shoulders. "Heavens, I don't know. He's off in his ship, I believe. Sam says talk is Jack's wedded to the sea and will never find a wife. I assume he's moving goods up and down the coast, which is what a lot of the ships here do—so Sam says. A risky business with the unstable weather we have down here." She glanced at Captain Carlyon's back. "It's odd, you know, but before we met up with you, Fitz was asking all about Jack. I've no idea why. Mind you, he's quite a nosy person and is always asking me about people I know. Anyone would think he was an old lady in her dotage, he's so fond of hearing all the gossip."

Odd, indeed, but then Captain Carlyon was in charge of the revenue men down here and perhaps fancied himself a bit of a sleuth. Harriet peered at where he had his head turned and his eyes fixed on Jack, an acquisitive expression on his face. What was it he was after? Surely not Jack himself? She felt an odd proprietorial instinct towards Jack, as though he might need protecting. She frowned. "He was?"

Ysella nodded. "But there's little to tell. Jack is such a private person with only a few friends—like Sam and me. And of course Nat and Caroline." She dimpled. "And I've yet to see him paying court to any respectable lady such as yourself."

Harriet felt the heat rise again to her cheeks. "He's not paying court to me. I'm a widow and still in mourning, and he knows I am."

Ysella chuckled. "My dear Harriet, if you think that makes you off limits to a man like him, then you are very much mistaken. Can you not see the look in his eyes?"

"The…?"

Another chuckle. "I may be young, but I know the look of love when I see it. He's smitten."

Harriet's hand shot to her mouth. "Oh no. I didn't mean him to… I-I didn't think I was encouraging him in any way. This is terrible."

Ysella chuckled again, her eyes twinkling in amusement. "Well, if it's not reciprocated he's gentleman enough to back down. But do you not think him quite the catch, with Rosudgeon, his own ship and his aristocratic father?"

"His what?"

"His own ship. Did he not tell you?"

Harriet, still reeling from the revelation that Ysella thought Jack interested in her, clutched the reins so tightly poor Peggy curvetted in discomfort. "Not the ship—the father. I didn't think there was a Mr. Trevelyan. His mother gave me the impression she was a widow, like me." The words came out little above a whisper.

Ysella leaned towards her with the air of someone about to impart a big secret. "I would not tell you were it not common knowledge. But you are right in one way, there never was a Mr. Trevelyan. Jack is the son of Sir Austin Trengrouse of Trengrouse Castle. Jack's mother was his mistress." She glanced furtively at the backs of the three men. "Sir Austin wanted to marry her, but his father refused his permission and forced him to marry a woman who brought with her a fortune—and gave him just the three daughters. No son and heir."

"Good heavens." And the man had set up his mistress and son in Rosudgeon House only a mile or two from where he must now live with his wife. What sort of a man did that? If she hadn't met Talwyn, she might have felt sorry for the legal wife, but she couldn't. And for Jack to have seen his father from afar as he grew up, but perhaps never had anything to do with him; that, too, seemed cruel on the part of his parents.

They had reached the lane down to Rosudgeon by now, and Jack and Harriet had to take their leave of the party from Carlyon Court, Jack with evident relief, Harriet wishing she could have heard more from Ysella.

"You must come over to the Court with your daughter," Ysella said to Harriet, as they parted. "I should love to meet with her. And your little boy, of course. I have a little girl of my own, and a baby boy. Merrin loves to see other children and gets so few opportunities to do so. We can send the carriage for you, if you like."

Caught unawares by this flamboyant offer, Harriet hesitated, but before she could answer, Jack did so for her. "I'm sure Harriet needs to settle in first, Ysella. We'll send a message to you when she's done so."

Annoyance rose in Harriet's breast, but she didn't contradict him. It had been bad enough when Ben answered for her, and he'd been her husband, but to now have a man she hardly knew doing the same made her hackles rise. However, ingrained into her through her years of marriage was the inability to contradict what a man had said. She bit her lip instead.

Captain Carlyon managed an approximation of a bow to her from his horse and a nod to Jack. "If you don't mind, Harriet, I would like to call on you. It worries me to think of you in your isolated cottage so close to the cliffs. No," he forestalled Jack who had clearly been about to butt in again. "I insist. It's the least I can do. I feel a responsibility as your late husband was in the same regiment as me. An officer always helps the family of a fallen comrade-in-arms. Nothing you can say will change my mind."

Harriet managed to bestow a weak smile on him, yet again falling foul of her inbred inability to refuse a polite request. "Thank you, Captain. That would be most kind of you." Only it wouldn't, would it? Surely what the smuggler-hunting captain really wanted was a closer look at Bessie's Cove and her house just happened to be close to it.

"Shall we say tomorrow, then?" He smiled his wolfish smile at her, showing too many of his white teeth. "We'll all be staying overnight at Roskilly, so I can call on my return journey."

"Won't that be a long way out of your way?" Jack got in, speaking as though through clenched teeth. "After all, aren't you based in St Ives?" He frowned. "Indeed, it seems odd to me that Sam and Ysella met you near Penzance. Where were you headed?"

Captain Carlyon's upper lip curled. "Oh, I was checking on the new customs men I've set up in Penzance. It was only when I met Ysella and Sam that I decided to return home via Roskilly. It's been such a long time since I've seen Nat."

"Well," Jack said, his brows furrowed as he turned Shadow away. "No doubt you'll enjoy your stay at Roskilly. Good day to you all." And he trotted away.

Did he know more about the smuggling than she'd suspected? With a wave to Ysella, Harriet hurried Peggy after him.

Chapter Fifteen

A FULL TWO minutes passed before Jack remembered he had Harriet with him. He slowed Shadow to a walk, and she brought Peggy up beside him, her expression puzzled, but some of the earlier wariness dissipated.

"Do you not care for Captain Carlyon?"

Well, she could speak her mind when the inclination took her, that was for certain. What to say? "The man irritates me." Something of an understatement, but he could hardly tell her the truth, could he? He didn't want her guessing why he didn't want Fitz Carlyon poking about near Bessie's Cove, or she might go poking about herself.

"I gathered that." A hint of wryness in her voice. Had he been that obvious? At least she'd lost her look of a dog waiting to be beaten, but that might have more to do with Ysella's cheerful influence and the fact that their ride was nearly over. She was now studying him with a small frown between her eyes as though he himself was a mystery waiting to be solved. What had Ysella said to her? Not that she knew anything of his more clandestine activities, because she didn't. Not with the way her tongue was inclined to run away with itself when she got excited.

He shrugged. "The man doesn't like me, either."

Harriet smiled, this time a natural smile rather than a forced one, her face transformed for an instant into a vision of loveliness.

"I had the impression on our brief acquaintance that the person the good Captain is fondest of is himself."

Jack couldn't help a grin. "You have hit the nail right on the head. He is indeed a man very fond of his own importance and also of his 'successes' with the fairer sex. He sees himself as irresistible. And as that importance is, shall we say, *important*, then I suppose I have to say he has the right to be. Or, rather, he sees himself as having the right."

They'd reached where drooping trees, still heavy with summer foliage that was just beginning to turn, overhung the track down to the coast, and Jack was forced to duck. Harriet steered Peggy around them with neat aplomb. "Is that the only reason you don't like him?"

Her forthright questions took him aback, forcing him to consider the real reasons why he didn't like Captain Carlyon. Fitz, as he liked to be known by his acquaintances, although he probably wouldn't encourage such familiarity from Jack, the man he was pursuing. Jack wasn't about to reveal all of those reasons to Harriet, whom he'd known only for the blink of an eye, although rather puzzlingly that blink of an eye felt like forever.

"I, er…" he floundered. "He's a sight too curious for his own good." There, that was an answer without having lied. It would have to do.

Harriet tilted her chin towards him. "And you are a very private person?"

Was he? He'd never thought of himself that way but perhaps it was how others saw him. "Yes." Easiest to admit it. "How astute of you."

"I don't know you well enough to have worked that out for myself. Ysella told me. She revealed *all* your secrets to me." She fixed him with a direct gaze, as though willing him to come clean to her himself.

Not all of them, hopefully. Neither she nor Sam knew of his cross-channel trading. Kit, Ysella's brother knew, because he'd been in the trade himself until he'd found himself a wife and a musket ball in the arm, much at the same time. Sam and Ysella, of course, knew what Kit had been up to, before that midnight raid by the revenue men, led by Fitz Carlyon, had put a stop to it. However, they knew nothing of what still went on, and Kit would never have welched on someone else's involvement. Jack frowned. If he could, he intended to keep it that way, even if it led to people calling him a 'very private man'.

He managed a smile. Impossible not to smile at her, in truth. "For someone who only knows me through her husband and brother, Ysella presumes a lot to think she's revealed all my secrets."

Harriet dropped her gaze and patted Peggy's sweaty shoulder. "Perhaps I should have said she told me what she knows. That you live with your mother, that Rosudgeon is yours, bequeathed to you by your father…" Here she paused, as though waiting for him to add something.

He didn't.

She gave an infinitesimal shrug and kept going. "And that she has never seen you riding out with a lady." The smile edged its way onto her face for a moment, almost conspiratorial in its nature. "Everyone has to have a few secrets they keep only to themselves."

Damn it. What had Ysella, with her love of gossip, revealed? But… did Harriet's words mean she had secrets as well? That she didn't want anyone to know? Something that made her as wary, in her way, as he was. Something that brought that look of fear into her eyes before she could veil it.

He'd consider that later. But for now, damn Ysella. Might she have let slip about his father? It wasn't a secret amongst his friends, and many of the country folk knew as well, and no one seemed to hold it against him. Did Ysella even know? She'd not been brought up down here, and she was a good eight years younger than he was. But, rumor being what it was, even if you did live right on the westernmost tip of Cornwall as she did, she might have heard talk and gained an inkling, even though his mother had done her best to keep it quiet. Servants, on the other hand, could rarely keep juicy secrets.

Making the decision to ignore the possibility Harriet knew of his parentage, he guided Shadow around a large pothole before replying. "There are very few ladies who would dream of being seen riding with me, Harriet."

She peeked sideways at him, for once almost coquettish and the hunted look gone. "Have I made a faux pas in agreeing to ride out with you, then? Will it ruin my reputation?"

"Undoubtedly. I am seen as a ne'er do well by the landed gentry in this part of Cornwall, unless they happen to be my friends. A ne'er-do-well who has chosen the sea over the ballroom and turned my back on society. And as for my friends, I pick and choose who those are."

This didn't appear to have disturbed her as he'd expected it to. Was she warming to him? "These landed gentry who turn their noses up at you, if they don't know me or see me riding with you, they will not be at liberty to consider my reputation damaged. Let it be our secret."

With the end of their ride in sight, her confidence appeared to be mounting. Had she been afraid he might do something untoward, heaven forbid ungentlemanly, when they were riding alone? She did indeed seem different now to how she'd been at the start of the ride. Confident enough to tease him. "You take this in your stride, as though facing a fence out hunting."

She nodded. "I have had many fences to face over the years, and not just on the hunting field." Her brow furrowed as though a memory troubled her. "But I won't bore you with my tales. Look, we're nearly at Rosudgeon. I'll dismount here and walk down the track to Keynvor."

"We can ride down there together, and I can bring Peggy back afterwards."

She shook her head. "No. I insist. I think my legs would appreciate the walk, as this was quite a long ride for my first time in the saddle in sixteen years."

Irritation coursed through him. Damn it. He wanted to have the chance to ride longer with her, to walk slowly down to her cottage and perhaps tarry a little for refreshment provided by the inestimable Bertha. And yet here she was, giving him the brush off as though he were just a casual acquaintance. Which he supposed he was. He searched for something to keep her with him longer as she placed her reins into one hand and unhooked her right leg from the pommel.

"You must have been a child bride."

She hesitated, that haunted look back in her eyes. "I was seventeen."

"A child indeed."

She made a little moue with her mouth. "It was that or say goodbye to the man I fancied myself in love with." Her hand went to her mouth as though she hadn't meant to say this, and she shook her head. "Perhaps you have experience of the hot-headedness of girls?"

He barely heard her last words. *Fancied herself in love with?* Had she not, then, loved her husband? Might she not be as deeply in mourning as he had thought? With his scanty knowledge of marriage, gleaned only from his working-class friends, he had little idea how those from the upper classes undertook it, but he'd always understood marriage to have been for love. He'd learned that at his mother's knee, and from watching his friends like Sam and Ysella and the Treloars. His mother had loved his father all Jack's life, and still did, more fool her.

He slid down from Shadow and came around to help Harriet down from Peggy. She slid into his arms and, for just a moment, he allowed himself to hang onto her, the urge to crush her to his chest waxing strong.

Beneath his hands, her body stiffened at his touch, and she stepped out of his hold, her cheeks a little pinker than they had been. "Thank you so much... Jack, for allowing me to indulge my love of horses." The words came out stilted, as though forced between her teeth, and she took another step back from him, her eyes lowered, all the old barrier built back even higher than before. "I very much enjoyed our ride." She hitched up the spare fabric of her habit and turned away.

"Will you be all right walking that far in your habit? You won't trip?" Now he sounded like an idiot, babbling on, when clearly, she was in firm control of the situation. Just for a few minutes, he'd felt a kind of ease beginning to grow between them, and now she was all bristling hedgehog again, curled in a fetal ball to keep him away.

She hitched her skirts a little more. "I shall be quite all right. It's not far, and the walk might ease out any aches and pains that are creeping up on me after my ride." She bobbed her head to him in a dainty curtsey, still without meeting his eyes. "Thank you again for this treat."

And she set off down the track without a backward glance. He watched her out of sight around the bend by the farm, willing her to turn around and look back at him, but she didn't. She must have put him out of her mind straight away. No doubt with ease. He stood a little longer considering how he was feeling, the two horses swishing their tails at a few flies.

Confused. Puzzled by her sudden change. Had it been when she'd felt his hands on her waist? Had that done it? Had she perhaps sensed his desire to hold her close and been shocked?

He shook his head in frustration. What was it about her that had him this way? His first instinct, on hearing she'd taken Keynvor Cottage, had been one of horror at finding some outsider right on the doorstep of the two hidden coves where he usually brought ashore his contraband. His next instinct had been to involve her family in their deeds in some way and thus frighten her into keeping silent, in the nicest possible way. This third instinct, which had overwhelmed the other two at startling speed, was not one he was used to. An instinct to protect her that he'd never felt towards any other woman.

She'd be heading down the hill now and nearing where the track forked, going right towards her cottage and Old Tummel's hovel on the headland. Turning away from the left fork, which led towards Bessie's kiddley and Will's house at Porth en Alls above Prussia Cove. The bits he didn't want her prying into, for all their sakes.

His mind wandered. That maidservant of hers, Bertha, would be waiting for her with the kettle singing on the hob, wanting to know how her ride had gone. Her children too, perhaps with eager questions about where she'd been. Would she tell Theo what his great-aunt had in mind for him? Probably not.

The children placated, she'd be going upstairs to take off her habit... Here, Jack's imagination began to run away with him somewhat, his tight breeches becoming uncomfortable and sweat standing out on his brow. No. She was a lady, not some girl from a tap room with morals looser than her drawers. He'd best not go there.

Shadow nudged him in the back, dragging him out of his speculative musings and back to reality. Grabbing Peggy's reins, he led the two horses in at the gates of Rosudgeon and up the gravel drive, steeling himself for his mother's inevitable inquisition.

Chapter Sixteen

CAPTAIN CARLYON, TRUE to his word, came calling on Harriet the very next day. Bertha was busy with the housework, and Lydia and Theo, begrudging being kept indoors on such a fine morning, were seated at the kitchen table working at their schoolbooks. Harriet, dressed for work in her oldest gown and an apron, was digging the weeds out of the overgrown beds at the front of the cottage in the hope of one day growing flowers there. The ramshackle, wobbly-wheeled and woodworm-infested barrow she'd found in the tumbledown woodshed stood beside her, rescued from being consigned to firewood and now piled high with leggy greenery.

The sound of a horse's hooves on the gravelly track had her straightening up, her heart, quite out of her control, doing a kind of somersault of emotion that was an odd mixture of fear and excitement as she stared up the track. But it wasn't Jack. That she'd been hoping it was dawned on her as she felt her heart sink, and a wave of guilty heat surged to her cheeks. Instead of Jack, the singularly more disturbing Captain Carlyon, on his fine gray gelding, came riding towards her, an expression of amused interest on his face.

"Good morning, Harriet," he called, as he halted the gray ten yards distant. His gaze ran up and down her attire in obvious speculation. Why did he make her feel as though he knew every secret she kept close, as well as what she looked like naked? Again. Most disquieting. If only they hadn't bumped into him yesterday. But she was going to have to be polite.

The memory of how Jack didn't like Fitz Carlyon rose swiftly, followed by the unnerving thought that she herself might know more than she should about smuggling activities here, just because the children had seen the ship. She should have been insistent yesterday that she wasn't ready to accept callers.

She smoothed down her skirts and untied her apron, plastering a welcoming, but not too welcoming, smile onto her face. She'd have to pretend she was pleased to see him. She'd had plenty of practice at pretending.

Fitz Carlyon swung down from the saddle and glanced around himself as though searching for somewhere to tether his horse.

Harriet remembered herself. "Good morning, Captain. I believe there's a tethering ring at the side of the house." Although that would mean he could stay for longer than if he had to hold onto his horse. Unless, of course, he took recourse to hitching the gray's reins to a branch of one of the low trees, as Jack had done.

"Fitz. Please call me Fitz. Everyone does and, as I'm already calling you Harriet, I feel there's no point in you persisting in calling me 'captain' every five minutes." He led the horse round to the side of the house.

A movement caught Harriet's eye. Both her children, and Bertha, had their noses pressed to the kitchen window. She waved a hand at them and scowled, having to wipe the scowl off her face in haste as Fitz returned, now without his horse.

Taking his hat off and executing a smart bow all in one fluid movement, he smiled, but the smile didn't reach his cold and calculating eyes. That he was here for some reason other than to merely call on her seemed glaringly obvious. Or maybe she was just being too suspicious. Maybe she should try accepting people at face value. Or maybe not… she'd done a sight too much of that in the past and look where it had got her.

He pulled off his gloves and tucked them into his hat. "I said I'd call, and here I am. Too much talk of babies going on at Roskilly for me. My cousin Ysella, charming and pretty as she is, can be quite boring when she brings up the subject of her offspring. I'm very much of the 'children should be seen but not heard' school." He glanced at the window, now thankfully empty of those eager faces. "And of course, Nat's wife is just the same as Ysella. Even Nat's sister, little Hetty, pretty as a picture and as yet unmarried so quite a distraction, joined in. I don't know what it is with women and babies. So, with no one to talk to who wasn't drooling over a baby, I remembered you'd extended a welcome. Hence, here I am."

She hadn't exactly extended a welcome to him. More he'd invited himself. Instinct warned her to be wary of this rather predatory gentleman; that perhaps he might prove himself to be less of a gentleman than she thought, if she were caught off her guard. She'd invite him in where there was company. That would be her safest move. "Pray come inside and I'll ask Bertha to make some tea. You do like tea?" It was mid-morning, after all. Surely he couldn't want brandy, which was still the only spirit she possessed. But you never knew with men.

Fitz set his beaver and gloves on the bench by the kitchen door and followed her inside. Lydia and Theo kept their heads down, but the pens in their hands remained suspiciously motionless. They were watching out of the corners of their eyes and listening like bats, and so was Bertha, with her back turned and a duster in her hand as she attacked the shelves above the range.

"My children," Harriet said. "And my maid. Bertha, can you bring tea into the drawing room, please, for Captain Carlyon and me?" And before Bertha had time to respond, Harriet ushered Fitz into their rather bare parlor, conscious of the fact that had he ever been on friendly terms with Jack or his mother, he might have seen some of this furniture before. She left the door deliberately ajar and sat where she could see Bertha at the stove, pouring boiling water into the teapot.

To do Fitz credit, he made no reaction, but took a seat when offered on a faded, highbacked wing chair close to the empty fireplace. The sight of the cold grate almost made Harriet shiver, as this room, unlike the cozy kitchen, had a definite chill to it.

"How nice it is to see you again," she began with, judging it best to stick to polite inanities with this gentleman.

His eyes shone with something that might have been a mix of amusement, admiration and… was that desire? The heat that had ebbed from Harriet's cheeks renewed itself. In Bath, she'd not dared venture into society for fear of accusations from Ben, unfounded though they would have been. She'd scarcely met any men in the last ten years other than Ben, his friends and the occasional tradesman. Even when he'd been away with the regiment, she'd not dared deviate, for fear someone might tell him she'd been out socializing. He would have taken that the wrong way.

So, being desired by someone, even though she felt nothing for him, was both frightening and a little pleasing, so long as it went nowhere. She sat up all the taller at the thought of it, and pushed thoughts of Jack, who'd looked at her in quite a different way, out of her head.

"In truth," Fitz said, "I could hardly wait to get away. The memory of your beauty stayed with me all night long, preventing me from sleeping any more than fitfully."

Good heavens, but he was forward. With her lack of experience with men other than Ben, Harriet recoiled a little in shock at his words. Of course, she knew she had once been pretty, but Ben had instilled into her that only a hoyden exploited her own good looks, and he would not have his wife disport herself like one of those. Plus, she was still confined to wearing black, a color she felt she never wanted to abandon as up until now it had served her as a suit of armor, rendering her untouchable and sacrosanct. Besides, she'd always viewed her looks as not the sort men would fall for. Ben had said… No, she wouldn't think about that.

"I must apologize for having caused you a problem." She didn't look up but regarded her fingers, forcing them to resist the impulse to twist themselves together in her lap.

He laughed, a deep, rolling laugh that was not unpleasant and seemed to reverberate around the cottage's parlor, filling it to the smoke-stained rafters. "No need for apology, Harriet. It was a pleasant night, if not a restful one. I would have had it no other way. You are quite the distraction to a man."

She looked up to find him gazing at her out of those speculative dark eyes. There was no denying his attractions, but they were not the sort likely to hold her in thrall. This man was too used to getting his own way—over everything.

She was saved from replying to his declaration by Bertha coming in with the tea tray. This she set down on the low table with a clatter of crockery. She took a step back and stood her ground as though expecting to be asked to do more, or to stand as chaperone to her mistress.

"Thank you, Bertha, that will be all." With the door left open, Harriet nurtured the illusion of safety.

Bertha gave a harrumph of displeasure and shot Fitz a heavy glare. Despite her instant liking for Jack, she appeared to have taken a just as instant dislike to Fitz. Possibly with good reason. "I'll just be in the kitchen if you need anything else, Miss Harriet. I'll leave the door open, in case you call." She spun on her heel and departed, leaving the door open to its full extent.

"I fear your maidservant has taken against me," Fitz said as Harriet poured the tea. "I seem to have that effect on some people. I can't think why." His tone gave the lie to that. Captain Fitzwilliam Carlyon knew exactly why he wasn't liked.

"Ignore Bertha," Harriet said, a little guilty at her disloyalty to her friend. "She's been with me since my childhood and is of the opinion she's my second mother and can tell me what to do." She poured the tea and handed him a dish.

He grinned, more wolfish than ever, making Harriet wonder if she should comment on how pointy his ears were or what long teeth he had, like the fabled Little Red Riding Hood in Theo's chapbook. "Then you should send her packing. If a servant becomes too familiar, it's time to say goodbye to them."

Harriet shook her head. "I could never do that. She's been my rock these recent months and before that as well." Very true, although Bertha still didn't know the extent of what had gone on between her master and mistress. No, that secret still lay clasped tight within Harriet's heart.

Fitz's eyes narrowed. "Ah, yes. In your loss." He was looking at her as though he wanted to extract every ounce of her story from her and would know if she told him an untruth. "I'm sorry this has happened to you. It must be very difficult with two children to bring up."

"I am managing tolerably well, thank you. Jack's mother, Mrs. Trevelyan, very kindly has taken me under her wing."

His eyes sharpened. "You have been inside Rosudgeon House?"

Harriet hesitated, the feeling that he was only here to mine her for information increasing. "I have. I walked up there to thank her for her kindness." She sucked in her lips. "Have you not been there, Captain?"

"Fitz. Please call me Fitz."

Why was it calling Jack by his Christian name felt natural, but calling the captain by his did not? Puzzling.

He shook his head. "Never. She occasionally might organize a dinner or a soirée, but I've never been lucky enough to receive an invitation in the three years I've been stationed down here in St Ives. Although I've dropped enough hints." A sly look crept over him and his eyes narrowed still further. "Perhaps, if you were to be invited, as you are now friends with Mrs. Trevelyan, I might escort you there?"

The sensation that she was fencing with him grew, and so did the rate of her heartbeat. "If I am lucky enough to receive an invitation, then I shall most certainly think of you." Oh no she wouldn't. Far too dangerous. She managed to force a smile to cover the lie, the feeling of being naked under his gaze returning.

He encompassed the room with a quick glance. "How cozy you have made this cottage, and how fortuitous for you that you have it. I believe I've encountered your Aunt's man of business down here in Penzance. Boase, a partner in the bank I use. A man with ambitions to be mayor. A bit of a dry stick of a fellow, but honest as the day is long. That's what you want in a man who manages your business interests."

Harriet bit her lip, cold sweat standing out down her back at the memory of her meeting with Mrs. Bolitho. "I had the pleasure of meeting my aunt by marriage while I was in Penzance yesterday. I called to offer her my heartfelt thanks for the provision of this cottage."

"Ah, so you've met the old woman." He set down his empty teacup and glanced up at the front window and the blue sky without. "You have my commiserations. But never mind that. She's not here now. And we're lucky it's such a glorious day. Might I tempt you to a walk along the cliffs?"

From the sounds emanating from the kitchen, Lydia and Theo had finished their lessons and were helping Bertha. For some reason, she didn't want Fitz anywhere near Lydia. The fear that her youth would not render her out of bounds to him had arisen. Perhaps she was maligning him, but best not to find out. "A little fresh air would be most welcome." No, it wouldn't, but she could see no other way to get him to leave. "I'll just fetch my bonnet and shawl."

Outside, the sun was still shining as Fitz picked up his hat and gloves from the bench and drew Harriet's hand through his arm. He glanced in the direction of the kiddley. "Shall we head east?"

No. *Not* a good idea as she was sure he wanted to spy on it. The instinct to protect her neighbors, no matter what they were up to, rose in Harriet's breast. Jack was undoubtedly a customer, and knew more than he should have done about the smuggling. "I haven't explored the path to the west as yet," she said, giving him a firm little pull. "Perhaps you could satisfy my curiosity by walking that way? I should very much like to see the headland views. My children tell me they are spectacular."

A small frown marred Fitz's all-too handsome face, but he acquiesced. He could have done nothing else and remained polite. "Very well. We shall explore territory unknown as yet to man nor beast. As though we were in the wilds of the Americas."

She suppressed a smile. Despite the aura of danger surrounding him, there nevertheless remained a physical pull, a charm that some women, not her of course, might find difficult to resist. He probably had little trouble winning over the ladies he met. Not much chance of him charming her, though.

The narrow path west wound along close to the cliffs, which for the most part hid the tiny cove below the cottage. No sign of any ships approaching it today. Jack's ship must be in Plymouth by now, unloading their cargo. Hopefully a legal one.

Ahead, Harriet's attention was drawn by a decrepit, one-story, thatched cottage where it crouched against the heather-covered hillside. An old man sat outside it on a low stool, his skinny, gaitered legs outstretched before him, and a fishing net spread over his knees. Wielded by his gnarled old hands, a shuttle darted in and out of the net in a rapid weave.

He must have been deaf, as he didn't look up until she and Fitz were almost upon him. Shaggy eyebrows jutted over a wizened, bearded face, and a toothless grimace that might have been a smile split his face. Not an edifying sight, but Harriet had seen worse amongst the beggars of Bath. She smiled back at him. "Good morning to you. A fine day to be sitting outside in the sun."

The old man nodded a head whose shagginess matched his eyebrows, although the beard on his chin was wispy and thin, as though nature, having bestowed upon him such a fine, thick head of hair, had skimped elsewhere. "G'mornin' to you, too, my luvver."

The greeting, made with as broad a Cornish accent as Harriet had ever heard, might have offended a person less accustomed to

Cornish vocabulary, but Harriet knew the term 'my luvver' was a much-used address amongst the working classes. Her own mother had used it from time to time, having learned it from her old nurse, and Bertha often said it to the children.

The old man's faded blue eyes slid past Harriet and came to rest on Fitz, suddenly sharpening, as though in recognition. In a hurry, he bent his head over his net and resumed his job. "Gotta get on wi' my work. No time to sit and pass the time o' day, Missus."

How odd. For a moment, it had seemed as though he was about to be friendly, until, that was, he'd laid eyes on Fitz. If Jack didn't like Fitz, it seemed this old man didn't either. But why? She could understand why Jack might see Fitz as someone to dislike, but why would some strange old man in the middle of nowhere look at him as though he were the devil incarnate? Did he, perhaps, know what Fitz represented? Did everyone locally know?

Fitz gave her arm a gentle pull. "Let's move on. I don't like the look of this character. A little disreputable for you to have for a neighbor. I hope your front door has a good lock."

The old man grunted but didn't raise his head at this insult, which he must have heard as Fitz hadn't bothered to lower his voice. Perhaps not so deaf after all.

With only one quick backward glance to where the old man was now staring after them from beneath those shaggy brows, Harriet allowed herself to be escorted away from the hovel to where the path climbed onto the headland. Below the cliffs, surf thundered onto their rocky feet, and gulls wheeled in the breeze, calling harshly to each other. The wind snatched at Harriet's hair, making her glad she had her bonnet.

"I believe there's to be a ball at the assembly rooms in Truro very shortly," Fitz said, his eyes scanning the coastline as though searching for something.

Should she consider it an insult that he wasn't looking at her while he was talking to her? "Oh?" was all she could think of to say in reply, as she, too, scanned the horizon. Far out on the blue-green expanse, the red-brown sails of a few small fishing boats looked tiny. But no sign of any larger ships. An odd feeling of relief settled on her.

"I was wondering," Fitz said, still not looking at her. "I was wondering if I might prevail upon you to attend? That is, unless you'd planned to go with Captain Trevelyan."

Oh no. This needed nipping in the bud. "I fear, Fitz, that you have not fully understood my position here in Cornwall." The sea breeze blew a strand of her hair across her face, and she had to tuck it behind her ear. "I am not at liberty to attend any social gatherings, either with you or with Captain Trevelyan, whom I do not know at all well, as not only am I still in mourning, but my... income... does not extend further than our day-to-day expenses." It was oddly easier to admit this to him when he wasn't looking at her. "So balls of any kind are out of the question."

Indeed, they had been ever since she'd married Ben. As a girl of seventeen barely out of the schoolroom who'd only been to the one ball where she'd met him, she'd longed to attend some of the enticing social events in Bath, but he'd forbidden it. She was his, he'd said, and would not go disporting herself in public, especially not when he was away with his regiment. Which he had been most of the time. The one time she'd disobeyed him... well, she'd not done it again. The thought that she could disobey him now suddenly arose, but not temptingly enough to make her want to accept Fitz's request.

He turned to look at her. "I'm sorry. I didn't mean to make you feel awkward. And I wrongly assumed that you and the brave Captain might already be friends as we came upon you riding together."

So he did have some fellow feeling for others. She shook her head. "He merely offered to escort me to Penzance so I could see Mrs. Bolitho. His mother has been kind to me." A small lie but an expedient one. "I don't feel awkward. Apart from my lack of funds, as I said, I'm also still in mourning. I would not in all propriety be able to dance, so it would be a waste of time."

He didn't look at all bothered, so perhaps his question had been to find out her relationship to Jack. "Perhaps when you are out of mourning?"

She bowed her head. "Perhaps." Only if she had her way that wouldn't be for a very long time. If ever. With a little shiver, she drew her shawl closer about her shoulders. "This wind is chilly. Do you mind if we walk back now? It must be time for the children to have their luncheon." As good a way as any to inform him that his visit was over.

Chapter Seventeen

A FULL WEEK later, Jack stood on the cliffs with Will Richards, outside Porth en Alls, the house Will shared with his wife, Eliza, and elderly mother-in-law. Raising a leisurely hand, he shaded his eyes from the brightness of the evening sun as they watched *The Fly* slip neatly into harbor in Bessie's Cove. A narrow channel that was never empty even at low tide, ideal for a shallow drafted lugger, existed under the western cliffs, and it was to this berth that Daniel Bussow was expertly maneuvering the neat little ship.

As they watched, young Harry, holding a rope, stepped nimbly off the deck and onto the iron rungs of the ladder fixed to the rocks to swarm nimbly up to the makeshift quayside. The sailors furled the lowered sails, and *The Fly* settled into her temporary dock like a gull returning to its roost. Jack couldn't deny that he was glad to see her back after so long away. His feet itched to feel her heaving deck beneath them.

He wrinkled his nose. "I hope they've got rid of the stink of fish down below."

This remark made Will chuckle. "Don't fret yourself. They'll've been in barrels, as usual, so they won't have left no stink on your precious ship. And anyway, Dan'l will've picked up a cargo of baccie from the Channel Isles, ready to take across to France. That's strong enough smelling to overpower fish any day."

Jack's turn to laugh. "You've said that before, and it's not been true. We've a long voyage to make tonight, over to Roscoff, and I don't want the smell of fish oil disturbing it."

Ignoring his friend's fussiness, Will turned towards the cliff path. "Shall we go down?"

The two men strode down the narrow path, their booted feet scuffing up the dust and pebbles, and their view of *The Fly* vanished, hidden by the vegetation that edged the cliffs. They wouldn't be able to see her again until they were on the path to her mooring.

Over to Jack's right, a column of smoke wound up into the darkening sky from Keynvor Cottage's chimney. Hopefully, Harriet and her brood would be safely indoors at dinner, and not intending to make any evening sorties. He'd seen the boy out and about with young Cado Bussell from the kiddley, but so far he'd been no problem.

Old Tummels came out as they passed his tumbledown cottage and fell in behind them without a word, as though, without having to be told, he knew the ship was back.

The three of them took the path opposite Tummels' hut, where it performed a sharp switchback to run below the cliff path down into the rocky inlet, a steep drop to the rocks on its right. *The Fly* came back into view, her crew busy making her ship-shape. No smell of fish as yet.

Over on the other side of the cove, more smoke and the top of the kiddley roof showed above the trees, but not a soul was in sight. Coming in to moor in the cove brought with it the risk of being spotted by someone unfriendly to their cause, but, as he'd said to Daniel a few days ago, it would be best to come in by night. Unfortunately, the tide had meant coming in by evening's fading light, but at least it was the tail end of September, and full darkness would soon be upon them.

He and Will swung themselves down the ladder onto the ship's deck. Daniel appeared from the stern and Jack shook his hand. "Good trip? Any trouble?"

Daniel grinned. "Sold all the fish. Got a good price for our friends in Penzance. Then we picked up the tobacco as planned over to St Helier. Paid a good low price for that, an'all. Didn't see sight nor sound of a revenue cutter. It's all down in the hold ready to set sail. Picked up a few trinkets, as well, to sell as a sideline."

Jack didn't ask what they were. If Daniel wanted to make a few extra francs selling things to the French that were still hard to get over on the continent, then that was up to him. No doubt all the crew had a few bits and pieces they planned to sell to supplement their wages.

"Lovey's got a stew going for you men," Will called. "Soon as you're ready. Then we'll be off about ten, as the tide goes out. Mind you don't get tap-hackled. I don't want no slubberdegullions on my ship tonight."

A chorus of agreement echoed round the men, some of it a little unwilling as they all liked a drink when in port. "Can we go now, Cap'n Will?" Silas Finn asked. "My belly thinks as it's bin cut off from my mouth."

Will laughed. "Off you all go then. You, too, young Clemo. Cap'n Jack's going to keep watch for an hour or so, as he's been playin' landlubber while you all were all off a-fetchin' and carryin' for him. You all go get your bellies filled."

The men, Tummels and young Clemo included, wasted no further time and were up the ladder and gone in a matter of minutes. The sound of their voices faded away, drowned out by the rumble of the waves rolling up the beach and onto the rocks.

Jack checked *The Fly's* ropes. A good captain always made sure for himself that his ship was secure, and the men knew it. None of the ropes needed adjusting. "You can get off too, Will," he said. "I'll be fine here on my own, and I've already eaten up at Rosudgeon."

Will swung himself up the ladder. "I will that, and thankee for saying so. That stew did smell right fine when I was in the kiddley. Lovey's a good cook."

Jack laughed. "Better than your Eliza?"

Will leaned down from the height of the rocky wharf. "A lot better than Eliza, but don't you dare go tellin' her that. She'd have my guts for garters."

Jack shook his head. "Sailor's promise. Get off with you."

When Will had gone, Jack walked forward to the bows and checked nothing was chafing, running his hand over the gunnels as he went, reveling in the sweeping lines of his little ship. A boat was never silent, and the little noises she made served to give the impression of a living creature. The mooring ropes creaked, the waves slapped along her sides, and overhead the halyards groaned. Strong in his nostrils, the smell of tar from the rigging was enough to cover any remaining aroma of her previous cargo.

Jack loved his times alone on board *The Fly*. A sense of calm washed over him, and his worries about Fitz Carlyon's nosiness drifted away. Very shortly, he'd be out at sea again, with his ship curvetting beneath him, as responsive and spirited as his horse and even if the revenue cutter hove into view, it would never catch them.

"Cap'n Jack!"

A piping voice disturbed his reverie.

He turned his head.

A small figure stood at the top of the ladder, gazing down at him out of earnest hazel eyes. Theo Penhallow.

Jack made his way back to amidships. "What're you doing down here?"

Theo beamed, full of childish confidence that if he liked someone, they were bound to like him back. "I saw your ship come in from up there." He waved his hand vaguely up towards the clifftop. "I asked Mama if I could go out after supper, and she said I could. So I came down to find you." He paused, suddenly not quite so sure of himself. "You said the other day that when your ship came back, you'd take me on board and show me around." His voice rose in question towards the end of his words.

Jack looked him up and down. "Come aboard, then, and I'll show you *The Fly.*"

Theo needed no more encouragement. On nimble feet he scrambled down the ladder and landed with a thump on the deck in front of Jack. "Yessir, Cap'n."

The boy's evident enthusiasm made Jack smile. "I suppose I did say I'd show you my ship. What would you like to see first?" He well remembered the first time he'd been aboard one of the old King of Prussia's ships, as a boy younger than Theo, and the impression it had made on him. Who was he to deny Theo the same pleasure?

It seemed Theo required to see everything, from one end to the other, and then, if he'd had his way, up as well. "Can I climb the rigging?"

Jack, thinking of Theo's mother, who would have undoubtedly seen climbing the rigging of any ship as too dangerous an undertaking for her precious son, shook his head. "You're not old enough."

Theo put his head on one side. "How old do I have to be?"

How old was he already? Jack didn't want to give him an estimate that was too close. Probably by the look of him about eleven. "Fourteen."

Theo's face fell. "That's two years away."

So, he was a small twelve. "When you're a sailor, you have to learn patience. For instance, the wind doesn't always blow, and when it does it's not always the wind you want."

Theo frowned. "But the wind's hardly blowing, and I'm really good at climbing trees. And cliffs." He paused. "Please don't tell Mama that last bit."

Jack shook his head. "Being good at climbing has nothing to do with it. I don't take boys of... twelve... to sea. That's too young. I didn't go to sea properly until I was fifteen." No need to mention the little single-sailed crabbing boat he'd sailed in by himself, or occasionally with Nat Treloar, from the age of nine.

Theo appeared to be digesting this information. Until the

sight of the hatches caught his eye. "Can I go in the hold, then? Can I see what it's like?" He grinned conspiratorially, as though accepting Jack into his coterie of young boys. "I've always wanted to see inside a hold, don't you know."

The baccy was down in the hold. Could Theo be relied upon not to mention what he saw? Suppose Captain Carlyon called at Keynvor and spoke to Theo? The boy might not mean to betray them, but it might come popping out of his mouth without thinking. Jack shook his head. "You've seen enough now, and the sun's almost vanished. It'll be dark in no time. You go on back up to your house or your mother'll be coming down here looking for you, and I'll be in trouble."

Theo's lower lip jutted in rebellion. "Will *The Fly* still be here in the morning? Can I come back and see her again?" He paused. "Can't I just stay here a *little* bit longer? I love the way you can feel her moving under your feet. It's like magic."

As this was much how Jack felt about being on board a ship, he softened a little. "Well, I was going to sit here on the hatch cover and just look at the stars for a bit, as they come popping out. I suppose you can sit here with me. Stars are important things for sailors. You can navigate by them."

Theo sat down with alacrity, probably in case Jack changed his mind. "You can? Will you teach me how to do it? I'd like to be able to do that."

Jack shook his head. "Not tonight. Maybe another time." He sat down beside Theo and gazed up at the stars where they were just beginning to prick out in the darkening sky. A few at the moment, but it was a cloudless night and very shortly the sky would look like sequined velvet. He heaved a sigh. Watching the stars come out had always been something he loved.

"Mama likes to watch the stars," Theo said. "But in Bath we couldn't see that many. Mama said it was because there was too much light. I wish I had a telescope so I could see them better."

Jack rubbed his chin. "I can fix that."

A minute later he was back with his own short telescope

which he handed to Theo. "Lie on your back and take a look up at the sky."

Seizing the telescope, Theo did as he was told. "Thank you, Cap'n. Oh my goodness. They look so close."

Jack was watching the moon coming up in the east. She'd been on the wane a few days now and her pale hemisphere glowed like a lantern in the dark sky. "Take a look at the moon."

Theo obeyed, gasping in appreciation as he focused in on it. "I can see its face."

"That's not a face. Those're craters."

"Craters?"

"Impact sites where meteors have struck the surface. A man called Johannes Hevelius studied the moon closely and made maps of it. They're in a book he wrote called *Selenographia*. I have a copy in my library at Rosudgeon."

"Might you show it to me?"

Jack chuckled. "I expect so."

He lay on his back beside Theo, gazing up at the stars. What would it be like if he had a boy of his own to show the world to? That thought needed shrugging away. He would have to make do with showing Harriet's boy instead. Which brought his thoughts to Harriet. Why not ask Theo a few gentle questions? He seemed the sort of boy who liked to talk.

"Do you miss your father?"

After a moment's silence, Theo answered, his voice strangely taut. "No."

Not the answer Jack had been expecting. "Oh. Why's that?"

Theo shifted the telescope. "Well..." He paused. "He was hardly ever there."

"I suppose as a soldier he was often away fighting."

Theo nodded without removing the telescope from his eye. "It was nicer when he was away."

Trust a child to be this candid. "Was it?"

Another nod. "Mama was happiest when he wasn't at home."

Things began to slot into place. "And when he was home,

what was she like?"

Was that a shudder? Theo gave a grunt. "She was unhappy. No... she was frightened all the time." He paused. "Is that one a planet? I'd like to see a planet. I know their names."

Never mind planets. Jack wanted to know what had happened to frighten Harriet in that house in Bath when Theo's father had been home. "What was she frightened of?"

"Of Papa." Another pause. "She thinks me and Lyddie didn't know, but we did. He didn't like us getting in his way, so we were mostly upstairs in the nursery when he was home. But we're not deaf." He lowered the telescope and turned to look at Jack. "We heard him shouting at her." Another pause. "Lyddie still liked him because he brought her presents, but I didn't. He was nicer to Lyddie than he was to me. I don't think he liked me at all."

So her husband had been a bully. That he hadn't wanted his children around was nothing new. A lot of men felt like that, and a lot of children were kept confined to their nurseries. And a lot of men bullied their wives. A woman in that situation had no recourse. She was her husband's chattel and had to do as he said. Unlike his own mother, who'd always done as she wished and never even considered confining Jack to his nursery.

"And now he's gone? How is she now?"

Theo sat up, drawing his knees up to his chest and hugging them. "She's much happier, and so am I. Lyddie misses him, I think. He sometimes used to call her 'his little angel,' when he was in a good mood. But that wasn't often. Mostly he was just cross all the time. I don't miss him at all." He set his lips together in a firm line and his brow furrowed. "I'm glad he's gone because now I'm the man of the house and I'm never going to shout at Mama ever. Then she'll be happy all of the time."

Jack sat up too and held out his hand for the telescope. "A good resolution. I'd like to see your mama happy as well. It sounds like she deserves some happiness. Now, we're off at ten, and my men'll be back soon from the kiddley. I'm probably going to have to go and winkle them out, so off you go now, back to your mama before she gets worried about you out here in the dark. We've cargo to deliver. *The Fly's* a working ship and has to earn her living."

"What sort of cargo?"

Now he was getting too nosy. Perhaps befriending him like this wasn't such a good idea, even if it had led to an explanation of some of Harriet's wariness. "None of your business. And it wouldn't interest you anyway. Now, off you go."

With obvious reluctance, Theo climbed the ladder while Jack watched, just to make sure he didn't slip and fall in. When he reached the top, he turned to have one last try. "I could come with you when you go? Be your cabin boy?"

Jack chuckled. Full marks for persistence. "No. I already told you you're too young, and anyway, I already have a cabin boy. Go home and do some growing. I'll take you out when you're fourteen. Life on board any ship isn't easy. Good night."

Theo sighed deeply, and with shoulders hunched, he set off back up the path towards Tummels' house, which would be empty now its occupant had repaired to the kiddley with his sometime shipmates.

Jack watched him out of sight, then sat himself down on the hatch again and took out his hip flask. All around him night was gathering, the lights of Porth en Alls a faint twinkle on the far headland. He could have been anywhere, so deep was the peace. From the little beach just over the rocks the deep swooshing of the waves pulling on the sand echoed over to him. A sound he loved to hear. He'd just have a quick swig of brandy then nip across to the kiddley and reclaim his men. They'd all be replete with Lovey's stew and a few jars of ale and would no doubt have forgotten the time.

Once he had them back, they'd let *The Fly* slip her moorings and glide silently out into the night, her cargo of tobacco, something that carried a high tax in France, ready to trade in Roscoff for the barrels of brandy the local squires hereabouts loved.

Five more minutes and then he'd go.

Overhead, more stars sprang out in the blue-black of the sky, and Jack lay back on the hatch covers again, staring up at them as they blinked between the gently rocking spars and rigging. Best not close his eyes or he'd be asleep in the cradle of the sea and then they'd never get to Roscoff.

···❧···
_______ ✦ _______

Chapter Eighteen

"WHERE'VE YOU BEEN to in the dark?" Harriet asked Theo as he breezed in through the kitchen door. "I said you could go out for ten minutes, not two hours. It's autumn and the nights are drawing in. I was worried."

"Sorry, Mama." Theo gave her his most innocent look, one she recognized of old and which in all probability meant he'd been up to no good. She'd think about that later. At least he was back now and still in one piece.

"Well, go and get yourself ready for bed, then. Lyddie's already gone up, and Bertha and I won't be far behind you. Off you go. And don't forget to wash behind your ears. Bertha left a bowl of water up there for you, but it's probably cold by now."

Bertha, who was sitting at the kitchen table mending a pair of Theo's stockings, looked up with a glint in her eye. "And no clumping about up there like a baby elephant. Your sister's trying to sleep."

Still looking suspiciously angelic, Theo bestowed a kiss on both Harriet and Bertha's cheeks and took himself off into the parlor. A moment later his footsteps clattered on the stairs, causing Bertha to emit a long sigh.

"That boy'll be the death of me," Harriet said. "I don't think I'll let him out after dinner again. He takes too many liberties."

"He's a boy," Bertha opined, as though Harriet might not

155

have noticed. "And boys will be boys."

Harriet frowned. As nurse to Harriet, who'd been an only child, and then to Harriet's children, Bertha only had experience of the one boy, so her sage words held little weight. And Harriet had to admit that she herself possessed little knowledge of boys, bar Theo, who'd been far less trouble when they lived in Bath—before he'd met Cado and Yves, the latter of whom he'd visited several times by himself now. Perhaps she might ask Jack's advice if she saw him again. Not Fitz Carlyon though. A boy needed the guidance of a man from time to time. So long as it wasn't a man like Ben… and she feared Fitz was more like him than he'd have liked to admit.

She got up from her seat at the table. "You know, we can save on lamp oil if we go to bed now, don't you think? And sewing in this light isn't good for your eyes, Bertha dear."

Bertha set down the half-mended stocking. "Aye, you're right about that. My eyes aren't what they were. I'll finish this mending in daylight tomorrow." She heaved herself to her feet. "I'll just damp down the range and put the bolt across the door."

Harriet watched for a moment as Bertha pushed the kettle off the heat and closed the dampers. Left like that, there'd still be glowing embers in the morning that would catch with a bit of dry driftwood put on them. No need to have to relight it. "Good night, Bertha."

"Good night, Miss Harriet."

Holding a candle, Harriet went upstairs, every tread creaking under her weight, but as yet showing no signs of collapsing, not even under Bertha's considerable weight several times a day. She tiptoed along the landing to the door of the bedroom she and Lyddie shared and opened the door just enough to squeeze through. Only a hump under the bedclothes and some heavy breathing hinted at Lyddie's somnolent presence. By the flickering candlelight, Harriet undressed quickly, braided her hair and hopped into bed, aware that the nights now had a definite autumnal chill to them. A sure sign of rapidly approaching winter. She snuggled down, glad to take the weight off her feet and was asleep in minutes.

The creaking of the stairs woke her to a darkness punctuated by shafts of soft moonlight filtering through the bedroom's one window. She lay still for a moment, wondering if this was Bertha coming upstairs to bed. But no, the creaking was definitely moving away—going down the stairs, not up them. She glanced at the vague hump that was Lyddie, still breathing the heavy breath of sleep. Not her. And as there were chamber pots under all the beds, no one had any reason to be up in the night. Was it Bertha or Theo? It had to be one of them. Most likely Theo in search of extra nutrition. That boy had hollow legs.

She lay and listened, waiting for Theo, or Bertha on the off chance it was her, to come creaking back up the stairs. But no one did. Instead, she heard the unmistakable clunk of the bolt being drawn back on the kitchen door, echoing through the silent cottage. Whoever it was, they were going outside. The door clicked shut behind them, right under Harriet's bed.

She sat bolt upright. It had to be Theo. Bertha wouldn't get up in the night and go outside. Whatever was he doing? The disturbing thought of how close they were to the cliffs and how dark it must be outside sent shivers through her body. Might he be sleepwalking? Without another thought, she jumped out of bed and pulled on her woollen dressing gown over her long nightgown, luckily a far more robust garment for late night autumn sorties than her old chiffon peignoir would have been. Slipping her bare feet into her shoes, she picked up her unlit candle and let herself out of the bedroom.

Having no windows, the short landing corridor was far darker than the bedroom had been, so she had to grope her way to the stairs and down them, afraid at any moment of stumbling and falling. The palely illuminated kitchen was empty, of course, the bolt on the backdoor drawn back. Drat that boy. What could he be up to?

Her cloak was hanging on the peg by the backdoor, so Harriet added that to her ensemble and let herself out into the cold night air. A light bobbed a hundred yards away where the path headed west towards that old fisherman's cottage. At least that meant Theo was less likely to take a tumble than she was, although the half moon's kindly light illuminated the path quite well. She hastened in pursuit of Theo.

The flickering light gave away the route he was taking. Opposite the old man's hut, the light bobbed to the left and disappeared from view, making Harriet hurry her steps. But, as she caught up with where it had disappeared, she spotted it below her, heading down a narrow, cliff-edge path towards the waters of the cove. Careful not to tread on a rock and twist her ankle, she started down the path behind her errant son.

Looking up from her careful watching of where to put her feet, she was greeted with the spectacle of Theo's objective. The moonlight glimmered over a narrow, shimmering inlet where a ship lay berthed, the soft light reflecting off anything metal on it and giving it an otherworldly glow. The sound of water constantly running up into the little inlet and lapping around the ship's sides muted the rumble of waves from the nearby cove. It must be the same ship the children had seen on their first day here. Jack's ship. Had Theo been out spying on it earlier that evening? Perhaps he and Cado had been together.

Even as she watched, Theo reached the ship. The light thrown by his lantern illuminated his face as he turned to climb down what looked like a rusty ladder embedded in the sheer rocky side of the inlet. Then he was gone.

Harriet stumbled down the track, careless now of the stones underfoot. A sense of urgency drove her. She had to stop Theo before someone on board that ship, some black-hearted, desperate smuggler, caught him trespassing. She reached the top of the ladder and halted, courage waning like the moon and uncertain what to do next. "Theo!" His name came out as a hiss. Fear pressed in on her that there might well be men stationed on the boat's deck who'd hear her. Were they really smugglers?

Were they the men Fitz had come sniffing about after? Might they be dangerous? More than likely. "Theo!"

Nothing.

She was going to have to climb down that precarious looking ladder towards the uninviting black water and look for him on board. She eyed the gap between the ladder and the ship's sides. The waves kept drawing the ship further away from the ladder, then letting it float in closer, rope fenders preventing it from damage against the rocky wall. She'd have to time her jump onto the deck, which looked a long way away, to perfection, or she might end up in the water, which could be deep. And was inky black. And on top of that, she couldn't swim. In fact, had never been in water even up to her ankles in her entire life. Apart from in a bath, of course.

Steeling herself, she turned around and, hitching her hampering clothing out of the way, went down on her knees. Then, bending her body forward, she groped with her right foot for the first rung of the ladder. She had nothing to hold onto to steady herself, and for a blood-chilling moment couldn't find the ladder's rung. Afraid to put her full weight down, she tipped forward until her hands rested on the flat rock of the jetty and drew a steadying breath. Then her foot found the rung. Thank goodness.

She got her second foot on beside it, still with her hands flat on the rock. She was going to have to keep going. What if she slipped and fell in? Would anyone hear a shout for help, or would they leave her to drown? Under her vise-like grip, bits of rust came away from the ladder onto her hands. Suppose it broke under her weight? Another step down. The ladder was damp, as well, with bits of weed clinging to it. Another step down.

She glanced over her shoulder as the ship swept in closer, her mooring ropes hanging slack. The waves slapped against her wooden sides and the rocky side of the inlet, threatening and loud. Theo had done this with ease. Could she?

Now or never.

Harriet released her hold on the ladder and made a leap for

the ship's deck as it drew near. But, as she jumped, the waves began to suck the ship away from the side again, and the dreadful realization that she should have jumped before it was up close dawned on her. She landed on the ship's wooden rails with her legs kicking in empty air, and the air shot out of her lungs. Gasping for breath and scrabbling in desperation for a hold, she felt herself slipping towards that black water. No. With very little breath in her lungs, the scream was in her head but loud enough like that. No. She refused to fall in and drown like this.

With an enormous effort, she hauled herself over the rails of the ship and went sprawling onto the hard wooden deckboards, fighting to draw air back into her battered body. At least she wasn't in the water.

For a few long moments, she lay where she'd fallen, still gasping and expecting at any moment to be surrounded by angry smugglers. But no one came. Not even Theo. A little insulted that no one, not even a smuggler, had emerged to pick her up and check she was all right, she pushed herself upright. Ouch. She'd banged her elbow and both knees and her ribs felt bruised. She rubbed her sore spots as she regained her feet.

Now what?

"Theo? Where are you?" She kept her voice barely above a whisper. If she'd made it so far without alerting the ship's crew, then she should take advantage of that.

The hemisphere of the moon, which had briefly hidden itself shyly behind a cloud, peeped out, illuminating the ship's deck. Midway down it, situated halfway between each side, lay a wooden hatch, partly pushed to one side. From inside came the unmistakeable glow of a light. Aha.

She crossed to the hatch and peered down into it. "Theo! What on earth do you think you're doing?"

Theo, caught in the act, stared up at her from not far below, his eyes shadowy black holes in the glimmer of his oil lamp. "Mama!"

She kept her voice to an angry whisper. "You have to come

up here right now, before someone catches you. Someone other than me, that is. I don't know what you think you're playing at here. This isn't your ship, and you've no right to be poking around in it."

"It's Cap'n Jack's ship," Theo said, showing no inclination to do as he was told and not keeping his voice down. "There's no one here but you and me, so you don't need to worry. He showed it to me this evening, but he didn't show me the hold, so I came back to take a look for myself. He said it was none of my business, but I wanted to see…" His voice trailed off. "Because, if you want to know the truth, I think he *might* be a smuggler, and I want to be one too, when I'm older." He patted a shadowy shape. "I think these must be his smuggled goods. It smells like the tobacco Papa used to smoke."

The thought sent a shiver down Harriet's back, and not just because of the threat of being caught by desperate smugglers. "Well," she hissed. "*If* they are smugglers, then you'd best get out of there quickly before they come back. Come up this ladder. Now."

Theo's light swayed back and forth. "Must I? It's a big hold and I haven't seen all of it yet. There might be other things… like treasure."

"You're mixing up smugglers with pirates. Smugglers don't carry treasure. Now come up here now before I get really angry."

She would have said more, but just then a flash of light drew Harriet's attention. On the cliff path above their heads, lights were swaying, making dark silhouettes of the overhanging vegetation.

Oh no. Had Theo not been present she might have used one of the words Ben had been wont to utter in anger whenever he perceived things as not going his way, which was often.

Who was that? The crew, most likely and not some innocent passersby in the middle of the night. Wherever the crew had been, they must be back. And they were about to catch her and Theo in what would look very much like spying, something she'd suspected Fitz of wanting to do. She swung round and slithered down the wooden hold ladder, landing with a thud next to Theo in the cramped space. All right for him, as he was so short, but she couldn't stand up straight. "The sailors are coming back, and we mustn't let them catch us. Put out your light. Quickly. Let's hope they'll only stay a short while and go off back to their homes and beds."

Theo extinguished his light, and she took it from him, standing it on the wooden boards. Without it, the entire hold was too dark to see anything. "We need to hide." Instinct had her pushing Theo toward where she thought the back of the hold must lie, her hand feeling along the soft bales of tobacco to her left. She came to a gap between the bales and pushed Theo into it, then crammed herself in after him and sat down. "Now keep quiet and hope they soon go away."

"They wo—" Theo began, but she put her hand over his mouth. He wriggled for a moment then went still. As she clutched him to her, she could feel his heart hammering in time to her own. Oh, please let them be quick on board and then go away again so she could get Theo home. How attractive her own cosy bed seemed right at this moment.

Muffled voices sounded from on deck, the ropes creaked, and the ship rocked gently on the swell. Heavy footsteps moved back and forth as though a lot of people had boarded. Theo lay quiet in her arms, his curly hair tickling her chin. She sat motionless, trying to steady her breathing in case anyone ventured down the ladder into the hold. But no one came.

The ship rocked a bit more, bumping against the rocky jetty. Soft calls sounded up on deck, but she couldn't make out what they were saying. More creaking. The sound of the sea grew louder.

Was that the flap of sails?

Were they at sea?

Harriet clutched Theo closer to her body and shrank between the bales of contraband goods. Whatever was she going to do when they found her?

Chapter Nineteen

J ACK STRODE ALONG the path from the secret mooring to the kiddley, annoyed that his men hadn't abided by his orders. *The Fly* would be perfectly all right left alone in her little harbor, but it still went against the grain to leave her unwatched, and he didn't want to be long away from her. The old King had drummed it into him as a boy that a good sailor always thought of his ship before anything else, even his wife.

Smoke was rising from the kiddley's chimney, pale against the darkening sky, and from inside could be heard the carousing of his crew and whatever locals might be present. Yes, they'd had little time for this lately, but nevertheless, they had a run to make tonight and he didn't want any of them falling overboard drunk halfway across the English Channel.

He pushed open the door and stepped inside. A fug of smoke, a mixture from the fire, men's pipes, ale and sweaty people, greeted him. Oil lamps hung here and there, but the taproom was still for the most part gloomy, and his men kept their heads down, indistinguishable from their friends and neighbors and probably hoping he'd ignore them.

Lovey, situated behind the bar polishing tankards with a grubby rag, met his gaze and gave him an eloquent shrug. She jerked her head towards a table in the corner where Will could be seen, in the act of draining a flagon of ale, a telltale empty brandy glass on the table in front of him. He set his flagon down and met Jack's accusing stare, an expression of guilt suffusing his face to be quickly followed by a wry grin.

Jack stepped up to the bar and, seizing the wooden mallet Lovey and Daniel used to call time, not that they often did, banged it hard on the bar top. Heads swivelled in his direction and a low, rumbling silence fell. A lot of guilty faces stared at him. Not just his own men's but those of their neighbors, too.

"Crew of *The Fly*, out," was all Jack said, standing with his hands on his hips and glaring at them all. "The tide's on the turn."

To do them credit, apart from the odd mutter, there were no complaints, and they all downed the dregs in their flagons or brandy glasses and got to their feet, abandoning their friends, one or two of them a sight unsteadily. Will, sheepish as the others, emerged from behind the table he'd been sharing with young Harry, grabbing his son by the arm and pulling him with him. "Sorry, my luvver," he said, addressing Jack. "Clean forgot the time, we did. Lovey serves such good eats and such fine ale."

Lovey, still polishing tankards, gave a snort. "Telled him to get the men back down to the mooring twice, I did, but he don't think he should listen to what a woman do say."

By the fire, occupying the warmest seat in the taproom, old Bessie hawked and spat into the fire. "A man needs to know when a woman's right." And she fixed Daniel, her nephew, with a jaundiced eye. "Time you boys learned that."

Will tipped his hat at first Bessie and secondly Lovey. "Sorry, my luvvers. But you do serve the best ale and the best stew around."

"Don't let your Eliza hear you say that, Will my lad," called a voice from one of the darker corners. "She'll string you up from the yardarm, that she will."

General laughter all round.

Looking more than a little sheepish, Will pulled his hat down more firmly over his ears and headed for the door.

Jack followed him out into the fresh night air to find his men lighting their lanterns and muttering together about how chilly it had got. Like a load of old women. They needed to be thankful they weren't laboring down one of the local tin mines. Then they'd have something to complain about. Smuggling had its faults and dangers, but at least they all enjoyed the work.

He shepherded them in the direction of the path to the mooring, irritated by their whispers, burps and heavy footsteps, Will's included. "Pipe down, can't you. Or you'll have the widow in Keynvor Cottage awake and staring out of her window. You're already enough of a spectacle with all these lights."

"Want us to fall down and break our legs?" Phoby Geen grumbled. "We wouldn't be much use to you if'n we did."

Jack chose to ignore this, and, thankfully, the rest of the men fell silent. Only the scuffing of their boots, loud enough in itself, broke the silence of the night. It was to be hoped the never-ending sound of the waves on the hidden shore, and the wind blowing from the west, would be enough to muffle these noises.

They negotiated the steep path down to the harbor without anyone falling and breaking a leg, to find the tide had dropped enough that a good six feet of the ladder was now exposed. One by one, Jack's men descended the ladder to the deck and set about preparing the ship to sail.

"I think I'll go below for a bit," Will said with a sheepish grin. "You can call me if you need me, but I'm doubting you will." He disappeared down the narrow companion way at the back of the boat that led to the ship's one cabin and pulled the hatch over it.

The men had already undone *The Fly's* mooring ropes, but left the gig moored where she was, and were now poling her out into more open water. They'd put the sails up once they were clear of the narrow harbor. Jack went to the tiller and took over from Young Harry who went to grab a sweep and help row her out a bit further.

The wind freshened as they emerged from the shelter the headland had afforded them, and at his quiet order, the men soon had the sails unfurled and the spars raised. The wind billowed them out and *The Fly* came alive, careening across the waves like an excitable filly. Yes. This was just how Jack liked it. Life was for living, and living meant sailing. He didn't care where to or what for, he just wanted a rolling deck under his feet and the wind in his sails and his hair.

DOWN IN THE hold, Harriet had uncovered Theo's mouth but now rested a finger against his lips. He moved his face up close to hers, his excited whisper barely audible. "Are we going to sea, Mama?"

As the only answer to this was yes, she had to nod. "I fear we are."

Theo wriggled. "Can I go up on deck then and help the men?" His voice rose a little in anticipation, so she jammed her finger harder against his lips.

This time it was she who put her mouth against his ear. "No, you cannot. I don't think you realise the seriousness of this situation, Theo. This is a smuggler's ship, I'm certain. Otherwise it wouldn't be lurking in a secret harbor with a hold full of dubious goods and leaving in the middle of the night. It's got to be the same ship you and Lydia saw on the day we arrived, and it can't be a coincidence it's back here again. Not twice in such a short time. And you're right about this smelling like your father's tobacco. It is tobacco, and I daresay it's being smuggled into France."

"Are we going to France?" His voice rose again and this time she put her hand over his mouth.

"Keep your voice down or don't speak at all. Yes. I think we're bound for France."

Theo digested this for a minute, and she relaxed her hold on his mouth. "Mama?" This time he did keep to a nearly silent whisper. "Are… are the smugglers *dangerous*?"

She nodded. "I think they probably are."

"Is Cap'n Jack a smuggler too?"

She bit her lip. Was he? Or were they just using his ship for their clandestine activities without his knowledge? She'd not heard his voice on deck, so how was she supposed to know? She managed a shrug, difficult in the space between the bales. "I have no idea. But if this is his ship, he most likely has some idea what's going on."

Another short silence from Theo. "He didn't say anything about it when I saw him this evening."

She froze. "When you saw him this evening? What did he say? You'd better tell me everything."

Theo shifted as though uncomfortable. "I watched it come in, and the men go off to the kiddley, but Cap'n Jack was still on board, so I walked down and said hello. He let me come on board and showed me round and wouldn't let me climb the rigging. So I asked to see in the hold, but he said the cargo was none of my business and wouldn't let me see in the hold. That's why I came back."

Her turn to digest the information. So Jack knew what was in the hold and hadn't wanted Theo to see it. Fitz Carlyon was inordinately interested in Jack. Jack frequented the kiddley and lived only a mile up the track from the cove. He kept himself to himself. It all added up. Jack had to be a smuggler too. There was no other explanation. And they were stuck hiding on his ship, amongst a cargo that would have to be unloaded at some point, during which event they would be discovered. At least, however, it was likely to be some port, so they might not risk being thrown overboard by angry smugglers.

But then what?

Harriet held Theo closer. "Wherever we're going, it's going to take a long time. We might as well get some sleep. Close your eyes."

Theo yawned, and with the resilience of youth snuggled closer to her. Probably he couldn't imagine a future where Jack didn't remain his hero and where their discovery heralded anything but pleasure on everyone's parts. Harriet, however, could imagine all sorts of terrifying outcomes to being discovered, in none of which did either of them remain alive. But the rocking motion of the ship, and the comparative comfort of being squashed between soft bales of tobacco, had the effect, at last, of lulling her to sleep.

JACK WENT BELOW when his pocket watch told him it was three in the morning and woke Will up to take over command. A little groggily, Will climbed the companion way and disappeared into the starlit darkness. Jack eased his stiff shoulders. With very little room on board, and most of below decks given up to their cargo, the cabin area was not just tiny but low roofed as well. Bent almost double due to his height, he slipped his boots off and climbed into one of the hammocks, where he settled down for a short sleep. Beside him, Daniel Bussow, the bo'sun, snored contently, but Jack was used to communal sleeping arrangements and ignored him. In a few minutes he was asleep.

He woke exactly four hours later, as he'd planned, to the sounds of agitated voices on deck. The ship was rocking with renewed vigor in what must be mounting waves, but the hammock had shielded him from the worst of that movement. With a skill born of years of hammock sleeping, he extricated himself from its embrace and found his boots where the ship's movement had sent them skidding into a corner. Having put them on, he rubbed the sleep from his eyes and seized the first rung of the companion way ladder.

Above him, the hatch, that had been nearly fully closed, slid open and early morning light spilled in, hazy and gray with cloud.

Will's anxious face peered down at him. "We've got a problem."

Jack swarmed up the ladder and climbed out onto the deck. "What kind of trouble?"

Will nodded towards the now half open hatch to the hold. "We've got stowaways on board."

"What?" In the plural as well. Who on earth would even have found *The Fly*, never mind stowed away on her? And who in their right mind would want to stowaway to France, even though Boney had been defeated and the new king put in place? It defied all logic.

Will nodded. "Harry heard'em retching."

"Seasick stowaways?"

Will nodded again. "That's right. And feeling a darn sight worse than I did when you got me up in the middle of the night to take the second watch, by the sound of them."

Harry, a good-looking lad, stepped forward. "Stinks a bit down there too."

"Who are they?" Jack asked. "And how many are there?"

Harry shrugged. "I'm not going down there in that stink to count'em. No thankee, Cap'n."

This was a problem Jack had never faced before. Here they were, a good halfway across the English Channel on their journey to Roscoff, their hold full of the tobacco the French wanted and a cargo of brandy awaiting them, and only now they found they had extras on board.

"Better get them up," Jack said. "See what they're like. And being up on deck might make them less sick."

Will nodded. "Make'em clear up the mess they've made more like. If any o' that's got on the baccy and ruined it, I'll be more'n angry." He grunted at his son. "Might decide to throw'em overboard. No one'd ever know we'd done it."

Jack shook his head, not quite sure Will hadn't been joking. "No one's being thrown overboard on my ship. I have final say here. If you ever get stowaways on *The Black Joke*, you can have them thrown overboard, but not here on my ship."

Will chuckled. "It's too kind a heart you have, Jack me boy."

"Who's going down to get'em?" Harry asked, leaning forward and sniffing at the hold. On the whole, the smell of fish might have been an improvement.

"No one," Jack snapped. "They can come up on their own."

He too leaned forward, but not to sniff. Instead, he shouted down into the hold. "We know you're in there. Come on out right now and show yourselves. Get up here on deck and let us see you."

Chapter Twenty

HARRIET HAD WOKEN to a feeling of rising nausea some time in the middle of the night, as the ship began to pitch and roll. At first, Theo slept on in her arms as she lay between the bales of tobacco fighting the rising inclination to cast up her accounts. Before long, the movement of the ship grew more violent, and, but for the fact she was wedged, she might have been thrown about. This woke Theo up, and the first thing he did was groan and throw up all over her.

That was enough for Harriet. She struggled out of their dark little nest, the horrible smell of vomit in her nose and throat, tried to stand up in the pitching hold, failed and fell over, and was herself horribly sick all over the floor. The hope that having thus cleared out her stomach prevailed, and she crawled back towards where Theo was lying moaning. Luckily his stomach contents had gone mostly over her cloak, so she divested herself of the offending garment, and climbed back in with Theo.

Peace was not to be hers. The ship appeared to be in the grip of a violent storm, sometimes almost upending itself as though plunging headfirst into the troughs of the waves and about to sink, sometimes tipping towards its stern. And her hope that having cast up their accounts once they would feel better for it was unfounded. As the night progressed and the tossing of the ship only grew worse, Harriet felt worse in parallel, and so, it seemed, did Theo.

When the hatch jerked open letting the morning light spill in, Harriet had reached the point where she no longer cared if a hundred ferocious smugglers discovered her whereabouts. She just wanted to get out of the noisome hole she was stuck in and preferably right off this ship.

"I don't think I like boats anymore," Theo murmured, blinking at the brightness.

A demanding voice shouted down to them. "We know you're in there. Come on out right now and show yourselves. Get up here on deck and let us see you."

Harriet froze. Surely that was Jack's voice? All hopes that he was playing an unwitting part in the smuggling vanished. What was she to do?

Beside her, Theo retched again, but without result, as for some time now he'd had nothing to bring up. He gave a little whimper of discomfort.

The voice, Jack's voice, called out again. "You'll feel better in the fresh air up on deck. Come on up. We've no intention of hurting you."

That was reassuring, at least.

Harriet extricated herself from between the tobacco bales and hauled Theo to his feet. He came reluctantly, one hand hanging on to the tobacco bales for support as though his legs wouldn't hold him up properly. At least the pitching of the ship wasn't quite so forceful right now. She stepped into the square of light thrown by the open hatch and stared up at the face of the man looking down at her.

His mouth fell open. "Harriet?"

She nodded, her stomach roiling with the continual rocking motion, and sent up a silent prayer that she wasn't about to disgrace herself by retching bile in front of someone she knew. She'd retained that tiny scrap of dignity and didn't want to lose it.

He recovered himself quickly and held out a hand to her. "And Theo, I see. You'd better come on up."

On legs as wobbly and weak as Theo's seemed to be, Harriet climbed the ladder, ushering Theo ahead of her, ready to catch him if he fell. But he didn't. As he emerged, strong hands took hold of him and sat him down on the other half of the hatch cover. She took Jack's offered hand, and he pulled her up the final few steps, out into the blessed fresh air. Overhead, the wind snapped the sail canvas and, to right and left, she could see the white tops of what looked like enormous waves still. Immediately, though, her stomach began to feel better.

She became aware Jack was staring, and a glance down revealed why. She'd quite forgotten she was only wearing her long nightgown and woollen dressing gown, but at least both were voluminous and thick, even if they were festooned with the remnants of vomit.

"What on earth are you doing on my ship?" Jack asked, avoiding the obvious question of what she was doing on it dressed for bed not a voyage.

Harriet looked around at the sea of swarthy faces staring at her, all of whom must have had the same question in mind. Apart from Jack, six other men regarded her in open curiosity, none of whom she'd ever seen before. Four, of varying ages, looked like common sailors in rough, homespun clothing, but two were cut from a different cloth. The older of the two, an imposing middle-aged man whose sizeable gut did nothing to detract from his fierce good looks, had his graying hair confined in an old-fashioned queue. The other, due to his close facial resemblance, had to be his son, a handsome lad not a lot older than Lyddie, who'd fixed an appreciative gaze on Harriet's lack of suitable clothing.

Harriet swallowed, not at all sure her dry, vomit-ravaged throat could manage speech.

"Water for the lady," Jack said, and a moment later a bone cup was being pressed into her hands. She drank deep, relishing the liquid as it drained into her empty stomach.

"Some for Theo," she croaked, a little ashamed that she

hadn't thought of him first, and the beaker was filled up and handed to him, where he was sitting half-supported between the two oldest sailors. He sipped it warily, probably afraid that if he drank it dry he'd end up seeing it again all too soon.

Jack cleared his throat. "I'll ask you again. What are you doing on my ship?"

Theo, bless him, piped up, his voice barely a croak, like hers. "It's my fault, Cap'n, sir. I wanted to see in the hold. So I came back here while you were fetching your men from the kiddley and I knew you wouldn't be on board, and Mama must have followed me." He glanced at Harriet. "But you and your crew came back, and we were frightened they'd be angry if they caught us, so we hid. Mama didn't think you were going out in the ship, and she wouldn't let me speak in case your men heard me." He pulled a face. "I don't think I like going to sea. I've changed my mind about being a sailor."

From a second hatch forward of the mast, a sandy-haired boy maybe a year or two older than Theo emerged, barefooted and untidily dressed. He came to stand behind Jack, balancing as easily as they all were and eyeing Theo with open curiosity.

Jack looked at Harriet and raised his eyebrows.

She nodded. "That's about it. Now can I please sit down."

Jack nodded to the boy. "Clemo, close the other half of the hatch. It'll be your job to go down there and clean up the mess."

The boy pulled a disgusted face but slammed the hatch shut.

"Take a seat," Jack said, indicating it. "While I think what to do with you."

Harriet sat down close to Theo.

Jack jerked his head at the large middle-aged man. "I'd best introduce you. This is my partner, Captain Will Richards. His son, Harry. My bo'sun, Daniel Bussow. My crew—Uncle Billy, Silas, Phoby, and our cabin boy, Clemo." He nodded at Captain Richards. "And this is Mrs. Harriet Penhallow, of Keynvor Cottage, and her son Theo." He waved a hand at his men. "Now, back to work. Cap'n Will and I will sort this out."

"You too, Harry," Will said with a grin. "You can stop ogling the lady just because she's in her nightgown."

Harry grinned at his father and turned away, but not without an appreciative wink for Harriet. Good heavens. Did he think her some kind of light-skirt?

The two sailors who'd been supporting Theo got up, and Harriet slid closer to him, thankful to be off her feet, and bristling with annoyance at the wink. Her stomach roiled anew and for a moment she feared the hastily drunk water was about to reappear, but it didn't. She reached out a hand and took Theo's and he hung on tight, very much her little boy and not the brave adventurer he'd fancied himself. As spray kept coming over the edge of the boat to strike the deck, Harriet gripped the edge of the hatch with her free hand, not at all confident she and Theo wouldn't be tossed over the side by the ship's movement at any moment.

Jack and Will exchanged glances, and Will gave a shrug. "It's your ship," he said. "You decide, but we don't want them interfering with the business we have to do, now do we? And I doubt we've time to take them back."

Jack shook his head. "You're right. Look at them. What they need is clean clothes and a wash more than anything. The sea's calming down a bit now, but they'll be best out here on deck in the fresh air."

Calming down? Was it? Harriet hung onto the hatch tighter than ever.

Will nodded. "We don't want them stinking up the cabin, that's for sure, or we'll have complaints."

The embarrassment of the situation washed over Harriet anew as she began to feel a little better. The fact that she and Theo were smelly, and everyone had noticed, bore down on her.

"Clemo," Jack said to the boy. "D'you have clean trousers and shirt?"

Clemo managed a heavy scowl. "I does, but they're me Sunday best."

Jack frowned back at him. "Go and get them." He nodded to Theo. "You can go behind the mast and take off your soiled clothing and put on Clemo's Sunday best. Chop chop."

It didn't take Clemo more than a minute to return with items of clothing that looked nothing like the sort of Sunday best Harriet was used to, but Theo, after a reassuring nod from her, went behind the mast and struggled out of his dirty clothes and into the new ones, remaining barefoot like Clemo. The expression on his face told Harriet how much he approved of his new clothing and the effect it was having on his morale.

"Go and give these a soak then hang them out to dry," Jack said, again addressing Clemo, who again looked as though this order was an insult. But obedience must have been ingrained, and he took the clothes and departed to where a bucket on a rope sat by the side of the ship. A quick dip into the water produced an almost full bucket into which he immersed Theo's soiled breeches, shirt and jacket, holding them delicately between finger and thumb, like an old duchess with her teacup, and poking them in with a long stick until they were submerged.

Jack, no doubt satisfied with this attempt at laundry, turned his attention back to Harriet. "You'll need clothes too, but you won't be able to change behind the mast like a boy. Can you go below decks into the cabin, do you think? Without further upset?"

Could she? Immediately the ship seemed to pitch more violently as though the weather knew she was about to go below decks again. Or that might have been her imagination. "Perhaps if you have a bowl or bucket I might take with me?"

He did. She followed him down the ladder into the cabin and found herself in a small, low-roofed space equipped with half a dozen hammocks, rocking gently with the motion of the ship. Better not look at them or she might feel sick again.

Jack pulled a shirt and a pair of breeches out of a small chest and held them out to her, although whose these were this time she had no idea. "These're all I have, I'm afraid. We can get your own clothes…" and here he looked up and down her night attire again, "washed and dried, but I don't think they're suitable for wearing on board a ship."

"Thank you… Jack." She took the bundle of clothes. As she did so, her fingertips brushed his hand and a current of unexpected electricity shivered up her arm. Jack's eyes widened for a moment, and he snatched his hand back at the same moment she did the same with hers. Had he felt it as well? And what had it meant? Her whole body felt as though it had come alive in that instant, suddenly aware of the proximity of this man and the intense masculinity he was radiating in such a small space. It should be frightening her, but it wasn't. Instead she felt as though she were holding her breath, waiting for something good to happen. What an idiot she was. She stepped back until her shoulders came up against the side of the cabin, holding the clothes to her chest like a shield.

"Well," he said, suddenly looking as awkward as she felt and rather pink about the gills. "I'll leave you to change. Come up as soon as you're dressed. Being in the fresh air is the best way to get your sealegs." And he departed, closing the hatch behind himself as he went. This plunged the tiny cabin into near darkness, but Harriet had little trouble getting into the unaccustomed breeches and shirt. A buckle affair on the back of the breeches tightened them sufficiently not to fall down, and a pair of braces finished the task. She tucked the tails of the shirt into the breeches and shrugged into the waistcoat. Deciding bare feet might make gripping the spray-doused deck easier than her own impractical shoes, she started back up the companionway. The moment she touched the hatch, it opened for her.

Jack. He must have been waiting for her to finish her toilette.

"I didn't need the bowl," she said, with some pride, handing it back. "I think your ship isn't tossing about quite so badly."

He nodded. "We get a lot of ocean swell here in the west, because we're almost in the Atlantic. And the wind's behind us, driving us on, building the waves. You should be all right now, as long as you take it easy. Come and sit by your boy and keep an eye on him for me. He's in danger of falling asleep sitting up."

Harriet moved to the middle of the deck and sat down on the hatch again, next to Theo, whose skin had lost some of its alarming pallor. He was chewing on a hunk of brown bread as though he'd eaten nothing for days.

Jack nodded at him. "Best thing to do if you feel sick on a ship. Eat. Then you at least have something to bring up."

Harriet shook her head. "Please don't talk about that. I'd rather not think about it."

Jack grinned and, pulling a coil of rope over, sat down opposite them. "Took me a while to get my sealegs, Theo. No one gets them straightaway. Takes time."

"I feel better now," Theo said. "Where are we going? I don't see any land."

"France," Jack said.

Just as she'd been fearing.

Theo swallowed another mouthful of bread. "Are we smuggling? That's what's in the hold, isn't it? You didn't want me to see in case I gave you away, but I wouldn't do that. Not ever. I want to be a smuggler one day, too. Just like you."

Harriet suppressed a smile at his use of the word "we." Did he fancy himself a party to this now they'd been discovered? What boy didn't dream of adventure on the high seas. What mother didn't fear it becoming a reality.

"No, Theo," Harriet said. "*We* are not doing anything of the sort, and you are never going to become a smuggler. Captain Jack, on the other hand, seems to be doing just that."

Theo frowned. "But I'm on board now, and I want to help." He glanced at where Clemo was doing something to the end of a rope. "And *he's* not fourteen, is he? You said I had to be fourteen to sail with you, and that boy isn't that old. He's not much bigger than me."

Jack opened his mouth to reply.

"Where in France are we going?" Harriet asked, swiftly changing the subject. "I mean, where are *you* going?"

Jack leaned his elbows on his knees. "Roscoff."

As Harriet had no idea where this was, she was none the wiser, but she wasn't about to let Jack know that. "And what are you going to do there?"

He tilted his head to one side. "What do you think? But I'm not sure it's something I should divulge to you. After all, you were seen in company with Captain Carlyon not so long ago. Did he ask you to find out about me?"

Harriet's body stiffened at his own change of subject. "Do you have people out *spying* on me?"

Theo's eyes widened.

Jack chuckled and shook his head. "Not especially. But everyone in Cornwall knows what everyone else is up to. I'd've thought you'd have known that, being from Truro yourself. Or maybe up there they're not so nosy. But they are down here. You'd be wise to bear that in mind."

Harriet bristled. Whatever he said, only a spy could have reported this. "While it is true that Captain Carlyon came to call on me last week, I can assure you it was not a welcome call." Above her head, the sails snapped in the wind. "I could not in all politeness turn a visitor away without seeming rude and churlish."

"Lyddie and me were doing our lessons," Theo said. "We were listening. I don't think he asked about you."

Harriet held up a hand to hush him. "I was most surprised that he chose to call. He suggested taking a walk along the cliffs to the east, which would have passed the alehouse—the kiddley— and that big square house on the point. But I suggested we should head west as I hadn't seen that part of the coast yet."

"Cudden Point," Jack said. "Yes. You were seen."

Harriet bristled again. "You say you weren't spying on me and yet it seems you were. You have your informants in every corner of the countryside. If you knew that was the way we'd walked, why not just come out and say it?" She glared at him. "Did you think I might try to lie to you? Was this a test of some kind?"

He had the grace to blush. "Nothing of the sort. But in my line of business it's well to cover every eventuality. And to keep an eye on those we don't trust."

Did he not trust her? "Well, as it happens, he did ask me questions about you. But I told him I scarcely knew you, and you'd just been kind enough to allow me to ride out on your mother's horse to visit Mrs. Bolitho. Because I'm a friend of your mother." She paused. "She's not a smuggler, too, is she?"

This served to make him laugh, and Theo joined in. "No, my mother most definitely is not a smuggler," Jack managed. "She would be horrified if she thought you believed that."

"I don't. I just wanted to check. I didn't think you could be a smuggler until last night."

"What did you think was going on, then?"

"That others were using your ship for their own ends, unbeknownst to you."

He laughed again. "I'd like to see them try."

"You haven't answered my question yet. What do you plan to do in this Roscoff place?"

He got to his feet. "Well, now you're a smuggler yourself, you might as well know. We're more than halfway there and should be moored up in harbor by early evening. We'll dispose of the goods we have stored in the hold and take on the cargo for the return journey. Then we stay the night and return tomorrow morning, so we'll be back in the dark with the rising tide to unload."

Harriet's mouth fell open. "Theo and I are most definitely not smugglers any more than your mother is, so please don't include us in your deeds."

Jack grinned, suddenly as wolfish as Fitz. "You'd rather we just put you ashore in Roscoff and left you there? I think you'll find that all the English craft that put in there are about the same business as we are, so you'd be hard put to find a berth on a return journey that doesn't see you as implicated as returning with us will."

"So, we're truly smugglers now?" Theo's satisfaction at this prospect shone out of him, banishing the last dregs of seasickness. "Oh boy!"

At the side of the boat, Clemo lugged up a fresh bucket of water. "If'n you wants me to clean up the hold then you'd all better shift," he said, banging the bucket down in front of them, a surly expression on his young face.

Harriet and Theo rose to their feet and Harriet grabbed Theo's hand before he could get away. "We are *not* smugglers. And you, Theo Penhallow, are staying right beside me. The sides of this boat don't look anywhere near high enough for safety." He wriggled but she had him tight.

Clemo threw them both a pitying look. "Sit on the spare sails up in the bows, why don't you? I likes to sit there when I's not workin'. Makes a good place for forty winks."

"Thank you." Theo's hand still firmly clutched in hers, Harriet turned away from Jack and walked carefully up the rolling deck. Sure enough, there were the sails, although they didn't look as comfortable as Clemo had implied. She settled herself on them with Theo beside her. At least here, they were mostly out of the wind, and if she tried hard she could pretend she wasn't on a boat at all. Maybe...

Chapter Twenty-One

HAVING WATCHED THEIR two passengers teeter up to the bows and take up residence on the spare sails, Jack retired to the stern, where Will had taken charge of the tiller and sent the early morning watch down to kip in their hammocks.

"That's her, then, is it?" Will said, without taking his eyes off the horizon. Western Brittany would be coming into view before too long.

"What d'you mean by that?" Jack leaned on the gunnels and squinted up towards the top of the mainmast at the way the topsail was straining in the following wind. That was what he liked to see—a strong wind and a foaming wake trailing behind the ship.

"You know what I mean," Will said, nudging him in the ribs. "She's the girl you've got your eye on."

"I have not." But the moment the words were out of his mouth, Jack knew them to be a lie. He did indeed have his eye on Harriet Penhallow, deny it as he would.

Will, rather annoyingly, just chuckled. The wind blew a few wisps of his grizzled hair out of his pony tail and across his eyes, and he had to put up a hand to brush them away. "Pretty little thing when she's not covered in vomit." His gaze rose to a gull that had been following the ship, its back curved like a sickle against the wind. "And she do scrub up well in boys' clothes, enough to tempt a man. Don't you go tellin' my Eliza I said that, mind. She don't like it if I so much as look at any other woman, even if that woman might chance to be dressed like a lad."

Jack's turn to laugh. "Only if you shut up about me having my eye on Mrs. Penhallow."

Will shot him a sideways glance. "She was Harriet just now."

Jack folded his arms across his chest. Frequently, his friend didn't know when to drop a subject, and now felt like one of those times. Mrs. Penhallow… Harriet… Somehow, calling her by her married name and title helped to distance himself from her, whereas calling her by her Christian name had done quite the opposite. He hardly knew her. He'd met her only a few times, been intrigued by the mystery about her, ridden out with her once, and now found her hiding on his ship. None of this served to make her someone for whom he should be nurturing feelings of this kind.

That brought him up short. Feelings of what kind? What did he mean by that? He looked away from Will, who had a smug smile on his face, and stared out across the rolling, white-capped waves, trying very hard not to think about Harriet.

And failed.

At least he now knew why she was so reticent, thanks to Theo's indiscretions last night. Not that she was being nearly so reticent right now. The look of wary fear in her eyes had vanished, probably chased away by her severe seasickness and her instinct to protect her child. Something he had to admire in her. She'd found herself on board a ship with eight strange men, well, one she knew a little and seven strangers, and she'd stood up for herself and her son, despite her sickness.

He peered down the deck, but the sails were in the way, and he couldn't see her properly. Hopefully, she and the boy would have a sleep there until they arrived in Roscoff. It was the safest spot on board for them and would keep them out of the men's way. They must be exhausted after that bit of rough sea and being down in the hold, to boot. The first time he'd been to sea as a green fifteen-year-old he'd been sick as a dog. It had been nothing like the voyages he'd made along the coast in his little crabbing boat, checking his crab pots, and, like Theo, he'd at first decided it would be his one and only trip out of coastal waters.

He needed to stop thinking about Harriet Penhallow before he drove himself mad.

AFTER A BIT, Will went below to take a nap, and Jack took over at the tiller. The sea was still lumpy, and a strong wind drove *The Fly* onwards at a good speed. With any luck they'd be in Roscoff by early evening, and it should be high tide. They'd need that to get moored by the jetty. He didn't want *The Fly* ending up beached on the sand for hours on end. Far too vulnerable a position.

Occasionally, the sails shifted enough to give him a view up the boat of Harriet and Theo fast asleep on the sails in the bows, Theo nestled in the crook of his mother's arm. Enough to reassure him that they remained safe, at any rate, and unlikely to be any more of a nuisance right now.

At midday, Uncle Billy, the oldest crew member, his sparse white hair hidden beneath a knitted cap his equally ancient wife had made him, brought out some bread and cheese, and the men who'd been below came up, stretching and yawning, to take over duties on deck. With eight men on board, no one needed to work too hard unless the weather was bad. Worse than it had been overnight which had only been a high wind.

Carrying a tin plate of food and a flask of water, Jack wove his way forward to the bows. Theo had wriggled away from his mother and was now curled into a ball with his knees drawn up almost to his chest, but Harriet lay on her back on the folded sails as though in the most comfortable of feather beds. Her dark hair, that had been confined in a single braid earlier, had come undone, and now fanned out around her in a silky cloud that had Jack's pulse racing so much he had to tighten his hold on the tin plate and steady himself on the foremast.

The pastiness she'd had when she climbed out of the hold had vanished, and her cheeks had flushed a delicate pink, with her thick dark lashes fanned out across them. A veritable picture of delicate womanhood, and yet incongruously cast in the attire of a scruffy boy. Never had he seen boys' clothing so attractively worn, with the shirt open enough at the neck for him to see the all-too tempting rise of her breasts. Almost a shame to waken her, but she needed feeding, and so did her son.

Wary of touching her hand, for some reason, instead he poked Harriet's bare foot with the toe of his own boot.

She stirred and stretched, like a cat, and Jack's trousers took on a tightness he was becoming familiar with the more he saw of her. In a hurry to disguise his embarrassment, he sat down on the sails a couple of feet away from her, still holding the plate of food.

Her lashes fluttered on her cheeks, making him glad he'd sat down, and her eyes opened. For a moment, confusion reigned as she gazed up at the billowing sails above her head, then realisation dawned. Her eyes focused and she looked up at him. "Oh." She pushed herself upright. "I was hoping this was all a dream."

A little of the old wariness had returned to her face. Not so much as when he'd first met her, but nevertheless still lurking. Perhaps she'd decided that if he had been going to do anything nasty to her he'd have taken advantage of her position and done it by now. Likewise his men. Jack smiled at her. "I've brought you both some food."

"Thank you." She shifted a little as if to get more comfortable. "I think I'll let Theo sleep a little longer though. He's not used to midnight sorties."

He grinned. "I would have thought you weren't, either."

A little smile played across her face as he passed her the plate. "You are quite right. Not much call for smuggling in Bath, nor sailing ships."

"Highwaymen perhaps?"

"None that I ever met."

"Footpads?"

"None of them, either, thank goodness."

"But now you've met a smuggler, do you think more or less highly of the profession?"

She tore a small piece off the bread. "Butter would go well with this and make it less dry. And I have yet to form an opinion about smugglers."

He leaned back, resting his back. Standing for long periods at the tiller always made it ache, a constant reminder of a fall he'd had from a horse as a boy. A horse he'd not been supposed to be riding. The doctor had confined him to bed for several weeks of rest, which had done nothing for the pain and not improved his temper. When he'd finally been allowed up, he'd resumed riding the horse and mastered it, but the back pain remained. "Well, you've jumped in at the deep end where smugglers are concerned. You find yourself in a good position to form an opinion of what we do… and of us." What he really meant was for her to form an opinion of him and divulge it, but he refrained from saying so. He didn't want to admit how much it mattered to him that she thought well of him.

She shrugged her shoulders and set about eating a little of the cheese, breaking off dainty portions and nibbling them like the well-bred lady she was. Perhaps he should have provided her with a knife. Niceties like that didn't exist on board ship. In fact, plates rarely came out of storage, so she was honored he'd found one for her.

Gulls circled the top of the mast, silhouetted against the piercing blue of a sky marred only by a few fluffy clouds, their cries harsh. They must be nearing Roscoff with its far more favorable climate than Cornwall. Every time he was over, be it summer or winter, the weather seemed inclined to sunshine, as though the weather god had chosen that particular corner of the world for special treatment. The wind was dropping as well, and the sails were less full. The ship would be slowing down as she approached the coast of Northern Brittany.

Harriet set down the plate and uncorked the flask of water. "Well, as to what I think of smugglers, we shall have to see." She took a long swig. "I've seen your cargo of tobacco. What is it that you'll be returning to Cornwall with? Brandy, I presume? Even in Truro we often had brandy in the house that had paid no taxes. My father said it tasted better than the stuff that had paid duty."

"Of course. Brandy. And silks for the ladies, spices in all likelihood, coffee perhaps, and lace. All things on which the tax in Britain is set exorbitantly high. We're doing the people who buy from us a favor, and they know it. Most of the brandy drunk in the houses of Cornish gentry, just like your father's, has paid no import duty." He laughed. "Once upon a time, we used to bring over tea, but the tax on that's so low now it's no longer worth including. But it depends very much what's on offer when we get there. We never know for sure what we'll be bringing back."

She sat quietly digesting his words and her meal before taking another pull on the flask of water. "So you see yourselves as philanthropists?"

Well, maybe they were. He shrugged. "I don't do it for the money. I do it for the excitement. The thrill."

A frown marred her alabaster brow. "Aha, so that absolves you of all guilt?"

"No, of course not." How irritating she was being. "But what guilt should I bear? The guilt of putting food in the mouths of my crew's families? The guilt of providing the people of Cornwall with cut-price goods? Who am I depriving?"

"The government."

He'd not taken her for a goody-two-shoes. "And what do you care for the government? What do you even know of it? How has it ever helped you?"

Her frown deepened. "I don't think we're supposed to ask what the government can do for us. Surely it's what we can do to help them, and paying our taxes is one of them, so they can do things like defeat Napoleon, by paying the wages of their soldiers."

"Like your husband?"

Her face clouded and that hunted look returned. Damn it. He hadn't meant to upset her. Beside her, Theo shifted in his sleep and she glanced down at him, stretching out her hand before drawing it back. "Like my husband." But her tone had flattened, and her eyes were guarded.

Jack sat up again, stretching his back and rolling his shoulders. "Theo told me about your husband."

Her eyes widened. "Theo?"

He nodded. "Children notice more than you would think." Just as he had, as a child, when his mother had thought her sadness hidden.

She set down the flask and plate. "What did he tell you?" She'd thrown a mountainous barrier up between them at the mention of her husband that he'd have to gently demolish.

"That you were unhappy with him."

She glanced back at Theo. "He knew? I was so careful not to show it."

"Like I said, children pick up on everything, all too easily. It's hard to keep secrets from them."

"You speak as though you have children of your own." She paused. "Do you? Have children?"

He chuckled. "No, none that I know of. But I was once a child myself. Just as you were. Think of all the things you knew then that perhaps your parents thought you didn't. I bet you knew a lot of things you weren't meant to be party to."

She nodded. "You might be right. But tell me, what was it that you knew, that your mother thought she'd kept secret from you?"

Now she was asking. But he wanted her to be honest with him, so he'd have to be honest with her first. "About my father."

She pressed her lips together but didn't look surprised. This wasn't news to her. Ysella must have told her. She glanced at Theo again before she spoke. "Did she keep his identity secret from you, then?"

He shook his head. "No. Not at all. My father visited us at Rosudgeon every week when I was a child, and I thought that quite normal for a father. I had no way of measuring how a father should behave, and my mother told me his business kept him away from us the rest of the time." He paused, turning over how to put this. "But servants talk, and children's ears are always open. I found that he and my mother were not married and that I was his by-blow—a bastard."

She was watching him now, her attention held by the tale of someone else's childhood.

"I had to ask what that meant, of course, and the person I asked was my nurse. Instinct told me, guided by the way I'd heard it said, that my mother would not be the one to question. And so I learned that not only was my father not really my father in the eyes of the law, but he was married to someone else. And I had sisters."

"How old were you when you discovered this?" The hunted look had vanished again, to be replaced with what might have been compassion, which he didn't want. He wasn't being honest with her to gain her pity, but to invite her to open up with her own story. Finding out why she was so nervous and wary seemed the most important thing in the world right now. Finding out what Theo had only guessed at.

He ploughed on with his own confession. "I was nine. And I was curious. My nurse had told me that my father resided at Trengrouse Castle, and you must know how close that lies to Rosudgeon."

She nodded. "The castle just to the west. I've seen it in the distance. Very splendid with its towers and crenellations."

"The very one. Well, I decided I should go there myself and visit my father. Not, as it turned out, one of my best ideas."

"What happened?"

"My father was not at home. The lies I'd been told about him being often away on business turned out to have been true. But his wife was." He paused, the scene on the castle lawns replaying in his minds eye. The sunshine, the laughter of a little girl running with a small white dog after a ball, the woman seated at an iron-work table in the shade of a spreading cedar, the nurse cradling the shawl-wrapped baby in her arms.

"I walked over. If I'd taken my pony, I'd have had to take the long way round by the Penzance road, so instead, I walked over the fields. My way brought me to the gardens rather than the front of the house, and the sound of a child playing drew me. My father's wife was in the garden… with her children. Children who were not bastards like I was."

Was he playing for her compassion even though he'd told himself he didn't want it? His words were beginning to sound as though he was.

"Don't tell me if it upsets you too much."

Was he upset, still, at the way the haughty Lady Charlotte had treated him that day? The way she'd shouted at him and called his mother a whore as the nurse hurried the children away. His sisters.

He grinned. "Let's just say she knew exactly who I was, and she wasn't pleased to see me. She made that blatantly obvious when she had a footman throw me off her property."

"Oh dear."

He pulled a rueful face. "And of course, she told my father what had happened, and he told my mother, who was furious that not only had the gossip of our servants revealed my bastardy to me in the worst possible way, but also that I'd sneaked off to try and see where my father lived. And met my father's wife. The other woman in his life. The one who won him from her."

"Did your father say anything to you about it?"

He nodded. "The next time he visited, which wasn't for over a month, he took me into his study and gave me a talking-to about my duties to my mother, and that I was to keep away from his house." He grinned again. "That was the moment I decided to become a smuggler."

She smiled. "An act of rebellion?"

"You could say that. He'd made me angry, and I wanted to show him I didn't care. That I'd make a life for myself, and he could be damned."

"But you were only nine."

He grinned. "But I knew what I wanted."

Would she now feel she could reveal her own secrets to him? After all, he'd bared his soul to her, so to speak. And it had been harder than he'd expected. Even after all these years reliving those moments came hard. They weren't incidents he often revisited. He'd done it for her.

She was saved by the bell. "Land ho!" Uncle Billy shouted.

Theo stirred on his sail bed and sat up. "Are we nearly there?"

Chapter Twenty-Two

HARRIET WATCHED JACK walk to the back of the ship with mixed feelings. How long had it been since she'd had a conversation like that with a man other than her husband? Not since before she'd married, other than the man of business in Bath who'd offered her Keynvor Cottage, and that had been of very short duration. Ben had never encouraged her to speak more than to exchange the simplest of pleasantries if any of his officer pals had turned up at the house, and she'd never dared gainsay him. The thought of what he might do if she did had kept her eyes down and her mouth primly shut. No doubt Ben's friends had taken her for a mouse of a woman with no confidence in company. No doubt that was what Ben had wanted them to think—that his wife knew her place.

Well, she *had* been a mouse of a woman when Ben had been at home, and there was no denying that. The thought that Theo, and presumably Lyddie as well, had heard something of what went on between her and Ben made her stomach churn. If she wasn't careful, that bread and cheese was going to make an unwelcome reappearance.

"Mama?" Theo's hand crept over hers as he rubbed sleep out of his eyes with the other. "Are you feeling ill again?"

She looked down at him. His dark curls were all over the place and his previously ashen face had achieved some much needed color. And some dirt. "Nothing at all, my darling. Here, Jack brought you some food." She passed him the plate.

Theo fell on the food like a starving dog. "I feel much better now. P'raps I *will* still be a sailor myself. A smuggler, I think, for preference. That's the kind of sailor I shall be. Boats are such fun." He seemed to have wiped clean away the memory of their night in the hold puking. Such is the resilience of youth. Holding the bread in one hand and the cheese in the other, he jumped to his feet and made a beeline for the side of the boat.

Harriet leapt to her feet as well, hot on his heels. "Don't lean out. This edge is very low. It doesn't look at all safe to me. Hold onto one of these ropes."

But Theo wasn't listening. Instead, he had his gaze fixed on where the ship was heading. A thin gray line filled the horizon, clearly something quite different to the blue-green of the sea, luring the little ship on. "France," Theo said with satisfaction. "It has to be. I've always wanted to go there ever since Monsieur Bulot told me about it in our history lessons." He paused. "Although I don't want them to chop my head off with their guillotine."

As Harriet had been forced to dismiss poor M. Bulot, a French emigré, as soon as she'd been apprised of her straitened circumstances, his mention brought a pang of guilt to her heart. He'd been such a nice, earnest gentleman, and had even helped her a little with what had remained of her own schoolgirl French. Who knew, this might now come in handy if she got the chance to go ashore. She wouldn't have admitted it, but she was probably as excited as Theo at the prospect of setting foot in France. At least the war was over, and no one was likely to clap them in prison or try to guillotine them for the crime of being British. Unless, of course, they guessed they were smugglers and didn't like them for that reason. Who knew what the punishment for smuggling was on this side of the English Channel.

One hand scrunched firmly in the back of Theo's shirt, and the other on the sturdy rigging that seemed to be holding the masts and sails in place, she watched as the coast drew slowly nearer. At first, she could make nothing out, then she spotted cliffs and the glimmering white sand of beaches at their feet, little rocky islets, bigger islands, and the bright splash of painted houses crouching along the shoreline. Small, blue-painted fishing boats dotted the waters, and as *The Fly* drew closer to the shore, she gazed down into that water and saw the green of weed and the shine of rocks not far below the surface. The Fly appeared to be skimming in over rocky beds that might well be visible at low tide. Any ship bigger than her would have had to stick to the dark waters of the deeper channels where they wound between the submerged rocky platforms.

The wind licked at Harriet's loose hair, tugging it out behind her, and salty spray flew up from the wake the ship was leaving. It was going to be a nightmare to comb the tangles out when she finally got her hands on a brush or comb again. She'd have to ask Bertha to help her.

Oh no. Bertha. And Lyddie, too.

Oh no, indeed. Why, in all this adventure, had she not spared a single thought for those she'd left behind so precipitately when she'd raced out into the night after Theo? Lyddie would have woken this morning to find her mother's bed empty and probably assumed her already risen. However, it wouldn't have taken long for her to work out that her mother's continued absence was anything but natural. And Bertha would probably spot she'd departed without any of her outdoor clothes.

What would they think? And what would they do?

Might Bertha try to get in touch with the local constable, if such a worthy even existed? But how would she do it, with no transport other than her own legs. Or would she try the neighboring properties first, asking if anyone had seen her mistress, perhaps omitting the fact that Harriet had gone missing in her night attire? And then, of course, there was Theo's absence as well. Might Bertha add Theo's well-clad absence to his mother's night attired disappearance and fear they'd both fallen off the cliffs in the dark into the sea? That was what Harriet, in a similar position, would assume—the worst. How dreadful for them both to have no idea what had happened, nor that they were safe, if only for now.

Guilt ate at her, but she pushed it aside with trembling hands. With nothing she could do about it right now, she'd just have to think about it later. But how hard that was when all she wanted was to take Lyddie in her arms and reassure her that everything would be all right, and give Bertha an apologetic hug for having given her such heartache.

"Look!" Theo pointed a grubby finger towards the land, where by now the small fishing village that must be Roscoff was hoving into view, green hills rising behind it. A long stone breakwater or jetty, Harriet was unsure of the terminology, poked out into the sea across the submerged rocks, and, along the seafront, a row of what looked like some sort of boathouses stood, half the doors open wide. "And there's an island."

Still edging in over shallow water, *The Fly* crept closer to the land with every minute, half her sails lowered now, as she passed the biggest island and headed into even shallower waters.

But they weren't aiming for the boathouses. Instead, Jack brought his ship in along the jetty, close to the landward end, and his men leapt into action taking the rest of the sails down, slinging the rope fenders over the side and securing their ship with ropes at front and back. All done with great efficiency. *These men know their jobs well.*

"We'd better sit down again out of the way," Harriet said to Theo, pulling him away from the side and back to their previous seating. "Or we'll end up being shouted at."

He wriggled. "Can't we go ashore? I'd like to. Can we ask Cap'n Jack if we can go and explore? I want to see what France is like. Might we see Revolutionaries?"

She hung onto him all the tighter, having no intention of letting him out of her sight. "No, they don't exist any longer. That was years ago from when Monsieur Bulot was a boy. Now sit down and do as you're told, or I'll have to ask Jack to shut you in the hold again."

With a disgruntled scowl, Theo took his place beside her on the sails, his gaze fixed in envy on young Clemo as he helped to tie up the sails and make *The Fly* shipshape. He probably saw himself usurping Clemo's job at some time in the near future.

JACK, BUSY WITH Will organising the laying up of his ship, nevertheless kept a weather eye on Harriet and Theo, approving of her decision to take a seat again out of everyone's way. A sensible young woman. And she had tight hold of her boy. Just as well, as the lad had about him the look of adventure now his nighttime ordeal of seasickness was over. Amazing how the young could just bounce back as though nothing had ever happened to them. He'd been like that himself, or so Will, fifteen years his senior and already a seasoned sailor when Jack had first joined the crew, swore.

He'd just finished sorting everything out, when M. Bagot of Malabee, Lisle, and Bagot arrived ready to inspect the cargo. A small man, outfitted all in brown, with sparse brown hair and a sallow face, Bagot had the appearance of an earnest and efficient banker about him, which he was, if only in his spare time. Plenty of money to be found in Roscoff, although not all of it ended up in banks, of course, with her semi-permanent population of English smugglers, and no French customs men for miles.

Luckily, thanks to his job and all his English customers, Bagot spoke excellent if strongly accented English. Jack had enough French to get on in a bar or with a woman, but, for negotiations, he preferred his own language. Bagot hopped down onto the deck from the jetty, with an agility born of many such encounters, and Jack, having shaken hands with the little man, opened the hatch on the hold. The stronger aroma of tobacco seemed to have dissipated the lingering aroma of vomit, thank goodness. Clemo must have done a good cleaning up job.

"Let us 'ave a look," Bagot said, seizing the top of the ladder and swinging himself over. "But eef it ees as good as ze last shipment you 'ave brought for me, zen I shall pronounce myself an 'appy man."

Jack followed him down, conscious of Harriet's curious gaze. Bagot, being so short, barely had reason to bow his head in the hold, but Jack was straightaway reminded of how his back still ached and of how he would be delegating unloading their cargo to his and Bagot's men very shortly. Up close now, nothing remained to indicate their stowaways' mal de mer.

Bagot poked his long knife into the nearest bale of tobacco and drew out a sliver. Holding it to his nose, he inhaled, then rolled it into a ball and rubbed it between his fingers. A second sniff and his lugubrious face broke into an apology for a smile. "Of ze topmost qualitee, M. Trevelyan. I am pleezed to say zat my colleagues and I will indeed purchase your entire cargo. And we 'ave ze barrels of brandy already in our warehouse awaiting votr'arrivé. Let us go up on ze deck in ze sunshine to see M. Richards and discuss tous les détails."

Half an hour of ferocious haggling in a mix of French and English as they sat on the hatches, which was always to be expected, as well as the imbibing of most of a bottle of brandy between Will, Jack, and M. Bagot, and the deal was done. Bagot went off well-pleased to order his men to bring along the barrels of brandy, and Jack and Will started their crew bringing the tobacco out of the hold and from there up onto the quayside. Just for a while, *The Fly* bobbed higher in the water with the weight of her cargo removed.

Many hands made light work, as the old saying went, and before long the barrels arrived and were stowed in the place the tobacco had previously occupied. *The Fly* sat a little deeper in the water once more. The work had to be completed quickly, before the tide started to go out. If they left it too late, getting over the rocky entrance to the harbor would be impossible.

At last, everything was stowed, and the hatch lid shut. The sun was already sinking in the west and a trail of golden light reflected across the surface of the sea like a magical road to the distant horizon. They needed to get back to one of the deeper channels and drop anchor for the night, but Jack had always loved to see the trail the setting sun left across the sea even as a boy, and this time was no different. He paused just long enough to take the welcome sight in.

"Untie her," he called out, satisfied he'd paid the sea god enough attention, and his men jumped to it.

"Aren't we going ashore?" Theo asked as Jack returned to the bows. Sweeps had come out and the men were maneuvering the ship away from the jetty with the extra long oars and into the deeper water with alacrity and skill.

Jack nodded. "We are, but not from here. We have to be in one of the channels when the tide goes out, or we'll be stuck here on the sand. M. Bagot, my buyer, will send out a gig to collect us when we drop anchor. Have no fear, Theo, you'll set your feet on French soil tonight."

He glanced at Harriet, pretty as a picture in her boys' clothes but probably not dressed for a visit to the town alehouses, which were where he usually went. Neither was young Theo, who was far too young to take somewhere like that. Clemo would be staying on board, as usual, despite his obvious annoyance. He'd been told enough times by the other crew members that he'd have to be fifteen to go ashore and taste the wares on offer, and was used to being the butt of their constant jokes. Might it be better to leave Theo behind with Clemo?

Jack scratched his head. If he did that, he'd have one very disappointed boy on his hands, and Harriet might want to stay on board with him. What he really wanted to do was to show Harriet what a good host he could be, when not constrained by a ship's small size. To charm her, if he could, and get her to open up about her previous life. Now, where could he take Harriet and

Theo that was safe? For a meal in one of the more reputable establishments. Madame S's hotel, perhaps. She catered for the more genteel of smugglers, of which there were quite a few. She'd also in her time catered for a few of Jack's other needs, but he wasn't about to share that with Harriet. And besides, it had been a long time ago.

True to his promise, just as they were dropping anchor in the deeper water, Bagot's gig came skimming out to collect them with two men at the oars. It pulled up alongside The Fly, shipping the oars, and Silas Finn threw down a rope ladder. By the hatch, Clemo stood clutching the silver shilling Jack had just slipped him, which had not been quite enough to wipe the disgruntled frown off his face.

Harriet, who'd put her shoes on over a pair of disreputable stockings to go with her breeches, shirt and borrowed waistcoat, took Jack's offered hand with only a small amount of diffidence, for once, and allowed him to hand her onto the ladder and down into the gig to sit in its bows. Theo, on the other hand, was tossed down bodily like a bale of tobacco, which made him squeal with laughter, then Jack and Will climbed in last. Bagot's men handed the oars over to Silas and Phoby, who set their backs into it and pulled for the shore.

Chapter Twenty-Three

HARRIET WATCHED THE jetty draw nearer, glad it was long enough to reach the deeper water and prevent them having to pull the gig up on the sand and walk. As the gig bumped against the granite slabs, the man called Silas shipped his oar and grabbed a dangling chain. A minute later and they were moored against the wall of the jetty, right beside a rusty iron ladder.

"Mind you don't tie her too tight," Jack said, as his men fastened the mooring ropes. "The tides a way to go yet and we don't want to come back to find her hanging in mid air."

"Think we're greenhorns, do'ee?" Silas muttered, but he slackened the rope he'd been tying.

"Hold her close while our guests disembark," Will said, and Silas pulled the nose of the gig in, while the other man who'd rowed pulled in the stern.

"Up you go. Theo first, then you, Harriet, and I'll come behind you to catch you if you slip."

Did he think she was an idiot? She wasn't about to let herself slip, even though the rails of the ladder were slimy with weed from constant submersion. Hopefully the weed hid no seaborne creatures that might nibble her fingers.

Theo scrambled up the ladder with the agility of the monkey they'd seen last summer at the traveling animal show, but Harriet ascended with less speed and more care, aware every step of the way of Jack's close proximity behind her.

At the top she had to get onto her hands and knees before she could stand up, and by the time she'd done that, Jack was standing beside her. A few minutes later and all the men were on the quayside alongside them.

He turned to his crew. "You're all free to go off and sell your wares, drink your fill, feed your faces and find somewhere to lay your heads." He paused. The men regarded him with grins on their faces. "And whatever else it is you fancy to do. Remember. What happens in France stays in France."

Good heavens. Was he encouraging them to womanize? Surely at least some of them were married. No wonder he'd insisted on the youthful Clemo staying on board. But what were she and Theo to do while all this carousing was going on? Suddenly, remaining on board ship seemed a much more attractive proposition. But it was too late now. *The Fly* sat bobbing gently on the swell too far out to be accessible unless she could prevail upon the owners of the gig to take her and Theo back. Looking at the two swarthy Bretons with the well-wrinkled faces of ancient mariners, she doubted they'd oblige.

Jack turned back to her as Will and their men, the two Breton oarsmen included, swaggered off down the long jetty towards the distant harbor front with the air of men on a mission. He benefited her with a diffident smile. "I'm not including you in that, of course."

Did he look a tad disappointed that he wasn't going off with them? Or was that embarrassment, perhaps, that she might be thinking this was what he customarily got up to in Roscoff? Was it? Did he? She didn't want to think about that.

He held out his arm. "Shall we go?"

She took his proffered arm. "Well, I'm glad about that. Theo is a little young for drinking his fill as yet."

Was that a throaty chuckle? She ignored it, and, holding on tight to Theo with her other hand, as the jetty, or whatever it was called, had nothing to stop him falling over the edge into the sea, she allowed herself to be escorted in pursuit of his men.

Jack smiled, his booted feet loud on the granite. "I'm glad to hear you share my opinion on that. No, I thought we three could go to a certain establishment I know of that not only provides an excellent dinner, but also has passable rooms for the night. I'm sure you don't want to spend another night on board ship in company with my men. There's only so far that sails can go in providing comfortable bedding."

A small frisson of excitement coursed unwanted through Harriet's veins. A fraction of a second later she was cursing herself. What was she thinking? She, who had vowed never to allow herself to be browbeaten by a man again, had for just that moment felt the temptation of a man's body close to hers. But of course, smuggler or not, Jack was a gentleman, wasn't he? And he would not for a moment have meant them to share a room... a bed. What was she? A common, animalistic creature aching for a man's body? The sort of woman Ben had so often accused her of being. An unfounded accusation, of course, until right this moment... No. The thought of what Ben would have said had her stiffening with fear.

No, indeed. Her thoughts were not going to go that way. If she allowed herself for a moment to be tempted, Jack would turn out to be just like Ben and she couldn't bear that. She'd far rather he remained at a discreet distance and didn't darken her door with his masculinity. A friend and perhaps a mentor for Theo, but not for herself. No, never. Only now she was going to have to eat dinner with him. But at least she had Theo with her. Who could ask for a better chaperone than a curious twelve-year-old boy?

She groped for a change of subject. Anything to make herself stop imagining what might be possible. "Will the sheets be damp, do you think? I don't want Theo catching a chill." Keep the conversation to mundanities and she'd be on safe ground.

"Mrs. S is a fine English lady, the widow of a gentleman who once followed the same trade as I do. She knows how we sailors value a comfortable billet every once in a while." What was that flashing across his face as he mentioned this widow's name? But it was gone before she could recognise it. He must have caught her look, though. "And don't worry. She keeps a respectable house. You'll be quite safe there."

"Why's she called Mrs. S?" Theo asked. "Doesn't she have a proper name?"

"Because she was always called that by her husband's crew," Jack said. "Tradition. Habit. Everyone called her that when she was a bo'sun's wife and now she's a bo'sun's widow, no one wants to call her anything else."

"So Mama would be Mrs. P?" Theo sounded gratified at this pronouncement. "I think the baker's boy who called with deliveries at our house in Bath used to call her that. Just like she was a smuggler's wife and not a soldier's wife at all."

Harriet tugged him a little closer. "Be quiet, Theo. Jack doesn't want to hear about our old life."

Jack turned his head to look at her, slowing his walk down as the end of the jetty drew nearer. "On the contrary, Harriet, I would love to hear of your old lives. I have no concept of what it's like living in a city, with all the hustle and bustle of people." He chuckled. "And little inclination to find out, but it would interest me this evening to hear more of your time in Bath." He paused. "And why you ever left Truro."

Oh no. Having revealed himself to her earlier, he no doubt wished her to do the same for him. But how could she admit what had gone on? In front of Theo. Everything had been her fault. She'd been such a bad wife and Ben had been quite right to…

His right hand moved to cover the hand she had tucked into his elbow, somehow warm and reassuring. "Have I said something wrong?"

She shook her head, glad of the rapidly fading evening light. "Not at all. I just…" She glanced meaningfully at Theo, who was ogling the array of small fishing boats now lying where the water had been replaced with sand as the tide went out. "There are things I'd rather not speak of." She kept her voice down low, but Theo didn't turn his head. Too many things to fascinate a boy.

They'd reached the dockside at the end of the jetty by now. Lights were already flickering into life in the dockside inns and alehouses, and the sounds of men enjoying themselves carried into the cool evening air. The smell of seaweed and fish hung over the village like a warm cloak.

Never having seen a fishing village other than Penzance up close, Harriet gazed around herself with interest. All along the docks stood teetering piles of weed encrusted baskets, coils of rope, random bits of ships and upturned rowing boats. On the exposed sand below the high sea wall lay more rowing boats, strings of wooden buoys, a thick line of washed up seaweed, and here and there the weed-encrusted detritus of old fishing nets. The smell wasn't unpleasant as Harriet inhaled a deep breath.

"You like it?" Jack asked, his tone a little hopeful as though her opinion on this tiny French town mattered to him. "This way. Mrs. S's establishment is down a quiet side street."

The same cobbles as lined the harbor road also lined the side street, but with far less of a smell of fish about them. Halfway down it, a sign hung off a metal pole sticking out into the laneway. Someone had painted a picture of a witch with long green hair and wild eyes onto it, along with the name The Sea Witch. Behind her, colossal white-capped waves rose from a wild sea.

"The name of the ship her husband served on," Jack said, pushing the front door open. "She was unusual in having a figurehead—of the witch, of course."

The room inside was small, square, and low-ceilinged, with twisting stairs going up to the left, and a table and chair in the center back in front of a couple of doors. No one appeared to be about, but the smell of cooking food lingered in the air. Fish, of course.

"Hello!" Jack shouted. "Mrs. S? Anyone about?"

Footsteps sounded and the door beside the stairs swung open to reveal a middle-aged woman in a mob cap and clean white apron, who to all intents and purposes, but for the apron, could have stepped out of a society drawing room in Bath. Not that Harriet had much experience of them, but this was not how she'd been expecting Mrs. S, smuggler's widow, to look.

"Jack Trevelyan!" she exclaimed, her kind face breaking into a wide smile and her light blue eyes sparkling with pleasure. "You've been a stranger to us for too long. And you've brought company." Her surprised gaze ran up and down Harriet and Theo.

Mortified, Harriet attempted to look as though cavorting in boys' clothing was a normal thing for her. "Good evening," she said, and for want of being able to hold her skirts out and curtsey, performed an ungainly cross between a bow and curtsey and then wished she hadn't attempted it.

"My dear girl," Mrs. S said, her eyes full of compassion. "What *has* he done to you? Jack—what ever has happened? Did you fish her out of the sea like a mermaid? Or have you taken to dressing your ladies as lads?"

His ladies? Did he come here often with women in tow? The mortification of being just one of a line of ladies swept over Harriet and her cheeks blazed with heat.

Without waiting for him to answer, Mrs. S ploughed on. "A room for you, my dear, and for your son. I'm afraid you'll have to share. And I'm sure we can find something better for you to wear. Shame on you, Jack, for allowing a lady to come ashore dressed like this."

Harriet peeked sideways at Jack, but he'd perhaps wisely decided to remain silent and not argue with this diatribe, nor to reveal that the only other option had been a nightgown. At least he possessed discretion.

Not so Theo. Unfortunately. "It's not Cap'n Jack's fault. We stowed away on *The Fly*, and he took us out to sea by mistake. We were hiding in the hold like proper stowaways. Then the sea got rough, and Mama and I were foully sick because of the storm, and all our clothes were dirty. But Mama only had her night-gown."

Mrs. S's wide blue eyes widened to their furthest extreme. "My goodness me. Never did I hear such a tale. You poor dears. You go into the parlor, Jack, and Etienne will pour you a brandy. I'm taking Mrs...?"

"Penhallow," Harriet said, feeling quite weak and feeble before this onslaught of capability.

"...Mrs. Penhallow upstairs with me. And you, young man. You look to me a likely cabin boy."

Theo, who'd been forced by Harriet to put his shoes and stockings back on, looked most gratified at this praise. "I can stay down here with the Cap'n because I don't need to change. I'm going to be his next cabin boy. When Clemo gets too big."

"No you're not," Jack said. "And you need a wash. Your face is filthy. That's what comes of sleeping on sails."

"Sleeping on sails? What a to do." Mrs. S clasped her hands together. "Not that I've not slept on sails myself in the past. Comfortable bed they make and if it rains you can creep in under a fold. But tonight you'll rest in my best bedroom, my dears. Have no fear." She gave a shout through the door she'd emerged from, a stream of gabbled French issuing from her lips. "Marie Hélène. Tout d'suite. Apportez de l'eau chaude au premier étage—la grande chambre. Dépêchez-vous, paresseux, vite, ou je vous donne une gifle bien méritée."

Harriet hadn't the foggiest what she'd said, but it produced a distant reply. "Oui, madame. Je viens, je viens." The gist of which Harriet picked up. Someone was coming with something she'd been asked to bring.

Mrs. S shooed Jack through the door to the right, and, like a farmer herding recalcitrant hens, ushered Harriet and Theo before her up the spiralling stairs. On the first floor landing she opened a door on the right and Harriet went inside, pulling the still resistant would-be cabin boy after her.

For the best bedroom, it was not large, but the bed had the appearance of being well-mattressed, and there were flowers in a vase on the deep windowsill. How very English. "You won't mind your little lad sharing the bed with you, will you?" Mrs. S asked, turning down the covers. "'Tis a good big bed and most comfortable. The window overlooks the harbor, but there'll not be much noise overnight as the tide's on the way out right now and none of the boats can get in."

Footsteps sounded outside and Marie-Helène, who turned out to be a scrawny French girl in a grubby apron, arrived bearing a jug of steaming water and a china wash basin, cleverly managing to balance this while walking with a towel tucked under one arm and a lump of soap under her chin.

"J'arrive, j'arrive," she panted, as she set down the bowl and jug on the pine dresser.

Mrs. S waved an airy hand at her. "Descends maintenant. Francine a besoin de ton aide, j'en suis sûr."

And with a curious, wide-eyed glance at Harriet, the girl hurried off.

"Now," Mrs. S said with satisfaction. "Let's turn you back into a lady for your Captain."

Theo, who'd gone over to sit on the high bed, legs dangling, burst out laughing. "He's not *her* captain. It was me that stowed away. Mama was just chasing after me and got shut in the hold with me. She didn't want to be on the ship at all. I can't think why. Apart from when we were sick, it's been great fun."

Mrs. S raised a perfectly plucked eyebrow at Harriet. "Mais, bien sûr," she said, reverting for some reason to French. "He is quite definitely *your* Captain, Mrs. Penhallow. I never mistake that look."

─────────── ··◦❦◦·· ───────────

Chapter Twenty-Four

A GOOD THREE quarters of an hour later, Harriet descended
the stairs with Mrs. S, who then, with the air of a proud
mama presenting her daughter at court, escorted her into a small
parlor. A fire burned in a wide stone hearth and a table had been
set for two. This last was because, to Harriet's consternation,
Mrs. S had sent Theo off after his own wash and brush up and
before she started on Harriet's transformation, to eat in the
kitchens with the delighted Marie-Hèlène. Something he was
eager to do. He departed with her, before Harriet could say no, to
the sounds of him practising his schoolboy French on the
bemused servant. "Bonsoir. Je m'appelle Theo. Comment tu
t'appelle?"

Which meant that Harriet was going to have to dine alone
with Jack. No use complaining to Mrs. S. though, who seemed
delighted to be pushing the two of them together, like some old-
fashioned matchmaker who'd decided for herself they were
meant for one another. Harriet was just going to have to endure
the experience. She refused to acknowledge that a part of her, a
tiny part only, was quite looking forward to eating with the
handsome captain.

He was seated in a high, wing-backed chair by the fire when
she came in, but he jumped up with alacrity, his eyes wide with
surprise at the changes Mrs. S had wrought on his stowaway.

She'd had no black dresses at all, she'd insisted, and Harriet would have to put up with wearing either a prettily sprigged muslin gown or go back to her breeches and shirt. The lure of the gown had won. "Tres bien," that lady had said with delight, reverting yet again to French. "Parfait for dinner with a gentleman. A shame to hide your beauty in dull black."

Clearly remembering his manners a little late, Jack swept a flamboyant bow. He'd not changed the clothes he'd been on board ship in, but the flickering firelight bestowed on him an antique glow that was not unpleasing. His dark hair glimmered as though gilded, and those almost golden eyes... well, she'd best not look at them too closely or it might be hard to tear her own eyes away.

"Now," Mrs. S said, with even more satisfaction. "Your new young cabin boy is eating in the kitchens with my servants, so he won't be disturbing you. I'll have Gaston serve your dinner, and make sure young Master Theo goes up to bed when he's finished eating, although as he's a boy, that should be a while from now. My servants know how to feed a growing lad."

Jack gave her a small bow. "Thank you for that." Then he turned to Harriet. "Won't you sit down?"

As Mrs. S, with an elaborate wink aimed at which one of them Harriet couldn't work out, departed, Jack held out one of the two chairs. Harriet sat down, arranging the skirts of the gown Mrs. S had lent her with care.

Jack took the seat opposite and poured wine into two fine cut-glass goblets. He held his up. "To smuggling and all it brings us."

Harriet raised her eyebrows but lifted her glass. "To not getting caught while Theo and I are on board."

He clinked his glass against hers. "An admirable sentiment to which I would add—to not getting caught, ever."

She took a mouthful of the wine, which was full-bodied and strong, not at all like the watered wine Ben had insisted was all she could be trusted with. "I gather the punishment for smugglers is severe. I saw what remained of a few of them as a girl. They'd been hanged then tarred and left up as a lesson to passersby not to follow in their footsteps. It's a wonder you're prepared to risk your life and liberty when you already have a fine house and all you could wish for in the way of possessions."

"Ah, but I don't do it for the money."

She took a second mouthful of the wine, savoring its fruitiness. With her present impecunity, some time had passed since she'd drunk wine of any sort, even watered wine. "So, you see yourself as the gentleman smuggler doing it for the good of others?"

He had the grace to look sheepish. "I might."

"Or is there another reason for the trade you carry out?" Goodness, she was feeling bold. Perhaps it was the wine talking. In case it was, she took another long sip to fortify her nerves, liking the effect. The midday meal on board *The Fly* being a long time ago, the alcohol brought a pleasantly warming glow to her empty stomach, which she also liked.

He smiled. "Would you believe me if I told you I do it for the excitement?"

She set her wineglass on the table, and he topped it up for her. She'd have to be careful not to drink too much, but it was exceedingly pleasant and at the same time gave her the courage to speak her mind. For once. And, unlike Ben, Jack didn't appear to be too shocked or angry that she was questioning him. In fact, it was fun to question him. To spar with him like a fencer with an epée. Much as she'd felt Fitz was sparring with her. Only she preferred Jack as an opponent.

"I think I would," she said, picking up her glass again, partly to give herself something to do with her hands, which were bare, as Mrs. S's wardrobe had not run to gloves.

"Then that is what I shall tell you." He drained his own glass and refilled it, and the door opened to emit a stout man with a large tray on which resided a large platter. Of snails.

"Escargots, M'sieur," he said, with a flourish, as he laid the platter on the table between them. "Spécialité de la maison."

Snails. Harriet's nose twitched at the inviting aroma of garlic butter. But snails? Of course, she knew, as any child who'd learnt French from a tutor or in school did, that the French typically ate snails and frogs' legs. But to be presented with them? In this quantity? There must be two dozen of them occupying their neat little shells all sitting in little recesses on the pottery platter as if it had been specially made for them. What if the main course turned out to be frogs' legs themselves? M. Bulot had said they tasted like chicken when Theo had asked him, and Theo had wasted no time in informing both Lydia and Harriet of this delicious piece of information. But he hadn't been clear on what snails tasted like.

Jack picked up a little pronged fork and prodded it into one of the shells, lifting out the occupant, cooked and covered in garlic butter. With an air of nonchalance he popped it into his mouth and mopped up the excess butter with a slice of crusty bread. Harriet watched him in fascination. Had Theo eaten snails in the kitchen, or were they reserved for those in the parlor?

"Don't you like snails?" Jack asked, taking a second. "Don't think of them as that. Think of them as shellfish. We Brits have little trouble eating oysters, so why should snails be any different?"

"I've never tried them."

"That means nothing. They're an epicurean delight. Are you woman enough to try them?"

She took another reassuring gulp of her wine. Why not? When in France... Using the tiny fork, she prodded it into the nearest shell until she'd attached it to what was lurking inside. Lifting it out, she paused a moment, the melted butter dripping off the snail. Best close her eyes. She popped it into her mouth and swallowed without chewing. But the taste lingered and... wasn't at all bad.

"Not quite how I'd imagined," she said, and took a second one.

To her surprise she managed to eat half a dozen to Jack's much larger portion, which was enough for her. She'd have to tell Theo later that she'd been brave enough to try snails. If he hadn't been offered them himself, he'd be fascinated.

"Peasant fare," Jack said, wiping his mouth. "But too delectable to ignore. Mrs. S is an accomplished cook and thinks nothing of borrowing the recipes of her less affluent neighbors here in Brittany. A lot of peasant cooking over here uses the cheapest and most easily accessible ingredients and turns them into culinary delights."

What a surprise that Jack was turning out to be some sort of connoisseur of French food. Harriet dabbed at her lips with her napkin and managed a smile. Really, the wine was making her feel quite mellow and relaxed. A smile came readily to her lips and this time she didn't chase it away. "I wonder why our own peasants don't also dine on snails? Perhaps they've never thought of it. Or perhaps they do, and we're just ignorant of their eating habits."

Jack topped up their wine again. "Mrs. S has come up trumps with that dress." His eyes ran over her outline before reverting to her face, and, for once, she didn't feel as though she wanted to curl up in a ball and vanish. No wonder Ben had never let her have more than one glass of watered wine and banned her from drinking it while he was away from home. "It is rather pretty." She stretched out her arm to admire the delicate puffed sleeves. "Such a lovely color."

"And so becoming to your complexion."

She felt heat swarm up her cheeks but this time it wasn't embarrassing. The wine was depriving her of her inhibitions as well as giving her confidence. "Thank you."

He grinned. "Although I have to admit you made a pretty boy."

"I was in fear of having to return to Cornwall still clad as a boy. Mrs. S has kindly said I might keep these clothes until the next time you are here." She pursed her lips. "Which I imagine will be quite soon as you claim to be a man who is fond of the excitement of the trade." She wouldn't think of the familiar glance Mrs. S. had given Jack on their arrival. She just wouldn't. Could she be jealous? Drat it, she was thinking about it when she'd just sworn not to.

"It will indeed be quite soon. There are always goods to be taken back and forth, with the exorbitant taxes both our governments levy. But at least they don't match one another, which makes it easier for us to take over goods the French pay high duty on and bring back the ones our government charge high duty on. It works well for both sides."

Gaston reappeared along with the tray. "M'sieur, Madame." He swept up the platter of empty snail shells and set another bottle of wine and two fresh glasses on the table. "Je reviens, tout d'suite."

True to his word, he was back in a moment with the tray freshly filled with two plates of some kind of rich chicken stew. "Coq au vin, madame." He set Harriet's plate in front of her with a flourish. Steam rose from the hot concoction to waft the enticing aroma into her nostrils. At least no frogs legs were in sight. She waited for Gaston to leave before taking a forkful of the tender meat. Delicious.

They ate for a while making only small talk, but eventually both their plates had been emptied and the bottle of red wine held only the dregs. Harriet was replete with good food and glowing from the effect of rather too much of the wine. What a good thing she'd eaten enough to soak some of the alcohol up.

"Gaston will bring us coffee shortly," Jack said. "While we wait, come and sit beside the fire a while."

Surprised by her own lack of fear, she let him take her hand, feeling a little light headed as she stood up, but covering it well. Three steps took her to one of the two fireside chairs, and she sat down a little heavily. If he were to importune her now, she'd have no defences, and what was more, she probably wouldn't care. What a disturbing thought that was. She hiccupped.

JACK REGARDED HIS companion with a wary eye. She'd rather guzzled the wine, but he'd been powerless to prevent her. Besides, it hadn't occurred to him that she wouldn't be used to it until it was much too late. And a little inebriation suited her well. In vino veritas, his mother was wont to say, and she was right. The reclusive Mrs. Penhallow was emerging from her shell with a vengeance, and he rather liked it.

Gaston arrived bearing the coffee with young Marie-Hèlène in tow to clear the table. He drew a small circular table to between the two fireside chairs and set the coffee tray on it, before stoking the already blazing fire. With a discreet cough, he and the girl departed, Gaston having fielded a sizeable tip.

Harriet shifted in her seat and stretched, like a cat. "Goodness, I haven't eaten so much in a long time." She frowned. "Not since I was a girl after a day's hunting, I don't think. Ben told me I'd get fat if I ate what he said was too much. He told me didn't want a fat wife."

Nice of Ben. Jack was himself fond of a girl with curves in all the right places. "Nothing to stop you eating whatever you wish now."

She nodded. "He wouldn't let me drink, either. Nothing more than a single glass of ratafia, watered, of course."

So that was why she was so pie-eyed now. The temptation to lean forward and take her in his arms had never been stronger. Instinct told him she would probably offer little resistance. To tell her she was quite safe now and she could do whatever she wanted all the time. But of course, he didn't. How ungentlemanly would it have been to have taken advantage of a woman in her condition.

However, she took him by surprise by leaning forward herself. "Ben was very particular about what his wife was allowed to do."

"He was?"

She nodded. "Very. He didn't like it if I crossed him. He said I did it on purpose, but I didn't." She screwed up her face at the memory as if straining to recapture it. "I never meant to be a bad wife. To do the things he said were what bad wives did."

"How did you meet him?" Jack asked, avoiding asking the question he wanted to ask—what the departed Ben's definition of a bad wife was. Probably not the same as his own. If he wasn't about to take advantage of her virtue, he had no scruples about questioning her while her guard was down.

She sat back in her seat, legs stretched out towards the fire, and kicked her shoes off. She had dainty, fine-boned feet. The longing to lift them onto his lap where he could massage them swept over Jack, but he resisted.

She frowned. "At the assembly rooms in Truro. He was on leave from his regiment and was attending with some of his officer friends." She pulled a rueful expression. "He was so handsome in his regimentals."

Jack had seen enough of soldiers in all their regalia to understand why a young girl such as Harriet had been might get carried away by the sight of a young officer.

"He asked Papa for my hand in marriage the following week, and Papa agreed. He didn't want to, because he thought seventeen was too young for marriage, but I told him I was old enough to know my own mind and he gave in, at last." Her voice trailed away. "Ben was very handsome, you understand, when he was happy…"

But from what Theo had said, that wasn't all the time. Not by any means.

"When did he begin to bully you?" Jack asked, determining to be blunt.

Her eyes widened a little. "Not straight away. After Lyddie came along… after I found out I was to have a child… then, he wasn't quite so kind to me anymore. He didn't like me being… fat and unattractive. We had rooms in London, to begin with, but when Lyddie was born, we moved to Bath to be near his aunt, Mrs. Bolitho, who has allowed us to live in Keynvor Cottage. She lived in Bath at the time and Ben would go to visit her when he was home from the wars. He never took me... although he did take Theo, once." Her eyes clouded at the memory. "He never did again. He said Theo was a devil child and I was a terrible mother to indulge him so and that was why he was so badly behaved." She looked down at her hands in her lap. "That was the first time he didn't stop at shouting, but struck me."

Jack froze. Not for one moment had he expected this.

She turned wide, candid eyes on him. "He was sorry afterwards, of course, but it didn't stop him doing it again. And again. Every time he did it, he was always sorry, afterwards."

Jack groped for words. That men beat their wives, he knew all too well, but that the man who'd been married to the beautiful young woman before him had done it to her was beyond imagining. "I didn't know."

She shook her head. "No one does. Not even Bertha, although I know she didn't like Ben one bit, so perhaps she suspected. She didn't like how much he drank. Nor did I, for the more he drank, the more likely was it that he would strike me."

She told the tale with such equanimity, as though it was to be expected that a man would beat his wife, as though she took it for granted that he was right, and she was a bad mother and wife.

"No man should raise a hand to a woman."

She blinked up at him. "You think so?" Her words were almost wondering.

He nodded. "There is never an excuse for violence like that."

"But how does a wife learn to be better?"

What? He shook his head. "She doesn't need to be. She's her own person, and a man, her husband, should accept her for what she is."

She frowned. "Ben said it was the right of a husband to discipline his wife and children and make them how they should be to please him."

Jack sighed. This Ben had indoctrinated her well over the years they'd been together, since she'd been scarcely older than her own daughter. "That might be so, but it doesn't make it the correct thing to do. The law is not always right, you know." He paused. "I would never raise my hand to a woman."

She was gazing at him with such intensity now he almost wanted her to drop his eyes. "You wouldn't?"

He shook his head. "Never. I value women for their own importance. I value you, Harriet, for who you are, not who I might turn you into."

"Oh." She kept on staring at him.

Flustered, he poured the coffee, the thick black liquid trickling into the tiny cups. It might help to sober her up. He needed a little sobering himself. He handed her a cup.

"Did no one notice your bruises?" he asked, after he'd taken a sip of the strong coffee.

She shrugged. "He was careful not to strike me where it would show."

"Good God." He couldn't help himself. "The man was an animal. Why did you stay with him? Were you not afraid for the children?"

She shot him a pitying look over her coffee cup. "I am a woman, Jack. Where would I have gone if I'd chosen to run? Where would I have taken my children? My mother was already dead when I married, and my father died soon after. My husband had taken the small inheritance they'd left me and gambled it away. Although I didn't know this until after his death. He was an inveterate gambler—he could not turn away from a wager of any kind. He left me deeply in debt." She gave herself a little shake. "I sometimes wonder if the report I had of his death was accurate or whether he died by his own hand instead of face the debtors prison."

"Or someone he owed decided on revenge. Did you have no one to turn to? No friends?"

She shook her head. "He'd made sure of that. I was not allowed to attend social gatherings. All I had was Bertha, and I couldn't reveal Ben's behavior to her for fear of what she might do. For if she'd faced him with it, he'd have thrown her out, and then I'd have had no one."

Before Jack could stop himself, he was on his knees in front of her chair, his arms around her pulling her towards him. For a moment she resisted, before he felt her body sag into his and he folded her against his chest. There was nothing predatory about his movement, and she seemed to sense it. He held her for several long and silent minutes, rocking her gently and breathing in the familiar scent of Mrs. S's soap and the spray of perfume she must have applied to her protégé.

After about a minute he became aware that his shoulder was wet and her body was shaking, although she must be fighting to keep herself under control.

"Let it all out," he murmured into her hair, the softness of her pressed close to his chest doing embarrassing things to his own body that he wanted to keep from her. "Cry as much as you want. No one's going to judge you." And cry she did until at last she quieted, her body ceased to shake, and she lay quiet in his arms.

His knees were aching with so long on the hard floor, so he shifted her around a little so he could see her face. Her eyes were red-rimmed and puffy, her cheeks tear-stained, but she managed a little smile. "I-I've never cried like that before. I never dared to."

Oh God, how close her face was to his and how badly he wanted to press his lips to hers and show her that a man didn't have to be a bully. But common sense stayed him. If he did that now, it was tantamount to being as bad as the despicable Ben. Instead, he put up a diffident hand and stroked her cheek, pushing the few strands of hair that had escaped Mrs. S's hairstyling back off her face. She was just so beautiful, so delicate, so vulnerable and yet she must possess a core of forged steel to have survived this far. Every part of him was shouting out that he wanted to keep her safe and never let anyone hurt her again.

But nothing lasts, and eventually she must have become aware of the inappropriateness of their situation. She extricated herself from his embrace and stood up. Jack climbed back to his feet as well, resisting the temptation to rub his sore knees.

"Thank you for your kindness, Jack." She was all distant again. "I shall not forget it. But now I'm very tired, and I think I should retire. What time do you require Theo and I to rise in the morning?"

Hiding his disappointment, Jack managed a smile. "Mrs. S serves breakfast at eight. There's no need to rise early, as we have M. Bagot's gig to return us to *The Fly*."

"Then I bid you good night." And with that she was gone.

Jack sat back down. What had just happened there?

Chapter Twenty-Five

THE STAIRS SEEMED a lot steeper on the way up than they had done on the way down. And Harriet's feet felt curiously detached from the rest of her body, as though her knees didn't exist, but she made it to the top without disgracing herself and falling down in a heap. Luckily, the "best room" happened to be the first on the right, so she pushed open the door and slid inside, supporting herself on the wall. She didn't want to admit it, but standing up so hurriedly had done strange things to her equilibrium and support by something solid was a necessity.

Whoever had brought Theo up to bed had left an oil lamp burning on the dressing table, so at least she was able to see to undress. The nightgown Mrs. S had pressed on her earlier lay on the chair by the bed, so Harriet picked it up and sat down heavily on the chair in its place. Undressing while uncertain of which way up the room should be was going to be a major undertaking.

A tiny tap on the door broke the silence. The sudden fear that this might be Jack and that he'd decided to try his luck with her after she'd been so incautious as to allow him to hug her flooded through her. One glance back at the bed told her this couldn't be him. No man would try to press his attentions on a lady with a child in the room.

"Madame?" A small voice, barely above a whisper, young and unsure.

With an enormous effort, Harriet summoned up the school-girl French M. Bulot had attempted to improve. "Oui?"

"Voulez-vous que je vous aide? Madame m'a envoyée."

It must be the little maid, Marie-Héléne. Harriet struggled with the strongly accented French. Did it mean the girl had come to help her? With a wary glance at Theo, she kept her voice down. "Entrez."

Marie-Héléne opened the door a crack and slipped inside, a timid look on her face as though facing a strange English woman was on a par with facing a dragon. "Je peux vous aider?" She held out her hands.

Definitely she was offering help, and Harriet was not about to refuse. Undoing this gown and her stays by herself was not going to be easy, what with the way her head was spinning. She'd let herself get too carried away with the effect the wine had been having upon her confidence. And what was more, she was uncomfortably aware that she'd said rather too much to Jack about Ben. She'd have to think about that later. She couldn't possibly consider it right now when all she wanted to do was get out of this gown and her borrowed stays. "Merci."

Fifteen minutes later she was tucked up in the big bed wearing the flannel nightgown, beside the sleeping Theo, and Marie-Héléne had extinguished the oil lamp and departed. But sleep felt far away, which in itself was odd as tiredness had washed over her as Marie-Héléne had helped her prepare for bed. Now the maid had gone, she lay wide awake with sleep flown out of the open window.

Confusion reigned. She'd let him hug her. He'd gone onto his knees in front of her and taken her in his arms and she'd let him. Why? All those years of Ben and she'd never succumbed to tears, never turned to anyone for support, not even her beloved Bertha, and yet, she'd done so with a man who was tantamount to a stranger. And liked it, what was worse. She'd liked the feel of his strong arms around her, holding her pressed so close against his chest she'd been able to feel the pounding of his heart. And it had been pounding, as though he was feeling the same anxieties as her. She'd liked the feeling of safety that had surged through her as she'd nestled close.

But she'd been tipsy. No, that was a polite underestimation. What she'd really been was drunk. Her cheeks flooded with heat. She'd allowed a man to see her drunk, something Ben would have hated. He'd always said that women couldn't take their drink and she'd proven him right. He'd said that if women, by which he meant her every time, had too much to drink, they lost their inhibitions and became loose moraled. And she'd done just that. She'd allowed herself to be held by another man. A man who was not her husband, and she'd liked it. If that wasn't loose morals, what was? Everything Ben had ever said echoed inside her head, rattling between her ears. She was a bad woman and he'd been right all along. She'd done bad things last night. Wherever he was, he'd be laughing at her, jeering, poking his finger to jab her in the shoulder, raising his hand, taking off his belt…

Ben's sneering face appeared before her. His darkly curling hair, just like Theo's, his heathery green eyes like Lyddie's, but his mouth, curling and cruel, nothing like theirs. "You slut," he shouted at her as she cowered on their bed. "You shameless trollop. I know what you've been doing while I've been away." Spit flew from his lips and the smell of brandy on his breath was overpowering as he leaned towards her, pushing his face into hers. "You're no longer to speak with that French fop, Bulot. From now on, he only sees Theo in the music room or I'll be taking my belt to him as well as you. Bertha can deal with the boy's lessons. You're to stay out of his way. Do you understand?" The room whirled around her as he grabbed hold of the front of her nightgown and it ripped at the shoulder. "I won't have my wife the talk of Bath, with her name bandied around the drawing rooms coupled with that Frenchman's."

She cowered further. "I'm sorry, Ben. I didn't think."

He shook her, his face suffused with fury. "That's your problem. You never think, do you? If you thought a bit more you might be a better wife. You disgust me." He threw her across the bed and turned away. "I'm going out. You'd better think about what you've done while I'm gone. I'll want a better apology than that when I get back."

And he was gone. Only she wasn't quite sure what she'd done, only that it had been wrong. She'd thought Ben would have been pleased that she was improving herself by learning more French. She'd thought Ben quite happy with M. Bulot, who was a funny little man with such strongly accented English it was hard to follow what he said. Small, skinny, over forty and rather effeminate in his ways, but also witty and kind and fun to talk to. Had Ben really thought she'd been flirting with him?

The image drifted away, thank goodness, and she turned to peer at Ben's son, curled up beside her, his dark curls spread on the pillow. It had always been a great relief to her that although Theo looked like his father, he wasn't like him in temperament. Thank goodness, also, that when Ben had been on his infrequent visits home, he'd wanted the children to stay in the nursery. Especially Theo. Lyddie, he'd tolerated and treated as his favorite the few times he'd seen her, which explained why Lyddie missed him so much now. She'd built him up as the fantasy father she craved and set him on a pedestal of bravery, little knowing what he was really like, poor child.

Harriet rolled onto her side, her thoughts wandering back to Jack. How very different he seemed to Ben. A little like the way Ben had been when they'd first married. Although, not that much. Ben had always been demanding of Harriet's full attention... and total obedience. He'd not liked it one bit when she'd grown large with child, and made it obvious that he found her unattractive. She'd suspected back then that he was keeping a mistress somewhere, or at least visiting a house of ill repute, but she'd never dared to say a word. A husband could do as he liked and it was for the woman, who could do no such thing, to put up with it.

Might Jack be like that, too? She'd apprised that look between him and Mrs. S. Had it been more than friendship? Did something lie between them, some shared feelings? He'd said this was a respectable house, so it couldn't be a bawdy house, but that didn't stop the proprietor from taking herself a handsome lover. Were they lovers now? Was Jack at this moment lying in the arms of their hostess? And wouldn't that make him no different to Ben?

She heaved a sigh. Perhaps it was all her fevered and suspicious imagination, fueled by the wine and the embrace. Perhaps he might be different.

What was she doing? Daydreaming, even though it was dark night, of a man she could never have. A man she felt sure she didn't want. Did she? And he wouldn't want her. Men like Jack married an heiress for her fortune, or their mothers arranged it for them. They didn't choose penniless widows with two children to support. She'd better put that right out of her head.

Impossible.

What would it be like if he were here, now, instead of Theo. If he were sleeping beside her so peacefully just as her son was. Or maybe not sleeping at all. A little shiver of anticipation vibrated through her. Perhaps he would lean over and kiss her, take her in his strong arms again, let her feel the beating of his heart against her breasts, run his lips over her bare skin…

No. Absolutely not. She must not think like this at all. It was the effect of all that wine. She must remember that all men were like Ben. That all they wanted was their own gratification and a meek and mild-mannered wife who would do as she was told and let them slake their lust. Men of any other sort did not exist, much as she would have liked them to. Jack would be just like that.

Just like Ben.

JACK, TOO, SPENT a restless few hours with thoughts of Harriet foremost in his mind, but eventually he fell asleep and dozed fitfully until daybreak, his dreams tormented by visions of Harriet in various compromising positions. He rose at dawn, half an hour before breakfast was due to be served, took his time washing and shaving, then descended to the same parlor they'd occupied the night before.

Theo and Harriet were already seated at the table, Theo tucking in with gusto to a spread of different pastries and Harriet delicately nibbling at a slice of bread spread with apricot conserve. Her pale cheeks and serious expression might well mean she was suffering the aftereffects of her injudicious imbibing of the night before. Jack had drunk as much himself, or more, but he was used to it, and this morning, after his shave, he felt quite the new man.

However, she glanced up with a little smile as he came in. "Good morning to you, Jack. As you will see, Mrs. S has been more than generous in equipping the breakfast table, but you'd best hurry yourself or Theo will have cleared it. There's coffee and hot milk in the pots."

Jack pulled up a chair and helped himself to several pastries and a slice of crusty bread.

"Shall I pour you a coffee, Cap'n?" Theo asked. He had a milky mustache from the glass he'd been drinking.

Jack nodded. "As a potential cabin boy, I think that ought to be one of your duties. Thank you. And good morning to you both." He eyed Harriet. "I trust you both slept well?"

Theo beamed. "Like a log. I didn't even wake up when Mama came up. Can we stay here a few days?"

"I'm sorry, but no. We have to take our cargo back to Cornwall this morning. After breakfast we'll row out to *The Fly*. We should be back home by nightfall, if we're lucky with the winds."

Theo pulled a disappointed face but kept on going with his food. A wonder the boy was so small and skinny, but Jack wasn't so old that he couldn't remember being constantly starving as a boy himself. He was probably on the verge of a growing spurt, and all the fresh air of the Cornish coast and sailing was making him hungrier than normal.

"Will the crossing be as rough as yesterday's?" Harriet asked, sipping her coffee, the eyes that regarded Jack over the top of the cup wary. Probably wondering if she'd get a revisitation of her breakfast later, if the sea got rough.

He shook his head. "A little lumpy, but hopefully nowhere near as bad. And if you remain on deck in the fresh air, you should be less affected." He wanted to ask her about last night; if she was all right, how she felt now she'd cried it out of her, but he didn't dare. Not in front of Theo, at any rate. He drained his coffee cup and poured a second, noticing the furrowing of her brow. "I'd drink a couple of glasses of water, if I were you. It'll help your headache."

Her eyes flew to his. "How do you know…?"

He grinned. "An easy guess after last night."

Color rose to her cheeks. "I must apologize for my unseemly behavior."

Theo pushed the last of his bread into his mouth. "Might I get down now, Mama, and run down to the harbor to look at the boats?"

She looked a question at Jack. "Will he be safe?"

Jack nodded. "Plenty of English sailors down there if he gets into any trouble."

She nodded. "Very well. But don't go too near the edge. Don't talk to any strangers. And don't get into any trouble."

Theo planted a kiss on his mother's cheek, saluted Jack, and was gone.

Jack stood up. "We won't be far behind him. I've just to settle up my dues with Mrs. S, then we can leave."

Harriet's blush deepened. "Oh no. I hadn't even thought of having to pay for our room and breakfast." The hunted look returned with a vengeance. "I have no money with me. A nightgown does not lend itself to carrying one's reticule."

Jack felt his own cheeks warm with the realization that he'd put her in an embarrassing situation. "I'm sorry. I should have said that I would be settling this myself. I don't expect my stowaways to pay for themselves now I've virtually kidnapped you to France."

Relief flooded her face. "Thank you." To be followed by what looked like the realization that having a strange man pay for one's accommodation in a foreign inn probably wasn't the done thing. "Oh no. I would rather you didn't."

Jack reached his hand across the table and set it on hers. For a moment, she tried to snatch hers away, but he hung on. "Harriet. I promise you that no one will ever know that I paid for your billet. Let me do it and we'll have you back home in no time. This will all be a bad dream for you." Only it had been anything but a bad dream for him.

She raised her eyes to his. "You are sure? You will not tell your mother? I should hate for her to know. She might think I was…" Her voice trailed off. She probably didn't want to put into words what she thought his mother would think. Even though she was well aware his mother herself was not of the most respectable in Cornwall.

He rose to his feet and pulled her up with him. Impulse seized him and while he still had her hand in his, her lifted it to his lips and pressed a kiss to it. "Have no fear, Harriet. I have nothing but the most honest of intentions."

Her look of relief was fleeting. No doubt she was pondering his words.

Chapter Twenty-Six

JACK WAS QUITE right, as Harriet had been nurturing a hope he would be, and the voyage north from Roscoff was a far less bumpy ride, helped by being out on deck in the fresh air. He made a comfortable seat for her and Theo on the sails again, which also happened to be in the most sheltered spot in the ship, as the edging, which Jack told her was called the gunwales, rose towards the front. She settled there with a warm feeling of coming home that she couldn't quite identify nor fathom. After all, *The Fly* was not her home, so why should she feel like this?

Their day passed in comparative comfort, as the weather held fine, and a following wind chased what clouds there were across the sky much as it was doing to *The Fly* on the azure surface of the sea. Somewhere in the middle of the voyage, just after they'd eaten a welcome noonday snack of barley bread and cheese, washed down with horn beakers of Cornish cider, a new experience for Theo, a school of dolphins found the ship. They followed her for some time, leaping out of the water or skimming just beneath the surface like sleek blue-gray bullets.

Theo knelt, on Harriet's insistence, beside the gunwales watching this aquatic display with delight, and even the crew, who must have seen all this many times before, took time to ooh and aah over their followers. After a bit, with his friend, Will, taking a turn at the tiller, Jack came and stood with Harriet while

Theo admired the dolphins from his position of safety, bringing with him a flask of much-needed water.

He'd removed his coat and wore only an unbuttoned waistcoat over a white shirt open at the neck to reveal his darkly curling chest hairs. Harriet averted her gaze and fixed her eyes on Theo, to whose waist she'd insisted on attaching a spare rope, much to his disgust and the laughter of the crew, especially young Clemo who'd been particularly mocking of what he called 'the landlubbers'.

Jack settled on the sails a few feet away, stretching his long, boot-clad legs out in front of him. "We only take the tiller an hour at a time usually," he said. "Because it takes it out of you to stand there for too long at a time, keeping her as close to the wind as possible. A man can have enough of steering a ship." And there was she thinking a man liked nothing better than to pose with the tiller of his very own ship. She controlled the smile that threatened to appear.

Theo jumped up. "Can I go and help Cap'n Will with the tiller then? In case he gets tired?"

Jack nodded. "But no running on deck. Your mother'll likely kill me if you hurt yourself." He grinned. "Or fall in." Wise words. He must have a good idea what being a mother was like. Perhaps Talwyn was responsible for that. They seemed to have a close bond, with him growing up hardly ever seeing his father.

Theo, having prevailed upon Harriet to remove the rope from his waist on his solemn promise not to go near the sides again, departed in as close to a run as he could manage without actually running, and Jack leaned back on the pile of spare sails. Harriet regarded him in silence for a moment or two. It might be a good idea, before he brought up last night, to get him talking about *The Fly*, then he wouldn't be able to remind her of her reprehensible behavior. Or talk of anything else that might discomfort her. "She's a beautiful ship," she said. "How long have you had her?"

He was almost prone now, as though soaking up what

warmth there was in the fast fading sun now he was out of the wind, and she had to look down at him. At the provocative hint of hairs on his chest, the shadow of stubble on his firm chin, the way loose curls of his hair flopped over his forehead... Good heavens. She was getting carried away here. She straightened her spine with determination.

He'd closed his eyes. "Not long. Will has his own ship, *The Black Joke*, which is off right now doing legal journeys. We have to let them do that as much as possible so as not to draw untoward attention from the authorities. As for *The Fly*, I'd wanted a ship of my own for a long time, so I had her built round in St Ives, in Thomas's boatyard, to my own design. Well, I had input, but he had the final say as he's the expert. She's fast as she can carry so much sail, but she's also capable of carrying a good weight in cargo. Like we have today."

Having asked him about what was probably his favorite subject, she had to expect a full and detailed reply. "Why did you call her *The Fly*?" She brushed strands of hair out of her eyes. A bonnet would have been useful. Her face was going to be very tan if she wasn't careful, and Bertha would remark on it, for sure. A lady's complexion should be milky white, not tanned like that of a man or a farm worker. Only working women looked like that.

Bertha. No. She would not think about Bertha until that worthy was standing before her. What would be the point? *Lydia*. No, she had to put off thinking of both of them for now, as dwelling on them would do her no good but make her feel guilty when none of this was her fault. Events had swept her up into this seaborne adventure. Adventure? Was she now seeing this trip through rose-tinted spectacles? Was she, heaven forbid, enjoying it as much as Theo?

Jack opened one eye. "When I was a boy, my father gave me a little crabbing boat to sail about in near the coast. Blue painted, with a red sail, just like the bigger fishing boats. I loved that little boat. She was called *The Fly*, so it seemed only natural to call the ship I commissioned myself after her."

So his father had seen enough of him to furnish him with gifts. Maybe not such an absent father as he'd led her to believe, or rather, as she'd assumed. Possibly more active in his life than Ben had been with Theo. That wouldn't have been hard. Somehow, the image of Jack as a boy of Theo's age, off in his own little sailing boat, appealed.

"And did you fish for crabs with your boat?"

He nodded. "You don't precisely fish for them. You put down baited traps and wait for them to crawl inside. A bit like lobster pots. I caught a good few and made myself a bit of money selling them round at the market in Penzance."

At the stern, Will was allowing Theo to think he was in charge of the steering, standing behind him with his hand steadying the tiller where Theo couldn't see. Young Harry was sitting on a coil of rope, whittling at something with his pocket-knife. The boy Clemo was doing something to one of the sails that involved a rope. Goodness knows what, but the boat was fairly skimming along, water spraying up from the wake she was leaving. Harriet had never realized a ship could feel so fast—almost like a horse at a canter. From on land they appeared to crawl like snails.

"She is a sleek creature," Harriet said, reaching out to touch the gunwale. "Like one of those dolphins. A wild creature of the sea."

"A mermaid, maybe."

She smiled. "Indeed."

He'd closed his eyes again and now fell silent enough to be asleep, but he wasn't, because after a bit he opened both eyes again and looked up at her. "I'm glad you told me all of that. Last night."

Oh no. How could he bring it up and embarrass her so? Had he no sense of decorum? She bit her lip.

He reached out a hand and caught hers before she had time to snatch it out of the way. "I'm glad you trusted me enough to tell me."

Oh. She stayed silent, longing to pull away but knowing that if she did he'd just hang on all the tighter. He was that kind of a man.

"Have you never told anyone else?"

What? Who did he imagine she could ever have told about this? She shook her head, keeping it turned away from him and staring out over the gunwales. His hand was warm and a little rough on hers. The hand of a man who worked with ropes and sails alongside his men.

"You were very brave to tell me."

Would he not take the hint from her reaction and let the subject drop? Had he no sense of propriety? "It was the wine talking." Her answer came out in a tight mutter.

"There's truth to be had in the bottom of a bottle."

He was right about that, but that didn't excuse her for having imbibed too much. She'd shown herself up and now he was refusing to let her forget it. "I didn't realize I'd drunk so much."

"You didn't. You're just not used to it, I'd say. We only had the two bottles between us, and I drank the lion's share."

She gave a little shrug, part turning so she could see him better and peeking out of the corner of her eyes. "Nevertheless, I should have known better."

He didn't appear at all bothered. In fact, he smiled. "You did nothing to show yourself up, if that's what you're worrying about. You never could, in my eyes."

What? Her eyes widened at his words. What did he mean? His words held deep sincerity, she was certain.

He rolled onto his side without relinquishing his hold on her hand. "Harriet Penhallow, I believe I am growing fond of you." His golden eyes fixed on hers, trapping them in his gaze, so firmly she couldn't drag them away.

She stared, unsure how to reply to this. The deeper she looked into them, the less she could read in his expression. She floundered, her cheeks heating. Only once in her life had a man ever declared himself like this to her, and that had been Ben. And his proposal had been so overbearing. She hadn't thought it at the time, but now she knew it had been. He'd told her they would marry, that they would live at first in London, near to his aunt, from whom he hoped to one day inherit, and then, when he had amassed some money, they would move to Bath. She'd had no opportunity to refuse him. He'd spoken with her father already and her answer, had it been required, had been a foregone conclusion. And anyway, she'd fancied herself in love with the handsome officer.

What should she say? Something that wasn't trite and missish. Not that she'd ever been missish. What had Bertha once said to her? If in doubt, be honest. Was honesty the best bet here? She swallowed. "I own I am growing to like you a little too."

Those golden eyes flashed for a moment with something like triumph, but he had them guarded in an instant. "Something I am happy to hear." He smiled, relaxed once more. "I had feared initially that you held me in dislike and scorn. For my trade and for my manners in kidnapping you like this and taking you to France."

"It was hardly kidnapping."

He chuckled. "But I thought you assumed it was." He pushed himself into a seated position, a little closer than he had been when prone, still with her hand captured in his own. And now, of a sudden, she no longer wished to snatch it back. Her heart, which had been gradually speeding up, began to pound. This was so silly. She wasn't a green girl like Lyddie. She was a woman grown, married, widowed and mother to two children. She was not the sort of woman a gentleman of means, by-blow or not, would even consider. And yet here he was, staring at her out of his mesmerizing golden eyes as though she was something he greatly desired.

Another thought rose to the forefront. "I am not a woman to be trifled with," she managed, a little stiffly. "I am no man's mistress, and do not intend to be." There, she'd said it, even though it had made her cheeks flame.

"And nor do I want you to be."

"Oh." What else was there to say? Conscious that her mouth was hanging open, she closed it with a snap. What did he mean by that?

He took a deep breath. "Harriet." He closed his other hand around the first, her own hand trapped between the two, his thumbs gently massaging her skin, something that sent undeniable shivers coursing through her body.

"Yes?" She found she was breathless, her heart increasing its rate even more.

"Might I kiss you?"

The sails flapped overhead in the wind, a gull called and the wind whipped across the deck. Harriet stared at him in a state of absolute wonder. Ben had *never* asked for permission to kiss her. He'd just taken what he wanted when he wanted it with no thought to whether she shared his desires at that moment in time. But that was what men did, wasn't it? And in return for the safety of a home, a woman complied. That was what her mother had told her before she died, advice she'd not been able to repeat on the morning of her wedding but which had hung over the ceremony and what had come after. "There'll be things to put up with that you won't like, Harriet. But grin and bear them, because they won't last long, and in return a man will give you a home and children and keep you safe." Not all of which had come true. Hardly any of it, in fact.

She stared at Jack's slightly parted lips. Oh, she wanted him to kiss her, but that would mean she was doing just what Ben had always accused her of doing. If only she could take a swig of wine, or better still, strong spirit, right now for confidence. If only she could find it in her to say yes and let him fold her into his arms against that strong chest like he'd done last night. Only then might she feel safe. But she had to make a decision, because he was waiting for her.

"Yes." It came out as a strangled whisper, startling herself with her own boldness.

He shifted closer, but he didn't attempt to hold her. Instead, he leaned in, his face drawing closer.

She glimpsed his dark lashes, the stubble on his chin, a look in his eyes she didn't recognize, before she closed her eyes, feeling like a girl about to experience her first kiss. Which, in a way, she was. Ben's attentions had not often been so personal as to begin with kissing.

His lips brushed hers, soft, gentle, undemanding. Warm.

A little shiver of excitement ran through her. For just a fraction of a second, she was able to enjoy the sensation, and then, from nowhere, the specter of Ben's last visit home before embarking for the continent, Waterloo and his death, leapt into her head. The embraces he'd forced upon her, taken by right because, as he so liked to inform her, she was his chattel and nothing more and he could do with her what he willed. The embraces she'd had to steel herself to bear in silence, lest her cries woke the children or servants.

Suddenly, those weren't Jack's lips on hers. She jerked back from his kiss, her heart hammering with fear this time.

"What is it? What's wrong?" His golden eyes showed only confusion.

"I'm sorry," she gabbled. "I shouldn't have let you do that. It's all my fault. I-I—" Her words trailed away and she felt a sob rising in her throat. She'd spoiled the moment. Ben had reared his ugly head and driven a wedge between them before anything had even begun. He always would. She could never escape him.

She was saved from further explanation by an excited shout. "Ship to starboard side, Cap'n." Young Clemo, who'd rather daringly climbed onto the gunwales, stood pointing out to sea, one hand on the ropes that held the mast up, his bare, almost prehensile feet gripping the wooden railing.

The aborted kiss forgotten, Jack leapt to his feet, pulling a short telescope out of an inside pocket in his waistcoat. "Where?"

"There, Cap'n. East-nor'east."

Her dilemma also forgotten, Harriet scrambled up and stared in the same direction as everyone else. Sure enough, there, on the hazy, early-evening horizon, was the distinct shape of a ship with many sails up.

From down below came the sound of running feet, and in a moment the rest of the crew were on deck, rubbing sleep from their eyes. One of them took the tiller from Will, who then joined Jack.

Jack passed him the telescope. "That's a revenue sloop if ever I saw one."

A revenue sloop? Wasn't that like seaborne Bow Street runners? Heading their way? Wasn't Fitz Carlyon in charge of them? And *The Fly* had a hold full of contraband.

Will peered through the telescope. "Aye, it is that. I'd say it's *The Dolphin*, out of St Ives, by the cut of her."

"*The Dolphin?*" Harriet echoed. A nice name but for a ship with something not so nice on the minds of its captain and crew.

Will passed her the telescope. "She's a seventy-five-foot sloop with fourteen guns on her, heading our way. Here. Take a look."

She'd never used a telescope before but set it to her eye and peered through it. A moment or so later she found the ship, a little blurry in the gathering dusk and difficult to keep in focus as their own vessel bobbed up and down. How they could tell her name and intent from such a distance and in such poor light escaped her.

Theo appeared at her side, quivering with excitement. "Can I look?"

She handed him the telescope.

"With those fourteen guns, she's bloody dangerous," Will said. "We'd best hoist the spare sails and hope she don't reach us before full darkness falls. We've a head start and a good chance of outrunning her if we're lucky. It's the only chance we've got."

Harriet's heart did a little leap of fear. No, a large one. The authorities were on their tail.

"Sit here on the hatch and keep out of everyone's way," Jack said to Harriet. "We need the spare sails now. Theo, sit with your mother and make sure she stays there."

Harriet did as she was told. Sixteen years of marriage to a bully had inculcated obedience into her and it came in useful now. She put an arm around Theo's shoulders and pulled him as close as she could. "You stay with me, you hear? I don't want you getting in anyone's way. We have to do as we're told by the captain."

He nodded, somewhat overawed by the whole incident and forgetting that it was he who'd been asked to look after her and not the other way around.

The crew hauled up the extra sails with amazing speed and dexterity and the little ship cut through the darkening water, heading like an arrow towards the Cornish coast, as yet not visible on the horizon.

To their right, which Harriet had worked out by now must be the starboard side, the revenue sloop inched closer, growing steadily larger but no clearer as the gloom of evening drew in. That Jack and Will wanted to use nightfall to hide themselves from her was obvious, but did they have enough time to get far enough away?

She glanced about *The Fly's* open deck in anxiety. Only the hold and cabin offered any sort of hiding place and those would be searched by the revenue men if they caught up with the ship. Nowhere for even Theo to hide. If the sloop's crew boarded them, they'd assume she and Theo were smugglers too, and she'd be slapped in jail, or worse, transported to Botany Bay, or worst of all, hung in Truro and left in an iron cage to rot and put off other would-be smugglers. And Theo would be treated the same way. Age was no barrier to punishment

The newly raised sails filled with wind and the little ship strained on as the sun sank towards the western horizon, blazing a golden path across the top of the waves and no doubt silhouetting them as a target for their pursuers. Harriet hadn't prayed since before she was married, but she did now, muttering under her breath and holding Theo fast against her. He must have picked up on the urgency of the situation, because he didn't wriggle.

At last, the sun sank out of sight, just the few clouds above where it had vanished tinged still with pink, suggestive of a fine day to come. When she looked to starboard, their pursuer was all but invisible, just a dark blob on the sea, much closer than it had been and sporting a light fore and aft. Needless to say, neither Jack nor Will had ordered the lighting of any lamps on board *The Fly*.

Chapter Twenty-Seven

THE BOOM OF the gun, when it came, reverberated across the expanse of sea between *The Dolphin* and her prey. Water sprayed up about a hundred yards ahead of *The Fly's* bows. A warning shot only, to encourage them to heave to and allow the larger ship to come alongside them. Jack peered into the gloom, trying to make out their pursuer and only finding her by the lights she was showing. She had no reason to hide, unlike *The Fly*. But if that was all that made her visible to him, then her captain would have even more difficulty in locating *The Fly*. He'd be firing blindly in the direction he thought they lay, and he wasn't far off in his aim. In fact, he was even more dangerous if he couldn't see them than if he could.

"Prepare to come about." Jack kept his command to Daniel Bussow low. All the men were making as little noise as possible. Anything to stop the crew of *The Dolphin* divining where they lay. Not that he thought their hunter would be able to hear anything above the sound of the waves and the wind in the sails and shrouds. But caution was not to be scorned.

Jack glanced at where Harriet remained seated with Theo, holding onto him as if she thought at any moment he'd be snatched away. Good. One thing she possessed in quantity was common sense, even if she had hidden in the hold of his ship.

Coming about changed the line *The Fly* was following. Hopefully, *The Dolphin's* captain would assume they were still beating for the safety of the coast as fast as they could, where they'd be harder to spot with the cliffs behind them, even if it would be more dangerous thanks to all the hidden rocks. Perhaps, under cover of the friendly darkness, they could double back behind *The Dolphin* and lose her. Although her captain might decide to hang around nearer the coast hoping to catch them at first light. Jack would just have to make sure they were safely in harbor by then and empty of their cargo. Holing the barrels and chucking them overboard was a last resort he didn't intend to have to turn to.

A second shot fell astern of *The Fly*, a bit too close for comfort this time. They must be nearly a mile away, at the extreme range of their guns, but if they scored a hit they might sink *The Fly* without even knowing they'd done it.

Will swung down out of the rigging where he'd been trying to watch their hunter. "Shall we get the swivel guns out?"

Jack shook his head. "If it comes to an all-out battle, they vastly outgun us, and our little guns don't have the range their big ones do. We'd lose, and probably some of us would die." He looked again at Harriet and Theo. The last thing he wanted was these two becoming collateral damage.

Will nodded, his face a pale blur in the darkness. "We could put the widow and her boy below decks."

"Just as dangerous. When the master of the *Dolphin* realizes we're not stopping, he's likely to order his men to fire for the body of the ship as it's easier to hit. No, our stowaways had best stay on deck. We're not in danger of being caught yet, so they're safe enough there." He glanced around the deck. "And it's getting darker with every minute they don't catch up with us. Let's just hope the moon doesn't give us away."

Will nodded. "Which way d'you want to head?"

Jack grinned. "Towards them. But to the south. They won't expect us to do that. They'll be thinking we'll head west to run for the coast further along, to cut around the Lizard and Lands' End and get away from them. If we head east instead, and get past them in the dark, we can turn north again before they realize we've done it. In fact, I'm hoping they won't realize at all and will head for Lands' End themselves." He glanced up at their full set of sails straining in the wind, billowing out in their efforts to drive the ship forward. "We've two and a half thousand square feet of sail. We've speed and maneuverability on our side. They're bigger than us, but they don't have the minds of smugglers. We can do this."

Young Harry had been on the tiller a while, so Jack took over from him, and Will went to stand in the bows, staring towards where they both thought the sloop must be heading. Jack bit his lip. If they got it wrong… how ridiculous would it be to crash into the *Dolphin* in the dark? That would be bad luck indeed.

All the crew were now on deck, ready to adjust the sails at a moment's notice, all of them with their eyes straining into the darkness for any sign of their pursuer. Had she extinguished her lights? Jack would have done so himself had he been in her captain's place. Trying to sneak up on her prey. But her prey was wily as a fox.

"Shouldn't have a woman on board," Uncle Billy muttered under his breath, but just loud enough for Jack to catch. "She done brought bad luck on us."

Jack rounded on him. "An old wives tale. I'll have none of your superstitions on board my ship. If I hear that sort of thing again, this'll be the last time you sail with me. Now get below and fix us something to eat and drink."

Uncle Billy, scowling, shut up, but Jack could tell he hadn't stopped ruminating over the old saying.

Young Harry gave Uncle Billy a shove towards the cabin. "Give over. You're talking like an old woman. How d'you think passenger ships and packet boats manage? They take women, don't they?" He chuckled. "Show a bit of the common sense you might've been born with, can't you?"

With a grunt and a mutter about not being called old by a whippersnapper, Uncle Billy disappeared below to the cabin. It was his job to keep the crew fed and they were going to need it tonight.

Jack shook his head in bewilderment that anyone could think a woman could bring bad luck. But then again, this was the first time they'd encountered a revenue sloop on this bit of the sea…

The night wore on, only the flap of the sails above their heads breaking the comparative silence on board. Ears strained. Eyes strained. Everyone stayed quiet. Even the exuberant Theo remained silent, nestled against his mother's side.

Jack relinquished the tiller to Will and went to take his position forward. The clouds that had covered the horizon had spread across the night sky, obscuring the stars, and only now and then allowing the waning hemisphere of the moon to peek through. Which was both good and bad. Little light for their pursuer to see them by, but also little light for them to see her, or where they were headed. Would it be wise to try to get into the tiny inlet at Bessie's while as good as blind? He'd been sailing from there all his life, and knew the narrow passage as well as his own home, but if you couldn't see, you couldn't see. And he had Harriet on board… and a child.

He'd think about that when the moment came.

Instead, his thoughts wandered unbidden to that kiss and the way she'd reacted. For a moment, he'd thought she'd liked being kissed. He'd kept his hands to himself and made it gentle and undemanding, wary of frightening her off. He'd felt her mouth soften under his, her lips parting… and then… it had been as though he'd bitten her, not kissed her.

Jack was no head doctor or alienist to assess why she'd reacted like that, but he could have a good guess, and the answer he came up with didn't bear thinking about. But he had to. Whatever her husband had done to her, it had gone deeper than just bullying and a few blows. He's scarred her mentally as well as physically, and he was going to have to approach her even more gently than he'd first thought. If they survived the night without being thrown in jail… or sunk.

He grinned to himself. What was he doing, doubting his abilities like this? Of course they were going to get away from the revenue men. They always did. They were one tiny ship in a vast ocean of nothingness and for *The Dolphin* to come upon them in the dark, the luck of the sea god would have to be with her captain. And Jack was pretty sure the sea god was on his side, not theirs. He cast a glance back at Harriet and Theo, still sitting upright on the hatch cover, but now wrapped in a blanket one of the men had fetched them.

"I'M TIRED," THEO whispered.

Harriet nodded. "I am too, but I don't think it would be a good idea for me to go to sleep. Not just yet."

He stifled a yawn. "Are you frightened, Mama?"

She shook her head. "Of course not. Captain Jack will have us home and safe soon. But just in case he wants us to do anything, we have to stay awake. Well, I do. You lean your head on my shoulder and close your eyes." A lie, but she didn't want to worry him. He was too young to realize just how dangerous their situation could turn out to be.

He leaned his head on her shoulder as she suggested, and very soon slipped down until his head was in her lap, fast asleep. She tucked the blanket more closely around him. How lucky he was that he could just shut the tension of the night out and fall sleep. Probably better that he did. Sleep had never felt further away for Harriet.

Jack was standing in the bows still, staring out into the darkness, every inch of him alert. As the moon peeped out from behind a cloud, the pale oval of his face glimmered a little, a worried frown marring his brow. How often did a revenue ship come after them? She had no way of knowing and wasn't about to disturb his vigil. She stiffened her back and remained silent.

They'd sailed on in this new direction for some time before Jack and Will ordered another direction change, with the sails swinging above her head into their new position. By now, Harriet was growing more accustomed to the commands in use on board ship. "Prepare to come about. Keep your head down, Mrs. Penhallow. Spars comin' over."

With alacrity, the men swung the spars over and, in what felt like only a short minute, *The Fly* was headed in a different direction yet again. Perhaps they thought they'd gone far enough out of the way to avoid the revenue sloop. She hoped so. But as all around them the darkness of the night pressed in like a heavy, suffocating cloak, how would they know they'd escaped her? The waves reflected the dim glimmer of the occasional stars, and the moon when it peeked out from behind the clouds, but other than that, no light prevailed. Even the lights on the other ship had vanished, so perhaps her sailors had wisely put them out. Or perhaps they were already miles apart.

Tiredness ate into her limbs, and Theo weighed heavy on her lap, making it impossible to shift her position. Her back ached, but there was nothing she could do about it. She pulled the slipping blanket closer around Theo and it slid off her shoulders, bringing a chill with its loss. If only she could put on her woolen dressing gown.

Time dragged by, the rushing of the waves against the hull, the flap of the sails, and the quiet instructions from either Will or Jack the only sounds she could hear. Fear ate at her insides. Fear that they'd be caught, even though, surely, finding them out here on the wide expanse of the sea must be like looking for the proverbial needle in the haystack. Fear also that if they were caught, no one would believe her story. And fear that if they were caught, Jack might be the recipient of rough justice.

The fact that up until tonight she would probably have heartily agreed with the dispensing of justice to smugglers brought a smile to her lips for a moment, to be quickly dashed away when she remembered the danger they were all in. Now she was one of them. She and Theo were part of the crew.

She almost jumped out of her skin as someone draped a coat over her shoulders.

Jack stepped back. "I'm sorry I startled you. I saw you'd lost the blanket."

She had herself back under control in an instant. "Thank you. Yes, I have been feeling the cold a little. The breeze is fresh." His warm familiar scent clung to the coat, as though he'd just taken it off, reminding her of when he'd taken her in his arms only last night. How long ago that seemed. What she wouldn't give to be safe in that bed at Mrs. S's inn with Theo asleep beside her. She looked up at Jack.

He stood in front of her with his feet planted wide, the better to balance himself on the rolling deck. "You should have called to me. I'd have made sure to find you something to warm you."

She shook her head, breathing in the coat's distinctive scent. "It's nothing. But one thing I would like is to move a little. I've grown quite stiff with Theo in my lap."

"Easily remedied." He called softly to the boy, Clemo, to fetch some more blankets. These he laid on the deck. "Now, give Theo to me." As though Theo were feather-light, he extricated him from her arms, scooped him up and laid him on top of the blankets, then tucked another around him. "There. Now let me tuck this one in around you." He sat down beside her. At their feet, Theo didn't stir on his blanket bed.

"No one ever done that fer me," Clemo whispered, but he didn't sound as if he minded all that much, and departed into the cabin perhaps for a sleep himself.

"Have you lost our pursuers?" Harriet asked.

Jack shrugged. "That's the plan. The English Channel is a big place and the night's pretty dark. We've diverted a good few miles east of where we saw them, but now we're heading north for the coast, and we'll skirt it with caution heading back for home." He tapped his foot on the deck. "And as for the cargo we're carrying, I've decided it's a bit risky to try to get it ashore at

Bessie's. We'll unload it at another little landing site we some-times use, around Helston way. Porthkeverne. It's mainly used by fishermen, but they'll be ready and willing to unload an unexpected cargo and take the money for their help."

"Will you put Theo and me ashore there as well?"

"Do you want to go ashore? It's a long way back to Bessie's. And even if we run into *The Dolphin*, there'll be nothing on board to incriminate us." He laughed. "In fact, I'd like it very much if we do meet them. I'll be happy to stop and let them search my ship. It'd be worth it to see the looks on their faces."

"We'll stay, then, and you can deliver us home."

He nodded. "If I fetch you some blankets, do you think you can take a nap?"

"No. I'd rather stay awake."

"Suit yourself. I'm going below to get some food. Shall I fetch some for you?"

She nodded and he departed, leaving her sitting wrapped in his coat, but at least now able to stretch her legs and shift her position. Theo slept on, like the proverbial baby.

She glanced towards the entrance to the cabin, waiting for Jack to return. His manner now had changed entirely. No suggestion of him stealing another kiss. A little part of her was disappointed. If only she didn't have Ben's shade forever on her shoulder, but he was something she'd never get away from. He'd always be there, whatever she did to escape him. Like Banquo's ghost at the feast.

THEY MADE IT into Porthkeverne Cove just as the sky was beginning to lighten in the east. Jack, on Harriet's insistence, had carried Theo down into the cabin and stowed him in one of the hammocks, where he continued to sleep undisturbed, and Jack was rather wishing she'd join her son and stay out of the way.

The less she knew, the better. It went against the grain to have anyone know where his hidden drop-offs were located. Who knew what pressures someone like Fitz Carlyon could bring to bear on a witness to make them talk?

The tide was mostly out and the stony beach strewn with small fishing boats pulled out above high tide level. Several rowing boats took to the water and, as Jack's crew dropped anchor, they bumped up against the side of *The Fly*. Just the reception Jack had anticipated.

"Why, Cap'n Jack and Cap'n Will. What brings you up here this mornin'?" the grizzled oarsman in the first rowing boat called up, hanging onto a rope on the side of *The Fly* to steady his little boat. "Got somethin' for us, have ye?"

"Morning to you, Robbo. The St Ives preventitives're what brings us here," Jack called down. "We've been dodging them all night. We need to use your smoking sheds again."

"Best get the goods unloaded quick then, afore they come sneakin' along the coast after ye." The old man said. "Long Pete's gone off to get some help. We thought as you'd be in need of it as you was puttin' in here so early in the mornin'."

Will leaned over the gunnels beside Jack. "Thought you might guess that."

Harriet appeared on his other side, and Old Robbo's eyes widened. "You shippin' petticoats now, Cap'n?"

Jack laughed. "There's a long story to that which I won't bore you with now. We'd best get a move on."

Unloading in a hurry was the forté of not just his crew but also the fishermen. More small rowing boats arrived, and Harriet was moved out of the way up into the bows again while the crew, helped by a number of the hoary old fishermen, hauled the barrels of brandy up on deck and lowered them into their new transport. In a very short time everything was unloaded and being carried up the beach to the smoke house in a couple of two wheeled carts drawn by sturdy cobs. Jack had used this drop-off on several other such occasions, and his cargo would be safe here.

Best not to have all your bottles of brandy in one barrel, so to speak. He had several other such emergency drop-off sites all along Cornwall's southwestern coastline, and men eager to do his bidding and take a small cut in the profits for their trouble.

There was to be no waiting around to talk though, with the tide still falling. With the anchor hauled up and the sails unfurled, Jack turned *The Fly* westwards towards home.

Chapter Twenty-Eight

SHOUTS WOKE HARRIET. She'd gone below on Jack's suggestion and worked out, after one or two abortive attempts, how to get into a hammock. It had turned out to be the most comfortable bed she'd ever slept in, and after a night of tension and more than twenty-four hours without sleep, she'd nodded off within minutes.

With reluctance, she struggled up out of the depths of sleep to a cacophony of even more shouting, although it didn't sound as though it was coming from directly above her head, but rather, from somewhere not on board at all.

Getting out of the hammock proved just as difficult as getting into it had been, and it was a few moments before she had her feet on the wooden floor. She must look a sight. Having decided that putting on her nightgown in the morning, even if it was for a sleep, wasn't such a good idea, she'd gone to bed in all of her borrowed clothes minus her shoes. A hand to her head told her how her once neatly coiffured hair had suffered, and she felt in general rather crumpled.

The hatch was slightly ajar, to allow fresh air to circulate, and through it she now heard a loud voice shout. "Heave to and prepare to be boarded."

Whatever was going on? Should she show herself or stay hidden?

Theo. A quick glance told her he no longer occupied any of the other hammocks. Of course, he'd slept for a lot of their crossing and was probably now on deck with the crew. That answered her question. If her child was up there, then so should she be. She slid the hatch back enough to squeeze through it, and, hitching up her skirts while thinking that her previous boys' clothes would have been easier for shipboard living, climbed the narrow ladder.

The day was cloudy with a chill breeze blowing, but that wasn't what drew her attention. Towering over *The Fly*, or so it seemed, was a second ship, much bigger than she was and with grappling hooks holding the two ships close together. A man in the uniform of an officer stood with his back to her, facing Jack and Will. With a stab of shock, she saw he held a pistol in his hand, and it was pointed directly at Jack's chest. Where was Theo? She didn't move, but her eyes frantically searched for her son's face amongst the far too many men now on deck. Sailors in blue jackets and cream trousers, all carrying pistols, Jack's crew, and there, close beside young Clemo, she spied Theo's pale face.

"Thought we wouldn't catch you, did you?" the officer drawled, satisfaction in his every word. Wait. She knew that voice. That lazy intonation. Fitz Carlyon.

"Fitz?" His name was out of her mouth before she had a chance to prevent it.

He swung round, the pistol wavering. "Harriet?"

Never had she seen anyone so surprised. His mouth fell open and the tip of the pistol swayed about dangerously. Will's anxious gaze followed its movement, but Jack had eyes only for her.

Bravery rose into her heart, helped by the confidence that the entire cargo was safely elsewhere. She spoke up loud and clear, emboldened by her adventures as well as her secret knowledge that they'd find nothing aboard *The Fly*. "Why on *earth* do you have a pistol in your hand? And why are you pointing it at Captain Trevelyan?"

Jack's eyes met hers, twinkling with amusement and understanding. Will appeared to be just as confident, apart from his anxiety about the wavering pistol. Both of them stood with their feet braced apart, hands held a little out from their sides. Probably they didn't want to be seen as making any aggressive movements while being held at gunpoint by one of His Majesty's official preventative men.

"What are you doing here?" Fitz spluttered, once he'd overcome his shock. The pistol lowered until it was pointing at the deck.

Harriet bestowed her sweetest smile on him. "Why, Captain Trevelyan kindly offered to take Theo for a trip on his ship, and as Theo is only twelve, I thought it best to accompany him." How glad she was now not to be clad in boy's clothes still, despite how easy they'd make climbing steep ladders. Sleep crumpled she might be, but at least she had a gown on.

Fitz spun around to face Jack, whose smile had taken on a degree of well-deserved smugness. "Is this true?" He almost spat the words out.

"What? Did you think I might have kidnapped her?" Jack asked, his tone mocking. Harriet bit her lip to control the chuckle that wanted to escape. How close to the truth Jack liked to skate.

"I'll ask again," she said, enunciating her words with precision. "Why were you pointing a pistol at my escort? And why have you brought what looks to me like a squadron of armed men on board?"

Fitz raised the pistol toward Jack again, as if deciding this must all be a ruse. "I'm afraid I have to inform you, Mrs. Penhallow, that I'm empowered by His Majesty's Government to stop and search all vessels suspected of smuggling."

The fact that he hadn't called her by her Christian name hadn't escaped Harriet. She controlled that urge to laugh again, with difficulty. Jack appeared to be doing the same. Oh, how truly wicked this was. But she could quite understand why Jack had wanted them to catch up with him this morning. Or was it already afternoon?

"And you think *we* are smuggling?" Jack asked, his own voice a studied drawl. "Well, we are not. And you're welcome to search my ship from bilges to crows' nest. You won't find anything illegal on board her, I can assure you."

If only he'd stop looking so smug. Yes, he knew he'd outwitted Fitz and the preventative men, but he had no need to look as though he had and was well aware of it. She, at least, had managed to hide her own feelings. Feelings she wasn't sure she should be having. Shouldn't a respectable widow be on the side of the government? Not, it seemed, a Cornish one, at any rate.

Fitz emitted a growl of pure fury, and turned to the armed sailors who were standing guard over the rest of the crew, Theo included. "Seeing as Captain Trevelyan has so kindly invited us, we'll accept his invitation, which I'm sure he won't be happy about." He shot Jack a piercing glare. "Search every corner of this ship. Leave nothing unturned. Poke into every crevasse." His gaze returned to Jack's amused face. "If there's so much as a flake of tobacco or a bottle of brandy on board, we'll find it, mark my words." His lip curled. "Else why would you have run from us last night when we fired across your bow and stern? Only the guilty run from the preventatives."

Jack laughed out loud. "That was you firing on us? We took you for privateers after our ship. These waterways are still not safe, even though the war with France is supposed to be over."

Fitz spluttered with fury, his face reddening. "A likely story."

Harriet stepped up beside him and placed a gentle hand on his arm. "Captain Carlyon. Fitz. It's obvious no one on board this ship is resisting you, still less Jack or Will. And your pistol, and those of your men, are making me quite nervous. None of us are armed. Please put it away. Have a thought for Theo, who is quite overcome by your attack on us."

To be honest, Theo didn't look in the least bit overcome but, instead, brimming with excitement.

Fitz lowered the pistol and stowed it away, albeit with some reluctance. Maybe he thought Jack and his seven-man crew, nine if she counted herself and Theo, two of whom were mere boys, might suddenly all leap into the attack and overthrow his much bigger ship.

Fitz's men disappeared down into the hold and the cabin, making Harriet glad she hadn't slept through the shouting. Being awoken by several large, armed strangers arriving in the cramped space of the cabin would have been something of a shock.

Jack gestured at the gunwales. "Do you mind if we sit while we await your men's findings?"

Fitz glared at him. "Please yourself." He must realize that neither Jack nor Will would be so offhand if anything remained on board to incriminate them, and that Jack's claim they'd thought his ship a privateer was a barefaced lie.

With studied nonchalance, Jack leaned against the gunwales as *The Fly* rose and fell gently in the swell, her fenders rubbing against the hull of *The Dolphin*. On an impulse of solidarity, Harriet sat beside him, both hands hanging onto the ropes, just in case. She wasn't nearly as confident at sitting with her back to the sea as she wanted Fitz to think.

From the far side of the deck, Theo's eyes met hers, and the scamp grinned at her. He must know full well that what they'd been doing was illegal and was enjoying every minute of this delay.

A lot of banging ensued from down in the empty hold as the men fulfilled their duties and poked into every hole they could find. But the tobacco had been well-wrapped, and the brandy had been in barrels, so there could be nothing to find. Eventually, looking disgruntled, the men reappeared on deck. "Nothing, Captain."

Fitz shot another glare at Jack. "Don't for one moment assume that I've been fooled by your little charade, Captain Trevelyan." He nodded to the men who started to climb back on board their own ship. "And don't think that I won't be stopping you again if I come across you and your ship out at sea. I'm going to catch you red-handed in the end, mark my words."

Jack grinned at him. "The day you catch me red-handed doing anything will be a long time coming."

Dislike crackled between the two men, but Fitz was the one who had to give way. On this occasion. He pivoted on his heel, grabbed a rope and swung himself aboard his own ship, followed by the last of his men. The crew of *The Fly* hastened to unhook the grappling irons and the two ships drifted apart at speed.

"Hoist the sails," Jack called to his men. "Let's get Mrs. Penhallow back home again, shall we?"

Harriet stared at the rapidly diminishing deck of *The Dolphin*, where Fitz was standing staring at them as his own men readied their ship for departure. There went a man scorned and humiliated, something she doubted he would want to put up with.

IT MUST HAVE been the middle of the afternoon when *The Fly* finally tucked herself in to the narrow inlet in Bessie's Cove. The journey back had been uneventful, after the amusing hold up with the preventative men, but long, as the previously fresh wind had diminished and they'd had to raise more sails to catch it. Tired after no sleep in nearly thirty-six hours, and ready for his bed, Jack watched the men tie her up to the metal mooring rings in their little rocky channel. The crew would have time to get over to the kiddley for an hour or two before taking her round into Penzance to do some much needed honest carrying. With Fitz sniffing after them, and having brought the revenue sloop all the way round from St Ives to do so, they'd have to lie low for a while.

Not that Jack minded. He had other things on his mind, and one of them was Mrs. Harriet Penhallow and the interrupted kiss they'd shared.

With her and Theo's clean clothes wrapped in a bundle and tucked under her arm, she was now preparing to disembark.

"Couldn't I stay on board and go round to Penzance with you?" Theo asked, his face bright with hope. "I've quite got my sealegs now so I won't be sick again, I promise. You need another cabin boy. I could help Clemo lots."

Clemo, engaged in sweeping down the decks, glanced up. "I c'n learn'im how to be a cabin boy."

Jack chuckled. Probably Clemo thought that if he managed to gain an apprentice of his own, his role would be improved. He'd no longer be the ship's dogsbody.

Harriet shook her head. "Thank you, Clemo, but no. Theo has his lessons to do and isn't old enough."

"I'm nearly as big as Clemo," Theo, ever hopeful, tried.

"But not so old," Harriet retorted. "And what I say goes. There's to be no more sneaking out in the middle of the night."

Jack caught hold of the mooring rope and pulled the ship in closer to the ladder. "Do you need a hand?"

Harriet shook her head. "Now I'm an experienced smuggler, I feel I should be able to disembark by myself." And with that, she hitched up her skirts and climbed the ladder with aplomb. Theo swarmed up it after her.

Jack followed. "Let me carry your bundle, at least."

She eyed him with a slight renewal of wariness. "Very well."

He took the bundle from her as Theo raced up the track ahead of them and disappeared around the bend. At least if he reached home before her, Bertha and Lyddie would have advance warning of her arrival and not be quite so shocked. Guilt swept over her once again that she'd given them so little thought while she'd been away.

Jack smiled. "You look none the worse for your adventures."

They started up the path. "And what adventures they were. I feel I might keep them to myself though. And don't worry, I've already instilled into Theo that we have merely been out for a sail in your ship. He won't be telling Bertha and Lydia anything of what has occurred. He's quite pleased to be a keeper of secrets. I can only hope Captain Carlyon doesn't raise the subject in front of them."

"You think he'll call upon you again?"

She chuckled, the first time he'd heard her do so. "I imagine not. He probably thinks me a willing party to your smuggling. Although, I dare say he might return expressly to question me on what I know. There is that." She paused. "But I shall reveal nothing, have no fear." Her hazel eyes twinkled with amusement.

They reached the junction of the paths by Tummels' house. He was sitting on the bench outside it with a pewter tankard in his hand and a greasy, well-worn hat jammed onto his head. "Mornin, Cap'n." He glanced at Harriet. "If'n you're lookin' for your boy, he's gone runnin' home. And as for you," he nodded at Jack. "Your ma's bin searchin' for you high and low. Somethin's afoot over at the Castle, but her man dint say as what it were. He come here an' asked me but I dint tell him nothin'."

Jack shrugged. "If it's that important, I'll find out soon enough." Probably something to do with his father's other family. One of the girls. His sisters. He'd think about that later. Right now, he was far more interested in the woman beside him. On an impulse, he reached out and caught Harriet's hand. "Come along. I'll escort you home and help you face the music."

For a moment, he felt her stiffen as if to pull away, then she relaxed and fell in beside him, her hand warm and pliant in his. Just a short walk would take them to Keynvor Cottage, and he was just beginning to wonder if he dared renew his request to kiss Harriet, when Bertha and Lydia came racing up the path to meet them. Thwarted.

Harriet wrenched her hand free of his and stepped away from him, leaving his hand cold and empty, as well as his heart. A missed opportunity.

Lydia flew into her mother's arms. "Mama! Theo said you were back. Where have you been?" She shot a furious, accusatory glare at Jack. "Theo said you'd gone out sailing with Captain Trevelyan, but you must have left in the middle of the night! And you went without telling us. And Bertha said you'd gone in your *nightgown."*

"Miss Harriet, thank God you're safe." Bertha fixed as forbidding a glare on Jack as he'd ever seen, no doubt condemning him as someone who took ladies out in his ship in their night attire. Oops, he'd gone right down in her estimation at one fell stroke. But etiquette forbade her from berating him with more than that death stare. It was going to take a while to win her over again. Did he care? The person whose approval he craved the most was her young mistress.

He stepped back from the family group. "I'll leave you to it." Best to beat a hasty retreat before Bertha decided to search for a weapon. There were a number or rocks within easy reach. He touched his forehead in a small salute, and executed a deep bow to the thunderous Bertha.

Leaving them to their tearful reunion, he turned up the track for Rosudgeon, striding out in his haste to be back. Whatever news his mother had, he supposed it might have been more important than what dress to wear for the Assembly Rooms for her to have sent the servants searching for him. Well… possibly, but he never knew with her. Fifteen minutes later, his feet crunched the gravel as he approached the house.

The front door flew open as he stepped into the porch, and his mother catapulted into his arms, grasping at him much as Lydia had grasped at Harriet. "Jack! You're back! Thank goodness!" And she burst into floods of tears.

Odd behavior from her, as she was more than used to his prolonged absences.

He struggled to extricate himself but she hung on like an octopus. "Whatever's wrong, Mother?"

She gazed up at him out of eyes swollen with grief. "It's your father. He's suffered an apoplexy and Dr. Rescorla has pronounced him near to death."

Chapter Twenty-Nine

JACK STARED AT his mother's tragic face, a turmoil of emotions tumbling through his head. What was he supposed to feel? Sadness, shock, anger? Images of the times his father had condescended to spend with him flashed through his mind along with the emotions. An hour here, half a day there, a few minutes before bedtime, a glimpse from the nursery window. Had his father been any better a parent than Harriet's bullying husband? Probably not.

"When?"

His mother sagged against him, pressing her wet cheek to his coat. "Yesterday. I only found out because Mrs. Pike's nephew works there. He told his mother, Mrs. Pike's sister-in-law, and she sent her daughter over with a message for us." All the servants knew their secrets, of course, in both houses.

"Does he still live?"

She shrugged her slender shoulders. "I've had no news since, and I dare not enquire myself. Any servant I sent would be turned away and I refuse to give that woman the pleasure of so doing."

He held her away from himself. "Pull yourself together, Mother. He's not worthy of your grief."

She flashed angry eyes at him. "Oh but he is, he is. He was my one true love, Jack, and he gave me you. He still is my one true love. And he's your father, never forget."

"Inside," Jack said, ignoring this outburst. "Into the parlor and tell me what Mrs. Pike's relations told you, most of which will be servants' gossip, no doubt, and without foundation."

She let him guide her to the parlor, and he closed the door behind him then ushered her to her chaise long. A firm hand on her shoulder, he sat her down then took his place beside her. "Now. Tell me everything you know."

She seized both his hands in hers, the tears still falling down her cheeks and dripping onto the lace fichu she wore about her shoulders. "Mrs. Pike's family can't read or write, so the message was a little garbled. Young Bennath Carthew brought it yesterday evening. She's just a slip of a girl, but a fast runner. She said her brother, William, a gardener at the castle, told them there'd been an argument between your father and Lady Trengrouse on the terrace, and your father had fallen to the ground, his face purple, gasping for breath. Bennath said her brother saw it all happening, as Lady Trengrouse shouted for his help." She paused. "Bennath seemed inclined to think Lady Trengrouse had struck your father, but apparently her brother assured their mother it was an apoplexy. He heard the doctor say so."

An image of his father the last time he'd seen him, over a year ago, across the crowded Assembly rooms in Truro, leapt into Jack's mind. Many said that Jack resembled him as a young man, but that had been a long time ago and time had not been kind to Sir Austin Trengrouse. Now in his fifties, good living and lack of exercise had crept up on him, making him corpulent and slow, and his once abundant dark hair had turned to gray and thinned. Drink had left its mark across his face in a myriad of small broken blood vessels. He had not looked a well man.

That out-of-character visit to the Assembly Rooms at the persuasion of his mother had also presented Jack with one of his few opportunities to observe his half-sisters. He knew of them, of course, but that night had been the closest he'd ever got to them. The oldest, Horatia, a girl who closely resembled the harridan who'd driven Jack from her home when he was a boy, and who was married to a banker from Truro, had been there with her husband. The second, Honoria, who also resembled her mother, had been about to announce her engagement to a minor aristocrat from Devon. Only the youngest, Lavinia, had looked anything like Jack and their father. Rather a pretty girl but with a discontented expression on her face as though outings to the Assembly Rooms were beneath her. Needless to say, Jack had not had the opportunity to ask her why and had deliberately kept away from that particular part of the Assembly Rooms for the remainder of the evening.

His mother, however, had seen him staring at the little family group. "Lady Trengrouse grows no more attractive with age," she murmured behind her fan. "I swear she more and more resembles the pig Mrs. Pike is fattening with the kitchen scraps."

Which had made Jack laugh, and softened the blow of seeing his father out en famille with the girls who had taken his place.

He gathered his thoughts on the present predicament. "They will have sent for the best of doctors, I'm sure. And servants always exaggerate."

His mother shook her head, fresh tears falling. "I fear not, on this occasion. Bennath was quite sure her brother had heard the doctor say it was 'a matter of time' and 'nothing can be done.' She had the words off pat. They're not words a child of twelve makes up, at least, not a blacksmith's daughter with no education."

"Perhaps you're right. Perhaps my father is truly dying. If so, what do you expect me to do?"

She tightened her clutch on his hand, her eyes beseeching. "Jack, my darling. Remember how he used to bounce you on his knee and brought you Scout for your birthday the year you were five. You loved that dog. He went everywhere with you. It wasn't your father's fault we couldn't live together..." Her voice trailed off as her brow furrowed. What was she thinking? "It was his father's iron rule."

Jack frowned back at her. "He brought me Scout because his wife had just presented him with a child. My sister Horatia. His legitimate child. It was to make up for that. To assuage his conscience."

"But it showed how much he loved you."

Jack shook his head. "No. If he loved me, he would have married you and made me his legitimate son. He would have stood up to his father and refused to marry where he was told. He was a coward."

Fresh tears sprang into his mother's eyes. "He was just a boy, Jack. You know he was. Far younger than you are now. I've told you often enough. He loved me dearly but I wasn't his social equal. My father was a tenant farmer... Austin's father was a baronet. There could never have been any match for us. Not in the eyes of society."

"No, mother, you delude yourself. You only have to look at your friend, Lady Ormonde. She came from a family of smugglers, no less, and yet Thomas Carlyon didn't make her his mistress—he married her."

"That was different. Thomas was not the heir then. His father and his older brother still lived. He could marry where he wished."

The impulse to give her a sound shaking had to be controlled. "Nonsense. His older brother had already been consigned to the colonies, doing God knows what and most unlikely ever to produce an heir of his own, from what I've heard. The old viscount knew Thomas and his children would inherit. Thomas just had more backbone than my father ever did. He married the girl he loved and be damned."

Her voice dropped. "Do you want so much to be his heir?"

Did he? He shook his head. "I have never wanted to be his heir, Mother. All I've ever wanted is to be recognized as his son."

She seized on that. "Oh, but he did recognize you. Why do you think he visited us so often and settled Rosudgeon on you? Because he still loved us both." She paused. "Better by far than that woman who looks like a pig. And she's only ever given him daughters. I gave him the son he wanted."

"He visited you so often because it suited him to have a mistress on his doorstep. It saved him having to ride to Penzance and find one."

She pulled her hand free and slapped him hard. "Don't speak of him that way. I was never just his mistress. I was—" She stopped abruptly.

"You were what?"

"Nothing. I misspoke."

Jack eyed her with suspicion. That something had gone unsaid was obvious.

She gave herself a little shake. "I cannot go to Trengrouse, Jack. That pig-woman would relish having her servants throw me out of the house. But you can go. She can't throw you out. I implore you to. You have to see him before he dies."

"She'd relish throwing me out too, you know."

His mother shook her head. "No. She won't. He'd never let her."

"You're very confident of that."

She bit her lip. "I have reason to be. Your father left a letter for you. I was to give it to you in the event of his death, or his expected death if possible. He wrote it shortly after the birth of your sister Lavinia, when he said he didn't think he would ever get a son from Lady Letitia." She paused. "The pig-woman."

Jack couldn't help a smile. "Mother, you keep calling her that, and it's most unlike you to insult anyone in that way."

His mother frowned up at him, tears streaking her cheeks. "Because she is a pig woman."

"You've never called her that before."

She snorted. "I've thought it often enough. Now, wait while I fetch out your father's letter."

"You have it on you?"

She reached for her reticule. "Safe here." She loosened the cords and withdrew a folded piece of paper sealed with a blob of red sealing wax. "You will see I've not read it. It is addressed to you alone."

"And he wanted you to wait until now to give it to me?" Did he even want to read it? "Do you know what's in it?"

"No." She wiped her eyes on the sleeve of her dress, avoiding his eyes. Did she know more than she was letting on? "I didn't ask. He said it was for you and it would explain everything." She held out the letter. "It's for you."

Jack looked down at the spidery writing of his name on the letter and the indentation of his father's signet ring—a dolphin arching across waves. A ring he'd envied as a small boy and wished to have a similar one of his own. His father always wore it.

Did he want to hear his father's excuses for the way Jack had been brought up, nearly fatherless? Yes, he'd had material possessions, but he'd lived for the days of his father's visits, which had never come frequently enough. To have that tall, jovial man swing him above his head or tickle him, to play with his puppy, Scout, to set him on the pommel of his saddle and gallop with him along the beach at Morgelyn: all of these things he'd longed for with passion and hope. Only to see his father at church with his humorless wife and three little girls in the family pew, whilst he and his mother sat in the far corner out of sight and mind.

"I hope," his mother said, "that when you've read it, you will understand him better and wish to go to his bedside. I know he would want you there. And she will not be able to turn you away. I swear it."

That was what his mother thought. Jack had a different opinion.

He broke the seal and unfolded the letter. His fathers scrawl covered the sheet from top to bottom in close packed lines, a little faded with age. It must be all of nearly twenty years old.

He began to read.

My dear Jack, my beloved boy,

If you are reading this then I am either dying or already dead. I ask that if I still cling onto life then you might come to my bedside that I might bless you with my dying breath, for I have wronged you and your mother.

Jack looked up and met his mother's eyes. Did she really not know the contents of the letter? He bent his head to continue reading.

I was twenty when I met your mother, and she seventeen, the most beautiful creature I'd ever set my eyes on. You will know that she was the daughter of one of my father's better-off tenant farmers, but what you will not know is that he had ambitions for her and she was well-educated and clever as well as beautiful. How could I not have fallen in love with her? And in return, to my amazement, she fell in love with me. I felt I was the luckiest man alive.

Jack had a sudden feeling of voyeurism at reading his father's inner thoughts about his mother. He hesitated, glancing up again at her, but she gave him a nod and he lowered his gaze and continued to read.

I told my father, your grandfather, Sir Montague Trengrouse, that I wished to marry your mother. He was so furious he forbade me to ever see her again. I was beside myself, but he sent me off to London to work in the import business he was a partner in, and refused to allow me back into Cornwall for a whole year. Your mother and I swore to remain true to one another while I was gone. Meanwhile, unbeknownst to me, my father evicted your mother's family from the farm they'd tenanted for centuries, as far back as our family had held Trengrouse. In London, I knew nothing of their fate.

This was information Jack had never heard before. His mother must have known it, but kept it from him. It had never occurred to him to enquire about her family, and he'd just accepted their absence from her life. Perhaps they lived yet, but elsewhere.

When I was at last allowed to return to Trengrouse, and had passed my twenty-first birthday, I fully intended to find your mother and her family and marry her, but my father forestalled me with threats and bullying that I couldn't resist. However, I don't believe he knew what had become of them after he'd evicted them from their farm, and he put me to work in the offices of Wheal Lucky. You will know its ruins, although it's been shut for some years now as I write this letter to you.

Jack did indeed know the ruins of Wheal Lucky, a tin mine that had been unlucky for many, standing just a short way inland from Trengrouse, on the far side of the Penzance road.

Your mother was working there as a balmaiden.

This brought Jack's head up with a jerk. His mother had been working at the surface of a mine? She'd been a lowly balmaiden, working for pennies? Breaking up the ore the miners were bringing to the surface? Jack's mouth fell open. "Mother. You never said. You once worked in a mine?"

She bowed her head. "He told you? It's not something I'm proud of, although in a way I am. I'm proud I could work like my father and brother to bring money in, but not of how low I had to sink to do so."

"What happened to your father and brother? Where are they now?"

Her chin shook. "They're still in Wheal Lucky, with the other men caught in the roof fall. The fall that caused the closure of the mine." She heaved a sigh. "Keep reading."

He tore his eyes away from her back to the letter in his hand.

After the mine disaster that took your grandfather and uncle and left your mother alone in the world, I determined to keep her safe. I had my allowance which permitted me to set her up in a small house in Penzance and visit her whenever I was there on my father's business. We loved each other and your mother was a virtuous young woman. She was never my mistress. I obtained a Common License from the Bishop of Truro and she and I were married in secret. She has and always will be my dearly beloved wife.

What?

Had he really just read that? His father and mother had been, possibly still were, if his father still lived, man and wife? He wasn't illegitimate after all? No by-blow bastard-born, but a legitimate son of Sir Austin Trengrouse. A mixture of emotions churned through his head, foremost the pressing question of why his father had always treated him as a dark secret when he could have acknowledge him in public as his son. He glared at his mother. "You knew? All this time you knew? That I'm no bastard? That you're his wife? And yet you stood by and let him marry someone else—bigamously?"

She met his angry gaze. "He's told you, I see, but you don't fully understand. You must read on and let him speak."

Jack had almost crumpled the letter into a ball and thrown it into the hearth where a fire burned, but a mix of common sense and open curiosity kept him from doing so. He read on.

But I dared not reveal this to my father. He was old and ill, and I thought that once he was gone, I could bring your mother to Trengrouse and she would be my wife in name as well as fact. But my father knew his end was coming soon, and, before he went, he determined to see me well married—a marriage that would increase the land holdings of Trengrouses for generations to come. I could not fight him for fear of his health and my mother's fury. I was forced, very much against my will and in full knowledge that I was committing the foulest of sins, to marry Miss Letitia Egerton, the only child of Mr. Zachariah Egerton, a man of considerable means.

So, his spineless father had spurned his true love, ignored his marriage vows, and married bigamously for money. What further depths could this man sink to, blaming his own father for them at every turn? Jack read on, his anger growing.

I had no sooner married Miss Egerton than my father died, leaving me as the new baronet. I did not dare repudiate Miss Egerton, for now, if my crime came to light, I would be either branded, or worse, transported to the colonies. And my poor Lady Trengrouse was quite innocent in this deed and already about to present me with an heir I would be forced to pass off as legitimate. I persuaded your mother to remain silent, for love of me, and installed her in Rosudgeon without my wife's knowledge. Things never came by halves for me, though, and your mother informed me that she, too, was about to produce a child—my true heir. I have never been so conflicted as I awaited the birth of these two babies. And when Lady Trengrouse's son was born dead, I recognized it as punishment for my sins. You, however, were born alive and kicking and screaming loud enough to wake the dead. A true Trengrouse, although your mother had taken her own mother's maiden name of Trevelyan. You, my darling Jack, are Jack Trengrouse, not Jack Trevelyan.

Jack let the letter slip to his lap. "Why did you let him do this? Why did you let the world think you his mistress?"

She shook her head. "Because I love him, Jack. I loved him then and I love him now." Tears trickled down her cheeks. "How could I have betrayed him by telling the world he was a bigamist? What good would it have done? He would have been sent to Botany Bay and I would have been more alone than ever. At least I had him from time to time, when he could get away from Trengrouse Castle."

"But effectively he prevented you from living a fulfilling life as someone else's husband. You could have married and had other children. Just *lived*."

"You think that my life was not fulfilling? You can say that, when I have loved you with all my heart and gloried every day in how closely you resemble your father?"

Unconvinced, he lifted the letter again.

And now I'm writing this in order to give it to you when I'm either dead already, or about to die. For I must do right by you, and you are my true heir. You will be Sir Jack Trengrouse after me, and Trengrouse Castle will be yours, for Lady Trengrouse and I will have no sons. But I pray that you will be gentle with your stepmother and sisters. She is not the guilty one here and nor are my daughters. I am. I have treated your mother badly, but I've also treated Letitia despicably. She knows nothing of this, and it will be a terrible shock to her to discover her marriage was a sham. Break it to her as gently as you can. Please. And remember, Jack, that I have always loved you, and it has broken my heart not to see you as often as I would have liked to. You are my boy, and you always will be.

Austin Trengrouse, Bt.

Jack looked up at his mother to find her earnest gaze fixed on him. She licked her lips. "You will go to him?"

He nodded. "I will go."

Chapter Thirty

DOWN IN THE stables, Shadow greeted his owner with an excited nicker as Jack carried saddle and bridle down the passageway towards his horse's loosebox. He'd turned down his groom's offer to saddle his horse for him, preferring the activity to standing waiting with nothing to do but think. Instead, he'd sent the groom down to the kiddley to tell Will a little of what had happened, and to take *The Fly* round to Penzance without him. However, even the activity of tacking up Shadow didn't stop his brain from reeling.

He'd always been legitimate. The mockery and often outright bullying he'd suffered at Truro Grammar School for being born a bastard had been unfounded. He and his mother could have lived with his father all this time, if only his father had possessed a backbone. And now, too late to try to mend the past, his father's dying wish had been to reveal all.

He slipped the bit between Shadow's teeth and pulled the headpiece over his long, velvety ears. What of Lady Trengrouse? Only of course, she wasn't Lady Trengrouse at all—his mother was. What of her three daughters? Two were already married to men who thought them the legitimate daughters of a baronet. One remained at home, as yet unwed. How old might she be? Eighteen, nineteen? Of an age to come out into society, but a society which would now sneer at her and turn its back. Much as it had done on occasion to Jack himself. No wonder he hadn't liked to move in Cornish society's circle.

Could he do this to her? Make her suffer in the way he had himself, knowing she was just a girl and couldn't find the kind of escape he had, with his fists. He fastened the throatlash and noseband, hooked up the curb chain and led Shadow out of his box. His horse's hooves skittered on the cobbles, eager for the off.

Out in the stableyard, Jack tightened the girth then swung himself up into the saddle and turned Shadow towards the archway onto the drive. What he wanted to do was gallop round to Trengrouse Castle, but Shadow had been too long idle in his loosebox and needed walking for a good ten minutes to loosen up his muscles. He'd have to take the long way around via the Penzance road, and that irked him more than ever. His hand overly heavy on the reins, he headed Shadow down the drive and turned left.

His horse pranced and curvetted, as though he felt the urgency of their mission and Jack's anxiety, but Jack tightened his grip and held him to a walk. Besides, it gave him time to think, although he couldn't be sure if that was a good or bad thing. Thinking hurt him.

What would he do when he arrived? Leave Shadow with a groom, or a footman, and march in through the front doors? Doors he'd never been through before. Apart from the one time he'd met Lady Trengrouse in the gardens, he'd never even been within the grounds. Of course, after that initial rebuff, he'd been back countless times to observe from afar, drawn by the spectacle of his father's other family. But eavesdropping or spying never brings happiness to those who do it, and, in the end, he'd given up before it made him bitter. Or more bitter than he already was.

So he didn't even know where in the grand house his father's room lay. He'd have to ask, or be escorted.

He'd walked long enough now. Time to trot. He gave Shadow a little more rein and the horse immediately burst into a long-striding trot, eating up the track to the main road. Jack turned west towards Penzance, and Shadow broke into a canter for the half mile to the turning down to Trengrouse, hooves pounding along the grassy verge beside the road.

That his father had set up the woman the world thought of as his mistress so close to the one they thought his legal wife was no surprise. His father had been pleasure loving and hedonistic, always the one to arrive with some toy or another as a gift, always willing to play with Jack, to laugh and flirt with his mother. He frowned at the thought of what his father had inflicted on his mother, just because of the accident of her birth and his fear of his own father. She'd not been unhappy, though, at least not while his father was with her. And she'd always shown a happy face to Jack.

But when she'd been alone, had she then wondered what her life would have been like had Sir Austin thought to stand up to Jack's grandfather? That she would have been a lady. Not that she was totally spurned by the high society of Cornwall, because she wasn't. She had her limited circle of friends, she attended the Assembly Rooms, she invited these friends to dine with her, mostly when Jack was absent. But did she dream of being by his father's side? Had she nurtured pangs of sadness and jealousy when she saw him with the woman who had all unknowingly usurped her place?

The track to Trengrouse was not as long as the one down to Bessie's Cove. It sloped downhill but was well-maintained enough for Jack to allow Shadow to trot. In all-too-short a time, he was riding up the wide, graveled drive to the front of the castle. Not that it was really a castle, being more of a grand house with the embellishment of crenellations and a few fancy towers. Something one of his father's ancestors must have added on. One of his own, legal ancestors now.

He halted Shadow near the front door and was just dismounting when that door swung open and the sturdy, black-clad figure of a butler appeared, his face the picture of shock. He must be well aware of who Jack was. Everyone for miles around knew, and if they didn't know, they could have guessed, from Jack's close resemblance to his father as a young man. "You can't—" the man began.

Jack held out Shadow's reins to him. "Here, take my horse to the stables. I shall be at the castle for a while."

The butler's mouth fell open, but long years of obedience to the upper classes had him holding out his hand and taking the reins. Without further ado, Jack was past him and through the front door, leaving the man gaping and in charge of the restless Shadow.

Trengrouse Castle was even more ornate within than without. The marble floor beneath Jack's feet echoed with his footsteps as he strode into the center of the enormous hall. Wide stairs rose to a half-landing then divided to left and right, heading for a galleried landing above that encircled the lofty hallway. Large, important looking doors opened to left and right and paintings hung on all the walls. There was one that had to be his father as a young man—the image of Jack himself. Jack dragged his eyes away from the portrait. Without the encumbered butler to ask, which way was he to go?

Upstairs. It had to be the way. He took the stairs two at a time, half-running to the wide landing where many doors and corridors opened off to different wings of the house. Where would the master bedroom be? He could hardly go searching every room.

The necessity to do so was removed as a gray-haired woman in a plain, dark-gray dress emerged from a doorway halfway down a wide corridor to Jack's right. She was balancing a bowl and jug in one hand and looking harassed. As she closed the door behind her, she raised her eyes and started back in surprise. "Sir Austin?" Her face blanched as though she thought she might be seeing a ghost. "But you're not dead, yet." The words came out on a horrified gasp and she glanced back at the door she'd just emerged from.

Jack took a few steps towards her and she retreated, the bowl and jug clutched to her chest. "No, keep away from me."

He halted, understanding dawning. "You're not seeing a ghost. I am not your master come to haunt you. I'm his son, come to see him."

The expression on her face changed in an instant. "You can't go in there. You can't be here at all. It's forbidden." Even though she no longer thought him a ghost, her low voice was rigid with fear. "You must leave. Now. Before you're seen."

Jack shook his head. "I've come expressly to see my father, on his deathbed, and you will not say me nay."

Glancing towards the stairs as though in hope of reinforcements in the shape of the butler turned groom, she drew herself up as tall as she could, which wasn't very tall, and set her jaw. "I shall call the footmen to have you removed if you do not leave." Perhaps she'd given up on the butler coming to help.

Jack ignored her outburst. "Is this my father's room?"

She stepped between him and the door, brave as a lioness defending her cub. "You shall not enter."

Jack took her by the shoulders. She was a small woman, and he was big and strong. With firm determination, he set her to one side. Her face darkened with anger and the bowl and jug in her hands wobbled. "Now go and do what you were told to do. Fetch some fresh water for my father. Now."

He turned the doorknob and pushed the door open.

"Wherever did you get this dress?" Bertha asked as Harriet sat down at the kitchen table. "It looks quite out of date. Here, get this hot tea down you." A dish of tea was pressed into her hands, Bertha's cure-all for every indisposition. There was no denying how welcome it was though. Harriet sipped the hot liquid and felt energy flood through her body along with the welcome warmth.

"Wherever have you been?" Lydia asked. "We were so worried. Bertha walked up to Rosudgeon to speak to Mrs. Trevelyan, but she had no idea where you could be. I stayed here, in case you came back, but you didn't. Then we went to the alehouse on the other side of the cove, and they behaved most oddly." She glanced at Bertha. "Bertha wanted me to wait outside, but I refused. I have no idea why men like ale houses so much—this one was so dark and smoky and altogether quite smelly. It didn't have many customers, and, frankly, I could see why, Mama. The woman in charge told us you'd probably gone out on the captain's ship. Why she thought that, I have no idea, but it does turn out she was right so she must have had some knowledge. She told us not to tell anyone else until the ship was back safely. She said it in an almost threatening fashion. I was quite scared."

Bertha grunted and sat down with her own tea. "Miss Lydia's right. It were more of a threat than advice. We decided to wait, as they said. If you weren't back today, we were going to walk along the cliff path over to Roskilly and ask the people there for help, seein' as how you know them and said as they was nice."

Thank goodness they hadn't. "I've only been gone two days."

Bertha refilled Harriet's dish of tea. It had been well-brewed and was strong and aromatic. "Nearer three, more like. We didn't want to believe as you'd both fallen over the cliffs into the sea, like that old man in that dreadful cottage along the cliffs suggested. He looked as though he'd have liked it if you had. Kept saying you'd be like the old man who used to live here. I forget his name." She sniffed. "He said if you was in the sea, then waiting'd do no harm."

"I'm glad you did wait, and I'm very sorry we worried you so. Theo and I had a very interesting sail in *The Fly*. Theo has decided to become a sailor, even though he was quite sick at first."

Theo, who'd been tucking into a large hunk of bread and honey, looked up. "No. I'm going to be a smug—"

"A sailor." Harriet shot him a frown. "And don't speak while you're chewing. We don't all want to share it with you."

Theo took another bite of his bread and shut up. Thank goodness.

"I've the kettle on the range," Bertha said, "for if you'd like a wash. I has to say that you looks like you could do with one." She flicked a finger over Harriet's hair. "And a hairbrush."

A scarce quarter of an hour later, Harriet was in her bedroom wearing only her undergarments and, with difficulty, brushing out the tangles in her hair. Who knew wind and salty spray could have such an effect on a lady's coiffure. What with having had no brush near her hair for the last twenty-four hours at least, nature had wrought devastation on her already somewhat unruly curls, not to mention her skin, which was not as pale as it once had been.

The door opened and Lydia slipped inside, an air of determination about her. "Would you like some help?"

Harriet handed her daughter the brush. "Only if you're feeling gentle. If you are, then perhaps you might brush out the back of my hair for me. It's terribly tangled."

Lydia took the brush and started on her mother's hair, humming gently as she worked, the effect being to lull Harriet into an almost somnambulant state.

"Mama?" Lydia interrupted their companionable silence. "Where did you sleep on the boat?"

Harriet bestirred herself. All that fresh air and tension and fear had made her far too sleepy. "On a pile of sails on deck, then later on in a hammock in the cabin."

Lydia shivered. "That sounds most uncomfortable."

"On the contrary, the hammock was one of the most com fortable beds I've ever slept in, and even the sails were more so than you would expect."

"And Captain Jack? What was he like?" The question sounded guarded, as though Lydia were probing for something she suspected might be there. Had she seen them holding hands?

"Very polite and courteous."

Lydia brushed on for a bit, teasing out the tangles with her fingers. "Mama? Might I ask you an impertinent question?"

She must have seen, or she wouldn't be probing like this. Heat climbed Harriet's throat to her cheeks. "So long as it's not *too* impertinent."

"Do you like Captain Jack?"

Now that was a question she'd been avoiding posing to herself because she didn't want to answer it. Did she? And what sort of liking did Lydia want to know about? "He is very gentlemanly," seemed the best answer for the moment.

"That is true. But I suspect he isn't quite what he seems. When I was at the farm getting milk from Mrs. Voas, I overheard some of her workmen talking, in the yard."

"You did?"

"Yes. They were talking about the brandy that was coming over from somewhere called Roscoff. Mama, I fear we were right from the start, and the captain's ship is being used for smuggling." She paused. "And I think the captain himself might be a smuggler as well."

Not at all a revelation, but how to react? "Have you mentioned this to anyone?"

"Who is there to mention it to? I don't see anyone here. Not like in Bath." For a moment, Lydia was back to being petulant.

"You're not to say anything to anyone."

Lydia stopped brushing. "Did you *know*?" She paused. "Mama! Did he take you smuggling?" She came round to face Harriet. "Did Theo go smuggling too?"

Harriet met her accusing gaze. She'd always inculcated honesty in her children. She couldn't then lie to them. And besides, Theo knew, and he was bound, at some point, to divulge this to his sister, even if only in wanting to show off to her that he'd done something she hadn't. "He did."

Lydia sat down on the nearest bed, which happened to be her own. "Oh my goodness, Mama. Does that mean you and Theo are smugglers now? Will Captain Carlyon clap you in jail?" Her eyes widened. "What will I do if you're transported, or... or hanged?"

Trust Lydia to think only about herself.

"No one will ever know," Harriet managed, remembering all too well the scrutiny Fitz Carlyon had given her when she'd come on deck. He knew. But would he do anything? He'd not been able to catch Jack and his men in the act, but he must have guessed she knew what they were about. What sort of a man was he? Would a gentleman consider reporting her?

Lydia fanned her face. "Mama, I feel quite overcome. I don't think I want to know any of the details. Just promise me you won't go out again in that ship with the captain."

Good heavens. Easy to mistake Lydia for the mother and herself for the wayward daughter. Could she promise this, though? Didn't she secretly want to go out to sea in *The Fly* again and visit France and stay with Mrs. S in her inn, even though she suspected Jack had been intimate with the lady in the past? For the adventure in it that had made her feel more alive than ever before... well, since she'd ridden to hounds as a girl. Well... more alive than that if she was honest with herself. More alive because she'd been with Jack.

What?

Guilt washed over her. She was not some energetic, romantic heroine from a sixpenny novel. She was the responsible mother of two children. She could not involve herself with a smuggler. And yet...

"Mama!" Lydia leaned forward, eyes accusing. "Mama—you liked it, didn't you?"

Harriet bit her lip. "Yes, I did. And I would do it all again." There. That was being honest and she should be proud of herself for it.

Lydia's eyes narrowed. "And you like the captain, don't you? And I don't mean because he's a gentleman."

Harriet swallowed. "Yes. I do like him." She managed the smallest of hopeful smiles. "Do you mind dreadfully if I do?"

Chapter Thirty-One

FOR A MOMENT, Jack hesitated on the threshold of the bedroom before him. Then he stepped inside and closed the door firmly on the woman in the corridor. The four people already in the room, arrested in their movement by his arrival, made a dramatic tableau.

The bedroom was huge, the walls lined with oak paneling that combined with the thick curtains drawn over the long windows, rendered it dark and gloomy. In the center of the wall opposite the door, a large four-poster bed stood, hung with heavy drapes of green and gold brocade. What little light there was came only from the plethora of candles that had been lit. They cast an eerie glow over the whole motionless assembly.

A rise in the bedcovers marked where Jack's father lay, his head upon a heap of pillows. To the right side of the bed sat two women clad in drab, dark colors, one of whom, easily recognizable as Lady Trengrouse, clutched his father's hand. The other had to be her youngest daughter. The only pretty one. On the other side of the bed, Dr Rescorla hovered in his somber black consulting coat, resembling nothing more than a thin crow come late to the feast.

For what felt like an eternity, nobody said anything and no one moved. Then, Lady Trengrouse, her spiteful face, as much like a pig's as his mother had suggested, made to step towards him, but Sir Austin's hand pulled her back. "No," was all he said, his weak voice carrying in the silence.

They were all staring at Jack. If Lady Trengrouse's look could have killed, he'd have been dead on the floor right now.

"What are *you* doing here?" she finally managed to spit out. The girl, his sister, on the other hand, was nothing but curious. Perhaps she'd long wondered about the half-brother who she must have known didn't live far away.

It was up to Jack to do something. To break open the ominous silence. "I've come to pay my respects to my father." Refusing to shrink under the accusing stare of Lady Trengrouse, Jack stepped up beside Dr. Rescorla and stood looking down at the figure in the bed.

Sir Austin peered back up out of eyes that should have been so like Jack's own, but now were exhausted, bloodshot and ringed by dark shadows. "You came." The side of his face nearest to Jack was pulled down and sagging and the words emerged slurred and difficult to hear. A trail of saliva ran from the downturned corner of his mouth.

Jack stared down at the man he'd always wanted to be closer to. Now it was too late. How could he be angry with a dying man? That his father had been so weak as to allow himself to be bullied into bigamy shocked Jack to the core, but the man was dying, and this was not the time for recriminations. It never would be.

A stool stood beside the bed, so Jack took it, drawing it close enough that he could take the pale hand where it lay on the covers, lifeless and chill, just a glove with loose bones inside it.

Across the bed, Lady Trengrouse released her husband's other hand and sat up straighter. "You have no right to show your face here."

Jack ignored her.

Dr. Rescorla cleared his throat. "Captain Trevelyan. I am afraid your father has lost the use of the right side of his body. His apoplexy has caused it. I've bled him, but there's nothing more I can do. It's just a matter of time, now. You are lucky he's retained the power of speech."

Sir Austin shot his medical man a venomous glare. So he wasn't as feeble as he looked. "I know I'm dying, man. You may go, all of you. I wish to be alone with my son." This time the words were clearer. He waved his left hand at Lady Trengrouse and Lavinia. "Go. All of you. Now."

Rising to her feet, Lady Trengrouse turned to her daughter, catching her arm. "Come, Lavinia, we must allow your papa his vagaries." The glare she shot at Jack could have had him in a smoking heap of embers on the floor.

The girl rose, but hesitated. "Might I not stay, too, Papa? I am your daughter as much as he is your son. You must know how much I love you."

The old man's eyes swiveled to take her in. "Very well. Not your mother. She must go."

Lady Trengrouse looked as though she would have liked to have argued the point, but Doctor Rescorla, who knew Jack well and had treated his mother on occasion, took her arm, tucked her hand into his elbow and ushered her out. "Your husband has little time left. You need to allow him his final wishes, my lady."

Did he know anything of the contents of the letter? He could only have been a boy at the time of Sir Austin's marriage to Jack's mother, but his father before him had been a doctor in Penzance. And the letter had said they'd married there. Someone must have stood as witnesses for them. Someone must have carried out their wedding. And yet no one had ever come forward to say so. Whoever those people were, they must have been in Jack's father's pocket not to have betrayed him as a bigamist.

The door closed behind them, and Lavinia returned to the far side of the bed, retaking her seat. Sir Austin's eyes had closed. "Papa, I am here." She took his one responsive hand in hers. "We both are."

Sir Austin opened his eyes. "My children."

"Mama has sent for Honoria and Horatia as well, only as

Honoria is in a delicate condition, Mama fears she won't be able to travel."

Jack watched Lavinia with interest. This was by far the closest he'd been to her and now they were facing one another, he could see even more clearly how much she resembled their father. Unlike her two rather sturdy sisters, she was slender and curvaceous, with a pale, oval face and the wide golden eyes of Sir Austin. And Jack himself.

She stared back at him in open interest. "So," she said, "you are my brother."

"Half-brother."

"I have always wanted a brother."

Jack bit his lip. If he were to speak the truth he'd have to say that he'd always wanted a sister, but he wasn't about to appear vulnerable in front of her. He was here to steal her name and her inheritance, and she'd not forgive him for that, brother or not. Not that it had ever been truly hers.

Sir Austin stirred. "I have not much time. Do you have the letter?"

Lavinia's brow furrowed. "The letter? What letter?"

Jack nodded. "I do."

"And you have read it?" His voice was weakening. Had he been holding on just so he could speak to Jack?

"I have."

"So you know."

"I do."

"And do you have any questions?" The sick man's chest heaved as he fought for breath. How sunken his cheeks were, how waxy pale, his eyes like dark holes in his skull.

"What do you want me to do with the information in the letter?" Let his father be the one to say whether Lavinia would love or hate her newfound brother.

"As you wish. But you are the rightful heir."

Lavinia's eyes widened. "How can that be, Papa? We thought it would be our cousin Henry? Surely he is heir to the baronetcy?"

Of course. The title and land must be entailed and could only go to the heir. The sudden realization that by taking the title he would not be depriving Lady Trengrouse and Lavinia of their home swept over Jack. They were to lose it anyway, to some cousin he'd never heard of.

"He is not." Sir Austin closed his eyes and his breathing shallowed. "Jack will inform you of what is in my letter. I do not have the strength. But he is the next baronet. He will see you are well cared for…" His voice faded.

For a moment, Jack feared he'd died, but then his chest rose in a shuddering breath. No. He'd just exhausted himself.

Lavinia fixed Jack with enquiring, intelligent eyes. "Are you going to tell me, then, or keep it to yourself? I fear it is something important that I need to hear. Mama as well." She spoke with intelligence and understanding, perhaps already guessing what he knew for fact. She was a sharp-witted girl, it seemed, not given to the vapors.

Jack rubbed his nose in an effort to give himself time to think. "Today, when I returned from my ship, my mother handed me a letter." He licked his lips, searching for a way to say this that wasn't too abrupt. "In it, my father told me that before he married your mother, he had already in secret married mine. In short, out of fear of his own father, he had committed bigamy. And after his father died, he was too afraid to admit he'd done so. He could have gone to jail, or been transported to the colonies."

Her eyes widened again. "Go on." She seemed a girl of quiet calm, perhaps not given to hysteria. Not so her mother, Jack feared. She was going to be beside herself with anger and shock.

"He told me that my name is not Jack Trevelyan, but Jack Trengrouse, and that I will be baronet after him and inherit all of the Trengrouse lands. He asked me to be kind to your mother and to you."

She pressed her lips together. "So, *I* am the bastard and not you? All this time while my mother has been sneering about you living so close with your mother, all this time it was your mother who was Lady Trengrouse, and my mother the mistress?"

That was one way of putting it. Not quite the way he'd have worded it himself. He nodded.

Sir Austin's eyes flickered. "You will take care of my daughter?"

Jack nodded. "I will."

Lavinia's eyes flashed. "I don't need looking after. As it would have been had my cousin Henry inherited, my mother will have the unentailed fortune she brought to the marriage and we will not be paupers, let me assure you."

So she had her pride.

Sir Austin nodded. "She is correct." He closed his eyes again and sucked in another breath. His eyes flickered open. "But I would like Jack to be as a brother to you, little Lavinia. You will need him."

She would indeed if she wanted to continue into society. She would need the approbation of her legitimate half-brother to get herself a husband, and even then, it would not be easy.

Sir Austin's gaze flicked to Jack's face. "Promise me you will take care of them."

A mountain of conflicting emotions surged through Jack. His father, whose lack of courage had brought about this mess, wanted him to forgive and forget everything that had gone before. Wanted him to be a better man than he'd ever been. He wanted him to put out of his head how Lady Trengrouse had made the gardeners throw him out of the grounds as a boy, to put out of his head the taunting he'd suffered at school for being a bastard. He wanted him to accept Lavinia, and presumably her absent sisters, as his family, when they'd never been forced to accept him.

What would his mother say to this? She didn't have a malicious bone in her body. She would forgive and forget for certain, or she wouldn't now be waiting at Rosudgeon, afraid to come to her beloved husband on his death bed. Afraid to intrude on the family she'd stood aside for. Afraid to cause them upset.

He had to do what his mother would have done. What his father wanted him to do. "I promise," he said.

His father's head lolled on the pillow and Lavinia bent her forehead to rest it on his hand. "Oh, Papa. Don't leave me."

But he had gone.

HARRIET WOKE THE next morning to rain pattering on the bedroom window. She lay for a few minutes in the bed's comfortable warmth, unwilling to throw the blankets aside and expose herself to the autumnal chill. A glance sideways showed her Lydia almost totally covered by her bedclothes, just the top of her dark head visible.

Then she remembered Jack, and her admission to Lydia last night that she liked him. Which had not been entirely honest. Not about how much she liked him, at any rate. To her surprise, this had not met with the disapproval she'd expected. Instead, Lydia had nodded with decision. "Good," she'd said. "I like him too, although I should like him better if he were to give up the smuggling when he marries you."

This had so shocked Harriet she'd been bereft of words for a full minute, and was saved from answering this declaration by the arrival of Bertha, come to tell them dinner was served. She'd had to throw on her dressing gown, that still held a faint aroma of tobacco in its threads, and run downstairs with Lydia to eat, putting off thinking about Jack until later.

Now, lying on her back and listening to the rain, she couldn't escape the image of him standing with his legs slightly apart on the deck, swaying with the movement of the ship under him. The image was so vivid, she could almost feel the movement herself and, for a worrying moment, feared the return of the mal de mer. But it vanished as quickly as it had arrived.

Instead of lying in bed dreaming about a man she couldn't

have, would in fact be afraid to have, whatever conclusion Lydia had formed, she'd best get up. So she pushed back the covers and set her bare feet on the floorboards. Brrrr. Too cold by half. The water in the jug on the dressing table had chilled overnight so her wash was perfunctory and hurried. She'd leave Lydia in bed a while. No need for the children to rise as early as her and Bertha, not with it now cooling down so much.

The single-handed struggle into her stays overcome, she donned a workaday gown, a clean apron and her lace-up boots and quietly let herself out of their bedroom onto the gloomy landing. Downstairs, Bertha was just finishing sweeping the floor after having lit the fire in the range earlier. She looked up as Harriet came in. "Tea's in the pot on the range."

Harriet poured herself a cup and took it to the table while Bertha finished the floor. It seemed she'd been up a while and all the chores Harriet had planned to help her with had been accomplished. She dismissed the guilt for this with a sense of further guilt at the dismissal. Bertha, oblivious to her mistress's conscience, sat beside her with a thud and poured herself a cup of tea. "Goin' up to see him then?"

"Excuse me?"

"You heard me." Bertha wiped her lips on her apron front. "Are you goin' up to the big house to see him today?"

What should she say? What had she done that had given away how she felt about Jack to her faithful servant?

Bertha placed a pudgy hand, still a little damp from the chores, on Harriet's. "Don't look like a frightened rabbit at me, my girl. I've known you all your life, don't you forget. Longer than anyone. I know when I see that look on your face. And I knows it when I see it on the face o' the man you've taken to as well. So, are you walkin' up there to see him or not?"

Harriet scraped around for words and failed. How had Bertha seen more than she had? Was she right and was Jack as enamored of her as she was of him? On the ship he'd asked to kiss her, after all, but that had come to nothing. Just the merest brushing of the lips before they were disturbed. A gentle kiss. Could she trust him to be gentle in all things? She couldn't risk repeating what she'd gone through with Ben again. And Jack was a man, after all, with a man's needs, and Ben had always insisted that his needs be met whenever he required it. Wouldn't Jack do the same?

That thought cooled her blood.

"No. I'm not running after him. If he wants to see me, then he can come here."

Bertha slurped her tea. "I'll lay odds that if you don't walk up there to see him this morning, then he'll be down here by teatime this afternoon."

Laying odds on a man did not sound the right thing to do. Might Bertha be right? Might he be thinking right now of coming down to see her?

Bertha set her teacup down with a bang. "I wouldn't play hard to get with him, if I was you. He's a keeper and a gentleman." She gave Harriet a hard look. "A sight better than the man you married."

Harriet's mouth fell open. She'd always been aware of Bertha's silent disapproval of Ben, but never had it been voiced before.

Bertha nodded. "Don't look so surprised. I'm not a fool. I saw what was going on when he was home from the army."

"You did?"

She nodded. "You can't hide anything from me. I had to hold my tongue though, or he'd've given me my marching orders and I wanted to stay close to you and the children. I had to keep quiet and just be glad he wasn't home often."

"So everyone knew except Lydia?" Shock cascaded through Harriet.

Bertha nodded. "That girl wouldn't know a fact if it jumped up and hit her on the nose. She sails through life with her head either in the air or in a book."

Harriet shook her head. "Not so vague as all that. She asked me about Jack last night before dinner."

"And you said what?"

"That I like him." She paused. "I didn't tell her how much, but she guessed. She said I was to marry him."

Bertha chuckled. "More sense than I thought she had. Well, I'll be. Fancy that. And she was right. So you should marry him. He's head over heels in love with you, but you're too silly to see it."

A delicious little wriggle of excitement coursed through Harriet, provoking the strangest of hot feelings in her very core. What might he be offering? Nothing, most likely, although he'd said he didn't want a mistress. No. She was fooling herself here, and Bertha and Lydia were just as addled. Nothing would come of this. Nothing at all. But a very large part of her was hoping something would.

Chapter Thirty-Two

LYDIA AND THEO appeared as if by magic as breakfast was being set on the table, Lydia with her hair neatly controlled in a long braid, Theo with his sticking straight up in the air as though no brush had been applied to it in days, which of course it hadn't. Bertha, used to Theo's early morning appearance, attacked him with a wet flannel, mainly to smooth his hair into some semblance of order rather than to wash his face. Theo struggled, but was no match for Bertha's strength and determination.

He sat at the table, a rebellious gleam in his eye. "Might I walk along the cliff path to Roskilly today, to see Yves Treloar? I want to tell him I've been out in *The Fly*. He'll be green with envy. And maybe he'll let me ride Blossom." He beamed at Lydia. "I'm getting good at riding now and I only fell off twice when we were cantering on the beach."

Lydia pulled a cross face at her brother.

Harriet set down the piece of toast she'd been nibbling. She didn't much like the idea of him falling off horses, but he'd assured her Blossom was very small so not far to fall, and the sand was always a soft landing. "Yes, Theo, you may go, so long as you don't ride up onto the cliffs. But I think I can trust you to be sensible, can't I?"

Theo nodded with vigor and took a large bite out of his own

toast and honey. "Thank you, Mama."

Lydia pushed aside her plate. "Can I go with you this time? Mama said Yves has a girl cousin. I'd like to meet her."

Theo's face crinkled in suspicion. "Not just to keep an eye on me and report back to Mama? And not to try and ride Blossom? You're far too big for her."

Lydia shook her head. "Not at all. I miss my friends in Bath, that's all. And I certainly don't want to ride a tiny pony like Blossom. I'd just like a walk, as the rain's stopped. Is it far?"

"About a mile and a half," Harriet said. "But don't mind me and your lessons, will you?"

Bertha snorted with laughter. "When did they ever mind you?"

"Can I go, please, Mama?" Lydia turned an appealing gaze on her mother. "And I can make sure he obeys you and doesn't go anywhere near the cliffs."

"I don't need minding," Theo interjected. "I'm twelve, not two. Haven't you noticed I'm not in petticoats anymore?"

Lydia ignored this outburst and took a sip of tea, eyeing her mother.

Harriet pretended unwilling acquiescence. "If you promise that this afternoon when you return you'll catch up with your schoolwork." As this was more than likely going to make sure they stayed for both luncheon and teatime at Roskilly, she doubted she'd see either of her children again until nearly their bedtime, but what did it matter? If they were happy, she was happy, and that was all she cared about right now.

"Thank you, Mama!" Theo and Lydia were up from the table in a trice, and after Lydia had run up and down stairs a few times for various things she'd forgotten, and Theo had stood tapping his foot with impatience by the kitchen door, they finally set off, almost, but not quite, an endearing picture of sibling cooperation.

Without their vibrant presence, the cottage felt suddenly quiet and bare. Bertha rose from the table. "Well, I'm away up to the farm to buy us some milk and eggs and to see if they've any more of that nice cheese young Theo likes so much. After I've washed up."

Harriet rose, too. "No need. Leave that to me. Here's some money." She fished in her reticule. "Why not spend the day with your friend? I'm happy in my own company here and will just clear the dishes and then sit outside in the sun while it's out and take the opportunity to read a book. You go on up to the farm and see Mrs. Voas. No doubt she'll be wanting to know what gossip you've got this time." She smiled. "Only be careful what you tell her about mine and Theo's adventures."

Bertha made a small pretense of wanting to do the dishes, but Harriet ushered her off to find her bonnet and shawl, took the kettle from the range and filled the sink. Immersing her hands in the hot water, she began to wash their plates and cups.

Having planted a departing kiss on Harriet's cheek, Bertha also departed, armed with a cake she'd baked for her friend, and now the house was really silent. Once the dishes were done, Harriet dried and put them away, then went to the table to sit and drink a second cup of tea.

The silence pressed in around her, almost heavy in its depth, as though it were shouting in her ears, and the tempting autumn sun shone in through the kitchen window. If she did what she'd told Bertha she was going to do and found herself a book, she could take a chair out onto the front and sit and read for a while, undisturbed. A pleasure rarely afforded her, even in Bath.

Now, where would Lydia have stored her small library?

She climbed the stairs to their bedroom and commenced a search. She soon found the small pile of books Lydia loved to read over and over again, mainly because they were the only ones she possessed, and selected Maria Edgeworth's Irish tale of *Castle Rackrent*. She'd read it before, of course, but so she had all of the books that had once been hers but had somehow migrated to being Lydia's possessions. Having found her own shawl, in case of autumn chill remaining, and with the book tucked under her arm, she descended the stairs, collected one of the kitchen chairs, and approached the kitchen door.

Setting her hand on it, she pulled it open.

Jack was standing on the doorstep, his beaver hat in one hand. His other hand was raised as though about to knock, and his expression was as taken aback as no doubt Harriet's was.

"Oh," she managed. "What a surprise to see you here."

"And you," he said, then uncharacteristically blushed, no doubt realizing the ridiculousness of having said it was a surprise to see her in her own house.

They stood for a moment, staring at one another, before Harriet remembered her manners. "I was about to sit outside and read a book." She gestured to the chair. "For once in my life I find myself quite alone and with time to do as I wish. The children are gone to visit young Yves at Roskilly, and Bertha has walked up to the Voas's farm for supplies. I said she could stay and talk to her friend for the day if she wished. I sounded kind but in truth, I just wanted some time to myself. But perhaps you would prefer to come inside and I could make a fresh pot of tea?"

Jack had about him an air of awkwardness that was quite unlike him. He shifted from one foot to the other, his grip on his hat tightening until the knuckles whitened. "I don't want to disturb you if you'd rather be alone…" He made to turn away in a half-hearted manner.

The disturbing thought that she didn't want him to leave shot through her. "No. Don't go. I should very much enjoy your company. I only meant I wanted time away from being a mother." She held up the book. "I was going to take the opportunity to read, but this is a book I've read before, several times, so it can wait."

He turned back, unmistakable relief in his eyes. "Perhaps we could sit outside together. With autumn well on, and winter close behind, it seems a shame to miss one of Cornwall's fine days by sitting inside." He waved his hand. "You choose your spot and I'll fetch another chair."

While he went in search of a chair, Harriet selected the most sheltered, sunniest spot, where a few hardy climbing roses that must once have been tended by the previous tenant climbed bravely up the wall of the cottage. A scattering of pink flowers remained from her dead-heading attentions before her trip in *The Fly*. The final blooms of autumn. She sat herself down and arranged the skirts of her work dress demurely. If only she'd known Jack was coming she'd have dressed with more care.

INSIDE THE KITCHEN, Jack stood for a moment, breathing deeply in an effort steady his pounding heart. The decision he'd made that morning to come straight down to Keynvor and propose marriage to Harriet now seemed an almost insurmountable obstacle. His confidence had slowly waned the nearer he'd come to carrying out his intention, and now he found his hands were shaking as he gripped hard to the tabletop. What was he, some lily-livered young beau with no experience of women and love?

That thought brought realization with it. He really did have no experience of love. He might know women, might have had his fun with a fair number of them in his time, but he had never loved any of them, and none of them had loved him. They'd been willing participants and so had he, but his emotions had never been involved, just his sense of enjoyment. So he really was the equivalent of a green young beau falling in love for the first time. Despite being thirty years old.

What if she turned him down? What if he couldn't get up the courage to even ask her? The damage her husband had done her might be too much to overcome. She might not want to risk herself with another man, and he wouldn't blame her. He racked his empty head for a way to prove to her that he'd be different. No inspiration came. But surely, now he was a baronet, to boot, she'd accept him?

She'd be wondering where he'd got to. He grabbed the nearest chair and carried it outside to set beside hers, as close as he dared. Then he flicked the tails of his coat out of the way and sat down.

The book rested unopened in her lap, and she was staring off into the distance, where, over the autumn-gilded treetops, the blue of the sea stretched towards the far horizon. And Roscoff.

"It's a beautiful view," he said. "I never tire of looking at the sea."

She nodded. "At first, I didn't think I would like living here. When I saw the state the cottage was in, my heart quailed, but I had to put on a brave face for my children."

Jack watched her delicate profile. She was a woman who'd no doubt had to put on a brave face many times and for many different reasons. "I'm glad you decided to stay."

She nodded, but didn't turn her head. "So am I."

This was at least going in the direction he wanted it to go in. "You've made this corner of Cornwall all the more beautiful by your presence."

Now she did turn her head to look at him, and he took advantage by reaching out and taking one of her hands. She made no attempt to snatch it back but regarded him out of her solemn, hazel eyes, as though seeking to see inside him to his very soul. "You say some pretty things."

He gazed into those eyes. "Pretty things about a beautiful woman."

Her lips parted a little, and he had to restrain himself from leaning forward to plant a kiss on them. She wasn't like his other women. He had to draw her in little by little, gentling her like a skittish filly.

Every part of him tingled with awareness of how close she was and he couldn't help his body's instinctive reaction. He crossed his legs in an effort to disguise his growing erection. Damn it, but she was so lovely he couldn't control himself.

Had she noticed? A little smile lingered around her mouth. "You are more than kind. I'm sure you've met many women more beautiful than me."

He shook his head. "Never."

The color rose from her breasts up her throat to her cheeks, but she never took her eyes from his. "Never?" Her voice trembled.

Exultation flowed through him. She felt as he did, surely. That couldn't be fear. Best to get his speech, that he'd been practicing on his walk down from Rosudgeon, out of the way. "Harriet." How he loved to speak her name aloud. "You must know that I have feelings for you. No. Don't speak. Let me say my piece. And I know that you suffered in your marriage to the father of your children to the extent that you feel real fear of allowing yourself to feel anything for another man." He paused, but she remained silent, watching him out of wary eyes.

"I've come here today to assure you that I am not like your husband. I know I could just be saying that, but believe me, it is quite true. I freely admit that I'm no saint. I've known a number of women in my time and I'll not deny it. But they were all willing participants and benefited from their association with me." Now he was making it sound like a business deal, which in truth, a fair few of them had been. "All of them would speak highly of me, I think. None would call me cruel or demanding." What was he doing? Offering her references? How hot his cheeks had grown. "In short, I want you to know that I would never expect anything of you that you weren't willing to give." He ground to a halt.

She hadn't dropped her gaze, but had caught the left side of her bottom lip under her teeth. Her breasts rose and fell with a rapidity that tokened deep emotion. Let it not be revulsion.

"Jack," she said, her voice gentle but, nevertheless, containing a tremor. "You speak of what you will and will not do, but I have no idea what it is you want *me* to do. In all your speech, you have not said."

Oh God. Nor had he. In one swift movement Jack dropped onto one knee before her, capturing her other hand as well. "Harriet, will you do the honor of marrying me?"

Chapter Thirty-Three

HARRIET STARED DOWN at the man on his knees in front of her, as her poor heart hammered against her ribs so hard she thought it might come jumping out. Was this not what she wanted? This handsome, dashing man who'd kissed her so lightly and gently, his lips like gossamer on hers. And yet… would he not assure her of all of this if he wanted to get her in his power? Men were liars. Ben had proved that to her with his promises of kindness and love. Might not Jack be the same?

She pressed her lips together as she gazed into his golden eyes, groping for an answer that wouldn't send him running. "I need proof of your good intentions," was what came out, surprising even herself.

His eyes widened. "Tell me how I can prove it to you, and I'll do it, willingly."

She swallowed, and rose to her feet. "I need you to show me how you will love me." She pulled him up. "Show me you're not like… him."

He was towering over her again, and for a moment she doubted the wisdom of her decision. He was so big and strong. He could take what he wanted in the blink of an eye and she'd be powerless to prevent him. Just as she'd always been powerless with Ben. "Bertha has gone to the farm and will be there talking to Mrs. Voas and drinking tea until this afternoon. My children have gone to Roskilly for the day. I am quite alone, here in the house."

His pulse beat fast in his throat, like a captured bird fluttering. Had she made herself clear enough? Did she even mean what she was saying? Her own daring left her trembling with something more than nerves—excitement, anticipation, and could that possibly be desire?

He must know what she meant. Glancing down, she couldn't avoid seeing the bulge in his breeches. He'd tried to hide it when they'd been seated, but she'd noticed. What woman wouldn't? The sight of it sent a fresh frisson of electricity purring through her. A large part of her wanted this, yet another part feared it.

Jack's tongue darted out to lick his lips, and he tightened his hold on her hands. "Might I, then, finish the kiss that was interrupted on board my ship?"

Her breath caught in her throat. He was asking permission again. Surely that showed he was telling her the truth? "You may." She could barely get the words out, so dry was her throat.

He lifted a hand to cup her cheek, his touch featherlight. "Harriet, you must know I would never hurt you." And he bent his head towards hers until their lips touched.

This time her memories of Ben didn't appear to frighten her off. She let herself press her lips to his, instinct parting them. His other hand clasped her waist, gently pulling her towards him. She allowed herself to be so drawn, until her body rested up against his hips, the bulge of his arousal more than evident.

She might have drawn back at the feel of it, but she stopped herself. She wanted this kiss, and maybe she even wanted what lay hidden in his breeches. What every man had, but in her experience did not use kindly. A shocking thought. Ben had told her only wanton women desired a man's body, and that it was natural for her to take no pleasure in something he seemingly so enjoyed himself, with his groaning and grunting over her.

The tip of Jack's tongue slipped between her lips and before she realized what she was doing, her mouth had opened wider under his and she was responding. The hand on her cheek snaked round to the back of her head, his fingers in her hair. Perhaps she should do that herself. She put a hand up to his head, his hair soft under her touch and a tiny groan issued from his lips.

Before she'd had her fill, he pulled away from her, panting slightly, but keeping a light hand on her waist. "Might I be so bold as to ask if you enjoyed that?"

She nodded, as breathless as he was. "I did." Although he'd held her intimately close, there'd been nothing of the predator about him, apart from that solid arousal pressed against her stomach. Nothing invasive, not even that questing tongue. Not for one moment had she felt violated.

She pulled away. "You need to come upstairs with me."

He held back. "Are you sure you want to do this?"

She met his gaze. "There's only one way for me to discover if I can marry you, and that is *this* way. I won't marry you if I can't do it. You wouldn't want a wife who couldn't."

His eyes lit up. "But you will if I prove myself? If you can bring yourself to let me…"

She nodded. "Come."

He let her lead him into the kitchen, through to the quiet, empty parlor and up the stairs, that creaked at every footstep they took. At the top, she opened the first door and led him into her bedroom. Sunlight slanted in across the wooden floor to strike the bed nearest the window, and dust motes danced in the air like fairy spirits. How different it looked to the room she'd left this morning, now she was entering it with Jack.

She turned towards him, determination in her heart. If she failed to do this with him today, the man she loved, she'd know she'd never be able to remarry. Ever. "Come, sit with me on the bed."

He sat down beside her, his bulk seeming to fill the room, his masculinity cancelling out the feminine touches she and Lydia had imposed. This had always been a man's room. They were only interlopers. "Show me, Jack, how you mean to be if I agree to marry you."

WHAT SHOULD HE do? That this was a kind of test he might fail bore down on Jack. He could see she wanted him. He wanted her himself, but the fear that he might do something wrong assailed him. How to make her feel at ease? Probably the boorish Ben, whose death he secretly rejoiced over, had never taken the trouble to ready her for anything. He'd been a soldier and had most likely gone in all guns blazing, ready only to satisfy his own lusts. A woman was a fine instrument that required constant tuning, and if only he could tune Harriet, she'd be his.

He drew her towards him. "Will you kiss me?" Make it sound as though everything was her decision, then she'd not feel the almost unavoidable dominance of a man over a woman. He must let her decide the pace.

Surprise showed in her eyes, but she nodded. Without a word, she leaned in for the kiss, one hand going to the back of his head as their mouths met. And this time her mouth was already open. He waited for her tentative tongue to come searching before letting his own meet it, and felt the sudden jerk as he did so. But she didn't pull away. Instead, she settled more closely into his arms and her mouth opened wider, her tongue fencing with his.

This time the kiss lasted a lot longer, and when they finally broke apart, both of them were panting. "How is it," she whispered, "that kissing you affects my entire body?"

Jack chuckled. "Because I'm good at kissing. That's how you should feel when a man… when *I* kiss you. I feel it too. A thrill that tingles every nerve."

"I've never been kissed like this before."

He nodded. "That's because you've never kissed me before."

For answer, she returned for another kiss, and this time, Jack put his hand on her leg, high up on her thigh. The heat of her body radiated through the thin muslin. For a moment, she stiffened in his arms, before relaxing back into the depths of the kiss. He moved his hand further up her thigh and she made no attempt to stop him.

This time when the kiss finally broke, he left his hand where it was, nearly at the apex of her legs. She was gasping, and so was he, the need for her body powering through him. He'd have to hold himself strictly in check, so as not to frighten her off.

"There's no need for us to remove all of our clothes for this," he said. "But if we do not, then I shall feel as though this was a common coupling without emotion. I would like to hold your body, naked in my arms. If you will allow it." Had he gone too far?

She regarded him out of her lovely eyes, a shadow of fear lurking there, but she must have been naked with a man before. She had two children, after all. Then she seemed to come to the same decision as him. She nodded. "I will remove my clothes."

He held up a hand. "No. Allow me to remove them. It's all part of the game and I can assure you, you will like it."

She hesitated, doubt flitting across her face. Had she allowed her husband to do this, or had the man shown no finesse at all and taken her fully clothed, as Jack refused to do. "Very well." Suddenly, she dimpled, a carefree girl for once. "I feel that *you* are wearing too many clothes for what you have in mind, and perhaps I should help you to remove them even as you remove mine."

Jack's cock leapt to greater attention than ever at her words. His throat constricted and he had trouble swallowing. The very thought of her hands on his clothes, brushing against his body, her breath warm on his skin sent a blaze raging through him. He let out a little groan and shrugged off his coat, letting it fall forgotten to the floorboards. "Turn around."

She turned her back to him, presenting him with the ties at the back of her bodice. His hands were shaking so much, he could barely undo them. She must be able to feel it. Heaving in a deep breath to steady himself, he slipped her gown from her shoulders and it pooled about her waist, leaving her in underslip and stays. He let his fingers trail down her shoulders to her wrists, the skin silky and soft.

Her turn to utter a little moan of pleasure. Yes. He could do this. She wanted him.

Before she thought to turn around, his fingers went to the laces on her stays—always an article of women's clothing Jack had stumbled over. And this time was no different. As he fumbled with them, she sat bolt upright before him, her shoulders rising and falling in quick breaths. The back of her neck, possessed now of a distinct line where she'd caught the sun on board *The Fly*, tempted him. He bent and pressed his lips to the soft skin of her nape and felt her catch her breath. He trailed gentle kisses down her back to the top of her stays, then back up again and she uttered another little moan.

The laces came undone at last, and he threw the offending garment to one side. Now, all that stood between them was her thin muslin shift, so light as to be almost transparent. He applied his lips to her neck again and was rewarded as she leaned back into him, arching her back. With his lips on the side of her neck, he had a view down the front of her slip, to where her nipples had hardened against the soft fabric. He slid a hand across her ribs toward her right breast, slowly, afraid she'd stop him. She didn't. He cupped her breast, his thumb gently rubbing the erect nipple and felt her stiffen for a moment before she relaxed again, her head back on his shoulder.

Now he really needed her, but he had, as she'd so rightly pointed out, far too many clothes on. No gentleman should make love to a lady with his boots on. With reluctance, he pulled himself away from her and hastily kicked off his boots. His waistcoat and shirt followed, and then his breeches.

She still had her back to him. Putting his arms around her once more, he caressed her slowly, far more slowly than his body needed. After this, he wouldn't last long, so she had to have her release before he had his, that was for certain, and there was one sure way of that. He slid his hand down her belly to let it nestle between her legs.

She let out a gasp as his fingers found her center. "Jack!"

He circled, rubbed, gently teasing her to a release he guessed might not be long in coming. Taking his time and fighting to control his own body, he slid her slip from her shoulders with his other hand, his mouth on her bare skin. Outside the window, in a different world, the call of gulls filled the air above the distant roar of the surf on the hidden beach. She arched her back against his chest, her head back, her breath coming in sharp pants. Then, beneath his fingers, her body throbbed, pulses shooting through her and into his fingers, and he knew he'd done it. She let out a cry that might have been a mixture of surprise and pleasure and pressed his hand between her legs. "Oh my God. Oh my God."

"God has nothing to do with it," he whispered in her ear. "This was all Jack Trengrouse."

If she'd heard him use his new name, she gave no sign of it, as her body arched more fiercely against his in her pleasure until finally she relaxed against him.

But now he was once more unsure of his reception, and with his cock digging into her back she must know of his need. A woman with two children certainly knew what went on between a man and his wife, and what a man needed. And yet, he couldn't ask her. It needed to come from her. He couldn't be like her husband, no matter how much he needed it.

She turned around and his breath caught in his throat at the perfection of her body. The smooth alabaster skin, the perfect breasts, the look of wonder on her face. "Can it be like that every time?" she asked.

He nodded. "Every time."

She dropped her gaze to his arousal. "Thank you, Jack. And now I'd like to try this as well."

FLUSHED WITH THE pleasure still coursing through her body, and with a newfound confidence, Harriet lay back on her pillows, staring up at the naked man before her. Above the waist his skin was tanned, as though he'd spent much of the summer on his ship half naked, and dark hairs curled across his chest. Her eyes descended further to his unmistakable erection. Of course, she'd seen Ben when he'd been aroused, but only ever briefly as there'd been none of what had gone on here. Neither of them had ever been fully naked together as she and Jack were now.

She opened her legs to him and he leaned over her, taking his weight on his arms. "You can tell me to stop any time you like. You understand that?"

She nodded. "I know."

"I don't want to hurt you."

"You won't. Stop talking."

She felt the width and length of him as he slid inside her and for just a moment was back with Ben forcing himself on her. Then Ben was banished, the door firmly closed against him, and instead, she stared up into Jack's eyes.

She gripped his shoulders and lifted her legs to wrap around his back as pleasure surged through her a second time. "Don't stop."

He needed no persuading to comply. She dug her fingers into his flesh, hanging on as tightly as she could as he pounded into her. "Definitely don't stop." And as the pleasure reached its mountainous pinnacle, and shudders cascaded through their bodies, he slumped against her, spent.

Their heavy breathing filled the quiet room.

Eventually, Jack levered himself up onto his elbows and then flopped over beside her. "Do I pass your test? And will you marry me?"

Harriet couldn't help but laugh. Never had she felt so happy, so fulfilled. "You have, and I will," she whispered. "But if we're to marry as respectable gentlefolk, then we need to get dressed before someone comes home unexpectedly and catches us naked in bed together."

Jack burst out laughing. "You think they'd care, my lady? For you are to be none other than Lady Trengrouse, although that's a story for later. I'd far rather concentrate on you and me right now." He rolled onto his side, his head supported on his elbow. "And if we could, I'd rather stay naked in bed with you all day."

Harriet burst out laughing again. "And I would rather not be found like this by either my children or by Bertha. It would give poor Bertha a heart attack. I swear she never looks at her own body when she's washing it and has never seen a man naked in her life. Other than Theo as a baby."

He grinned. "I'll win Bertha over, just you wait and see. She'll be putty in my hands and you'll be green with envy at the flattery I pour on her."

Harriet stretched, luxuriating at the feel of the cool air on her sweaty skin. "And as for you, you'd best explain to me why you're calling yourself Jack Trengrouse all of a sudden."

FINIS

About the Author

After a varied life that's included working with horses where Downton Abbey is filmed, riding racehorses, running her own riding school, owning a sheep farm and running a holiday business in France, Fil now lives on a widebeam canal boat on the Kennet and Avon Canal in Southern England.

She has a long-suffering husband, a rescue dog from Romania called Bella, a cat she found as a kitten abandoned in a gorse bush, five children and six grandchildren.

She once saw a ghost in a churchyard, and when she lived in Wales there was a panther living near her farm that ate some of her sheep. In England there are no indigenous big cats.

She has Asperger's Syndrome and her obsessions include horses and King Arthur. Her historical romantic fiction and children's fantasy adventures centre around Arthurian legends, and her pony stories about her other love. She speaks fluent French after living there for ten years, and in her spare time looks after her allotment, makes clothes and dolls for her granddaughters, embroiders and knits. In between visiting the settings for her books.

Social Media links:
Website – filreid.com
Facebook – facebook.com/Fil-Reid-Author-101905545548054
Twitter – @FJReidauthor

www.ingramcontent.com/pod-product-compliance
Lightning Source LLC
Chambersburg PA
CBHW060432310726
48977CB00001B/153